The Enemy We Don't Know

A Homefront Mystery

THE ENEMY WE DON'T KNOW

A Homefront Mystery

by LIZ MILLIRON

First edition

ISBN: 978-1-947915-51-0

This book was professionally typeset on Reedsy.
Find out more at reedsy.com

For Betty Lederman and Dorothy Milliron – the real Betty and Dot.

Praise for The Homefront Mysteries

World War II on the home front comes alive in Milliron's new-series debut as Betty Ahern solves more than one mystery even while toiling in a Buffalo airplane factory with other young women. The story is riveting, Betty's courage and persistence are a delight, and her sidekicks provide perfect support and caution. The Homefront Mysteries promise to keep you on the edge of your seat…and smiling as you read. — Edith Maxwell, author of the Agatha-nominated historical Quaker Midwife Mysteries

Liz Milliron gives us a charming new series that I absolutely love and think you will too. Betty Ahern is feisty, loyal, and determined. Finding her way in a traditionally men's world, she not only helps the war effort by working at Bell Airplane, she's following her dream to become a private eye with a little help from her friends. If Sam Spade and Rosie the Riveter had a love child, she'd be Betty Ahern. — Annette Dashofy, *USA Today*-bestselling author of the Zoe Chambers Mysteries

A lively, richly atmospheric novel, set in the defense plants and ethnic neighborhoods of World War II Buffalo, NY, *The Enemy You Don't Know* is "Rosie the Riveter Meets Sam Spade." With fresh, idiosyncratic dialogue from a charismatic narrator, Liz Milliron delivers a compelling, crackerjack of a novel. Betty Ahern is the irrepressible heroine. Smart, stubborn, and—yes—reckless, she works in a defense factory building airplanes for the war effort. At least when she's not investigating disturbing acts of sabotage at the plant, snooping into the murder of a co-worker's brother, or keeping her eye on some suspicious Nazi sympathizers. And all this while doing her best to circumvent her parents' strict Irish-Catholic house rules. Readers

i

will love this tale of derring-do on the home front. — James W. Ziskin, author of the Anthony and Macavity award-winning Ellie Stone mysteries

Chapter 1

November, 1942

I wish life was more like a movie. See, in the pictures, it's easy to tell the good guys from the bad guys. The good guys wear white hats and the music is real positive. The bad guys wear black hats and their music is grim. It's pretty easy in a war, too 'cause your side is wearing one kind of uniform and the other side's different. But it's messy in real life. The good guys sometimes dress like bad guys and, well, the other way 'round. It's much harder for me to tell who's who.

I folded Tom's note, the paper worn soft and thin, the creases deep, and slipped it back into my purse. I didn't need to read it, really. I'd memorized it long ago. "I probably won't be able to write for a while. Stay my girl. Love, Tom." Still thinking of him, I wandered toward the time-clock until a voice broke through my thoughts.

Anne Linden turned from the clock. "Betty Ahern. Good morning."

I tapped out a cigarette from my pack of Lucky Strikes and stuck it between my lips. Then I fished around in a pocket for my Zippo. "Morning." I flicked the lighter a couple times, hoping she got the hint I didn't wanna talk. Then I clocked in and headed for the coat locker.

"Must be a note from your beau. You were very careful putting it away." She followed a step behind me.

'Course I was careful. It might be the last letter I got from Tom ever. Not a full year after Pearl Harbor, who knew what the Nazis and the Japanese had in store for us? I might lose my fiancé to the hell of the battlefield before I was twenty. We shoulda gotten married before he shipped out, but Mom insisted eighteen was too young. "Yeah." The lighter refused to catch. Giving Anne the brush-off wasn't working. She acted like the starved cat that hung around our porch when we put the milk bottles out. A few other girls nodded to me, but once they saw Anne, they stayed away.

Anne looked a little like Marlene Dietrich with her wavy blonde hair and what my mother called "bedroom eyes." A little rounder than the actress. My friend, Dot Kilbride was pinup-girl curvy. But Dot's curves made her look friendly. For some reason, Anne's put me off. I mean, l liked Dietrich…on the big screen. Not trailing me around like a puppy desperate for a few kind words. She didn't play that character type.

I gave up on the smoke and replaced it in the pack. Then I stowed my lunch pail and bag. "Is there something I can do for ya?"

Her blue eyes widened. "Oh…no. I was only saying hello."

"Well, I gotta get to the line or I'll be late." It wasn't a lie. I was due on the assembly line and Bell Airplane didn't pay me to shoot the breeze. But I had more time than I let on. I rushed away, leaving her standing near the door to the cafeteria.

Poor Anne. Smart enough to realize she didn't quite fit in with the rest of us, but not enough to figure out how to fix it.

I hurried across the yard from the cafeteria to the assembly lines. The building was one massive floor that held five lines. Painted fuselages came in one side on dollies. I stepped carefully over the chain in the floor that pulled the dollies along, stopping only for installation of the various parts. Each line was far enough from the other that even once the wings were attached, the planes could be rolled through giant doors out to the yard. Someone had told me mass production had worked so well for Henry Ford, Bell had adopted the practice for planes.

I found Dot standing near the day's assignment. In the time I'd been at Bell, I'd installed all the parts of the P-39. Today's task was windshields. They weren't as complicated as other tasks, like engine or instrument installation. Since half my mind still lingered on Tom and the other half had been ruffled by Anne's presence, that was a good thing.

2

"Where've you been?" Dot asked as the conveyor chain shuddered to life. "I lost you when we got off the bus."

"Got sidetracked." The repetitive task of fitting the windshields and attaching them to the body ought to settle me down.

Dot took her place next to me. "You heard from Tom lately?"

"Not since he left Ireland. It's not like the US Mail makes stops in North Africa."

"You don't know he's there. You said they...whaddya call it?...censored that out."

I gave her my best Look, the one I'd learned from Mom. "Rommel is in North Africa. He leads the German tanks. Tom's in a tank division. I'm no dummy, Dot."

She had the sense not to say anything to that. "I saw you talking to Anne. What was that about?"

"Dunno. The conversation didn't get much beyond hello."

"I feel kinda sorry for her." Dot finished her polishing and moved to the next piece. "Nobody likes her. I dunno why. She seems nice, even if she is German. A bit reserved maybe. She hardly says anything. Is that it?"

"Are you talkin' about the same girl? The one who never leaves me alone?"

"But she doesn't talk to no one else. She sits by herself at lunch all the time. I've never heard her say two words to anyone 'cept you."

Lucky me. Girls who had family and friends in the war had a hard time accepting folks with German backgrounds, even in Buffalo with its healthy German population. But when it came to Anne, that was too easy an answer. "She tries too hard with me and not hard enough with everyone else," I said as I continued my work. "Maybe it's unfair, but she puts my back up."

"That is unfair. Not like you at all."

"I can't help it. I want to like her but...I dunno. Can't quite put my finger on it."

Dot cast a reproachful look in my direction as a fuselage stopped in front of us.

"Don't nag at me, Dot. I have enough on my plate without worrying about Anne's popularity." I snapped the windshield in and screwed it down.

3

Dot polished the Plexiglas to remove my fingerprints. "Do you know anything about her?"

"I once heard her say her family came here ten years ago. I think they have some money, too. That's about it." I looked over to where Anne stood on the second line, working away and keeping to herself. Being on an assembly line didn't give us much elbow-room, but the gap between Anne and the others looked bigger to me.

Anne wasn't shy about saying she didn't have to work. Was that it? Did Anne's family having money, while so many of the rest of us scrimped along, bother me?

***

The shift had almost ended when I heard a ruckus from the engine installation area from line number two. I grabbed the arm of a girl running by me, her face streaked with grease. "What's the fuss?"

She coughed. "Fire. Not a big one, but I gotta go call the fire department."

I let her go. A fire? How did that happen? I took a couple steps.

"Betty, it's not our place," Dot said. "Plus what if you get hurt?"

"They're gonna need help until the fire trucks get here. We don't need it getting worse than it is." I sprinted off weaving between girls coming from line two engine installation, many of whom were crying or coughing. Work stopped on the other lines as girls realized the problem with line two's engines.

I got over to the fracas and skidded to a halt. Work had stopped everywhere and a buzz of talk filled the room. Flames flickered around the engines waiting their turn for installation and girls beat at them with sacks. The smell of the greasy smoke made my stomach curdle like last night's milk. Ninnies. I grabbed an extinguisher from the wall. "Get outta the way. Drop the sacks and grab the sand buckets." They backed up, still flailing their burlap. I turned the nozzle of the extinguisher on the fire and let 'er rip. Clouds of white billowed from the hose. A couple of the others tossed sand on the engines for good measure.

By the time the firemen got there, we had things pretty much under control. Thankfully, the fire hadn't spread to the engines on the other lines.

A few of us poked around the edges of the oil and smoke-streaked metal. I mostly looked to make sure the flames were gone, but I also checked things out. Sure, there was a lot of grease and oil involved in engine installation. It was messy, which was why it was my least favorite assignment. It took forever to get my clothes clean and the smell gave Mom one more thing to gripe about. Another reminder that her daughter was doing a man's work instead of being a proper young woman. But engines didn't burst into flames on their own. Something had started it.

While Mr. Satterwaite, our shift supervisor, talked to the firemen, I snooped. Streaks and puddles of oil marked the floor, some charred lines where flames had followed the trail. Most of the damage seemed to be to the engine waiting for its plane, covered in soot and a thick layer of soda acid from the extinguisher. There was no way of knowing if the big Allison still worked, not without testing and running it. I heard male voices come nearer and I ducked down on the opposite side of the engine. Mr. Satterwaite and I didn't have a great history. He wouldn't appreciate me sticking my nose in.

"What do you think started the fire?" Mr. Satterwaite asked.

I listened hard. Work had restarted on the other four lines, noise echoing off the rafters and windows high above us, making it hard to pick out the words.

An unfamiliar, deeper voice answered. I guessed it was the lead fireman. "Don't know until we check it further. Could be a spark of some kind. Are these engines ever started?"

"Not here. This is just where they're installed."

The fireman's heavy black boots showed underneath the belt as he walked back and forth. "What about smoke breaks? Any of your girls ever take a puff while she worked?"

I glanced around the floor. No one would be stupid enough to smoke on the line, would they? No butts on the ground, but I couldn't see inside the engines and I didn't dare check. They'd see me for sure. I retreated a few feet to join the girls who'd stayed to help put out the fire. They'd prob'ly been told to stick around.

Mr. Satterwaite's outraged voice cut the air. "Absolutely not."

Girls on lines one and three elbowed each other, turned, and looked.

"Hmm." The fireman, a burly man whose body matched his voice, came 'round to where I'd been skulking and leaned over the engine. O'Leary, his name tag said. Figures. With a thick shock of red hair across his forehead and eyes as blue as the summer sky, he couldn't be anything but Irish. He paused over the engine, reached down, and pulled out something. "Then what's this?" He held out his find. It was a half-smoked cigarette.

Mr. Satterwaite's face turned beet red. "Why I never," he sputtered. "Let me see that."

The fireman held it up, but did not put it in Mr. Satterwaite's open hand.

Even from where I was standing, I could see the word Camel on the end. I preferred Lucky Strike Green, but some of the others smoked Camels. I looked around the group. Of the four who stood there, I knew Florence Anderson and Mildred Patterson didn't smoke. Helen Ackerman smoked Luckys, like me. I didn't know about Alice Whitfield.

Mr. Satterwaite rounded on them. "Does this belong to any of you?"

They all shook their heads.

"What about you, Miss Ahern?"

"I didn't work here today, Mr. Satterwaite. I was on line four, windshield installation."

His eyes narrowed. "Then what, pray tell, are you doing over here?"

Mr. Satterwaite hadn't liked me before the mess last October with Mr. Lippincott. The way that turned out didn't do much to change his attitude. I lifted my chin and stared. I wouldn't have backed down if it was just him. I sure wasn't gonna do it in front of a crowd. "I came over to help with the fire. There are other people to do the installation work. But I don't smoke Camels."

He glared, but didn't have any choice but turn back to the firemen. "I suppose you'll want to know who worked on this line during this shift."

"That would be helpful," O'Leary said. He stepped over to us. "There's also a red lipstick mark here. Any of you girls know who wears this color red?"

Lipstick was a prized possession these days. I had one tube of Dorothy

Gray South American Red I hoarded like the gold in Fort Knox. Wear it to work? I could only think of a handful of girls at Bell who fit that bill. Anne Linden, Catherine Ramsey, and Rose DeLuca among them. All three had worked engine installation that morning. Coulda been a coincidence, but I'd seen enough detective pictures to know coincidences weren't to be trusted.

Next to me, Florence bit her lip then spoke up. "Anne, Catherine, and Rose. Rose smokes Camels. I've never seen Anne or Catherine with a cigarette, but that don't mean nothing, I s'pose."

O'Leary nodded. "I'd like to speak to them, Mr. Satterwaite, if they're still here. Then I'll talk to anyone else who worked this line today."

Satterwaite hurried off to find Anne, Catherine, and Rose.

"You." O'Leary pointed to me. "What's your name?"

"Elizabeth Ahern, sir. Most folks call me Betty."

"Miss Ahern. You said you came over to help with the fire? What did you see?"

I told him about hearing the noise, seeing the smoke and fleeing girls, the fire, then grabbing the extinguisher. "I didn't see anyone smoking though."

O'Leary's face creased in a smile. "You're a feisty one, aren't you? Not many would run toward a fire. You remind me of my sister. Ahern. Irish?"

I lifted my chin. "Buffalo First Ward." And proud of it.

Mr. Satterwaite returned with his quarry. Anne's face was pale and she twisted the fabric of her shirt. Some of her hair, nearly white-blonde, had escaped her bun and stuck to her face next to a smear of black. Grease? Rose's dark brown hair was still neatly tied back, fire in her deep brown eyes. High-spirited, that was Rose. Pop would chalk it up to her Italian heritage. Catherine's dark eyes looked sly. If it hadn't been for her last name, I'd have sworn she was some sort of Slav because of her blue-black hair and dusky skin. But her last name, Ramsey, said English or Scottish. "These are the girls you wanted to speak to," Mr. Satterwaite said.

O'Leary moved over to them, holding out the cigarette. "Mr. Satterwaite said all of you were on engine installation for this line today. I found this in the engine. Were any of you smoking while you worked?"

"No, sir." Anne's blue eyes were wide as she shook her head. Her voice trembled. "I don't smoke."

"But you do wear red lipstick. I can see that for myself."

"I don't smoke," she said, voice still shaky. "Ask anyone."

O'Leary turned to Rose. "What about you, Miss…"

"DeLuca," she said, husky voice scornful. "Yes, I wear red lipstick and yes, I smoke Camels. But I don't light up on the job. I'm not dumb."

He turned to Catherine, but she didn't even wait for the question before answering. "Catherine Ramsey. I love a good red lipstick. But sorry, I don't smoke, not even on the sly."

O'Leary closed his hand around the half-smoked Camel. "Mr. Satterwaite, please gather all the girls who worked this line in the cafeteria building. The line is closed until further notice."

This sounded bad, no matter how you looked at it. If someone had been careless and didn't wanna admit it, well, she'd put her job and the safety of the others at risk. But if the fire had been set on purpose, that was even worse. Stuff like that could make Bell decide it wasn't worth keeping the plant open. This fire turned out to be small potatoes, but what if things were just getting started? Not only would it hurt the war effort, it could put a whole lot of girls, including me, out of a job.

There was only one way I could see to stop that from happening. Figure out where that half-burned cigarette came from.

Chapter 2

I missed the first afternoon bus back to Buffalo and arrived home late. So late the family was already seated for dinner, which earned me a sniff of disapproval from Mom. "I'm sorry. There—"

"Go change your clothes, Elizabeth," she said. "Then come eat your supper. It's cold by now."

I smothered a sigh. If Pop got home from Bethlehem Steel after food was on the table, she'd have offered to warm up his plate. She didn't approve of my working, so no such luck for me.

Pop had returned to work at the Steel at the end of October and Mom said that meant I could stop working at Bell. After all, nice young ladies didn't work at factories. But I had made good money that summer. On top of that, I felt useful, and work kept me from thinking about Tom, and my brother Sean in the Pacific. To my surprise, Pop sided with me. "The girl likes to work, she should work, Mary," he said. "With all the rationing and things getting more expensive, Lord knows we can use the money."

Fact is, Pop understood my working made things a whole lot easier on the bank account in a way Mom didn't. Yeah, I could have cleaned houses with her or played nanny to the Griffin twins down the street. Both jobs were more "appropriate" for a girl my age. But neither of those paid as good as Bell.

Not only that, everyone wanted to do her part for the war. Sean was in the Navy, the younger ones collected cans and paper…and I kept our allies in the air by building their planes.

On second thought, Mom prob'ly knew just fine. She didn't wanna admit it is all. She had a different vision for her daughter. I was s'posed to get married and start my own family, just like she did. Hopefully, I'd have a bigger house, maybe marry a guy who could afford to move us out of working-class First Ward Buffalo and into the suburbs. Buy a house with a yard and a picket fence. The American Dream. Every time I went with Mom to her ladies' group at church, I saw the looks she got. That I understood. Mom's generation didn't approve of girls donning pants and doing "a man's job."

That vision—house, family, picket fence, the whole shebang—was what I'd seen for myself before December 1941.

The Japs and the Germans changed all that.

I hurried to change into clean clothes and return to the table. I slid into my seat, said a quick prayer, and ladled some beef stew, more potatoes than beef, onto my plate.

"How was work today?" Pop asked. He liked swapping stories with me about our days.

Mom, Pop, my younger brothers, Jimmy and Michael, and my younger sister, Mary Kate, still sat at the table, plates scraped clean. Jimmy, twelve, and Michael, eleven, looked like twins, right down to the freckles and the mischief gleaming out of their brown eyes. Jimmy, the older one by only thirteen months, got better grades. We all knew he was our future college boy. Knowing my brothers, they'd finished eating in a hot second and wanted to go back out to work on whatever cockamamie idea they had cooking.

"Interesting." I mopped up some gravy with a thick slice of bread. It was warmer than I expected. I most likely had Mary Kate to thank for that. Brown hair tied into two neat pigtails, solemn brown eyes, her gingham dress immaculate, Mary Kate was the homemaker. She also had a sweet tooth, which made her easy to bribe when it came to ducking out of household chores. In between mouthfuls, I told him about the fire.

"Big?"

"Not really. It shut down one assembly line and I don't know if the engine is still in working order, but it wasn't like the paint area went up in flames or nothing." That would be a disaster.

He frowned. "Do you think someone actually smoked while she worked?"

"Dunno." I speared a potato and stared at it. "I thought about it on the bus ride home. What if it wasn't an accident? You wouldn't really have to smoke the cigarette, would you? I mean, light it up, a few puffs to get it going, put it in the engine, and something would catch fire eventually, I'd think."

Pop tilted his head, fingers steepled over his plate. "I suppose so. How burned down was the Camel?"

I thought as I chewed the potato. I made sure to swallow before answering. "I'd say 'bout halfway. It would keep burning after it was lit, I s'pose. Build up the ash until it fell off into the grease or oil, and the fire would start."

"Anybody get hurt?"

"Nah, just a lot of mess. Makes me think—"

Mom clucked her tongue. "Enough. Bad enough you two talk about work at the table. We don't need you sticking your nose in where it don't belong. Running around like a cheap dime-novel detective like you did when that supervisor died last month. Shameful."

"Now, Mary," Pop said.

Mom scowled. "Eat your supper, Elizabeth. Then you can help Mary Kate with the dishes."

Pop winked at me.

"Yes, ma'am." There was no further talk of the fire while I finished eating. Mom didn't remember, or didn't want to remember, that they'd caught Mr. Lippincott's killer 'cause of me.

Afterwards Mary Kate and I washed the dishes, and I listened to her talk about school and the new paperboy, who she pronounced "dreamy." I didn't laugh at her too much. After all, I had been sweet on Tom when I was fifteen.

We finished the dishes and I gathered up the trash. Taking it out back, I dropped the kitchen can to open up the heavy-duty metal one. Something yowled and streaked by me. I finished with the garbage, wiped my hands on my apron, and went looking for the owner of the noise.

One of the mangiest cats I'd ever seen cringed by our back step. The stray. A smoke-gray thing, swirls of off-white on its body, dabs of white on its paws, and enormous green eyes. I could count its ribs. We ate better and that wasn't sayin' much.

Mary Kate had come outside. "Aww, the poor thing." Mary Kate was a sucker for animals.

"We can't do nothing for it. Go back inside. It'll have to scrounge from the garbage. Maybe find some dead fish down at the lake shore."

"But Betty, look at her. She's so skinny."

"I don't think that's a girl."

"Can't we give her some milk? We have some left from this morning. Please?"

"If we feed it, it'll never go away."

Mary Kate's eyes widened.

"If Mom finds out, she'll tan our hides for sure."

Mary Kate's lip trembled.

Darn her. I could hold my own against anyone—Mr. Satterwaite, even my mother—but my sister could turn me to mush. I grumbled, went inside, and found a saucer we never used 'cause it had a chip on the edge. I filled it with the last of the day's milk, then returned to the back yard.

Mary Kate had teased the cat out from its hiding spot to sniff at her fingers.

"Careful it doesn't bite you." I set down the saucer. "Here you go, cat. You can't expect this every night, you hear me?"

The cat wouldn't come any closer until we stepped back, but as soon as we did it set to lapping up the milk like it hadn't eaten in forever.

"Aww, see? She's starving. I bet she's so thankful," Mary Kate said, hands clasped in joy. The girl was gonna grow up to save every stray animal in Buffalo.

I didn't bother pointing out I'd seen the animal's boy parts and shooed my sister inside. I figured the cat would be at it for a bit. I'd come out later to get the saucer so Mom wouldn't find it. In the meantime I wanted to talk to Pop. I found him in his chair in the front room by the radio, listening to the latest war news.

I sat on the floor in front of his chair. "Anything about…"

"Tom or Sean? Or more exactly, anything that could be about them?" Pop patted my arm. "No, my darlin' girl. Mrs. Flannery would have gotten a telegram if anything had happened to Tom and she'd have told you. The British beat the Hun at El Alamein and Rommel had to pull back. We'll just have to wait and see what happens next. Same with Sean, we'd get a telegram."

Nobody called the Nazis that, but Pop was a Great War veteran so I guessed they'd always be the Hun to him. I twisted my engagement ring and said a quick prayer. A few folks I knew said once America entered the war it would be over quick, but I wasn't in that camp. I couldn't see Hitler or Hirohito giving up easy.

"Anyway." Pop leaned back and carefully packed his pipe. "Tell me more about this fire. Now that your mother isn't listening."

"I already told you what I know." I watched him light the pipe and puff gently. "Could it have happened like I said?"

"Light the cigarette and wait? I don't see why not." Smoke curled from the pipe, the sweet smell of tobacco filling the air. "But why go to the trouble to start such a small fire?"

"The person thought it would turn out worse than it did?"

Pop murmured in agreement.

"Anyway, if I'm right about the way it happened, then it didn't have to be anyone working that particular line's engine installation. Someone coulda left it earlier, say lunch break. Maybe no one did smoke on the job, like they all said."

He puffed. "Hardly a foolproof plan."

I pondered his words. "Because the cigarette could've gone out without a fire. Or the fire could've done even less damage. All that happened is we got a burned engine and a mess."

He nodded, puffing on the pipe. "Did Dot tell you anything?"

"I haven't talked to her. She caught the earlier bus. I'll ask tomorrow, but she worked with me over on another line. The floor's so big and there's so much noise, I doubt she saw anything." The smoke relaxed me. Pop never went in for that fancy ring-blowing stuff, like in books, but it floated about his face. More lines creased the skin around his mouth since the accident

13

at the steel plant that had put him outta work last October and the start of the war, but his blue eyes still twinkled. I wished I'd gotten his eyes, real blue like cornflowers. Mine were paler, more like forget-me-nots. "Line two was closed when I left."

"Will it reopen tomorrow?"

"I s'pose. Guess it depends on what repairs need to be made and how much time it'll take to clean everything up."

Mom walked in, a basket of laundry on her hip. "That's enough lollygagging. Elizabeth. Leave your father alone. He's had a long day. The younger ones are doing homework, so you can help me fold."

Because I hadn't had a long day at all. But there was no point in saying that. I sighed, stood. "Yes, ma'am." I followed her out of the room. Mom wouldn't listen to me ramble. But she couldn't stop me thinking about what happened and, more importantly, why.

Chapter 3

Saturday morning, on the bus to Wheatfield, I didn't need to come up with a way to push Dot into talking about yesterday. She was all too eager to start gabbing.

"Who do you think started the fire?" she asked, sitting on her hands, brown eyes wide.

"What makes you think I have ideas 'bout that?" I picked my nails.

"Oh come on, Betty." She flashed a knowing smile. "You had ideas 'bout Mr. Lippincott, didn't ya?"

"That was different." Mr. Lippincott was our former supervisor. Last month, we'd found him dead at the start of the shift. I'd gone on to solve his murder.

"Not really. Couldn't that fire have shut down Bell?"

I told her my opinion, the fire was small potatoes. "I bet line two is already up and running."

"They won't be interested at all?"

"I didn't say that. I'm sure they wanna know if it someone set it deliberately or by accident. The muckety-mucks don't want anything, no matter how small, interfering with production. They want all five lines humming, you can bet on that."

She bounced again. "Then who d'ya think did it?"

I sighed. "They found a cigarette, a Camel, in the engine. And it had a red lipstick stain on it. 'Cept I was talking to Pop last night." I told her about my idea.

She pouted. "That don't really help."

15

She was spot on about that. If I looked at Bell as a whole, lots of girls prob'ly wore red lipstick and smoked Camels. Heck, if I was right and the firebug only needed the cigarette to start the blaze, she didn't need to smoke Camels or even smoke at all. It didn't even need to be a she. The lipstick could be a blind. "Who coulda been near the engine installation station, do you know?"

"Loads of people." She counted on her fingers. "I recognized Rose, Florence, Mildred, Alice, and Helen."

"They were there to help with the fire."

"I also saw Catherine and Anne. Plus Mr. Satterwaite." She wrinkled her nose. "I know you don't like him much, but I got a hard time seeing him starting a fire. He loves that factory."

True. I half-suspected Frank Satterwaite would sleep in his office if Bell would let him. "I'm friendly with Florence. She'll tell me who worked that station."

"But if the person only needed to light up, it could've been anyone. She coulda walked through the area. That means everyone who worked at Bell yesterday first shift is a suspect, aren't they?"

That was a lot of people. More than I cared to count. "I can't possibly know all those names. Bet no one does 'cept the payroll folks."

We watched the browning grass speed by outside the window as the bus belched clouds of black smoke. The snow hadn't started yet, but it wouldn't be long. Not around Buffalo in November. Mom had knitted me a new muffler for the winter and I had better dig out my winter shoes, too, just in case.

Dot broke the silence. "Anyways. You hear the news?"

I was afraid to ask. "News about what?"

"You know the Bund? Those nutters who think Hitler is the best thing to happen to Germany since sliced bread?"

"I thought the Bund was old hat."

"So did I. After all, the old leader, Kuhn, is still in jail and their new leader ran away to Mexico. Turns out there are some people left who think the Bund has it right."

I snorted.

"Some of 'em are in Buffalo."

Buffalo had lots of Germans, but it also had lots of Irish and Poles. "Who cares? Hitler wasn't too nice to a lot of people in Europe. Can't imagine he's got a lot of support over here."

She nodded again, curls bouncing. "Yup. But you weren't on the bus yesterday. Some of us got to talking. Helen Ackerman said some people in Buffalo are definitely trying to revive the Bund. She's German so she should know."

Like me, Dot loved the pictures. Unlike me, she always wanted to turn everyday life into a spy flick, like Bogart's *All Through the Night*. Her imagination was amazing. She was too excited for this to be idle talk, though. "Okay, I'll bite, Dot. Who is it?"

"Who is what?"

"C'mon." I poked her. "You're practically busting at the seams. Helen, or someone, said a name you know, or you think you know, and it's got you going. Who is it?"

She leaned forward. "George Linden."

It took a second to sink in. "Like Anne Linden? But Linden's not an uncommon name in Germany, is it?"

"Might not be. But Helen's pretty sure George is Anne's brother. According to her, he's right at the top of the list of people who want to revive the German-American Bund." She gave me a knowing look. "You know what that means?"

I sure did. If George Linden was trying to revive the Bund, one way get the group moving would be to figure out how to cripple American war manufacturing. Like Bell. And his sister Anne would be perfectly placed to give her brother some help.

***

Saturday shifts were never my favorite. It meant missing the afternoon matinee and I needed my serial fix to keep up with the latest adventures of Flash Gordon. With my current mission, I didn't mind so much today. 'Course, I didn't see Anne all morning. Typical. When you want to see someone, you don't. I knew a few German-Americans. They weren't too keen on what had happened to Germany after the Great War, but they didn't like Hitler either.

Line two was up and running, but I could tell enthusiasm lagged after yesterday's events. Over lunch, I cornered Alice. "They find out any more about the fire?"

Alice's pin curls were tucked under her bandanna, a bright yellow that contrasted with the gray of her shirt. She shook her head. "Not that anyone's said to me. Everyone who worked engine installation on two yesterday had to turn out her pockets and lunch pail, but no one said why."

"They're looking for cigarettes and lipstick." I noticed Alice's lips were pale.

"Well, they ain't gonna find nothing on me. They didn't find it on anyone else either." She took a bite of baloney sandwich.

"You don't smoke, do you?"

"Nuh-uh."

"Well, I figure whoever set that fire didn't need to smoke." I told her about my idea. "My pop thinks I'm in the ballpark."

"Are you accusing me?" Alice kept her voice low, but the outrage came through clear as day. "For your information, I hate the taste of cigarettes and I wouldn't do anything to ruin production. My cousin flies for cripe's sake. And I need the dough, same as you."

I didn't want everyone to know what I was up to, but even Sam Spade had to ask questions. I'd known Alice long enough that I trusted her to give me a straight story. "Relax, I'm not accusing you of anything." I made a shushing motion with my hands. "I'm just sayin' it's possible. Get my drift?"

She appeared satisfied. "Yeah, I s'pose so."

"Anybody say anything while you were waiting?"

"Rose and Catherine seemed to think it was a lark." Alice finished her sandwich in two huge bites. "Both of 'em talked about how they were going to spend their free afternoon, like it was some sort of holiday."

I played with the crust of my sandwich. "You ever hear anything about Anne's brother?"

"I don't talk to Anne if I can help it. She bugs me. Thinks she's better than all the rest of us if you ask me, just 'cause her family's got dough." Alice wadded up her garbage.

"Yeah, but have you ever heard anything?"

"I know his name's George. That's all." Alice stood and gathered up her lunch pail.

"Is she here today? Anne?"

"I haven't seen her." Alice walked away, leaving me alone at the table.

I asked a few other girls, but they were as unhelpful as Alice. Nobody had seen Anne that day. A few had heard of her brother George, but that was all.

"She's so unpopular," I said to Florence as we took a quick smoke break. "I mean, I knew she didn't have a lot of friends. Still, I'm kinda surprised. She's German, but I thought her family was glad to be in America."

"I think they are." Florence took a draw from her cigarette. "She told me once they left Germany after the last war 'cause of all the economic problems when France and England made Germany pay up."

"Then what's the problem? I've never heard her talk nice about Hitler neither."

"I don't see where she's your best friend. Why the sudden interest?" Florence lifted one eyebrow.

"It's just…" I took a drag and blew out the smoke. "I know she's not the most comfortable person to be around. But with all the girls in this place, I'd think at least one or two of them would be friends with her."

"If you ask me, she's too standoffish." Florence puffed and nodded like she knew something I didn't. "Lunch every day she reads a book. She never gossips. It gives off the air that she don't want to be around us and who likes that? I've never seen her anywhere besides Bell, have you?"

"Nope. I don't get to Kaisertown much." I understood where Florence was coming from. It's hard to like someone who keeps apart as much as Anne did. 'Course, if she had such a high opinion of herself, why did she follow me around like a shadow? Aside from being Irish, I wasn't any different than the others. Why key in on me?

"Yeah, but Buffalo ain't that big of a city. You'd think someone would have seen her, but zip. Not a movie or a dance...nothing. 'Course she said something once about her dad being real old-fashioned and strict, so maybe that's why she don't get out more."

Now that Florence said it, I realized I'd never seen Anne at the cinema or heard about her going to any of the dances where girls hung out with departing soldiers and sailors, or the boys who didn't make it into the service. "I guess. Say, Florence, what kind of cigarettes do you smoke?"

She stubbed hers out, held it up, and smiled. "Luckys, same as you, Betty." She tossed the butt onto the pavement and started to walk across the yard to the assembly line building. "I'm not your girl," she said over her shoulder.

Darn it, someone was. In the far corner, girls headed into the building where they painted and assembled the fuselages, before rolling them into place for final assembly. The cafeteria building was kitty-corner from paint, not that far from the big assembly line building. I decided to take a quick look where the fire started before heading back to work.

They'd moved the damaged engine off to the side. The Allison sat off in the corner, a misbehaved child, waiting for its fate. Prob'ly no one had had the time to figure out if it could be saved. I poked around it and saw lines of black soot where the flames had traveled. No one had bothered cleaning off the soda acid and sand, either. The engine didn't have much free space, but someone could have wedged a lit cigarette in there if given enough time. And if she hadn't been noticed. Not impossible, but the space was tight enough that I doubted it was completely accidental. The lines hadn't started up after lunch, so I got down on my hands and knees to check the floor and around the chain on line two.

Mr. Satterwaite's voice broke my concentration. "What do you think you're doing, Miss Ahern?"

I bumped my head trying to stand and my eyes watered a little as a I bit back a word Mom would definitely not approve of. I scooted back, then tried again. "Just lookin' around."

"Just looking, huh?" He sneered. "Still fancy yourself a detective. Last time didn't teach you anything?"

"Last time it worked out pretty well as I remember it. Pretty well for me, that is."

The sneer turned into a scowl. "Get back to work before I dock your pay."

I didn't scurry, but I double-timed it back to my place. I wouldn't put it past Mr. Satterwaite to make good on his threat. I didn't find anything at the scene of the crime, and I'd struck out talking to Alice and Florence. Seemed to me that I'd have to look for an opportunity to corner Anne somewhere other than at Bell.

Chapter 4

My shift started in the morning and passed quietly. I expected more of the same that afternoon. Maybe, despite what I'd observed, the fire truly had been an accident, the guilty party too scared to 'fess up. I was turnin' into Dot, seeing conspiracy at every corner like a low-grade spy picture.

After Mr. Satterwaite hustled me off, I went back to windshields on line five. A lot of the girls working with me were the same ones who'd been on engines over on two yesterday: Catherine, Anne, Florence, Mildred, Rose, and Alice.

Alice took her place beside me. "You look as jumpy as a cat on a hot tin roof, Betty. You expecting trouble?"

"No. I guess I'm jittery, that's all." I looked around. "Hey, where's Catherine?"

She appeared and squeezed in between Mildred and Florence across from me. "Right here. I had to use the bathroom. You'll never guess what I saw." Her gaze darted in Anne's direction, a few places down the assembly line. "I caught Miss Snooty poking around."

"Where?" Mildred asked.

"Right along the chain where the fuselage moves from instruments to windshields." Catherine readjusted her shirt sleeves. "I noticed her before I hit the john. She jumped about a mile high when I asked what she was doing. I tell ya, something's not right with that girl."

I glanced down the line. Anne stood by the spot where they installed brakes. She didn't look any different to me. Same closed expression, same stiff posture. The girls around her talked to each other like Anne wasn't even standing there. I debated running over to say a quick word, but the conveyor chain clanked as it started.

"Here we go," Catherine said, studying the oncoming plane body. "Another long, boring afternoon."

But the line didn't run for very long before a horrible grinding and the shriek of metal on metal split the air. The chain backed up on itself, bursting out of the channel on the floor where in normally ran smooth as a snake.

I had to shout to be heard over the racket. "Shut it down!"

Florence pulled the emergency stop. Everything rumbled to a halt.

Catherine, who had stepped back at the first sign of trouble, eyed the belt. "Well I'll be damned."

Mr. Satterwaite pounded into the room, huffing like a steam engine. "What the hell is going on in here?" He took in the bunches of chain poking out of the floor. "Someone better have a good explanation for this."

Except we didn't. Everyone looked at one another until I spoke up. "We got back from our lunch break. Started up the assembly line, it ran for maybe a minute, and then we heard an awful noise, like the chain links were banging against each other. Then it all started to back up on itself and jump the channel. I told 'em to shut everything down."

He glared at me. "Oh you did, did you, Miss Ahern?"

What did he expect us to do? Keep an assembly line that was obviously malfunctioning running and maybe cause more damage? None of us were dimwits. But I didn't say any of that. Instead, I fixed him with what I hoped was a defiant stare. "Yes, sir, I did."

He grumbled, but didn't reply to me. Instead he waved at the rest of the group. "Well, come on. Get this cleaned up. There weren't any problems this morning, so we need to get down there and see what's broken. Come on, snap to it."

Fortunately, the malfunction was contained to the floor. The fuselage hadn't run into any waiting equipment, and the one behind it hadn't been able to move far because the chain had stopped moving. Girls pushed aside parts and attempted to smooth out the links. I grabbed the part that wasn't crooked at attempted to place it back in the channel.

Part of the crooked chain was still in the floor, jammed on something that prevented me from pulling it out. Catherine and Florence came over to help. Between the three of us, we managed to wriggle it free. Overcome with curiosity, I looked at the floor, but I couldn't see anything. I knelt and reached in, feeling my way.

Florence grabbed my shoulder. "Betty, be careful."

"I will." I shook her off and continued my exploration, careful not to slice my fingers on the mechanism that moved the chain along. Eventually, I felt a long, smooth stick. Metal, no doubt. A stick that had no business being in the floor channel. It was wedged tight. I tugged until it came free, then pulled it out.

It was a long, gunmetal gray rod, chewed to bits where the teeth of gears had ground against it, twisted and bent by the force of the chain. "Well, now." I turned and held it out to Mr. Satterwaite. "I'm pretty sure this doesn't belong in there. Aren't you?"

His face got beet red and he mumbled something about everybody staying put. Then he stomped off.

"Like we'd leave after that," Florence said.

Catherine dropped to the floor, legs crossed. "I would." At Florence's stare, Catherine shrugged. "If I can't work, I might as well go home. You think anybody would mind if I cut out?"

"I don't think that would be a great idea," I said as I checked out the room. All along the other lines, girls turned their heads to spy out the action on line five. Movement on the other four lines never stopped, noise thundering on. But it was interspersed with a frantic buzz as they muttered, heads together and looking a bit anxious at the damage.

One person was conspicuously absent. "Anyone see where Anne went?" My words set off a storm of whispering among the girls on five. I double-checked, but Anne was definitely gone.

Catherine stretched her arms to the roof. "She must have skedaddled at the first sign of trouble." She tucked her hands behind her head, stretched out her legs and stared at me. "If you weren't suspicious before, Betty, I'd say you should be now."

***

They took this accident more seriously than the fire. Everyone who worked that particular assembly line was marched through yard, a frigid wind biting our faces, and back to the cafeteria, where a Niagara Falls police officer took our names and addresses, and asked what we remembered.

"Somebody's sure taking this hard," Alice said from where she'd slumped against the wall.

"It affects war production," I said. "I said before, management wants all five lines running full throttle. The fire just damaged one engine. This has torn up a whole chain. It'll have to be replaced and that could take a whole day. Or more. The more time we spend twiddling our thumbs waitin' for repairs, the fewer planes get shipped overseas to the boys."

Catherine scoffed. "The Americans aren't even using the P-39."

"The Soviets are. And the French."

"The Reds. Bah. Big deal."

"They're our allies last I checked. I'm sure they got sisters, and parents, and girlfriends who want 'em home safe." I craved a cigarette, but the cops weren't letting anybody go anywhere until they'd been interviewed. A lot like last time the police had been called out to Bell, 'cept that time we'd huddled in the open yard.

Florence crossed her arms on the table and rested her chin on them. "What do you think is going on, Betty?"

I straddled the table bench and sat. "I s'pose it's possible we're just victims of a string of bum luck. Accidents can happen anywhere."

"You don't think that's the case, though. Do you?"

"Not after this, I don't." At her quizzical look, I continued. "That metal bar wasn't part of the conveyor line. Someone put it there. Not 'someone thought they were fixing things and it came loose' putting it there, either. There's no way the chain would run smooth with a big stick of metal jammed in it. But it doesn't make a lot of sense."

Catherine spoke. "Sure it does. Someone wants to shut us down."

"Well, that person isn't very smart. Just like yesterday, they'll make repairs

25

and we'll carry on like nothin' happened. Sure, this is a bit more involved than a burned out engine, but all the same, not a huge setback. I bet line five is up by morning, maybe sooner."

Rose scowled. "Here I was hoping for a couple of free days."

Alice, who was sitting next to Florence, leaned in. "Who would have the opportunity to jam things up like this?"

"That's what I'm tryin' to think about." There'd been no problems that morning, so it was pretty clear to me that nothing had been tampered with until lunch. The chain had busted pretty fast when they turned it back on, so if the rod had been stuck in there while the assembly line was running that morning, the damage would have happened before we went to eat. "We turn things on, the racket starts, and we shut things down. Who all was there?"

Florence sat up. "Almost everyone. You and me. Catherine, Mildred, Alice, Helen, Rose, and Anne." Florence counted off the names on her fingers. "Those are the ones I know best. Plus the others on lines one, two, three, and four, but we don't need to worry about them, do we?"

I thought about that. "I'm not sure we can cross them off the list, but hold that thought. Of the names you just mentioned, who was always in sight?"

"I definitely never lost sight of Mildred, Rose, Alice, and Helen," Florence said. "Helen was standing next to me, Rose on the other side, and the others were right across the way. We all went to lunch, then came back together."

"I worked next to Mildred," I said. "I don't think she went anywhere. I was across from Catherine. Anne was down the line a bit." I looked at Catherine, who was sitting at the next table. "You said you saw Anne poking around? When?"

"Right after we came off break. I told you. I was on my way to the bathroom and she was standing by the dolly cart. Right where things got all jammed up."

"What was she doing?"

"I dunno. But she was wiping her hands on her pants, like she was cleaning 'em off. Maybe after she wedged that bar inside."

I thought about it. It was possible. But wouldn't Anne have attempted to be a little sneakier, not let herself be seen by anyone passing by?

Florence drummed her fingers on the table. "Two accidents and she's at both. You gotta admit it's fishy, Betty."

"I guess. But so were you, and Helen, and Alice, and—"

"All right, I get it. Sheesh."

I eyed Catherine. Of all of us, her and Rose seemed the least bothered by the work stoppage. "You said you went to the bathroom. Anybody see you there?"

She glared, but her voice stayed even. "No. I don't usually take a gang when I gotta pee."

I turned to Rose. "And where were you?"

Her face was smooth, but there was a glint in her eye. "Why? You think I had somethin' to do with this?"

Alice and Florence watched us both. Their expressions were similar, like they were getting ready to duck an explosion. Florence cleared her throat. "You said we can't dismiss the other line workers. What did you mean, Betty?"

I didn't want to back down from Rose's hard-eyed challenge, but I turned to face Florence. "The best time to put that bar in was when no one was around. Someone from one of the other lines could've nipped in, done the dirty work, and been back at her place like nothing had happened."

Catherine studied her nails. "Like Anne."

"Except you saw her," I shot back. "Not very sneaky. Actually sorta stupid, if you think about it. I don't think Anne is all that stupid. A pain in the butt, a little snobbish perhaps, but not dumb."

"Then why'd she take off after all hell broke loose?"

I couldn't answer.

Rose tossed her head. "Face it, Betty. She's the best suspect."

"What's her motive?" I asked. There was always a motive.

"Don't know, don't care."

Florence broke in. "You've all heard her brother is a Nazi sympathizer, right?"

My response was swift. "That's nothing but a rumor. Plus even if he is, it's not like that has anything to do with Anne."

"But what if it's true and Anne feels the same as her brother?" Florence tilted her head. "He backs the Nazis, his sister works for a company that's supplying the Allies, he gets her to cause problems here at the plant."

"Makes sense to me," said Catherine.

I shook my head. "Innocent until proven guilty. I admit Anne's a suspect, but that's all I'm willing to do right now. She isn't the most likable person, but we should talk to her before we decide she's guilty. Give her a chance to defend herself."

Catherine tossed her head again. "Too bad she isn't here."

I couldn't explain why, but the explanation felt a little too pat for my taste. But without any proof, the only way for me to either clear or convict was for me to hunt Anne down and force her to have a talk.

Chapter 5

They weren't able to bring line five back up after all the fuss. Anne disappeared. We were assigned to different areas for the day, so I wasn't able to tell if she was working another line or of she'd vamoosed. The others were convinced she'd left work on the sly. Since no one saw her after the accident, it was more than possible. Rose was the most vocal in her accusations. "Mark my words," she'd said. "They'll find out Anne was behind the whole mess."

As for me, well, I needed some more convincing.

I offered to go down to the Broadway Market for Mom when I got home Saturday evening. I admit, I wasn't just being helpful. Friday was payday at a lot of companies, including Bell, which meant folks did their shopping Saturday. Broadway offered meat and produce, as well as bread and pastries. It was one of the spots in the city where anyone and everyone could mingle. Since I hadn't cornered Anne at work, I figured it was the next best chance I had of finding her.

I wandered the stalls holding Mom's list, keeping an eye peeled for Anne. I'd almost given up when my patience was rewarded. I spotted her at one of the bakeries, looking over a selection of breads. "Anne. Hey, Anne!" I called over the crowd.

She glanced my way, dropped the loaf she was holding, and hurried in the opposite direction as fast as the crowd would let her.

Huh. Why was she running off? Dodgy, for sure. With my knowledge of the market layout, I knew where she'd most likely come out and how to get there faster. I cut across a couple of aisles, stopped, and checked out the crowd. Her blonde hair was easy to spot among the Poles with their babushkas. I waited.

She pulled up short when she saw me. "Betty, I didn't...how did you get here so fast?"

"Shortcut." I stepped out of the way of an old Polish woman, then closed the distance. "Where'd you go this afternoon? I was looking all over for you."

"Oh I...went to the infirmary. After the line broke down, I didn't feel well so they sent me home."

She hadn't "felt well"? She hadn't been close enough to be injured. "There was a lot of talk after you left."

"About?"

I crossed my arms. "What do you think?"

Her face turned a light pink.

I waited, but she didn't say anything more. "Why'd you run away from me just now?"

"I didn't." She shifted on her feet and clutched a bag containing her purchases.

Sure, like Jimmy and Michael didn't avoid Mom when they were up to no good. "How're you doing?"

"I'm fine." Her face and voice were wary. "To be honest, Betty...I couldn't stay. They all blame me, don't they?"

"What makes you say that?"

"I'm not stupid. The others don't like me. I'm not sure you like me, either." She looked around, plainly eager to go anywhere but that spot, but she was hemmed in by old ladies and families.

"Honestly? I don't like or not like you. One minute you act like you're above us, the next you're talkin' like you're my new best friend. I don't get it."

She said nothing.

"Tell me about your brother."

"Jurgen? Why do you want to know about him?" The wariness was still there, but also puzzlement. Interesting combination.

"No, your brother George. I didn't know you had two. Is George older or younger?"

"Jurgen is George. That's what Mama and Papa call him at home so it's what I'm used to hearing. He's older than me. And he's fine, although I don't know why you'd be interested." She hefted her bag.

"Is it true he's part of the Bund? You know, the Nazi supporters?"

The deep pink flashed to scarlet. "He's not...please, I need to go. I'll talk to you later."

We were interrupted by the approach of a guy not much older than me, fair like Anne and a bored expression on his face. With his blond hair slicked back, he looked a little like Fredric March. "Anne, Mama and Papa are looking for you," he said. "Who is this?" He looked me up and down. Checking me out, but not in a cheap way.

Another young man pushed through the crowd. He was also blond, but darker, with a square jaw and brown eyes. Gary Cooper, but without the leading man charm. He was shorter than the first guy by a couple of inches. "You found her." His attention turned to me and he straightened a bit. "Well, hello. Who's your friend, Anne?"

I waited for Anne to introduce me, but judging by the miserable expression on her face I'd be waiting until the end of the war. "Betty Ahern. I work with Anne. You are?"

The newcomer held out a hand. "Freddie Linden. This is George. He and Anne are my cousins." He threw a look at George. "We'll finish that talk later."

"There's nothing to talk about." George glanced at his wristwatch. "Come on, Anne. I have things to do tonight."

I studied both Linden boys. "I'm glad I met you before you shipped out."

George had half-turned away, but my words drew him back. "Shipped out? Did Anne tell you that? We're not going anywhere."

"Oh, I'd have thought two strapping young men like yourselves would be eager to join up."

"Sorry, but that's none of your business." George tugged on Anne's arm. "Let's go. I'm going to be late."

31

"I can help you out," Freddie said. "I told you—"

George let go of his sister and rounded on his cousin. "*Quietscte*! This isn't the place to talk and besides, how many times do I have to tell you the answer is no." He scowled at me, then snapped his fingers at Anne. "Let's go before I have to drag you out of here, both of you." He stalked off, Freddie hot on his heels. George might have been done with the conversation, but from the way Freddie was jabbering away, he wasn't.

Poor Anne had to hurry after the boys, arms drooping with her bulging shopping bags. I saw her mouth move, but the words were lost over the bustle of the crowd.

I stood rooted in place, barely noticing as people bumped into me and grumbled. The whole meeting left me floored. Anne was embarrassed. The men were arguing over something, and prob'ly something fishy, if George had been so tight-lipped. One thing was certain. I'd have loved to be able to tag along with the Lindens on their trip home.

***

I got off the bus and paused to light a cigarette. I held it between my lips as I balanced the bags in my hands. I was saved from looking like a puffing chimney as I walked down the street by the appearance of Liam Tillotson.

I'd known Lee forever, which is to say since we started school. First time we met, he told me he hated his name and if I wanted to be his friend I'd have to call him Lee. When we were in second grade, he and I competed to see who could land farther jumping off a tire swing. He broke his left leg real bad on his landing and it never healed straight. He'd limped ever since, which kept him outta the service. When he wanted to bust my chops, he'd say I wrecked his army career.

"Why don't you give me one of those bags before you swallow that thing." He didn't wait for a reply and took the sack from my left hand.

"Thanks," I said, after I took a drag and exhaled. "You just knock off?"

"Yep. Mom will be thrilled. I'll be home in time for dinner and won't have an excuse not to take out the garbage." He peeked into the bag. "Unless you're gonna ask me to eat at your place."

"Yeah 'cause I had enough ration coupons to feed your bottomless pit of a stomach."

He grinned. "What's shaking up there at Bell? I heard you had some excitement. You girls have all the fun."

"You want me to come down to General Motors and cause some trouble?"

"Nah, that's okay." Despite the hitch in his walk, Lee kept pace with me easily. "Joking aside, I saw Dot yesterday and she told me about the fire."

"And we had a problem on the assembly line earlier today." I filled him in on the details. By the time I was done, we'd reached my house. We stood on the sidewalk while I finished smoking. The cat appeared from the side of the house and poked his nose in the bag Lee set at my feet.

"They find out who's behind it?" Lee asked. He reached down to swat the animal away.

"Leave him be." I dropped my cigarette and smashed it underfoot. "Nah, not yet. I s'pose it's a matter of time, though. These problems haven't caused too much grief, but the higher-ups won't want it to continue."

"Since when do you have a cat?"

"He's a stray. Mary Kate's been feeding him."

Lee shook his head. "They got any suspects?"

"Management isn't saying, but of course everybody's talking. Most of the girls think Anne Linden is behind it." I told him about Anne, including the rumor of her brother's Bund involvement, and how I'd seen Anne, George, and Freddie up at the Broadway Market.

Lee watched the cat as he wound his way around my ankles. "This guy, George. What does he look like?"

I described Anne's brother.

"Is he really in the Bund or is that just guff?"

"I don't know. But George and Freddie were arguing about something. I'd bet my next paycheck on it. And if George had told Anne to jump, she would've been three feet in the air before she asked how high." I squatted down and rubbed the cat's head behind his ears. He stretched his neck against my hand, eyes closed. "Why the questions?"

"There were some guys handing out propaganda at GM the other day. I think they were with the Bund."

"Can you find out if George was with 'em?"

"Lemme ask." He raised an eyebrow. "You figuring on being a real-life Nancy Drew?"

I patted the cat's head and was rewarded with a meow. I stood. "I'd rather be Sam Spade, if it's all the same to you."

Lee's expression sobered. "I seem to recall Sam Spade gets in a lot of scrapes."

I picked up my bags. "Then I'll just have to be better than him, won't I?"

Chapter 6

I arrived at work Monday ready for trouble to strike, determined to keep my eyes peeled. I knew the saboteur was still on the loose because if anyone had been caught, it would have made the news. Lee had joked about Nancy Drew. I was dead serious about Sam Spade.

The morning part of the shift passed without a hitch. All lines were up and running, but I didn't see Anne until right before the noon lunch whistle blew. Was it my imagination or was she paler than usual? Did it have anything to do with the scene between her, her brother, and her cousin from Saturday evening? She hurried out of the assembly building and had fled the yard by the time I got outside.

When I got to the cafeteria, I sought her out. She sat by herself like always. A beat-up paperback was open in front of her, but the stillness of her eyes and failure to turn a page said she wasn't reading it.

I dropped onto the bench seat across the table. "Hiya. I barely got a chance to talk to you Saturday. Your brother all but dragged you out," I said as I unpacked my lunch pail.

No answer.

"Two boys at home. Lucky you." I watched her as I ate. "What do they do all day?" If I could get her talking about her menfolk, maybe I could learn something that would either put her in the clear for sure, or finger her as Bell's saboteur.

"Freddie doesn't live with us. He's got a job at a delicatessen in Kaisertown, on Clinton, and rents a little apartment."

"What about George?"

"He doesn't work."

I wondered what she meant by that. With so many men overseas, any guy who could stand up, breathe, and had a pulse could get a job. I waited, but she didn't elaborate. "I'm surprised neither of them is in the service."

"They both were 4F."

Not acceptable for military service. "That's awful. I can't imagine how that'd feel." Playing sympathetic about two strangers didn't feel like quite the right thing to say. For all I knew they and their families were overjoyed they were safe at home. "I mean, I 'spect they'd be disappointed, right? But there are other ways to support the war effort. My friend, Lee, has a bum leg, so he works down at the General Motors plant instead."

Once again, she didn't answer.

Was that George's problem? He was angry about being told he wasn't healthy enough to serve? It didn't seem to have bothered Freddie too much. "I've heard a rumor George is in the Bund. I can't imagine why he'd do that. I mean—"

That got her attention. "I told you it's not true. I don't know what you're talking about." She swept up her half-eaten lunch, the book, and stormed out of the cafeteria.

Nice going, Betty. Philip Marlowe would slap me silly. My skills as an interrogator needed work.

Rose DeLuca took her place. "What's her problem?"

"I'm not entirely sure." I watched Anne as she nearly bowled over some girls, including Dot, in her haste to leave the cafeteria. "I met her brother over the weekend. He struck me as a real peach."

"I know." Rose leaned in. "I saw him once down at that jazz club in South Buffalo. He was with a bunch of his friends."

I couldn't see George in a jazz club. Then again, if they were looking for a place to hang out without no one hearing them, the noise of a band would sure be the place. "You know any of those friends?"

"Nuh-uh." Rose unwrapped a sandwich and folded her waxed paper neatly into squares. "They were all talking German, though. Least I think it was German. And they all looked like those propaganda pictures you see on the newsreels, the ones the Germans use. Blond, tall, strong."

"That so?" It reinforced my opinion of George from the market. Could it be that he bought that whole superior Aryan race thing? Maybe he did sympathize with the Nazis. 'Course, as Pop would tell me, liking Hitler and his cronies wasn't proof of anything, especially sabotage. I wondered if Freddie had been with the group and described him to Rose. "Was someone like that there, too?"

"No idea. Gotta admit, they were lookers, all of them. Except for one guy. Skinny, dark hair, bad skin. I tried to say 'hi' and be friendly. But they didn't wanna have anything to do with me."

Dot made her way over and sat down with a huff. "I take back everything I ever said that mighta been nice about her. She didn't even say sorry." Dot grumped as she unpacked her lunch.

"Who?"

"Anne. Ran smack into me and didn't even apologize." Dot tore off a piece of her sandwich with a ferocity she didn't usually have. "If she wants to make some friends, saying sorry when you almost knock someone flat would help with that. She can take her pastry and stick it."

Dot's outrage was amusing, if only 'cause it was not like her at all. "What pastry?"

"She had some baked thing in her lunch last week and offered me some. She said her mother bakes every night."

Every night? "Was it sweet?"

"I dunno. It looked sticky. Why d'ya ask?"

"Dot, when was the last time your mother baked a sweet dessert? Just because?"

She stared at me, understanding dawning on her face. "Mrs. Linden bakes every night. That's what Anne said."

"Exactly. Where's she getting all the sugar?"

Dot shifted in her seat. "She could be trading."

Trading for coupons was pretty common. But enough to bake every night? Somehow, I just couldn't see it.

***

I made up my mind on the bus ride home Monday afternoon. I needed to find Anne and make her talk to me, by hook or by crook. "You don't know where the Lindens live, do you?" I asked Dot.

"Only that it's in Kaisertown." Dot took off her bandanna and shook out her hair. "I think they go to church at St. Casimir's. Anne said something once about it. I'd imagine she lives near there, but I don't know exactly where. Why?"

"There's a lot of guesswork going on about Anne and her brother. I was thinking I'd go ask her flat out what the deal is."

"You sure? I mean, if George Linden really is in the Bund and he's behind all the trouble we've had, accusing him could be dangerous."

"I wouldn't be accusing him. I'd be talking to Anne."

Dot didn't look convinced, but she knew me well enough not to argue.

St. Casimir's was on Cable Street, which was not real close to home. I figured it would be at least half an hour by bus one way. Fortunately, Mom worked with the Christian Mothers on Tuesday nights, so it was just Pop and us kids for dinner. Mom had made a chicken casserole for us before she left. "Hey, Pop. Would it be okay if I ate early? I gotta go over to Kaisertown," I said.

He looked up from his evening paper. "Where in Kaisertown?"

"Over by St. Casimir's." He didn't need to know I wasn't exactly sure of my final destination.

"Who's over there?"

"A girl from work."

"A friend?"

"Not really. Just a girl I wanna talk to."

He tilted his head. "This have anything to do with the problems they've had lately?"

Darn him. "Well, kinda. Talk is that Anne Linden's brother is involved somehow. Anne's always trying to get on my good side, chat me up and stuff. I figured if anybody has a chance at getting her to spill it's me."

Pop said nothing at first. I knew he backed me up on work. I wasn't too sure he felt the same about being a private dick. Then again, he was generally the more understanding of my parents. "You'd better be home before your mother gets back. You got enough for bus fare?"

I nodded and went over to kiss his cheek. "Thanks, Pop."

It had been warm earlier, but now that the sun was down there was a nip to the air. I got off the bus at the corner of Weimar and Clinton, the spire of St. Casimir's in plain view. There weren't too many houses on Clinton. It was mostly a business district. I decided to walk down Cable Street toward the church. If I didn't see her on Cable, I'd start walking the nearby streets.

I walked quick, both to keep warm and finish my trip as fast as I could. The bells at the church chimed the half-hour. Five-thirty. I needed to be back on the bus by six-thirty to get home before Mom.

There were a few people out on Cable, including an old woman setting out her milk bottles. "'Scuse me," I said from the sidewalk. "Do you know where the Linden family lives?"

"Why do you want to know?" the woman asked, not bothering to mask her suspicion.

"I work with their daughter, Anne."

"If you're friends with Anne, wouldn't you know where they live?"

"We aren't best friends, only friendly. She never had a reason to give me an address."

She gave me a hard-eyed look for a sec and I thought she was gonna tell me to scram. But then she nodded, apparently satisfied I wasn't gonna egg their house or nothing. "They live over on Casimer Street. Number 437," she said. "Go past the church and turn left."

Anne's home was a neat little white house that sat almost next to the sidewalk with a tiny strip of mostly-dead grass in between. There was a small patch of dirt with the remains of a Victory garden. Through the front window, I could see flimsy white curtains. No star, like the one we had for Sean. It made sense if George was a 4F. The Lindens had already put out their milk bottles for the evening. I knocked.

Anne opened the door. "Betty, what...you can't be here."

"Why? I've gotta talk to you."

"Not...I don't want my brother to see you."

"You can't have friends?"

She threw a frantic look over her shoulder and stepped out of the house, pulling the door shut carefully so it didn't make any noise. "It's not that. He...he wasn't pleased after I saw you at the market on Saturday. He doesn't like people snooping."

Which meant George had something to hide. I fixed her with a stare. "Anne, I know we got off on the wrong foot. I'm sorry 'bout that. I want to help."

"With what?"

"I'm gonna give it to you it straight. You're right. The other girls think you're involved with these accidents."

Her voice was bitter. "They only think that because I'm German. So is Helen Ackerman and no one is accusing her."

"That's part of it. You don't help your own cause. Some of 'em say you think you're better than everyone 'cause you hardly mingle."

"I'm not comfortable talking to people. I'd rather read. A book doesn't criticize you."

"But you keep following me, trying to be friends. Why? What makes me so special?"

"Because the others respect you. I thought if I could get on your good side, they'd at least stop talking about me, even if I couldn't be their friend."

I was flattered she thought I had so much pull, but I wasn't sure I'd agree. "If that's the case, tell me straight. Is your brother in the Bund?"

She paused, then wilted a bit. "George has friends. I know Mama and Papa don't like them, but he doesn't talk about them much. I don't like them, either. I don't know if they belong to the Bund or not."

I believed her. Unfortunately, it didn't help. "The others at Bell, they think you'd do anything to help George."

"I love my brother, Betty. No matter what he is or what he's done. I'm sure you understand that."

"Loving a brother? Yeah. But saying you love him doesn't help me clear you."

"That's what you want to do?"

40

Was it? Innocent until proven guilty was the American way. I'd heard stories of the Nazis dragging people off in the night. I didn't want this country to be that way, that's for sure. "I want to know who's mucking things up at Bell. If that's you, well, you're gonna have to deal with that. But if it's not you, I don't wanna see you take the fall for someone else."

I thought she might be on the cusp of confiding in me. Unfortunately, we were interrupted by Freddie Linden, who came out of the house before she said another word. "Betty Ahern, right?" he asked. "What are you doing in Kaisertown?"

I nodded at him. "I was talking to Anne. Privately."

"I see." He eyed Anne, who'd gone quiet and still as a mouse looking to avoid a cat. "I think you should go inside, Anne. Aunt Maria will need help with the baking."

Anne scooted off without another word.

Baking again? "They sure make a lot of sweet treats in this house. I'm jealous. Someone has terrific luck with the coupon trading."

Freddie drew his eyebrows together. "Coupon trading?"

"You know. Ration coupons." Was he joshing me? "For sugar. I mean, there are fewer people in this house than mine and my mother can't bake every night."

His face muscles relaxed. "Ah, well, there are other ways of getting what you need."

I rolled the dice. "Like the Bund?"

"The Bund. A group of deluded people with unrealistic fantasies."

"You're not a supporter."

"Me? No. I'm not a fan of fascism. I'm a red-blooded American capitalist."

"What about George?"

Freddie's expression turned cautious. "George is, well, let's say that George doesn't know what he wants. I'm trying to help him with that." He walked up to the house and paused with his hand on the doorknob. "I'd try and explain, but I get the feeling you wouldn't understand. Not your fault. You *are* only a girl. Good night, Betty." He went inside and shut the door.

Only a girl? I had been pretty committed to continuing to investigate the accidents at Bell and George Linden's possible involvement through the Bund before because it was the right thing for the war and I wanted to keep my paycheck. Freddie's statement made me even more determined. I wasn't gonna stop until I knew exactly what had happened and why.

***

It was almost seven-thirty when I got home 'cause I'd missed the bus back to the First Ward and had to wait for the next one. I decided to go in the back door. Better chance of getting inside without being seen.

I pulled up short when I saw a pair of glowing, green eyes skulking under the wilting vegetables in our Victory garden. The cat was back, almost certainly looking for another free meal. "What're you doing here?" He stared at me. "Go on, get out. No more milk for you."

The cat gave a pitiful meow and laid down, tail swishing back and forth.

I sighed, fetched the same saucer, filled it with milk, and took it outside. The cat slunk back when I stepped near it, so I set down the saucer and backed off. Again, as soon as I did it attacked the milk and lapped it up.

I was getting as soft as Mary Kate, being played like a violin. There was no other explanation. "This is the last time, cat. I mean it. It's hard enough feeding the six of us. I don't need to be taking care of you, too."

The cat lifted its head and blinked. A drop of milk clung to its whisker. But when I didn't say anything else, it went back to drinking.

I went inside and locked the door.

Mom's voice behind me was like a whip. "Elizabeth Anne. Where do you think you're going?"

She thought I was sneaking out. In a way, this was a good thing. If she thought she'd caught me before I got into mischief, it'd go easier on me in the long run. "I was going to check to make sure the garbage was safe. I heard stray cats fighting last night and I didn't want them making a mess."

"In your new muffler and mittens?" Mom grabbed a wooden spoon and swatted me across the legs. I hastened away from the door. "Let me tell you something, missy. Your factory friends might be able to sneak out to go to dances and meet boys, but I'll not be having it in my house. If you want to be engaged then act like it. Is that clear?"

"Yes, ma'am." I hightailed it to my room. She thought I was sneaking out to a dance? Thank goodness. If she knew where I'd really been, job or not I'd be locked in my room for a month.

Chapter 7

My foul mood the next morning must've showed because Dot didn't talk to me on the bus. I'd traveled all the way to Kaisertown, been busted by my mother, and hadn't learned a darn thing. Or had I? George and Freddie both acted like guys with things to hide. Freddie maybe didn't support the Bund, but what had he and his cousin been arguing about that George didn't want overheard? Anne might not know exactly what they were up to, but she knew enough to make her skittish, I could tell. Maybe it was a result of growing up with folks who remembered the old country, but she also came off as plenty willing to let the men lead the way, even if she knew what they were doing wasn't quite on the up-and-up.

Bottom line, she might not know everything, but she was smart enough to be scared of what could happen if it came to light. Whether or not it had anything to do with sabotage at Bell, well, that was the big question.

After we punched in, we went directly across the yard to the assembly building. But before we went to our assignments, Mr. Satterwaite called us together.

"Just how I want to start my day," I said, careful he didn't hear me. "Listening to Mr. Grumpy."

Beside me, Dot snickered and Florence rolled her eyes.

"Pay attention," Mr. Satterwaite said. "By now, you are all aware of the incidents that transpired last Friday and Saturday."

"Get him and his fifty-cent words," Catherine whispered.

Mildred and Helen joined Dot in her giggles.

"Quiet back there." Mr. Satterwaite glared at me, but as I wasn't doing anything all he could do is continue. "It is clear to those in management that these are deliberate acts of sabotage, aimed at damaging the war production at Bell Airplane."

Well, no kidding. I coulda told him that.

"While the investigation is going on, we will continue our work. But I must warn you. If the girl responsible is not caught, or there is further damage, the consequences will be dire. It might even lead to some or all of you losing your jobs. Pity, but maybe then Bell will bring back men who can be trusted to work and not cause trouble." He paused for effect, then clapped his hands. "Now get to it before we lose even more production time."

If Mr. Satterwaite had more in common with Conrad Veidt than a receding hairline and slicked back hair, I'd have been a little worried at his announcement. As it was, he was too cartoonish to be taken seriously. He also couldn't have said anything more likely to stop us in our tracks if he'd tried.

No one moved. As soon as Mr. Satterwaite was out of sight, the talk started. Everything from anger to worry to flat-out fear. I faced the group. Anne skulked in the back, but the rest huddled like sheep. Dot chewed her bottom lip. Helen, Florence, Alice, and Mildred bunched together, all of 'em talking at once. Others clustered in little groups of two and three. In the cavernous room, the yammering echoed off the windows, walls, and partially completed planes. Only Catherine and Rose looked like they were enjoying the commotion.

They all looked to me to lead, Anne had said. Time to find out if she was right. I put my fingers to my lips and whistled, a sharp, shrill sound that cut the babble like a hot knife through butter. "Everybody shut your yaps and listen." I put my hands on my hips. "I understand you're upset and things sound pretty bad."

"You're telling me," someone shouted.

"We need to keep our cool." I tried to look each girl in the eye.

Florence raised an eyebrow. "Easier said than done, Betty."

I nodded. "I know. I also know that it's Frank Satterwaite's dearest wish to kick us back to the kitchen and bring back the all-male workforce. It's not gonna happen."

Alice glanced around. "But this time—"

"Nothing's changed. There aren't any men, least not enough. Bell needs airplanes built. That's a cold fact. If most of the folks available for the job are women, well, that's who's gonna get the work."

Florence studied me. "They could fire us and bring in a whole new crew."

Florence didn't seem to be panicking, so I directed my words to her knowing that everybody else was listening. Why not? I brushed the thought aside. "That's a load of hooey. Bell isn't gonna fire an entire shift of skilled, trained workers just to bring in a bunch of greenhorns who don't know a lug nut from a washer. They need the planes built today, not three months from now. No, it'd be too big a hit on production. Mr. Satterwaite is talkin' through his hat."

Murmurs ran through the crowd. I didn't need everyone to believe me, I just needed to get one or two who would lead the others back to work.

Catherine spoke up, her voice lazy and scornful. "What do you propose we do?"

"Get back on the assembly line." I tried again to look directly at as many people as I could. "Everything like it usually is. Keep your eyes skinned for trouble and speak up if you hear or see anything. Simple as that."

"What about this saboteur?" Catherine asked. She didn't outright challenge me, but her tone said it all.

I took a deep breath. "You let me worry about that."

***

When the whistle blew for lunch, I went looking for Dot and found her in the admin building near the ladies' room.

"I gotta pee. I'll meet you in the cafeteria." She took a step toward the toilet.

I grabbed her shoulders and spun her in a new direction. "I need your help with something first."

"What kinda help?"

46

"I need a lookout." I quick-marched her toward the locker area, where we stowed coats and lunch pails. I stopped just outside the room.

To Dot's credit, she didn't argue. "What am I watching for?"

"Keep an eye out for anyone coming into this area. You see someone, whistle a few bars of 'Chattanooga Choo Choo' and beat it."

"I shouldn't stay?"

"Nah. I only need a little warning so I'm not caught grubbing through everyone's stuff." I paused at the door. "Thanks, Dot."

She grinned. "Whatever you need, Betty. But make it fast 'cause I do hafta pee."

I left her leaning against the wall where she could easily spot anyone who looked like they might be making a beeline for the lockers. The room was empty. I'd timed it so everyone would've grabbed her lunch and headed to eat.

The problem was I didn't know what I was looking for. I'd been awfully brash when I told Catherine I'd figure out who was our saboteur. It was time to put my money where my mouth was. Examinations of both scenes had coughed up precious little information. I didn't have much confidence my search of the lockers would, either. Surely the saboteur wouldn't be so stupid as to leave evidence in such a public place. Then again, I'd decided that the weak attempts so far meant the culprit wasn't all that bright to begin with, so maybe I'd get lucky.

All three shifts shared the same lockers, so none of them were locked, fortunately. I opened the first one. A worn, but nice coat, gloves in the pocket. I didn't recognize it. I shut the door and moved on. The next three lockers were a bust, yielding only more coats of varying lengths and quality. I rifled through the pockets, but all I found was lint, a couple of pennies, and a few odd buttons.

The fourth locker held a black wool peacoat. In the left pocket was a tube of red lipstick. I uncapped it and twisted it up. It looked like it might be the same color as what had been on the cigarette, but it was tough to tell. In the right pocket was a crumpled piece of paper. The handwriting was unfamiliar and there didn't seem to be any words, just letters and numbers.

After a quick read, I recognized M, H, O, P, A, E and the number three. But there was also something that looked like an O with a line through it and a backwards R. The letters were vaguely familiar. I didn't recognize the coat, but given the red lipstick, I'd give the paper a closer look when I was done searching.

I paused to glance at the clock on the wall. I'd been at it for five minutes. I had to hurry. Not only was I going to be missed at lunch, I couldn't leave poor Dot in the hallway ready to wet her pants. But I hadn't heard the notes of "Chattanooga Choo Choo" so I decided to search a few more lockers.

Four down from where I'd found the note was Anne's locker. I could tell because there was a dog-eared Jane Austen paperback on the shelf. She was the only one I knew who'd have such a thing. No lipstick, no cigarettes. Her lunch pail sat next to the book, which meant she wasn't with the others eating. More reason to pick up the pace.

The cheerful notes of Glenn Miller's springtime hit sounded clear and crisp. I quickly closed the locker and darted over to my own, stuffing the paper in my pants pocket as I did. I opened the door and pulled a compact out of my purse to pretend I was fussing with my makeup.

Anne came through the door a moment later and pulled up when she saw me. "What are you doing here?"

"Just fixing my face before I head to lunch. I had to hit the john." I replaced my compact and took down my lunch. I hoped Dot had scampered off before she'd been seen. "I'm surprised you aren't already in the cafeteria."

Anne retrieved her own pail and the book. "I had to clean up my area first, then wash my hands." She turned to leave.

I wasn't sure what made me continue speaking, but I did. "Hey, Anne."

She paused at the door.

"The other night, when I came to see you. Was there something you wanted to say to me?"

"No, why?"

"I dunno. I got the feeling if your cousin hadn't interrupted us, you had something you were going to tell me. Maybe about your brother and his friends?"

She stared at me for a long moment. "I don't remember. It must not have been very important."

"Look, I'm sorry if I came across a bit rude to you. About Freddie and George, and stuff. But what happened last week, it's got me on edge. So if you know anything—"

She tensed up like a violin string.

I drove on. "—or if you suspect something, please. Tell me. We'll figure out how to deal with it. No matter who all is involved. I just wanna help, that's all."

She didn't break eye contact, but it was forced, like she was trying to look more confident than she was. "I wish I had something to share. But I don't. I'm sorry if you don't believe me." She walked out.

I stared after her. She put on a good face, I'd give her that. But I'd caught the look in her eye. Anne Linden was afraid. Very, very afraid.

Chapter 8

We knocked off at three, leaving anything unfinished for the next crew. Over in the admin building, the usual crowd of girls mingled near the time clock, most of us punching out, but some stragglers just punching in. Under cover of the hubbub, I filled Dot in on the results of my search.

"I can't believe you went through people's things," she said.

"I had to. Not that I found much."

She buttoned up her coat. "You really think Anne is scared? Of what? Being caught?"

"I dunno. Yet. But mark my words. That girl knows something. Or suspects something. I bet she's afraid I'll find out so that's why she's skittish around me lately." Which of course made me even more determined to figure out what she was hiding.

Outside, I scanned the crowd. Maybe I could corner Anne before we left and give convincing her another shot.

Out of the blue, she rushed up. "Betty. I thought about it and I need your help. If you have time, could you meet me later? There's a soda shop on Clinton. Please?"

Before I could answer, a car pulled up in front of the plant entrance, which was shouting distance from the admin building. Girls stopped and stared. It was a 1930 Ford Model A, the two-door kind. Its appearance set off a storm of whispers. No one drove a car, not with all the rubber and gas going to the war effort.

George Linden got out of the driver's side. "Anne, come here. Now! We need to leave. *Eile!*" He snapped his fingers.

Her face creased in an apologetic frown. "The soda shop. Seven o'clock. I'll see you there." Without another word, she ran to the car. George barely waited for her to close the door before he pulled away.

Florence came up beside me. "Whoo-ee. Did ya get a look at that car? Must be nice to have money."

"It was hardly new," I said. "I recognized it, a 1930 Ford. A twelve-year-old car isn't that flash."

Dot raised her eyebrows. "We don't have a car. Neither do your folks, Betty."

No, we didn't. Pop and me, we took the bus. Mom and the younger kids walked mostly. Jimmy had his bike. No one in our neighborhood had a car of any kind.

Florence shook a cigarette out of a pack and tapped it on the box. "You're right, Betty. A twelve-year-old Ford ain't much to look at. But I got a better question." She shot me a look. "Where the heck is he getting the gasoline? My dad has an A-card and he can't hardly get enough gas to drive. He hasn't taken the car out of the garage in months. How's George Linden able to keep the tank filled?"

***

After dinner, I told my folks I was going to lay a wreath at my Uncle Patrick's grave at Holy Cross. Uncle Patrick had been Mom's brother. He'd fought in France during the Great War and Mom said he'd come home "funny," so she'd taken care of him until he died a few years ago. I had liked him. He'd always slipped me a nickel for penny candy.

Tomorrow was Armistice Day, but production wasn't going to stop for anything. There was a dance that night. This would be my only chance. Plus it got me out of the house so I could go meet Anne and get the scoop.

The younger kids hated to go to the cemetery. They said it gave them the creeps, being around all those dead people. I found it peaceful. The temperature had plunged as the sun went down, so I crouched before the tombstone, the grass being too cold to sit on. "What do you think, Uncle Patrick? Am I nuts to even try and talk to this German girl?"

There was a crunch of grass from an uneven step behind me. "You know, Betty, I hope you're not waiting for an answer. Catholics don't believe in that stuff," Lee said.

I stood and turned. "You're going to have to do better'n that if you want to scare me."

"Why would I ever do that?"

"Because you're a troublemaker. You always have been. Just ask my mom."

"You're the one who dreamed up that tire swing dare."

I stood and chucked him, but not hard enough to hurt. "How's work?"

He rubbed his shoulder and grinned. "Ow. You're gonna damage me."

"I am not, ya big baby. I'm toughening you up." Unlike me, Lee didn't have brothers, only two little sisters. Since I'd learned from Sean how to hold my own with the boys, I considered it my job to make sure Lee got the right amount of roughhousing in his life.

"There's a rumor we're getting a big order of Pratt & Whitneys soon, but nothing definite. Still, we're pretty busy." Lee's job at General Motors was perfect for a car fanatic. He'd dreamed of designing the next best-seller for them. Instead, the factory got converted over to wartime production and he spent his hours making engines for American planes.

"You prob'ly shouldn't tell me stuff like that."

"It's just you, Betty." He gave a lopsided grin. "But I didn't come down here to tell you about engines. I stopped at your house, and Jimmy and Michael told me you were here."

"I'm surprised they didn't hit you up for stuff first." Like most kids, my brothers were big into collecting paper, rubber, and cans for the war effort.

"They did. Said if I wanted to know where you were, it was gonna cost me. Racketeers, the both of 'em." Lee limped toward another row of headstones.

"Why'd you come find me? Did you learn anything out about the Bund?"

Lee knelt to brush dried leaves away from a stone I knew was his grandmother's. "You could say that. They were back at GM today." He stood and stuffed his hands in his jacket pockets. "Well, a pro-German group at least. I don't know if it was the actual Bund."

"Passing out leaflets again?"

"Yep. Most of the guys ignored them, but I took one." Of course he did. If a guy had him at knife point, Lee would strike up a conversation while handing over his wallet.

"I'm guessing it wasn't an invitation to a USO party."

"It was propaganda. All about how Germany was really the injured party in the war and how if America was honest, we'd be fighting with the Germans, not against 'em." He stepped back, then looked at me. "It said how we should all go on strike at GM in 'solidarity with our German brethren.' Some of the guys got real mad. They got brothers or sons overseas."

The pamphleteers were lucky they didn't get their butts whipped. "Did you see a tall guy, blond, icy blue eyes? Very fair skinned, thin face, sharp nose?"

Lee shook his head. "George Linden? Nah, didn't see him. At least he wasn't at the gates where I left. He mighta been at one of the others."

We headed out of the cemetery and I turned toward the bus stop so I could catch a ride to Kaisertown. "Would you ask your buddies if they saw him?"

"I already did. I'll ask a couple more of the fellas tomorrow, but so far zilch." The bus pulled up and he watched as the door opened. "Where are you going?"

"Kaisertown to meet Anne Linden. She wants to talk to me about whatever it is that's bugging her and it's important. I can feel it."

"You better be careful."

I dug a coin out of my purse. "It's a soda shop, Lee. I'll be fine."

"You want me to come with you?"

I paused getting on the bus. "Anne doesn't scare me. I can take care of myself."

"What if she brings a friend? Or her brother shows up and he's the one with the friend?"

"It's Tuesday. It's your night to watch your sisters." I poked Lee in the chest. "Relax. You know I'm no delicate flower. I jumped off that tire swing too, remember?"

He rubbed his injured leg. "How could I forget?"

***

I was late getting to the soda shop, but not by much. It was slightly after seven when I walked in, setting the bells above the door tinkling. There weren't many people in the joint, a few at the counter and only a couple tables occupied. I searched for Anne's blonde head and didn't see it. But I did recognize two of the guys at the counter who turned toward the door. George and Freddie Linden.

I strolled up to the soda jerk. "I'll have a root beer float, please."

George and Freddie came over to stand next to me, one on each side. "You've come a long way for a treat, haven't you?" George asked. "They don't have soda shops in the First Ward?"

I focused on the guy making my float. "I'm meeting someone."

"No, you're not. I told my sister to stay home."

Who did this guy think he was? I turned to him. "You sure do give a lot of orders. Maybe that's how it worked in Germany, but this is Buffalo, New York, in the good ol' US of A. If a girl wants to meet a friend from work and gab, she can."

George took half a step toward me. "You listen to me. My sister doesn't have anything to say to you. She might think she does, but she doesn't. Finish your ice cream and go back to your own neighborhood."

I wasn't going to give George the satisfaction of seeing me back up. Besides, I could feel Freddie behind me. They were trying to intimidate me, as though George was Jimmy Cagney in *Angels with Dirty Faces*. It wasn't going to work. "And if I don't? What are you gonna do to me?"

"It's not me you should be worried about." George's stare bored into my eyes. "Come on, Freddie." He headed to the door.

The soda jerk set down my float. I handed him a quarter, but Freddie pushed my hand aside and flipped the kid a coin. "Keep the change," he said.

"I don't need your money."

Freddie straightened and smiled. "I'm doing you a favor. Do yourself one. Drink your soda, get back on the bus, and go home. George won't warn you again."

"What's he so afraid of?"

"What makes you say that?"

"If he doesn't want me talkin' to Anne, he must be scared of what she'll tell me."

"Anne doesn't know anything." Freddie touched his forefinger to his eyebrow, then pointed at me. "It was nice meeting you, Betty. But I suggest you take his advice and don't come around again." He sauntered out of the shop.

Chapter 9

The mood at Bell on Wednesday could be summed up in one word: grim. Everyone, workers and bosses, walked around like we were expecting to be invaded. In a way, I guess we were. But despite a lot of whispering and jittery nerves, the day passed without a hitch.

News that the Allies had kicked off a major invasion in North Africa greeted me when I got home. It almost got me to back out of the evening festivities. After all, I didn't know exactly where Tom was. But the news radio reported the 1st Armored Division was facing off against Rommel. Tom's division. Surely my time would be better spent saying novenas, not dancing.

But Pop said I needed to get out of the house and Dot was counting on my company. I pulled out my last pair of nylons, careful not to snag them as I eased them on. Mary Kate helped me with the pin curls in my hair and made sure the seams of my stockings were straight. I used my coveted South American Red lipstick for the night. Mom frowned on lots of makeup, saying she didn't want her girls to look like tarts. I pinched my cheeks and studied the results. I'd do.

Dot and I entered the First Ward community center arm in arm. They'd done their best to liven the place up with streamers and such, all in patriotic colors of red, white, and blue. A sudden cold snap put a bite in the air and made Dot's nose redder than Rudolph's by the time we arrived. The inside of the center was warm and stuffy by comparison, almost like mid-summer. We shucked off our coats and handed them to the young girl manning the counter.

Dot snapped her fingers along with the beat of the band playing at the far end of the hall. "I'm gonna get something to drink. You want anything?"

"A 7Up would be swell, thanks." I tried to hand her some money, but she waved me off.

"You get the next one. Be right back." She bounced off, shimmying to the music.

It was crowded, more than I expected. Enlistments were taking a toll on the numbers of eligible young men, but a double-handful of guys in Cracker Jack sailor uniforms and Army browns danced with the many girls there.

A sailor sauntered up to me. "Fancy a dance, sweetheart, or are you rationed?"

"Not only am I taken, I'm engaged." I wiggled my left hand in his face.

He shrugged. "Is he here? 'Cause if not, I've got the next dance."

Dot returned with our drinks. "Didn't you hear? She's got a guy. But I don't." She batted her eyes at him. He held out his hand and she giggled, handing her glass to me. They whirled off to the center of the dance floor, swinging to the band, which had launched into Glenn Miller's "(I've got a Gal in) Kalamazoo."

Dot didn't need me at all. I could prob'ly leave and she wouldn't notice 'til they closed the place. But I didn't want to hurt her feelings, so I sipped my pop and looked for an empty table. Finding one, I sat down and watched the swirling couples. That would be Tom and me, soon as this stupid war was over.

"Betty? That you?"

I looked up to see Catherine. I didn't envy many girls, not really. But I was dead jealous of Catherine. She had thick dark hair, her pouty lips set off to perfection against her dusky skin by deep red lipstick. Her dark eyes were inviting and her figure was perfect femme-fatale curvy, just like Lynn Bari. Dot was pinup girl perky. Catherine was exotic. I was an inelegant stick. "Hiya, Catherine."

She sat down, cheeks red from either the heat or dancing, or both. "What's buzzin' cousin? Didn't expect to see you here, what with your guy overseas."

"Dot talked me into it." I nodded toward the dance floor, where Dot had taken up with a new partner. It was a good thing there weren't that many guys at the dance. She'd wind up with a reputation she didn't want.

Catherine, however, found Dot's antics hilarious. "She is such a sweetie. You known her long?"

"Almost my whole life. She's gonna be my maid of honor when, well, you know."

"Right." Catherine's gaze turned sympathetic. "You heard from him or your brother lately?"

"Nah." I sipped my 7Up to cover my expression. "Mail isn't regular and they cross out a lot because the generals don't want troop movements and junk known."

"Must be hard."

I stared at the bubbles in my glass. "It was bad at first. These days I try not to think about it much. Work helps. I say a Hail Mary for each of 'em every morning, though. And I light a candle when I go to Mass."

She watched the couples for a bit as the band started a new tune. "You learned anything more about the troubles at Bell?" She shot a sideways look at me.

"Not much." I held my tongue about my search. No one would be happy to learn I'd rifled through their stuff and Catherine didn't need any more ammunition against Anne. Dot had found a third partner. "I don't think whoever's responsible is a pro, though."

"What makes you say that?"

"This stuff's been penny-ante. Inconvenient and annoying, but not really disruptive. I think someone who was serious about putting a wrench in the works would be slicker."

"How so?"

"They'd hit something big, like paint. We can get more Allisons, or fix 'em. We can repair stuff like the assembly line chain. Heck, we already have. I bet our numbers aren't even down much. Nah, whoever the troublemaker is, he's an amateur and prob'ly acting on his own." As I spoke, I realized that description fitted George Linden to a T. The son of a German immigrant looking to cause trouble.

She tossed her head to get the hair out of her eyes. "Shame, though."

"What's a shame?"

"All those planes and they aren't even being used by our side."

"What're you talking about?" I'd heard stories that the P-39 wasn't as successful as the generals had hoped 'cause they didn't work well at high altitudes. But the newsreels said the French and the Russians used lots of 'em for attacks against German ground troops.

Catherine's voice dropped as much as possible and still be heard over the noise. "We talked about this. They're mostly being used by the Soviets."

"The Russians? Well, yeah but they're with the Allies. That's our side. Unless you've heard something I haven't."

"I guess, but..."

"But what?"

She leaned on the table. "They were with the Allies in the Great War, too. Until they had that revolution, shot all their royalty, and high-tailed it home. What's to stop them doing it again? With allies like that, who needs enemies?"

I was too young to remember the Great War, but Pop had told me a little about it, the trench warfare and the mustard gas. And yeah, the Bolsheviks and how the Russian front had collapsed after the February 1917 revolution. But that was the last war. "I don't think Stalin is a fan of the Nazis and Hitler isn't a big fan of the Communists. Didn't old Adolf go back on their agreement?"

She gave a graceful shrug and went back to studying the dancing couples. "It's the principle of the thing. They can't be trusted, the Reds. They're not on anybody's side but their own, Betty."

I sipped, trying to make my 7Up last. It was an odd conversation and, frankly, it made me edgy. Far as I was concerned, the Russians were Allies and talking against them was nearly as bad as being against the British or the French. All of us were fighting against the Germans and Hitler's quest for domination. That was enough for me.

"If it were me, though, I'd be looking at every girl there with German heritage," Catherine continued.

"How come?"

She tossed her head. "Who knows which of 'em has relatives back in the old country. Could be they're related to folks right in the Reichstag and none of us knows anything. Like Helen Ackerman. She's got family back there. Did you know that?"

Before I could say anything else, there was a ruckus over by the door. I craned my neck to see. "What's all the fuss?"

A group of men, maybe a half a dozen or so, had entered the hall. They wore khaki clothes and homemade white armbands. Against the white, the black of the swastikas stood out clear as anything. They were masked, but singing what I thought might be the German anthem, goose-stepping through the room, knocking over tables and chairs as they went. Some of the soldiers and sailors present rolled up their sleeves and got ready to fight, while others pulled girls from the dance floor and pushed them to the safe edges of the room.

I fought down bile. Here Tom and Sean were off fighting, and maybe dying, for these clods, and they were tearing up the hall like they owned it. The masked men on the edges scuffled with our boys, but the center of the group pushed on, still singing, tossing furniture aside, and setting girls to screaming. Some of the wannabe Nazis could barely keep singing they were laughing so hard.

One of them trailed the others and as the crowd rallied, his gaze darted around as though searching for an escape. I looked for something to throw, but all that was on the table was crumpled napkins. The only real object was my glass, still a quarter-full of 7Up. "Hey fat-head! Catch!" I made to throw the glass, but I didn't. The remaining pop splashed him in the face, catching him right in the eyes. He sputtered and clawed at his mask, pulling it half off.

The group stopped and fell back as our boys advanced holding whatever was handy as weapons. The one I took to be their leader pushed the others to the open door. "Let's get outta here!" They broke and ran.

But not before I recognized the one with the face full of 7Up. George Linden.

***

Needless to say, the dance broke up fast after all the hubbub. There weren't many injuries, but most of the decorations were torn, some furniture was smashed, and no one left felt much like dancing. I barely listened to Dot's chatter as we walked home, just enough to throw in a "yeah" when it sounded like the right thing to do.

George *was* in the Bund. That meant he had motive. It explained Anne's funny behavior, too. She didn't need to be helping her brother, like Catherine said. She knew or suspected he was getting into Bell to cause trouble, had come to me to confess, and he'd put a stop to that. Case closed.

When I got home, Mary Kate was on the back step all bundled up and trying to tempt the cat with a little bit of scrap meat, but it wouldn't come near her.

"You know Mom wouldn't like you feeding that cat," I said.

"Her name is Becuna, like in the Irish fairy tale." Mary Kate held out the scrap. "Here, Becuna. Come and get it."

"I hate to break it to you, but the cat's a boy."

"Oh." She paused, then made kissing noises. "I'll come up with a boy name. Hey kitty. Come here."

I went inside, refilled the saucer, and brought it out. I took the scraps from Mary Kate and put them on the edge. "Okay, cat." It looked at me. "My sister's a softie, so here you go." I set down the saucer and it trotted over to eat. "Maybe that's what it wants to be called. Cat."

"That's boring."

I laughed and ruffled Mary Kate's hair. "Names aren't all that important to animals, little girl. You use whatever it listens to." I went back inside. I was thinking of making tea to warm up when Pop came to the kitchen.

"You're home early. Anything wrong?"

I told him about the fuss at the dance. "Hey, Pop, I heard a crazy story from Lee." I told Pop about the German-supporting pamphlet guys at GM. "I can't imagine they thought a lot of people would go for that shtick."

"If they believe that much in their cause, they'll try anything."

"You ever see anyone trying that at Bethlehem?"

His forehead wrinkled as he thought. "They did, once. It wasn't any more popular, but a few of the men were rather more vehement about making them go away. Blows were exchanged."

"You saw it?"

"Yes, but I wasn't involved."

"Did you see a blond guy?" Once again, I described George Linden.

"I don't remember anyone like that. Are you sure he was there?"

"No, but he was at the dance tonight. Pop, d'you s'pose he could be sneaking into Bell? Maybe he strong-armed his sister into getting him onto the property. She felt guilty, tried to confide in me, but he got to her first."

"It's one idea." Pop crossed his arms. "At this point, I think you should take these suspicions to your supervisor or someone else at Bell. Let them handle it."

"Pop, it's just talk. Not facts."

"Someone else can gather those. You've done your part." He kissed my forehead.

"Yes, sir." I watched him as he walked out. Pop might think I didn't need to know, and I could simply hand over my suspicions and that would be enough. But Sam Spade wouldn't be happy with half a job. And neither would I.

Chapter 10

The next morning, I confided all I'd learned from Lee and Pop to Dot.

"I'm surprised they had the nerve," she said. "To walk up to American factory workers who they know are supplying the U.S. Army?"

"Pop says when people really believe in something they take all kinds of risks."

"What I don't understand is why the different approaches? I've never seen anyone with propaganda at Bell."

I'd thought about that, too. "GM and Bethlehem are bigger facilities. Could be they need help, so the pamphlets were a way of identifying sympathetic insiders."

"Like recruiting accomplices?"

"Exactly. Bell is smaller, so they can move straight to action."

"And if George Linden is involved, he's got a built-in helper."

I didn't want to think about that. Truth was, the whole thing was easier to swallow if the fact that George Linden's sister worked at Bell was just a coincidence and Anne wasn't involved at all. I didn't want to think I'd been working next to a traitor.

I was counting the minutes to lunch when a group of men striding across the floor toward line five drew my attention. One was Mr. Satterwaite. The smug expression on his face matched the oily gleam of his hair. The other two were strangers, men wearing dark suits and crisp white shirts who I'd never seen before. Girls turned their heads as the men walked by, leaving a sea of whispering in their wake. They strode up to Anne.

63

"This is her, sir. Miss Linden," Mr. Satterwaite said.

"Anne Linden?" Suit One asked.

Her mouth moved, but no sound came out. Her peepers were as big as the saucer I used to feed Cat.

"I'm sorry, I didn't hear you."

"I said—" Mr. Satterwaite interrupted.

Suit One held up his hand. "I'd like to hear it from her."

Anne found her voice. She wasn't loud, but activity had dropped so much it was not hard to hear her in the cavern-like room, even over the hum of the motors that powered the chains in the floor. "I'm Anne Linden, yes."

"We have some questions. This way." He stood aside and seemed to take it for granted Anne would obey. Which she did. Suit Two followed them.

Mr. Satterwaite clapped his hands. "Okay, no gawking. Back to work." He bustled away after the little group.

I glanced at Dot. "Cover for me. I'll be back."

Dot checked for Mr. Satterwaite. "You're gonna snoop, aren't ya?"

I grinned. "Of course."

Nobody looked at me as I two-timed it in the direction the suits had taken with Anne. They'd gone into a small room off the main floor. The door was cracked open. I pressed myself against the wall and peeped in. Anne stood between the two suited men, twisting her fingers together, an expression of fear pasted on her face.

Mr. Satterwaite stood in the corner. The smug look on his face oughta been illegal.

Suit Two consulted some notes. "Last Friday, were you working on engine installation?"

"Yes."

"You left the line rather suddenly, didn't you?"

"Yes, I...I jammed my finger and went to the infirmary."

"And not long after that, the fire started?"

"I don't know. As I said, I was in the infirmary."

"I see." Suit Two consulted another page of notes. "On Saturday, November seventh, where did you work?"

Anne looked like a cornered mouse, but she answered. "On the brake installation. The fifth line."

"That would be the line where the chain was tampered with?"

"Yes."

"You returned to the line after the whistle blew for lunch, is that correct?" Suit One asked.

"Yes. I had left a kerchief behind. I use it to wipe my forehead when it gets hot when I work. I didn't want to lose it."

"Were you alone?"

"I think so, yes. Most of the girls had gone to eat."

The only interrogation I'd ever heard in person was when Detective Sam MacKinnon of the Buffalo Police Department had interviewed me last month. I didn't need a lot of experience to know this was going real bad for Anne.

Suit Two confirmed my opinion when he put his notes away. "Miss Linden, I'm sorry to inform you that your employment at Bell has been terminated, effective immediately."

"Why? I haven't done anything. I'm a good worker."

"You're being fired due to suspicion of sabotage," Suit One said. "Please, Miss Linden. We will escort you to your locker to retrieve your belongings and then to the exit."

"But I didn't do anything!"

"Obviously, we don't have the authority to arrest you, but we have enough suspicion to remove you from employment. We will be handing over the results of our internal investigation to the authorities." Suit Two took her arm and tugged, but Anne must have locked herself in place because she didn't budge. "I have no doubt they will want to talk to you further."

Tears slid down Anne's cheeks and she continued to protest, her words now sprinkled with the occasional German.

"Come on, you silly girl," Mr. Satterwaite snapped and grabbed her other arm. "Stop making a scene."

Suit One pushed him aside. "Mr. Satterwaite, let go of Miss Linden. We will handle this." He turned to Anne, his voice firm, but not unkind. "Miss

Linden, don't make us call the police to remove you from Bell property. Let's go."

I scurried away from my listening post. They must have some pretty solid proof if they were firing Anne.

Dot moved aside to make room for me. "What's goin' on?"

"You'll find out in a sec," I muttered.

Not a minute later, the suits appeared, Anne between them. They made a little parade across the floor and work stopped as they passed. A hissing wind of whispering followed them.

As they passed our line, Anne glanced at Catherine. Or was it Rose or Helen? All three of them were huddled together. When she got to where I was standing, she stopped and faced me. The plea in her blue eyes was clear as day. *Help me.*

But I couldn't.

Suit One put his hand on her back. "Keep walking, Miss Linden." He led Anne, looking as skittish as Cat had that first night, away from the assembly line and out of sight.

"All right, ladies. Back to work! Or I'll dock the lot of you." Mr. Satterwaite prowled around, snapping at anyone who wasn't working fast enough for him. No doubt he was peeved from the suits putting him in his place.

I still didn't know if Anne was guilty or not. But the forlorn look in her eyes tore at my heart.

***

The talk at lunch had been nothing but Anne being fired and escorted off the floor. "Think the problems will stop now?" Florence asked.

Catherine broke the carrot sticks from her lunch in half. "Well, they obviously think they got the right girl."

"But did they?" Alice asked, eyebrows puckered. "Anne never struck me as having enough courage or smarts for this kind of thing."

"They must have information we don't." Rose shrugged as she ate. "Besides, if it's her brother who's the Nazi, it might be his idea and he just made her do it. Didn't you see the way he ordered her to that car the other day? She'd do anything he said."

I didn't participate in the conversation. I was too busy sorting facts in my head.

"You're awful quiet, Betty," Dot said as the others chattered away. "What'cha thinking?"

"Something's not right, Dot. I can't explain what it is, but I know it's not square." The whole thing was too easy.

I'd only been home a few minutes when the phone rang. I heard Mary Kate answer it. She came into our room as I was changing. "It's for you."

"Who is it?"

"She didn't say. Just that it was important."

Not many people called me. Lee and Dot lived close enough they skipped the phone call and came to the house. Buttoning my shirt, I went to the hall and picked up the phone receiver. "Hello?"

"Betty, it's Anne."

I smothered a surge of surprise. "How'd you get my phone number?"

"I looked it up. I have to talk to you. In person."

My gaze darted around the hallway. "I don't know if I can get away long enough to come to Kaisertown."

"I'd rather come to you. Less chance of being interrupted. Is there a place we can meet?"

I thought a moment, then gave her the address of a drug store nearby.

"I'll be there in an hour." She hung up.

I replaced the phone in the cradle. What was so gosh-darned important that Anne would not only call me, but travel to the First Ward for a meeting?

I left in plenty of time to meet her. "Mom, I'm going up the street to the bakery. I got a little extra pocket money for a treat." I didn't wait for her answer and bolted outside, nearly tripping over Cat on the back step, which earned me an indignant meow. "Sorry, Cat. I don't have time to feed you now." I swept away a twinge of guilt at the plaintive yowl in response. If I paused to feed Cat, Mom would catch me and put a crimp in my plans.

I hustled my way to the drug store, hoping to get there first. But when I walked in, I saw Anne seated in a corner booth. I almost didn't recognize her. Her blonde hair was tied in a low ponytail and she wore a neat dark skirt, pale blue blouse, and a cardigan sweater. "All right, I'm here," I said as I slid into the opposite seat.

"Thank you."

"Before you say anything, I wanna tell you I'm not positive you aren't guilty. Those men sure made it sound like you had plenty of opportunity."

"I understand."

"Plus, I'm not all that sure I like you that much."

"But you don't hate me, either." Her blue eyes were solemn.

"Shoot no." I didn't hate anyone. Okay, maybe old Adolf.

"That's good enough for me. Besides, I can give you a very good reason to help." She pushed an envelope across the table. "I want to hire you."

"What for?"

"To investigate and find the truth."

"Why me?"

She folded her hands on the table top. "You did pretty well with what happened to Mr. Lippincott last month. Maybe you don't truly like me, but you're fair. And you're smart."

I opened it and peeked inside. Cash, a stack of crisp, new five-dollar bills. I quickly counted them. "Fifty dollars? Holy cow. Where did you get so much?" It was more than a week's wages.

"It's all the money I've saved over the last six months. It was going to be for a wedding dress someday. But this is more important."

"Anne, this is too much. Way too much. I can't take it." I tried to hand it back. It was a bold move if she was guilty and figured she'd come off to the good if I poked my nose around. Either that or she was telling the truth.

"You have to."

"But this is everything you have." I stared at the envelope. We could eat like royalty for a long time on this. All for asking a few questions. Who knew detecting would pay so much?

"The money won't do me any good if I'm arrested for something I didn't do." Her hands were still clasped and her knuckles were white.

"You could use it to hire a lawyer."

"I'd rather you take it so I can avoid the need for one."

Something the Irish and the Germans had in common. We were both stubborn. I folded the money and put it in my purse. How would Nick and Nora Charles do this? "All right. You win. For now."

"Where do we start?"

I paused. "Let's talk about the day of the engine fire. You said you went to the infirmary. About how long after you went would you say the fire broke out?"

"I don't understand. Why would that matter?"

"The way the suits were talking, it's like they thought you wanted to be away from the scene when the fire broke out. That means you'd have an idea of when that would happen."

"I see." She frowned. "I don't think it was that long. I went and had the nurse look at my finger. She said it wasn't broken, wrapped it, and sent me back to work. I was almost there when I heard the alarms and fuss."

"I didn't see you on the floor."

"I didn't make it that far. I didn't get farther than the doorway."

Where she could have snuck off without anyone seeing her. Except wouldn't she have wanted to stay put? Be seen by as many girls as possible, so someone could back up her story? "What about Saturday? You went back for a kerchief, you said. Did anyone see you?"

"Yes, Catherine." Anne paused. "I also passed Helen and Rose on the way. Catherine was the last one out of the room."

"Did she say anything to you?"

"No. She never speaks to me unless she has to." Anne smoothed her skirt.

"You think any of them wanted to wreck things?"

"I don't know." She brushed her skirt again. "I don't know much about Catherine. Rose, well, she's Italian. That's the Axis, isn't it? Helen is German, like me. I guess she could secretly support the Nazis."

I tried to think what else Sam or the other movie detectives would ask, but I came up blank. No matter, I could always come back to the accidents. "You asked me to meet you Tuesday at the soda shop. Why?"

She hesitated. "I'm worried about George."

"Worried as in you think he's responsible for the sabotage?"

"Yes…no…I don't know." She studied her hands, which she had clasped again and rested back on the table. "George has always been very nationalistic about Germany. Mama and Papa always thought it was because he was proud to be German. So did I."

"But something changed."

"He started hanging around with new friends. They're not good people."

"Members of the Bund?"

"I don't know, but I think they support the Nazis. They mock Jews. Papa caught them doing the Nazi salute and laughing, so he threw them out of the house. I worry about their influence on my brother. George hides it, but he wants people to like him so he does things he shouldn't."

I thought about it. George looked exactly like a recruiting poster for Hitler's Aryan race. If his new pals were Nazis, no wonder they sucked up to him.

"Earlier this summer, George turned secretive. He began taking the car a lot, going out at night. One day, I found some boxes in the garage. I tried to move them, but they were heavy. George saw me and got angry."

"What was in them?"

"I don't know. But he said I was never to touch them, ever. The next day, they were gone. Then he started bringing a new friend around, a Jewish friend. They spend a lot of time huddled in George's room talking, but if anyone interrupted them they stopped. I asked once what they were up to and George told me to mind my own business."

"Did the groups ever meet, the Jew and the Germans?"

"Not that I know of. Oh, George argued with one of the Germans recently. Dark hair, thin face, I think he's the leader. He told George to stop seeing the Jew-boy or George would be sorry."

"What did your brother say?"

"That he wasn't sure he wanted to be on their side anyway."

It didn't sound like George was all that keen on his Bund friends. "What about Freddie?"

"What about him?"

"Does he hang out with the same friends?"

Anne rubbed at a spot on the table. "No. I've never seen Freddie with anyone other than George. I think George finds it irritating. I know I do. Freddie is around all the time and he acts like he knows everything. I think he wants in on something with George, though."

"Why d'you say that?"

"I've overheard a couple of conversations where Freddie begged to be cut in and George brushed him off. It's another reason I think George is up to something."

If George was hanging with the Bund, that could connect him to the sabotage at Bell. But being friends with a Jew would definitely not go over well with a bunch of Nazi sympathizers. It sounded like George was ditching the Germans in favor of his new pal. When I'd seen the group at the dance, George did look like he was hanging back. Was he there against his will? Could the Jewish guy be the one behind the sabotage? But why would a Jew want to hurt American war production?

"Betty?"

I realized Anne had continued talking, but I'd been so lost in my thoughts I hadn't heard her. "I'm sorry. What did you say?"

"George is involved in something and I don't think it's good. If I go to the police, they'll arrest him. I'm not ready to do that. That's why I need your help. In addition to clearing my name."

"I'll do my best. What if I learn that George is involved?"

"Then he has to face the consequences." She glanced at a slim wristwatch. "I must get home." She stood. "I promise you, Betty. I didn't have anything to do with these incidents. Find out who did, please. Even if it turns out to be my brother. I would do a lot for him, but not this. You know where I live. If you need me, come to my house."

Chapter 11

Since I told Mom I was going to get a family treat, I went to the bakery after Anne left and bought a little cake. Then I wandered to the bus stop at a decidedly slower pace. I needed the time to think.

Now that Anne had given me money, this was real work. I'd better get serious. Everybody thought Anne was the saboteur at Bell, either on her own or because she was obeying her Nazi-loving brother. Thing is, I believed her when she claimed innocence. I figured I was a pretty good judge of character. Anne's denials felt right to me. So did her claim that she wouldn't follow her brother on this count. Maybe in other things, but not sabotage.

Had George even asked her to help, though? He played at this Bund malarkey. Anne said she heard him threaten to quit the group. Did he? I needed to find out. How would Sam Spade do that?

The pamphlet guys at GM. Lee hadn't recognized my description of George, but he said he'd talk to his friends. He'd only promised two days ago, but the money made it important I find out.

Fifty bucks. That was a lot of lettuce. I don't think I'd ever seen that much at once before. Remembering Anne's face when she handed it over made my conscience prick. It was all the dough she had. She was saving for her wedding dress. And I'd taken it. True, she'd insisted. I decided I wouldn't keep it unless I could clear her name. That definitely wouldn't be right. Even if I did succeed, maybe I wouldn't. Well, not all of it.

I got off the bus onto Louisiana and turned onto Mackinaw. The streetlights were on and I strode to the Tillotson house. I'd get the cake home soon enough. "Evening, Mrs. Tillotson. Is Lee home?"

"Betty, how are you? Yes, we just finished supper. Would you like to come in?" She held the door open and warmth rushed out to meet me.

"That'd be swell." I stepped in.

She closed the door and pointed at the cake box. "For Liam?"

"Oh, no. I'm taking this home." I let her peek in the box. "I only gotta ask him something real quick, then I'll be off."

"Looks delicious. I'll go get him." She went off to fetch her son.

Lee appeared maybe a minute later. "You making home cake deliveries now?"

I stuck out my tongue. "No. Remember that conversation we had on Tuesday?"

"Yeah, why?"

"You talk to any of the guys yet?"

"Boy, you sure are pushy." He headed for the living room. "Come sit, my leg aches."

I followed and perched on the faded floral-print couch. "Okay, spill the beans. What did they say?"

He had dropped into a matching arm chair and stretched out his legs, rubbing the left one. "What's the rush, Betty? Why're you so keen on this?"

I held out the envelope of money. "Anne Linden paid me. This is for real now, not a game. What'd they say?"

He whistled, then handed back the envelope. "There was a group of those pamphlet guys at every gate that day. I asked all the fellas if George was in any of them. He was at the gate on Lakeshore Road."

"You sure?"

"Well, a guy was there who matched that description down to the eyebrows." Lee reached for the box.

I slapped his hand away. "Don't even think of it, pal. I don't come home with this cake, I'll have a lot of explaining to do."

He grinned. "My buddy Steve saw him. Steve also said George didn't look all that happy."

"How so?"

"George was kinda loitering off to the side. The leader of his group, some dark-haired guy, real pin-head, had to keep pushing George forward to talk to the plant workers." Lee reached for the box again, but snatched his hand back before I could swat him. "Steve said the leader got real mad at one point. 'You gotta talk to them, you idiot. Pass out the pamphlets, or I'll have Marcus beat your ass.' He said it a couple times."

George definitely sounded like he was less than happy about the propaganda gig. "What did George do?"

"He tried to talk to a couple guys, but when they blew him off, he shrunk back again. That really pushed the leader over the edge. Steve said the last thing he heard was the guy promising to give George a thorough whipping after they left."

Anne told me her brother didn't talk much. Was he not happy about passing out the Bund stuff because he was shy? Or did he like the Bund as a social club, but not so much when it came to doing real work? "Thanks, Lee. I owe you one."

"I know how you can pay me back."

Uh-oh. "How's that?"

He reached for the box again. "Gimme some of that cake."

Chapter 12

I filled Dot in on my new job on our bus ride to work Friday morning. "She gave you how much?" Dot's voice spiraled up so high several people looked up from their morning papers to frown at her.

"Shout a little louder, they didn't quite hear you up front." I tugged my coat.

"You didn't take it, did ya?"

"She wouldn't take 'no' for an answer." I couldn't meet Dot's eyes. First time ever, I think. "I don't think I'm gonna keep it. Not all of it. If I can't clear Anne's name, not any of it."

"That's good." Dot sat back. "But, Betty, you're not a detective. How do you plan on doing this?"

"By being smart and asking questions. That's all being a detective is, really. I already started." I told her about my talk with Lee.

"Maybe George is shy, or he don't like talking to people. Have you thought of that?"

"As a matter of fact, I have. What I need to do is talk to some German folks. See if they know anything about the Bund or a Bund revival. If so, could be they can give me the straight dope about George." The idea had come to me last night.

Dot cocked her head. "Yeah? How're you gonna do that?"

"Helen Ackerman is German. She doesn't talk about it a lot, but she is." Helen didn't stand out 'cause her family had been in America for ages, the turn of the century at least. When we first met, she'd mentioned how her pop had some tough times during the Great War 'cause of their last name. "Her

75

family might be members of the German-American Club in Kaisertown. If so, maybe she'd take me as a guest so I could talk to people." I didn't mention the possibility Helen had Nazi relatives and might be helping them out. Dinner with her family could help me learn more about that, too.

"I dunno. Sounds like you're setting yourself up for trouble, if you ask me."

"Yeah, well, then good thing I'm not asking, isn't it?"

Dot stuck out her lip in a pout. I avoided looking at her. I didn't want to risk having that face talk me out of what I had planned to do. I'd hoped she'd support me on this. I guess not, but I was gonna do it anyway.

Step one was to search the scene of the crime. That was always the first thing. At least it seemed that way to me when I went to the pictures. I'd taken a quick look before and a few days had gone by, but I figured it was worth another shot. The equipment had already been fixed of course. That was an unlucky break for me, but something might have been overlooked.

I started with the floor chain in the windshield installation area. Fortunately, that's where I was assigned to work today, so I didn't have to make an excuse to be there. I thought back. We'd come back from our lunch break, taken our places, and started the line. It had been a good minute or two before things went haywire.

"Anybody know where that rod went?" I asked. "The one they pulled outta here last week?"

Rose pointed at a bunch of junk piled up against the wall. "Prob'ly over there. Why?" Her eyebrows lowered in a suspicious look.

I glanced around for Mr. Satterwaite. "Be right back." I went over to the pile. Trash, bits of leftover framing, scrap metal, and a twisted steel rod. That had to be it. I picked it up. It was heavy and thick, smooth except for the deep scoring where the gears of the chain had bitten into it. The ends were not threaded. It wasn't pipe, just a piece of metal like what would be used in framing. Straight, not curved; that meant it coulda come from wing assembly or one of the interior structural pieces. I carried it back over to the line.

Rose nodded toward the rod as she continued to work. "What on earth are you looking at that for?"

"I dunno." I turned the rod over in my hands. "It's not the most flexible thing in the world, is it?"

"Not really."

"Then how'd it get in there?" I looked as the dolly ran smoothly, pulled along by the chain. The fuselage moved down the line, stopping at various places for installation of all the things needed to make a functioning plane. "When we found this, it was in the middle of the works, right?"

Rose frowned in thought. "Yeah, jammed right up against the gears." She halted her work to come over to me. "I see what you're on about. It'd be hard to jam it in. You'd almost have to take the chain out of the floor, put the rod in, then refit the chain." She glanced at the door. "Here comes Mr. Satterwaite."

I took my place and shoved the bar under the dolly holding the plane body. I didn't need our supervisor getting in the way this early in the investigation.

He prowled among us as usual, making cutting remarks. When he came beside me he said, "Surprised to see you standing there, Miss Ahern."

I concentrated on the plane in front of me. "Where else would I be?"

"A month ago you fancied yourself Bell's personal detective. A big mystery right here in front of us and here you are, just working away."

"Girl's gotta make a living."

He sniffed and moved on.

I waited until I was sure he was well away before I pulled the bar out again and went back to what I'd been doing. How did one get an unbendable bar deep inside machinery like this? I turned my focus from the bar to the floor.

It was like Rose said. You'd have to lift the chain out of the floor, put the bar in, then reset the chain. That would take time. How much?

The metal plates surrounding the channel in the floor were dirty, streaked with grease, not only from the hanging parts, but from anything applied to keep it running smoothly. "How long d'you think it would take to pull out this chain, then reset it?"

Rose looked over. "They lubricate the chain pretty regular. Can't take that much time because it's not like it takes down production. And you aren't pulling out the whole section. A minute, maybe two? That's just a guess, mind."

Two minutes. It didn't sound like a long time, but anybody who'd spent two minutes waiting for a bus in a Buffalo winter knew how long it could be. But what if you were good at it? Could you be faster? "Do you know when they lubed it up?"

"They oiled it two weeks ago. That's the last I know of." She sure knew a lot about the maintenance schedule. Huh.

I pushed that thought aside. Two weeks. I'd bet things were checked no more frequently than once a month, which means the rod wouldn't have been noticed by a maintenance worker before it had time to wreak havoc. "Tell me, who'd you see that day?"

"The usual. Catherine, Helen. I think Dot might have been here."

"Anne Linden?"

"Yeah."

We'd worked all morning. The problem had happened immediately after lunch. That narrowed the window. "Anybody hang back at lunch time? Or show up late?"

She shrugged. "I don't remember. The whistle blew and I beat it pretty quick. I seem to think it took Anne a long time to show up. Catherine and Helen took a bit, too. But I could be wrong."

"See any of them fussing down by the floor, maybe with tools?" Catherine had mentioned seeing Anne, I remembered. Had she really or was that a cover?

"Nope."

I needed to scope out the engine area. "Hey, cover for me? In case Mr. Satterwaite comes back?"

"Where should I say you went?"

"The bathroom. He already believes women need to go every half-hour, so he should believe you."

She grinned and I dashed off.

Engine installation was dirty and noisy. There was grease everywhere, puddled on the floor, streaked on the dolly, and on hanging chain. Grease was flammable, not as much as gasoline, but it would burn if given enough time and heat. I approached one of the girls on the line. "Hey, you know Anne Linden?"

"Yeah, I know her."

Another who didn't think much of Anne, judging by the girl's voice. "The day of the fire, was she around here?"

"Yep. Stood off by herself, well as much by herself as you can, same as usual. I said hi to her. She didn't answer, like always. Stuck up little priss."

The girl across the line jumped into the conversation. "She never talks to no one. She obviously never worked before she came here, either. Lily white hands and skin. She didn't like installing engines 'cause of all the mess."

"Does she smoke?"

"Her?" The second girl sniffed. "No way. She hated cigarettes. If someone lit up around her, she'd wrinkle her nose and walk away."

"But the fire was set with a lit cigarette." I looked between the two of them. "You think she could do that if she hated smoking so much?"

They exchanged a guilty look and returned to work.

"She work here the day of the fire?"

"I don't remember," the first girl said, a bit sullen.

"Anybody see her that day? It would have had to be a while before the fire started, maybe as much as an hour. Did you see anybody poking around?"

The first girl shook her head, but her friend spoke up. "I did, actually. I thought maybe someone was trying to sneak a smoke, you know? She was skulking around where the planes come off the line and are wheeled out the door."

"She look like Anne?"

"I…maybe. I don't know. Her face was darker, but she was in the shadows and was all dirty, so I can't rightly say. I thought maybe she had dark hair, but I guess it could have been covered by a dark bandanna."

I thanked them and left. Anne hated dirt and I'd never seen her with any kind of bandanna, which made it really unlikely she was the firebug. But then again, if she was responsible, wasn't that exactly the image she'd want, squeaky clean and a non-smoker?

Catherine had dark hair. So did Rose. Helen's was dark blonde, but in the shadow maybe it could look dark. Hmm.

I glanced at the clock. Almost noon. The whistle would blow and that meant Mr. Satterwaite would be making his final rounds. I needed to get back to my place. I wasn't near good enough at this private detective business to risk my job. Not yet anyway.

***

At lunch, I tracked down Helen. I slid in next to her at the cafeteria. "I've been lookin' for you all morning."

"Oh yeah? What for?"

There was a lot of noise and I didn't think anyone was gonna hear us, but I lowered my voice anyway. "Your family's German, right? I mean, German heritage?"

She took a bite of apple. "So what if they are?"

"Look, I'm not accusing you of anything so relax." At least not yet. I leaned over. "Do they belong to a social club?"

"Yeah, the German-American Club."

"The one in Kaisertown?"

"Why do you want to know?"

I fidgeted on my seat. "D'you think you could take a guest for dinner?"

"You mean you?" She set down her apple. "Why on earth would you want to go there? You got places in the First Ward to hang out. They must be loads more convenient than going all the way to Kaisertown."

"Well, yeah, but...Anne Linden lives over that way. I think her family goes to the club. I want to go so I can ask some questions."

"Whatever for?"

I had hoped to keep my side job a secret, except for Dot, but it didn't sound like Helen was going to do anything without a reason. I told her.

Her voice cut the air. "Anne hired you to do what?"

"Shush!" A few girls glanced our way. "To do some detecting. Will you help me?"

Helen thought a moment. "Sure, why not. You gotta give me some of the money, though."

"What for?"

"Expenses." Helen grinned. "Aren't detectives always buyin' information and stuff?"

I grumbled, but I agreed. What else was I going to do? I needed to get into the club. "Fine. When can we go?"

"Ma and Dad always go for dinner on Fridays, so tonight. I'll meet you there at six. Wear something nice. Not flash party nice, church nice will do."

"Deal." The visit might turn out to be a bust, but at least I'd get a meal.

Chapter 13

Now all I had to do was come up with a reason for missing dinner at my own house. It turned out to be surprisingly easy. "Your father is pulling a double tonight," Mom said when I walked in the door after work. "I need to go over to the church. The Christian Mothers are getting together for an evening prayer service after the news today."

"What news?" I took one look at Mom's thin line of a mouth and the tears in her eyes and I knew it had to be war news. Any other kind, even the death of someone in our neighborhood, and she would have told me straight off. "What happened?"

"You didn't hear?"

"I've been on the bus, remember?"

She paused. "We…we lost the *Juneau* at Guadalcanal. There were no survivors." Her eyes were downcast and uncharacteristically shiny. Mom never cried that I'd ever seen. Even when we buried her father, she'd been iron-willed and silent.

I sagged, Anne and her problems banished. The U.S. Navy had lost an entire ship? "What about Sean?" I whispered.

"As far as I know, he's still on the *Washington*. No visit and no telegram, not yet anyway."

"I'm coming with you to church." The whole detecting thing could wait. My brother and all the men with him needed my prayers.

Mom's no-nonsense attitude returned. "Absolutely not. You're going to stay home, and watch your brothers and sister."

I'd go crazy staying at home. But I knew better than to argue with Mom when she gave an order. "Yes, ma'am."

Mom gave a brisk nod, went to get her purse, and left.

In the end, I decided to meet Helen's family, after first kneeling and saying my own prayers. The activity would keep me from going nuts thinking about what might be happening at Guadalcanal. Helen had told me to wear church-nice clothes. I settled on a deep red dress with white polka dots, a sweetheart neckline, and a red ribbon at the waist. It had short sleeves and a swingy skirt that skimmed my knees. I'd worn it often when Tom and I went out dancing. I pulled on my precious pair of nylons. Then I slipped on my nice pair of shoes, black pumps with an open toe and a little bow.

"Golly, you almost look like a girl, Betty," Jimmy said when I came into the kitchen.

"Shut your trap, buster." I fluffed my hair and swiped on some of my favorite South American Red lipstick. "I gotta go out. You three won't tell, right? I shouldn't be gone too long."

"Whatcha gonna give us?" Michael asked from atop the table.

"I won't tell Mom you were sitting on the table," I said.

"Not good enough," Jimmy said.

"Oh really?"

"Really." The boys exchanged a look and Jimmy nodded. "Get us an ice cream and we promise we won't tell."

Mary Kate came into the kitchen. "Who's buying ice cream?"

"Betty." Michael hopped off the table top. "So's we don't tell she went out and left us alone. You're included, Mary Kate."

I threw up my hands. "Fine. I'll buy you all some after church on Sunday. But not one word, d'you hear me? Or you get nothing." More expenses. This job was gonna cost me some money.

Cat came out from behind the garbage cans to wind his way around my feet, meowing as he did. I'd been adopted, no question. "I'll take care of you when I get home, promise. I got a bus to catch."

The German-American Club was a squat brick building on South Ogden Street. I supposed at one time a German flag flew on the empty pole next

83

to the one that displayed the Stars and Stripes, but it was bare right now, the rope slapping against the metal in the evening breeze. A tiny flag with a black double-eagle showed in the bottom corner of the window, barely noticeable. These folks might be proud to be German, but they sure were keeping it out of sight. I went inside. "'Scuse me," I said to the woman at the greeter's stand. "I'm looking for a friend of mine. Helen Ackerman?"

"This way." She led me to the doorway and pointed to a table off to my left. "The Ackermans are over there."

I thanked her and went over. Some of the families were in fancy duds, but most were dressed like me. Nice, neat clothes, suits that looked a little shiny at the lapels from age, shoes that were scuffed from use.

Helen noticed me and waved. "Ma, Dad, this is a friend of mine from Bell. Betty Ahern. I invited her to join us tonight."

"Pleased to meet you both."

Mr. Ackerman stood and pulled out a chair, while his wife said hello. "Of course. Ahern. Irish?"

"Yes, sir."

"Have you ever had German food?" Mrs. Ackerman asked.

"No, ma'am. This is a first." I unfolded a napkin. *Manners, Betty* I heard Mom whisper in my ear. "It's real nice of you to let me come."

Mr. Ackerman retook his seat. "Any friend of Helen's is a friend of ours. So you work at Bell, too?"

"Yes, sir."

"Helen told us about the problems you've had," Mrs. Ackerman said, smoothing the napkin in her lap. "How terrible. But they arrested a girl, I understand?"

"They didn't arrest her, Ma," Helen said. "They fired her."

A platter of sausages and another of sauerkraut arrived. Mr. Ackerman served us. "A German girl, Helen said."

"Yes, sir." I wasn't sure about the sauerkraut, but the sausages smelled delicious. "Anne Linden. I don't know if you know the family. Pass the salt and pepper please?"

While Helen handed me the shakers, little ceramic things shaped like a

84

girl and boy in what I took to be traditional German clothes, Mr. Ackerman answered. "I do. Helmut Linden works at the bank."

Of course they knew each other. Kaisertown wasn't that big a neighborhood. "Don't they have a son, too?" I tried to sound like I was simply curious.

Helen kicked me under the table.

Fortunately, her father was the trusting sort because he didn't blink. "Yes, George, I think his name is. I saw him once or twice. He's a very difficult young man. Helmut waited on me at the bank one day. He asked if I had a son and I said yes, but much younger than Helen. 'I hope he does not give you problems when he grows older,' Helmut said."

"Is the boy a troublemaker, Gerry?" Mrs. Ackerman asked.

"Not exactly." Mr. Ackerman paused to pile sauerkraut on a piece of sausage. "He's never been in trouble with the law, but he has some problematic friends, I take it. Young men who support the German-American Bund and want to see it revived."

"I'm curious about that, Mr. Ackerman." No, I definitely did not like sauerkraut. But Mom had raised me to eat without complaint, so I did. "Do all folks of German heritage support the Bund?"

"Betty!" Helen hissed.

Her father waved her off. "No, no, Helen. It's a perfectly natural question." He speared another bite of sausage before answering. "No, Miss Ahern, we don't. In fact, I would say the majority of us don't, especially men like Helmut who know that Hitler's rise to power is fraught with problems. He makes promises he can't keep."

Mrs. Ackerman tutted, but kept eating. No need to ask what her opinion of Hitler was.

"It is the young men, I think, who are drawn to the Bund. Young men are proud and quite often very foolish." Mr. Ackerman's smile was a bit too knowing. Perhaps he'd been one of those proud, foolish young men once.

"You don't let them in the club, then?" I asked.

"We cannot keep them out, but there are no Bund activities tolerated," Mr. Ackerman said.

I poked at my sausage. "Do you still have family over in Germany?"

Helen kicked me again. Her father's peepers narrowed. "Why do you ask?"

"Oh, just conversation. Only," I thought fast, "it would be hard, wouldn't it? You being American and all, having family on the other side."

He seemed to relax a bit. "I suppose so. I have a cousin in Berlin. Helen used to be pen pals with his son, but they haven't written in a while, have you, Helen?"

"Not for ages," Helen replied and changed the subject. "I didn't know you were so familiar with the Lindens, Dad."

Was it me, or did she sound eager to get off the topic of family in Germany. I followed her lead. "Are the Lindens ever here with their nephew, Freddie?"

"I've seen him a couple of times, but not spoken to him very much. I gathered from Helmut that the boys are very close. Almost like brothers." Mr. Ackerman scooped up a bite of sauerkraut. "Why all the questions?"

Rats. He wasn't as trusting as he seemed. "It's so foreign to me why anyone would support Hitler."

"Betty's brother is in the Navy. And her boyfriend is in the Army," Helen added.

Mr. Ackerman patted his mouth with his napkin. "I certainly understand your confusion. However, Ireland has declared itself neutral in the war and even given sanctuary to Germans. They are not, I think, overly fond of the British."

"Maybe not, but they're more foolish than the Bund if they think the Germans will be any better to them," Mrs. Ackerman said, her temper flaring a bit.

"I agree, Mrs. Ackerman," I said. Best put myself on solid footing before continuing. I'd raised enough suspicion. We ate for a bit before I spoke again. "Anne doesn't think her brother is truly supportive of the Bund, though. She said he's always found making friends hard, that's how come he hangs around with the others."

"She may be right about that," Mr. Ackerman said, pushing away his empty plate. "One of the few times I saw George, I asked what he thought of Hitler and he professed to not like the man very much. When Helmut brought up the Bund, George said, 'Those are just friends, Papa. I like them for their company, not their politics.' Later on, I think one of them came up to say hello and young George looked very uncomfortable."

A waitress came by and set down a pastry dessert that smelled heavenly, apples and cinnamon with a perfectly browned crust. I inhaled deeply. "That smells good. What is it?"

"Apple strudel." Mrs. Ackerman cut a slice and passed me a plate. "I think you will find this more to your taste than sauerkraut."

***

Mrs. Ackerman was right. I liked apple strudel a lot more than sauerkraut, although I'd tried to convince her I liked both. But she was as good at reading expressions as my own mother, so there was no fooling her. Best of all, the club served real coffee with dessert, something that was increasingly hard to find.

After dinner I thanked the Ackermans and headed for the bus stop. If all went well, my folks would never know I was gone. There wasn't much traffic on South Ogden, foot or vehicle. While I waited, I thought about what Mr. Ackerman had said. He didn't think George Linden was all that keen on the Bund's political activities and that kinda went along with what Lee had told me about George's behavior at GM. All that supported what Anne had told me. If George wasn't really all about the Bund, he wouldn't be likely to ask his sister to help him wreck stuff at Bell.

What about these relatives in Berlin? Helen had been awfully keen not to talk about 'em. I thought of Berlin as the center of Nazi activity. Had she kept up with her childhood pen pal, maybe believed in his politics? How could I find out without asking her?

I looked down the street, checking for the bus. Instead of my ride home, all I saw was a guy walking toward me, a fedora pulled low over his face. In fact, he looked downright shifty, keeping close to the walls and avoiding the streetlights. I clutched my purse closer.

A strong gust of wind blew down Ogden. It had warmed up some, but I shivered, pulling my coat close. Across the street, the wind plucked the guy's fedora right off his head and he chased it down the sidewalk as his pale blond hair gleamed in the yellow lighting. He picked it up, dusted it off, and looked around. I sucked in my breath. It was George Linden.

Yeah, it was dark and he was across the street, but my eyesight was pretty darn good. Before he could catch me staring, I averted my gaze. Keeping my face down and lifting my eyes, I could still see him. He jammed the hat back on, tugged the brim down, and disappeared down an alley.

When I'd left the club, it had been almost seven. What was George doing walking around Kaisertown in the dark? Alone and obviously trying not to be noticed, or at least not identified. And going down an alleyway no less. Was the Bund so hard up for meeting spots they were skulking in unlit city alleys?

My bus still hadn't come and George didn't come back into view. I wasn't all that familiar with this area of the city, so I didn't know if the alley was a dead-end or opened on to the parallel street. Except wasn't the next street residential? Not likely an alley would cut straight through.

Minutes passed and still no George. I took a risk, got off my bench, and hurried across the street to stand at the mouth of the alley. As I suspected, it was a dead end, but I did see a low wall with a few garbage cans against it. Maybe George had jumped on the cans to hurdle the wall and exit that way. I took a step.

In the low light, I could see a dark pile on the ground. Garbage? Clothing? I stepped closer, but stopped when the pile groaned.

There was a bottle nearby and I picked it up to hold it like a club. It wasn't much, but if that pile was George and someone had smacked him on the head, I wanted to be able to defend myself. I inched closer. "George Linden?"

The only response was another groan. It sounded weird: wet and bubbly. Amidst the stench of trash, I detected something else, sour and metallic, like I'd put a penny in my mouth.

I didn't see any one else, so I put down my bottle and rolled the person over. It was George. His jacket had fallen open to display a spreading splotch of red on his chest. Blood bubbled at his mouth. I hadn't heard a shot. Had he been stabbed?

He tried to speak and I leaned in, but his voice was too faint for me to make out words. He was alive, but he had to be losing blood fast. I needed to stop it long enough to call the cops. "I'm gonna try and take your jacket off." I wrestled him out of it and he moaned when I pushed him over. I wadded the coat up, placed it on his arm, and shoved him over so he was lying on the bundle. Hopefully that would be enough to keep him alive until I could get help.

I ran back to the club and yanked on the door. The same woman was at the greeter's stand. "Do you have a telephone I can use?" I asked, while I tried to catch my breath.

"In the office. Do you need to call a cab?"

"No. The police."

Chapter 14

I stood on South Ogden, watching the gathering of cop cars, a dark sedan, and an ambulance. The headlights of the patrol cars and the ambulance bathed the street in a yellowish glow, but no one had rushed off anywhere. I suspected I hadn't been fast enough and George was beyond needing a hospital. As I watched, two guys walked out of the alley. They got in the ambulance and left, no wailing siren.

Yeah, I hadn't been fast enough. I wished I had my cigarettes.

The next guy to leave the alley was a familiar figure in a dark suit, also with blond hair, but darker than George's. Detective Sam MacKinnon. I knew his eyes would be dark blue, his attitude polite yet direct, and he prob'ly wouldn't be all that amused to see me again. One of the uniformed cops pointed in my direction and he strolled over. He stopped for a split second when he recognized me, then continued, a rueful look on his face. "Miss Ahern. Second time we've met because of a murder. How are you?"

Detective MacKinnon and I had first crossed paths during the investigation into Mr. Lippincott's death last month. Hopefully that meant he wouldn't treat me like a dumb woman, since he knew I was anything but. "Fine, I guess. He's dead then?"

"Oh yes. The patrolman tells me you called it in. What happened?"

I told him about waiting for the bus and seeing George go down the alley. "When he didn't come out again, I went after him."

"Kind of risky on your part. What if you'd run into trouble?"

"I found a bottle. I know how to take care of myself."

"I remember. I also remember telling you that solving crime in real life isn't like the movies."

I shrugged. It had worked out pretty well last time, but I didn't see the need to remind the detective of that.

He jotted notes in his little notebook. "How do you know the victim?"

"He's the brother of one of the girls at Bell." I paused. "Well, he was her brother, I guess, and she used to work for Bell. She lives around here." I gave him the Lindens' address.

"What happened to her job?"

"She got fired."

He looked up. "Why?"

I didn't know how much to say. The events at Bell hadn't made the front page of the paper since they'd been reported as simple accidents and there hadn't been any injuries. If it was really sabotage directed at war production, I didn't think the Department of Defense would appreciate me yakking to a Buffalo homicide detective. Then again, no one had told me not to talk about it.

Philip Marlowe didn't go blabbing everything he knew to the cops at the drop of a hat. It might be better to hold something back for now. On the other hand, building a little credit with Detective MacKinnon might help me in the future. "There was a fire that ruined an engine and someone jammed a metal bar in the chain that pulls the dolly along the assembly line. When Anne, that's George's sister, got fired, they said it was 'cause they suspected her."

"Sabotage?"

I nodded.

"Why would she sabotage production at Bell?"

"The family is German."

"They're Nazi sympathizers?"

"Not the parents, but you've heard of the Bund, right?"

"The German-American Bund, yes. Their leader is in jail and the organization is falling apart."

"George Linden is, was, a member. He and a couple others busted into a dance last weekend all dressed up." I told him about George's supposed involvement with the pamphlets at GM and the Steel, his snotty attitude, and how he bossed Anne around.

Detective MacKinnon tapped his notebook against his hand. "The management at Bell thinks she's involved and her brother was directing her."

I pulled my coat tighter, cold seeping through the seams. "Anne claimed George wasn't really all that enthusiastic about the group's mission. It was more of a social thing for him. My friend Lee works at GM. He told me George was definitely part of the pamphlet group, but he was yelled at a couple of times by another guy and was threatened with a beating if he didn't step it up."

The detective narrowed his eyes. "How do you know this?"

I didn't think he would be real impressed if I told him I'd taken up private detective work. Not at a murder scene. "Lee and I were gabbing one day and he mentioned it. Lee's got a bum leg, that's why he's not in the service." I don't know why I felt pressured to justify Lee not being overseas, 'specially since Detective MacKinnon hadn't said anything, but I did. "Oh, George had argued with his cousin, too." I told him what I knew about George and Freddie, including what I'd heard at the Broadway Market.

Detective MacKinnon wrote it all down. He didn't look like he believed me about how Lee and I had been "gabbing," but he let it go. "Did anyone go down the alley after Mr. Linden?"

"No, sir. If he was meeting someone, the other guy musta already been there. Which means George knew him, 'cause who goes down a dark alley to meet a stranger? That's a dead end so it's not like George was taking a short cut home."

"Did you see anyone come out of the alley?"

I didn't miss the fact he didn't answer my question. Part of me took that as agreement. "No. I 'spect he stabbed George, and used the garbage cans to climb up and hop the wall at the end of the alleyway."

Detective MacKinnon didn't say nothing, just wrote some more.

"Do you think that's what happened? I mean, if a guy wanted to dish out a beating, he mighta told George to meet him. I don't know why George would wear a nice shirt and a fedora if he expected a fist-fight."

"Miss Ahern, we discussed this before. Leave the detective work to the police. I will have one of the officers drive you home since you've missed your bus." He tipped his hat and turned away.

"Wait, there's something else." I didn't know for sure it was important, but it couldn't hurt to say something. "The other day, George came to collect Anne from work. He came in a car."

MacKinnon paused. "Unusual given rationing, but not impossible."

"Florence, another girl at Bell, said her father doesn't drive much 'cause it's too hard to get gasoline."

MacKinnon said nothing.

"I was thinking. Where'd George get the gas? I mean, he could be stockpiling A-cards, or maybe they don't drive much, but Wheatfield isn't exactly around the corner from Kaisertown." The detective still didn't say anything, so I continued, the ideas coming as I talked. "Maybe he stole the ration card from someone or it could be a black market deal. If that's the case, maybe that's how come he got killed."

"Miss Ahern." Detective MacKinnon drew his eyebrows together and his voice had that no-nonsense tone it had the last time he told me to mind my own business. "Thank you for your information. If you think of anything else, you may reach me at the downtown precinct. One of the officers will drive you home. Good night." He beckoned to the uniformed cop, who came over and led me to one of the patrol cars.

Poor Anne. First she was fired for something she most likely didn't do and now her brother was murdered. If I was going to clear her name, I'd have to make sure George wasn't involved and that meant finding out who killed him.

***

I knew I was in trouble the minute I walked into the kitchen. Mom and Pop were both at the table. The younger kids were nowhere to be seen. "Pop, I can—"

"Sit." He pointed at a chair.

I sat.

"Elizabeth Ann Ahern." The measured tone was way worse than if he'd been yelling. Heck, it'd almost be better if he pulled out his belt, but that wasn't Pop's way. "Where have you been? It's almost nine o'clock."

"You left your brothers and sister alone, you didn't make dinner, and they were all up listening to the radio." Mom's voice was just this side of yelling, but she wasn't near as scary as Pop. "Plus, there's this." She held up the chipped saucer. "You're feeding a stray cat from our back step?"

Cat musta been prowling around, looking for his evening meal. Sean always told me it was better to keep quiet in these situations, not that he was ever a troublemaking kid. I got in way more scrapes than he did. But he was spot on with the advice, so I held my tongue.

"Where have you been?" Pop asked, folding his hands on the table.

"I went to dinner with a friend of mine, a girl who works at Bell," I said.

"Where?"

"The German-American Club on South Ogden." I didn't look at Mom. "I'm sorry. I shoulda told you I was going."

"What you should have done is stayed at home with the younger ones," Mom snapped. "And why, may I ask, did you come home in a police car? Don't bother to tell me you didn't because I saw you out the front window."

Pop held up a hand. "Mary, let me handle this." He held my gaze. "Answer the question."

Think fast, Betty. Pop had already told me to pass on my suspicions and stay out of the investigation at Bell. Not only would I be in hot water for disobeying, he and Mom would be mad as all get out if they found out one of the subjects of my investigation turned up dead in an alley. I hated deceiving my folks, but I couldn't back out on my promise to Anne, and not just 'cause of the money. I owed her.

"I left the club in plenty of time to get the bus home," I said. "But then I thought I'd dropped my lipstick, so I went back inside to look for it." I glanced at Mom, but kept most of my attention on Pop. If I convinced him, I'd be home free. "You know lipstick's real hard to come by, so I spent a good amount of time searching. It was in the ladies' on the sink. When I went back outside, there were cop cars across the street. They found a body in the alley across the way. I had to stick around and give a statement 'cause the detective thought I mighta seen something. By then I'd missed the bus, so the detective had one of the cops give me a lift home." First step to a successful fib, Sean told me. Keep it as close to the truth as you can.

Mom opened her mouth, but before she could say anything, Pop spoke. "I'm very disappointed in you, Betty. I thought you were more responsible. If this is the kind of behavior the girls at work are going to encourage, then I will have to rethink my opinion of you being at Bell. For the time being, I'll take your word that this will never happen again."

I had to answer, but I didn't want to lie, not anymore than I already had. "I won't get in trouble again. I promise."

He nodded, stood, and left the kitchen.

"And there will be no more feeding of stray cats, is that understood?" Mom banged down the saucer so hard it was a miracle it didn't shatter. "It's hard enough to put food on our own table. We don't need to be feeding every scrawny animal in this neighborhood." She swept out of the kitchen.

I slumped on my chair. I'd have to be more careful, that was for sure. If Pop was willing to make me quit Bell because he thought it was a bad influence, what would he say if he knew why I'd really been in Kaisertown tonight?

Chapter 15

I checked the *Courier-Express* Saturday morning for any news about George. His death only rated a small story in the local section. A man identified as George Linden of Kaisertown was found stabbed in an alley off South Ogden Street around seven-thirty the previous night. The police had no leads. I wasn't mentioned at all, thank goodness.

I had no idea what kind of funeral customs the Germans would have, but I knew the Lindens were Catholic. The day after would be too early for a wake, but I was pretty sure I'd find Anne at home, most likely helping her parents make arrangements. Fortunately, I only worked every other Saturday so I was off. With any luck I wouldn't run into Detective MacKinnon. I wasn't ready to see him again, although he couldn't fault me for visiting a friend whose brother had just been killed.

I decided I'd better get permission this time. Pop had already left for work, but Mom was in the sitting room, patching the knees on a pair of Jimmy's pants. "Mom, may I go out this afternoon?"

She didn't look up. "Out where?"

"Over to Kaisertown, to see my friend, Anne."

She paused in her sewing and fixed me with a stare. "Isn't that were you were last night when you had to get a ride from the police?"

"The same neighborhood, yes. It turns out that the man they found was stabbed. He was Anne's brother."

"Why on earth do you want to go back there?"

"I thought it would be nice if I went and paid my respects, see if she needs anything. She doesn't have a lot of friends."

Mom went back to sewing. "Dinner is at five sharp. You better be home by then."

"Yes, ma'am." I rushed to my room. I didn't expect a formal wake, but I couldn't show up looking like a slob, either. I decided on a pair of gray flannel pants and a white-and-red striped cotton button down shirt. I pinned back my hair and dabbed some powder on my nose to take off the shine. I wished it covered up my freckles, but a girl couldn't have everything. Then I grabbed my purse and headed out. Cat was prowling around the back step. "You better watch out," I told him. "Mom found that saucer and she won't hesitate to swat you with a broom if she catches you here."

Cat flicked his tail, blinked green eyes, and disappeared behind the garbage cans.

I got to the bus stop just as the bus was pulling away, but I managed to wave it down and jump on. I paid my nickel and found a seat. Bus fare. Another expense.

At the Linden house, I knocked on the door. It took a minute, but Mrs. Linden finally answered. Dressed all in black, her color had drained away. Hers was a face meant for smiles and laughter, I could tell. But now she was a faded imitation of a woman. She prob'ly wasn't much older than Mom, but her grief had clearly aged her overnight. "Yes?"

"Mrs. Linden, hi." I was an intruder. This woman didn't know me from Eve. But I pushed on. "My name is Betty Ahern. I work, that is I used to work with Anne. I'm real sorry to hear about your son."

She sniffled.

"Is Anne home? I need to talk to her."

"Ja, just a moment." Mrs. Linden called over her shoulder for her daughter.

A few seconds later Anne appeared. Her pale face was splotchy and her red eyes told me she'd been crying, prob'ly since last night. If someone had brought me news of Sean's death, that's what I would have done.

"Oh Betty!" She rushed to hug me, a fresh wave of tears overwhelming her.

Mrs. Linden gave me a weak smile and slipped back into the house.

I patted Anne's back. The way she acted, it was like we were best friends.

But no other girls from Bell would visit her when they found out about George, not even Dot, so maybe I was her best friend. "I heard about George. I'm sorry."

She sobbed for a bit, then pulled back. "I got your shirt wet."

"'S okay. I didn't want to intrude, but—"

She wiped her nose with a handkerchief. "You're not intruding. Some of the older women in the neighborhood came to help Mama. I've been trapped with them all morning."

Where were all the girls, those from church or her neighborhood? "Didn't any of your friends come?"

"I don't have many friends." Her eyes were wet and her smile was bitter. "Most of Mama's friends and their daughters don't think it's ladylike to work in a factory."

"Well isn't that swell of them." I bristled. Ladylike. "I'm glad they can afford to think that way. The country is at war and they're worried 'bout being all proper? Didn't know Kaisertown was Delaware Park." Not that Anne's neighborhood was a slum, but it wasn't near as flash as where the industrial bigwigs lived.

Anne hiccupped and tried to giggle.

"Why don't you and me take a walk?" The sun was shining though the air was crisp. But the clear skies and lack of wind meant it didn't feel all that cold, 'specially if we kept moving. "We can talk and you'll get out for a bit. Unless your mom needs you."

"I don't think so, the women are still here. Let me tell her where I'm going."

A couple minutes later, we walked down Casimer Street toward South Ogden. Our breath came out in clouds. "Are you okay?" I asked. What a stupid question. 'Course she wasn't okay.

Anne, her nose and cheeks pink, blinked against the sun. "No. But I'm better than Mama and Papa. I guess you don't expect a police officer to knock on your door to tell you your son's been murdered, especially late at night."

"Did you know where George was last night?"

"He left earlier in the evening, right after dinner. He said he was going to meet some friends."

"His Bund friends? Did he say why?"

"Maybe and no. George comes and goes as he pleases. Mama and Papa don't ask questions. I did once, but George made it clear it was business and I should stay out of it." She bit her lip. "What I don't understand is how the police knew where he lived. He left his wallet at home, so he wouldn't have had his driver's license. All they said was a witness had seen him go into the alley and had gone after him when he didn't come back out."

"They didn't give you the witness's name?"

She shook her head.

I could stay nameless, but it didn't sit right. "It was me."

"What were you doing up in this neighborhood?"

"I went to dinner at the German-American Club with Helen Ackerman and her family last night. I was asking questions about George, if you gotta know."

"What kind of questions?"

"About his Bund friends." I told her about Lee's information from GM, how George had been with the pamphlet guys, and how his dark-haired friend had threatened him. "Look, I know you don't think he was serious about all this pro-Nazi stuff. But I'll tell you straight. The rest of the girls, and prob'ly the management at Bell, think the reason you caused those so-called accidents is because your Hitler-loving brother told you to do it."

Anne stopped. "I told you I would never do such a thing."

"I know. Remember, you hired me to find who's behind the sabotage, even if it was George."

"You think he's involved, him and the Bund?"

"I don't know, but I can't ignore the possibility. That's why I went to the club, to see if the Ackermans could give me any information."

Her cheeks were red and I thought she was gonna storm off home, but after a moment she kept walking. "What did the Ackermans say?"

"Not much more than what you've told me. And Lee said George didn't look all that comfortable in public with his buddies. The only reason you look that way with someone is if you're embarrassed to be seen with them."

"If George was really friends with those boys, he wouldn't be embarrassed."

"Exactly." We walked a bit without talking. "So lemme ask you. The dark-haired guy. Do you know who that might be? And who's Marcus?"

She frowned. "Marcus Hoffman. He's not very bright I don't think."

"You know any other names?"

"George mentioned a William Dunkel once. I think they're muscle. I know George didn't have a very high opinion of them. And there's one they call the Mick, but I've never seen him."

"I don't suppose you know where they live."

"No, I'm sorry. George often mentioned he was meeting friends at Dingens Park, which isn't far from here. Hoffman and Dunkel are both German names, so I'd guess they live in or near Kaisertown."

"The Ackermans said they've also seen Freddie at the club. He spend a lot of time with your family?"

"Of course."

We'd covered several blocks by now. "You mention George and Freddie *were* like brothers. What happened?"

Anne turned around and began walking back home. "I think something had come between them. Maybe the Bund. Freddie came around like always, but George seemed impatient with him lately. As though Freddie was nagging at him. I suppose even the closest brothers argue."

I thought of Jimmy and Michael, who could go from best pals, to a knock-down fight, and back again within minutes. "He doesn't live with you, does he? Freddie?"

"Not anymore. His parents left him money, and when he turned eighteen he got his own apartment. Freddie has worked for years. He's very money-conscious. I think Papa often wished Freddie's work ethic would rub off on George." She tried to smile as tears filled her eyes again.

"If you give me Freddie's address, I'll go talk to him. Meanwhile, I'll scope out the park, maybe on my way home." I was aware that the sun was slipping further toward the horizon, but if I hurried I'd have time before I needed to catch the bus. "Did you know Helen has family in Berlin?"

"No. I told you. None of the girls at Bell talked to me much."

Dead end there. "Next question. George picked you up from work the other day in a Ford. Is that his car?"

"Yes, he's very proud of it."

"Does he drive it much?"

"He goes everywhere in it."

"How's he getting the gas?"

She stopped. "I don't know what you mean."

I folded my arms. A light breeze had picked up, and blew some old dried-out leaves and a crumpled newspaper down the street. "They started rationing gasoline last May 'cause of the war. You've seen all the stickers, haven't you?"

She nodded.

"The A-cards are the lowest priority. You only get four gallons a week. You say George drove everywhere. What does that mean?"

"He drove me to and from Bell, he took Mama grocery shopping, he went out with his friends."

Driving back and forth to Wheatfield six times a week would use more than four gallons, never mind all the rest, and I told her that. "Somehow, he's getting more than his rationed share."

"But how?"

"I was hoping you could tell me." Whatever the answer was, it wasn't nowhere legal.

Chapter 16

Anne and I finished the walk back to her house without talking much. Once we reached her front door, she turned to me. "Betty, I think you should stop. It's too dangerous. When I asked you to look into this mess, I didn't plan on it involving murder."

"You don't know it does. George's death could be unrelated."

She brushed back her hair. "You won't know if it is unless you keep investigating, right?"

"Yeah, I s'pose."

"Then it's too dangerous." Her eyes were still red-rimmed, but she was just as stubborn as the day she hired me.

Except I was determined to out-stubborn her this time. "I promise I'll be careful, okay? You hired me to get to the bottom of these accidents and clear your name, and I'm gonna do it. Money or no money, but you did give me a lot of dough."

She permitted herself a small smile. "I thought you didn't like me."

"Yeah, well, turns out you're not so bad, I guess." I hadn't planned on it, but I admired Anne's grit. I scuffed the ground with the sole of my shoe.

"Thank you." She laid her hand on the doorknob. "You're a good friend. Dot is a lucky girl. But Betty?"

"Yeah?"

"You must promise me you won't do anything foolish. If something were to happen to you over this I'd never forgive myself."

"Cross my heart and hope to die."

She shook her head and went inside.

I fished a cigarette and my lighter out of my purse. On the sidewalk, I lit up and took a long drag, exhaling the smoke slowly. Mom had told me to be home by five. I checked my wristwatch. It was only a little after two. Dingens Park wasn't that far of a walk. I had plenty of time to go down, enjoy the sunshine, and maybe catch a glimpse of George's so-called "friends."

I didn't hurry, but I didn't dawdle, either. As I made my way back to South Ogden, I smoked and thought. Anne really didn't think about all the gas George had been using, but I was sure it was way more than the standard A-card allotment. Another thing to look into, if I could figure out how to do it.

Down South Ogden, across Clinton, to Dingens Street, and over to the park. The cold weather coupled with the lack of snow meant it wasn't crowded, but there were folks there. Mostly families with young kids taking the opportunity to escape the house while the sun shone. How long until the first snowstorm of the season kept everyone inside was anybody's guess. I strolled around, careful where I was flicking the ash of my cigarette so as not to accidentally burn any of the little ones running around. They looked to be playing some complicated game of tag, not a care in the world. Kids. I didn't see anyone who looked like they were up to shady dealings of any sort.

I finished my cigarette and ground the butt under my shoe. Maybe it was too nice a day for a Bund meeting. This William and Marcus, they might have siblings to take care of, or jobs, or something else that was busying up their Saturday. Perhaps they only met in the evenings, when there was less chance of them being seen. Except two guys, or more, hanging out in a park at nighttime would surely catch the attention of any passing cops. They'd want to make themselves less noticeable, not more.

I decided to do another round of the park before calling it quits. I was nearing the far corner near Glidden and Dingens when I saw them. Two guys that sure looked like the description provided by Lee: dark, close-cut hair, beefy arms, barrel chests. They were with a third, smaller guy. Shorter, thinner, with dark blond or light brown hair, depending on how the sun hit it. I slowed, pretending to be watching some of the little kids. Out of the corner of my eye, I kept tabs on the threesome, who were huddled together talking up a storm. I took a few steps closer, straining to hear them.

"That's not the plan," one of the heavier guys said.

"Then the plan's gotta change, don't it?" said the other heavy guy. He had a scar on his chin. It was the only way I could tell the two of them apart.

The third guy stepped in the middle of the other two. "We ain't gonna jaw about it here. Not in the open. Let's go to the garage and talk about what we do next." He looked a little weasel-like. Sounded like it, too. He had the kind of voice that grated my nerves, where everything sounded like a complaint, even if it wasn't. Like my Aunt Peggy.

I couldn't believe my luck. It was pretty clear to me that these guys weren't up to anything good, but what were the chances they'd spill the beans right here in the park?

Heavy glowered at Weasel. "Whatever you say. But this one," he jabbed his finger at Scarface, "is giving me a headache with his yammering."

"All I'm saying, Will, is that it happened and we have to deal with it," Scarface said.

"Enough." Weasel looked around.

I was sure he saw me. Hopefully he thought I was a concerned older sister or something.

He must have, or at least he figured I wasn't anything to be worried about. He grabbed a handful of Heavy's shirt with one hand, and Scarface's shirt with the other. He pushed them both toward the park exit on Dingens. Despite being the smaller guy, he got both of them stumbling forward. "Get going. Stop yapping and act cool. We'll talk more at the garage."

I waited until they were out of the park. Then I took off after them. Reaching the exit, I saw them on Dingens, heading back in the direction of South Ogden. Perfect. As we got closer to a bigger street, there'd be more people about and I'd be even harder to notice. Melting into the background on a tail was important. I wished I'd worn a shirt with less color.

I stayed about a block behind them until I reached Cambria Street. I was intent on my pursuit and not watching where I was going, when the screech of brakes and yelling broke my concentration.

A milk truck making the turn off Dingens onto Cambria collided with another truck waiting at the corner. I leapt back onto the sidewalk. Steam hissed from the engines of both vehicles and the drivers got out, yelling and cursing at each other. A crowd gathered to watch the show.

Ahead, I saw my trio turn right at the corner and onto South Ogden. I had to hurry. I tried to push my way through the mass of people, but it was no use. I darted across Dingens, up to South Ogden, and back across the intersection.

The three men had disappeared.

The crowd I'd been counting on to mask my presence was now an obstacle, one I couldn't see around. I craned my head and stood on tiptoe, searching for Heavy, Scarface, and Weasel. Nothing. The delay at the accident meant I'd lost them.

Well, shoot. Weasel had mentioned a garage. I could look for that. It had to be nearby and somewhere on this stretch of street, but looking around I realized it could be any number of buildings.

Doggone it. Now what?

***

I got back to Mackinaw as the sun was well on its way down in the sky, coloring the faint streaks of clouds with fire-red and orange against the deepening blue. The air was dry, but without the scent of snow. There'd been nothing all month, even the weather was conspiring to be unnatural. Murder, sabotage, pro-Nazi activities, no snow in November—everything was end over teakettle as my gramma would say.

Jimmy and Michael raced down the street, arms outstretched and making engine noises loud enough to be heard down on the lakeshore. "Betty, did ya hear? Did ya?" Jimmy asked, breathless as the two boys circled around me.

They were too keyed up for it to be bad news. "No, I haven't. Did Mayor Kelly stop to have a beer with Pop?" Buffalo's new mayor, Joe Kelly, was a tried-and-true Irish boy.

"No, silly. Did ya hear the war news?"

Michael continued to swoop around, yelling "raaawwwr" at the top of his lungs.

"Haven't been at home, have I? Why don't you tell me?" I wasn't gonna get a step closer to home until the boys got whatever had wound them up off their chests.

"We sank a Japanese battleship at Guad...Guad..."

"Guadalcanal." My heart leapt. That's for the *Juneau*, I thought.

"Yep. Sent it right to Davy Jones's locker." Jimmy joined his brother in circling. "C'mon, Mikey!" They swooped away, running down the street now adding the "rat-tat-tat-tat" noises to mimic the gun fire as they sank their imaginary enemies.

I'd get better details inside. Pop was at work and Mom was nowhere to be found, but Mary Kate was taking down washing in the back yard, the sheets half-frozen.

"Betty, you're home. Mom's at the rectory helping Mrs. Grady clean. Did you see the boys?" She unpinned a sheet from the line.

"I could hardly miss 'em. Here, lemme help you with that." I unclipped the other end of the sheet. "Cold day for hanging out the wash. Best warm these up and dry 'em out before you put 'em away. What was the ship that sunk?"

"I can't pronounced the Japanese ship, but the one from our side was the *Washington*." She put more laundry in the basket.

My heart stopped. Sean's ship. But Mary Kate wouldn't be casually taking down laundry if something happened. "The *Washington* sank?"

"Nah, it did the sinking." She stretched her back. "I can do this. Mom says you're to start biscuits to go with dinner. Oh, there's V-mail for you on the table."

Mary Kate was a gem. I dashed inside. There was only one person in the world who'd send me V-mail. It had been ages since I'd heard from Tom. Sure enough, I didn't even need to look at the postmark. The familiar cramped lettering was enough. I slit open the envelope and unfolded the single sheet inside.

Dear Betty - I only have a minute, but I haven't written in a while. They've got us working from sunup to sundown, hardly a second to breathe. I've been wearing this uniform so long it'll walk off me soon. We got a destination now, but I'm not s'posed to tell. Remember when we was at the beach last summer and you buried me up to my neck? I can still feel the sand in places where a Joe shouldn't feel sand. I bet you won't recognize me when I get home. I stopped burning long ago and now I'm as brown as a well-oiled baseball glove. Seems like the sun don't ever set. I can't wait to see a Lake Erie sunset arm in arm with you. Gotta go. Stay my girl. - Tom

He was safe. Well, he was safe a month ago. The censors were always careful to block out any sensitive information, but Tom was smart. He could write so I knew enough of where he was. All that talk of sun and sand meant he was in the desert. The 1st Armored Division was in Algeria, so he'd have been part of that Operation Torch I'd heard about on the newsreels.

I re-read the letter. What would Tom think of dating a detective? Would he be proud or would he send me back to the kitchen? I wanted to think the first. He'd always said my spunk is what caught his eye.

I folded the letter, kissed it, and said a quick prayer. *I'll stay your girl, my Tommy. You come home to me safe.* I went to the bedroom I shared with Mary Kate to change.

There had to be a better way of finding that garage, short of roaming up and down South Ogden checking every building that looked like a place a pro-Nazi group would hang out. I'd think of something.

Chapter 17

We went to Mass Sunday morning at Our Lady of Perpetual Help. After the service was over, I stopped to light two candles, one for Sean and one for Tom, like I always did. When we got back home, we had breakfast. Then Mom and Mary Kate settled in for some Sunday sewing. I paced the front room, my skirt swishing as I moved.

Mom huffed, but didn't stop stitching. "Betty, for the love of all the saints, stop fretting and sit down. There's mending to do."

"Last time I put a button on a shirt you told me I did it wrong," I said. Mom was particular about her sewing.

"Then sit and read your Bible. But please stop flitting about like an overactive bird."

I stared out the window, the sunshine beckoning. On our way back from church I could tell it was going to be another mild day. "I'm going for a walk," I said, grabbing a light coat and my purse.

Mom set down her sewing. "Where to?"

"Just around. I'll prob'ly see if Dot can go with me. I'll be back in time for dinner." I buttoned up my coat and headed out.

Dot answered when I rapped on her door. "You come by to tell me you can't go to the social tonight?"

"You want to go for a cup of coffee? I've gotta do something or I'll go nuts."

She studied me for a sec. "Sure, let me get my coat."

Ten minutes later we were seated in a booth at the drugstore, steaming cups in front of us. Dot dumped in a generous amount of condensed milk.

"Only way it tastes decent," she said and took a sip. "What's on your mind?"

Even at home, when it was weak and stretched with chicory, I preferred my joe black. "Can't I go for a cup of coffee with my best friend?"

She flashed a knowing look. "Yeah, because this is what you like to do on a Sunday afternoon. C'mon, Betty. I know you better'n that."

I told her about my conversation with Anne, then seeing Heavy, Scarface, and Weasel in Dingens Park. "I lost 'em at South Ogden. I've got no idea how to find this garage without looking up and down the entire street."

"There's gotta be a lot of garages on South Ogden. You sure there's no way to narrow it down?"

She was right. There had to be a way. "They turned right at the corner. That means they were headed north."

"They were going straight to the garage?"

"That's what Weasel said."

"How far up does Ogden go at that point?"

"A couple of blocks. Maybe three."

She sipped. "Do you think they'd leave Kaisertown?"

"No. They'd stay on friendly turf." I drained my cup and set it down. Then I stood. "Which means we have plenty of time."

Dot followed me. "For what?"

"A little side trip."

***

I had to bribe Dot with bus fare and a Coke, but she agreed to accompany me to Kaisertown. I went directly to the corner of Dingens and South Ogden. The Sunday foot traffic was light, automobile traffic almost non-existent.

Dot shaded her eyes as she scanned the street. "Okay, we're here. Now what?"

I glanced around. "When I followed 'em, we came from that direction." I pointed toward the park. "They got here, then turned right. Let's walk up the street and see what's what."

Dot shrugged her acceptance and fell in beside me. On the right side of the street, we passed houses with neat yards, some with toys. Across from us were more business-type stores and open lots. More than a few of the houses had garages.

"You think they went to a home?" Dot asked, pausing to examine a white house and garage, both with streaks of dirt on them. A wilted Victory garden was in the back, a sign with a blue star in the front window.

The door to the garage was down. For a second I considered peeking in the grime-crusted window, but decided not to. "I don't think so. They'd want to meet somewhere they wouldn't be disturbed. Anyone could bust into a home garage."

"Unless one of their families owns the house and they've all been told to keep out."

It was possible. But the Bund was not exactly a popular organization. I couldn't shake the feeling Weasel, Heavy, and Scarface would want someplace more secret for their meetings. And I didn't even want to consider they could be meeting in the home of a service member. "Put that idea on hold. We'll check commercial buildings. If we don't find anything, we can look at likely houses. Not this one."

Dot started to argue, but she must've noticed the star in the window because she fell silent.

We kept walking, bypassing more houses and small shops without gathering spots. Just as I saw the end of South Ogden and was about to give up, Dot pointed at a ramshackle building surrounded by a fence. "What's that?"

I jogged across the street and over to the fence. A faded sign proclaiming the place Walden Auto hung from the chain link at a lopsided angle. The enclosed lot was a combination of gravel and weeds. The owner prob'ly didn't get much business these days. A rusty Ford pickup occupied the near corner, sad with its faded paint and dry, cracked rubber. I was sure it hadn't been driven in a while.

"Windows are blacked out." Dot crossed the lot to try and peer in. Paint peeled off the door, giving it a faded gray color. She jiggled the doorknob. "Locked."

"I'm not surprised. Looks like the perfect place for a secret meeting, don't ya think?" I circled the building. Every window was covered with tar paper.

A garage door was padlocked shut. "I don't think anyone's here."

"Good thing or else we'd be busted for sure." Dot kicked at the limp, brown grass at the building's corners. "Betty, there's paper over here. Take a look."

I headed over to where she stood. "Anything written on it?"

She stuffed her hands in her pockets. "You pick it up. You're the snoop."

"Detective." I stooped and nabbed a pink pamphlet before it blew away. "Support the true victims," it read in large black letters. "Join forces against the imperial oppressors of Europe - Britain, France, and Russia. Join the German-American Bund and fight for the Fuhrer!"

Good grief. No wonder this thing had fallen flat. I couldn't imagine Pop, Lee, or any of their co-workers supporting this muck. At best the pamphlets would get the brush off, at worst a broken nose. I folded it up and put it in my pocket to show to Lee later and confirm it was what had been handed round at GM.

"Now what?" Dot asked.

"Ten to one this is the place. I'd love to see inside. Maybe get some names."

"You're off your rocker. Picking up paper on the ground is one thing, but I'm pretty sure breaking in would be illegal."

"Still, it'd be interesting." I tapped my finger against the window. The only sound was the wind ruffling dead leaves and grass, and the occasional squawk of a seagull.

"Yeah, well, you'll have to get someone else to help with that. Bus fare isn't worth going to jail. Come on. We gotta get back home and clean up before we go to the social tonight." She walked away without a backward glance.

I studied the forlorn building for a moment. Dot was right, it wasn't a good time to try my lock-picking skills. Yet I was certain this was the meeting place for the Bund, and where Heavy, Scarface, and Weasel had gone after leaving Dingens Park. Now I had to get inside and prove it.

Chapter 18

Sunday dinner was always served at five. Afterward, I helped clear away and wash the dishes. Then I fetched the pamphlet from my room. I had enough time to run one errand before I had to get ready for the night's social. "I'm goin' down the street to talk to Lee. Be back in a few minutes." I was out the door before anyone could object. While I'd cooked, I'd put out Cat's saucer, this time tucked around the corner next to the drain pipe where Mom wouldn't see it or Cat. Funny how it hadn't taken long for the gray-striped animal to grow on me.

He looked up from his dinner when I rounded the corner. I squatted so I could scratch behind his ears. "Maybe next time I go to the market I'll see if they've got any fish they're getting ready to throw away." He purred as he butted his head against my hand. I stood and took off down the street. When I looked behind me, Cat was following. Silly thing. It didn't think I meant I'd go right away, did it?

Lee was outside on the sidewalk smoking when I got to his house. I pulled out my own gasper. "Gimme a light?" I lit up off his cigarette. "Any new shenanigans at the plant?"

"Nope." He blew out a stream of smoke. "Either the Bund don't work weekends or they gave it up as a bad job. You come over here to ask me that?"

"Not exactly." I held out the pink sheet. "This what they were passing out?"

He took it, careful not to set the paper on fire. "Looks like. I didn't read it all that close."

"But you took it?"

"Easier to do that and pitch it." He inhaled and blew out another cloud of smoke. "Hey, you picked up a tag-a-long. You must smell like fish or something." He jabbed his cigarette at Cat, who was winding around my legs.

"He's our stray. Mary Kate and I've been feeding him. Looks like I've been adopted."

Lee grinned, took a final puff, and flicked his cigarette to the gutter. "Not sure what that says about you, Betty. Adopted by a scrawny old cat."

I gave him a little shove. "Can it. Is that the same paper?"

"Pretty sure." He held it just out of my reach. "Question is, where'd you get this one? You're not working at GM too, are ya?"

I tried to snatch it back, but he continued to taunt me. "I found it," I said.

"Oh yeah? Found it where?"

"On the ground outside a garage on South Ogden."

His arms dropped to his side. "What the hell were you doin' up there?"

I took the opportunity to take the paper. "I think I found the local Bund headquarters." I told him about seeing Heavy, Scarface, and Weasel at the park, my busted attempt to follow them, and the discovery of the meeting place. I was pretty proud of my skills.

Lee didn't find it nearly as admirable. "Are you crazy? What if they'd seen you?"

"I'd have pretended to be out for a walk."

"And if they didn't buy your act?"

"C'mon, Lee. It was the middle of the day. What were they gonna do in broad daylight? Besides, I had Dot with me."

He stared, mouth open like a landed fish. "Yeah, because crimes don't happen at three in the afternoon. I love Dot, but she's not much of a deterrent to violence."

"I don't see what you're so steamed about. Not like I was checking out a deserted building at nine at night." He was stealing my sense of adventure. "Although, I might hafta find a way to do that if I wanna catch them actually doing something."

"You wouldn't."

"I sure would." Clearly, Lee did not believe I was serious about my new profession. "In fact, I was gonna ask if you wanted to go with me, but since you're gonna get all persnickety maybe I'll just go by myself."

"Betty, you listen and listen good." He took a step closer and grabbed hold of my arm. "You know you're like a sister to me. We go way back. I never told you, but Ma was pretty mad at you over that tire swing. How could I let you talk me into it?"

"Lee—"

"Be quiet." The expression on his face was unfamiliar, a seriousness that he'd never shown before. "Before Tom shipped out for Ireland, we went out drinking. 'I need a favor, Lee,' he said. 'Something only you can do. You'll look after Betty for me, won't you? She gets headstrong and I know you love her like I do. Someone's gotta watch out for her and keep her safe.' I said of course I would." His eyes softened. "I know you like all those movies, Sam Spade and all that. You know they sometimes get into trouble."

All I could do was nod. Lee had promised Tom he'd look after me? Neither of them had mentioned that. 'Course they wouldn't. I doubted Lee would have said anything if I hadn't taken up private investigation as a side job.

"When you see Bogie, that's just the movies. It's all fake," Lee continued. "When the bad guys come after you with a knife, Betty, that'll be real. If Tom were to find out I'd let you get hurt, he'd kick my ass into Lake Erie from all the way over there in North Africa. And I'd deserve it."

"Lee, I didn't know."

"You weren't s'posed to." He let go of my wrist. "Anyway, if you won't leave it be for your own sake, do it for Tom."

Of all the low-down sneaky tricks. 'Cept I wasn't sure Tom would ask me the same thing. "I can't."

Lee leaned against the house and crossed his arms. "How would you feel if you got a telegram saying Tom had been injured in battle? Or worse, killed?"

Unfair. "I'd feel awful. Worse than awful. You know that."

"Okay. Now think how he'd feel if things were reversed. He's over there, fighting, thinking about the day he gets to come home to you. Then he learns you've been hurt with all this detective stuff. And he wouldn't be able to do anything about it. Did you ever think about that?"

The words cut like a whip and I fought back tears.

"If it were Tom standing here, right now in front of you, would you still insist on doing this? Be honest."

I swiped my hand across my eyes. "Yes, I would. No, now it's your turn to listen. This girl, Anne. I think she's getting a bad rap. I don't like her much. Well, I didn't like her, but I've changed my mind I think. She's been set up to take the fall and I can't let it go. And her mother. Lee, you didn't see this woman. Seein' her all in black and crying 'cause her son is dead and not knowing why? I can't stand back and do nothing. Tom wouldn't expect me to, either." Tom wouldn't, and if Lee knew his buddy half as well as he claimed, he'd see it was true.

After a moment, Lee shook his head. "Nothing I can say will change your mind, huh? How do I keep my word to Tom if I let you do this?"

"Tell you what. Help me out. I promise if you think I'm getting carried away, I'll step back. Even Sam Spade had a partner, right? You saw *Maltese Falcon* with me."

"His partner was killed in that one."

True. "That just means you'll be better at your job. Deal?" I stuck out my hand.

He sighed, but he shook on it. "Betty Ahern, you're gonna be the death of me."

115

Chapter 19

I spent the better part of Sunday night and Monday morning on the bus arguing with Dot, wheedling her into playing ball with me. I think what swung it was telling her Lee was coming with me. I got the impression she thought he'd keep me in line or something.

Fat chance.

Dot and I were at his house as soon as he got back from GM, and I explained our plan to examine the garage.

"Sounds good to me," he said. "Just let me toss my stuff inside and tell Ma I'll be out for a bit."

Dot's eyes got as big as saucers. "Lee! I can't believe you're gonna go along with this. I thought you were just playing."

He faced her. "What? You think I'm gonna let the two of you run off on your own? You're crazy."

Dot huffed. "You were s'posed to say 'no way' and talk her outta it."

"You *are* crazy. I already tried that." He shifted the lunch pail in his hand to rummage in his pocket for keys. He found them, unlocked his front door, and turned to me. "If I said I'd changed my mind and Dot bailed on you, would you go anyway?"

I glanced at Dot. "Yep."

"See? You and I need to team up, Dot. It's the only way to keep her out of trouble." He opened the door. It only took him a minute to disappear inside, drop his work gear, and return. "Let's go."

Lee and I came up with the final details while we rode the bus to Kaisertown. Dot didn't contribute, but at least by the time we'd arrived she lost most of her grumpiness. After making sure we could hear her, we stationed her at the bus stop on South Ogden close to the garage.

"What am I supposed to do again?" Dot asked.

"Just stay at the corner, like you're waiting for a bus," I said. "If you see anyone heading for the garage, give a sharp whistle so Lee and I get a warning."

"What if someone asks why I'm whistling?"

"Tell them you're searching for your dog," Lee said, tugging his cap down.

"I thought I was waiting for a bus."

Lee rolled his peepers. "Dot, you're a quick-thinker. I have faith in your ability to come up with a good story. Betty, you bring the hair pins?"

I held them up.

"Then let's get this show on the road."

After making sure no one was in sight, we strolled over to the garage's front door. "You see any lights inside?" he asked.

"Hard to tell with all this paper over the windows. Hold on." I circled the building. The paper in one of the back windows had a tear in it. Not a big one, but enough to let me know there weren't any lights on. To be sure, I put my ear up close to the glass. Nothing. I went back to the front. "The place is deserted."

"You do realize this is against the law, right?"

Yeah, I knew that. Neither Lee nor Dot seemed to understand I'd argued with myself over this. If we got caught, we'd be in deep trouble and might even get arrested. But if I didn't, I'd never be able to connect or clear the Bund, find out who offed George, and Anne might be locked up for something she didn't do. "Stand right there, so people can't see me real good from the sidewalk. Hopefully it'll look like I'm having trouble with the lock."

"Won't you be?"

"I don't expect to."

The door lock looked simple and a bit worse for wear. I inserted the pins and fiddled with them, waiting to hear the lock snap open. A full minute passed without anything.

Lee's grin teased me. "You know, Sam Spade would be inside already."

I straightened up and blew hair out of my eyes. "Okay, smarty pants. You do it."

"With pleasure." He took the pins. Less than fifteen seconds later, he opened the door. "Piece of cake."

We slipped inside. "Do I want to know where you learned that little skill?" I asked.

He handed me the hair pins. "I work in a machine shop. It's all leverage and tumblers."

I made a note to ask for lock-picking lessons. Later, after we'd finished our snooping.

Lee closed the door tight behind us and I searched for a light switch. There wasn't one on the wall, but my fingers found a chain hanging from the ceiling, hopefully attached to an overhead light. I pulled.

A yellowish glow filled the room. Another door led off to the left, most likely to the bays where they worked on cars. "This must be the office," I whispered. There was a counter and a cobwebby cash register, along with a battered wooden table and a couple ladder-back chairs that needed a fresh coat of paint.

"You don't have to whisper," Lee said, laying his cap on the counter. "No one will be able to hear you from the street unless you start yelling."

I stuck out my tongue at his back. He might be right, but he didn't need to rub it in.

"Tell me again what we're lookin' for?"

"Anything that links the Bund to the sabotage at Bell, or something that might show the Bund had a motive to kill George."

Lee nodded. He opened a drawer in the battered file cabinet and winced at the metal-on-metal squeal. "You think George was murdered by his Nazi buddies?"

I sat and opened a desk drawer. "I think it's possible. He was definitely good friends with whoever did it."

"What makes you say that?"

"One, he went down a dark alley to meet the person. Two, it was someone he was comfortable standing close to, or at least didn't think was a threat."

The drawer contained nothing except old receipts and auto repair orders, so I closed it and moved onto the next one.

Lee turned around. "I don't see how you figure that."

"You gotta get close to someone to stab him. Think about it. You're over there, I'm here at least three feet away. Only way I could get you with a knife is to throw it. To get you in the heart my aim would have to be perfect. But if I'm standing right next to you..." I made a quick jabbing motion. "Easy as pie. 'Cept if you were afraid of me, or if we were total strangers, you wouldn't let me get close enough, would you?"

He considered it, then turned back to the cabinet. "Makes sense. But it's not only the Bund members that fit your idea. Could be another friend or even a family member."

"I know, but I gotta start somewhere. And I don't really wanna think a member of the Linden family coulda done this. At least not yet."

There were papers all over the table, as well as tacked to the walls. I moved over to look at them. "Lists of names," I said. "Names and addresses. Think they're members?"

Lee joined me. "Or potential members. It's pretty foolish to leave their rosters lying around, even if this is the headquarters."

"The Bund isn't operating in secret."

"You said those guys at the community center dance last week were masked."

They had been. "They aren't a secret organization, but maybe those involved don't want folks to know they're members. It can't be real popular to be seen supporting the Nazis with our troops overseas."

"Prob'ly not." He started sifting through the papers on the table.

"What's that?" I came over to stand at his shoulder.

"If I had to guess, it's their plans for recruiting and activities." Lee pointed. "Look, here's the pamphlet campaign, along with a list of who would be at which plant and when."

"It include George Linden?"

Lee scanned the sheet. "Yep, right here at GM like I said." He tapped a line. "This here says they want to have a membership drive at the German-

American Club."

"Good luck with that. I didn't get the feeling from Mr. Ackerman that many of the folks there would be keen to join up."

He shuffled through the papers. "These here are meeting minutes. Fund raising, more ideas for events, and the date of their next meeting."

"When is that?"

"Tomorrow at seven."

"Then I was right. Nobody is here and we're perfectly safe." Now that I knew I was right, I could afford to be smug.

"Yeah, but you didn't know that before we saw this."

Lee and I continued to read, but the rest of the paper wasn't very exciting. More lists, samples of a couple different flyers, and a bus schedule. I left him to sort through it all, while I looked on the shelf by the register. A few receipt books, a calendar from 1939, and an auto parts catalog. And cobwebs, lots and lots of cobwebs. Whatever the Bund was doing when they were here, they weren't working the register.

"Have you found anything?" I shoved a box containing old newspapers back on the bottom shelf.

"Like 'here are our plans for industrial sabotage'? No. Nothing to indicate they were up to funny business at Bell or anywhere else, for that matter." He put down the papers he'd been holding. "This is all pretty tame. My Boy Scout troop was better organized than these fat-heads."

I stood and dusted my hands. "Maybe they don't keep it here. Could be—"

Lee clapped a hand over my mouth. "You hear that? Dot's whistle."

Despite my failure to hear anything of the kind, it didn't occur to me to doubt Lee. His sharp ears had saved us from a lot of scrapes when we were kids. Just as I was about to pry his hand off my face, a jumble of voices got my attention.

"People outside. Quick, we gotta hide." Lee scanned the room, but hiding places were scarce.

"We're gonna be in major hot water in about thirty seconds."

Lee tugged my arm. "The repair bay."

We slipped through the door into the open space of the garage in the nick of time. We no sooner crouched behind a rusting truck when we heard the office door creak open.

"Okay, which of you mooks forgot to lock the door?" Weasel's nasal voice.

"Wasn't me." That was Heavy.

"Don't look at me." Scarface. "I don't even got a key."

Sounds of shoving. Then Weasel cut in. "Knock it off. I'll just make sure to do it myself next time." The desk chair creaked as someone sat down. "Who left his hat here?"

Lee squeezed his eyes shut. I could imagine the words goin' through his mind and they weren't nice ones. How did we forget the cap?

"Ain't mine," said Heavy. "Maybe left behind after the last meeting? I could do up a flyer—"

"Oh, for chrissakes, if it's someone's they'll claim it next time." Weasel blew out a breath. "Flyers. Sheesh."

Whew. I raised up to try and peer in the dirt-streaked window. But all I saw were three shapes before Lee pulled me back down. I opened my mouth, but he laid a finger over his lips.

"Now what do we do?" Heavy asked.

"You think George told anyone else what we was up to?" Scarface asked. "We could be in big trouble if that's the case."

"Yeah, maybe he blabbed to his sister."

The chair creaked as Weasel answered. "I don't know. Maybe we should pay her a visit to make sure."

My heart clenched. Anne. If these three thought George had spilled the beans about the Bund's plans, she could be in danger. Especially if that's what got George stabbed.

"And if he did?" Heavy asked. "What do we do then? I know she don't like us. I heard her crabbing at Georgie-boy one day. She ain't gonna play ball and leave us be."

I stared at Lee. His expression was solemn. Were they threatening Anne? Sure sounded like it to me.

"We'll deal with her if we have to," Weasel said. The chair creaked some more.

The garage bays and the old truck were coated in dust. My nose itched. It would be a bad time for a sneeze. Of course, the second I thought that, I felt an uncontrollable urge. I buried my face in my elbow and fought down the sneeze as I squinched up my face.

Lee noticed and his eyes widened. He reached over to pull me close and press me against his chest.

I sneezed, a small but squeaky sound.

The chair squealed and snapped. "Did you hear that?" Weasel asked.

"I didn't hear nothing," Scarface said.

Lee and I froze. There wasn't anywhere else to hide. All we could do is stay quiet as mice and hope the three in the office decided not to search for such a small disturbance. Or decided they imagined it.

The wait was crushing. Longest five seconds of my life.

"Mice, maybe. Let's get outta here. I want you two to go watch the Linden house," Weasel said. "You see anything that makes you think the sister knows something, you tell me. And don't forget to lock the damn door this time."

I heard scraping and heavy steps, the snap of a lock and the thunk of a door. I pushed myself off Lee.

He crossed himself. "Thank God they aren't the sharpest knives in the drawer."

We stayed in the garage bay for another couple minutes, to make sure the three Bund members didn't come back. Once we felt comfortable that the coast was indeed clear, we went back to the office. "I gotta check in with Anne," I said.

He grabbed his cap and jammed it on. "You think she knows anything?"

"I don't know. But it doesn't matter. If those three think she does, she's in trouble for sure."

Lee shook his head. "Don't s'pose I could convince you to call the cops and leave it alone."

I held his gaze. "No. You heard 'em. Besides, nothing we heard was illegal. What can the cops do?"

"I s'pose you still want help."

"I won't lie. But I understand if you want out. I've gotta do this 'cause

I don't want anything bad to happen to Anne. But you don't know her and neither does Dot, not like me. If you two would rather call it quits, I understand."

"I doubt Dot is gonna abandon you. You two're as thick as thieves." He sighed. "I may not be Army material, but I'd be a poor friend if I didn't at least try and keep you out of trouble."

I hugged him. "Thanks."

"Yeah, whatever. C'mon, let's get out of here, collect Dot, and catch a bus back to the First Ward. There's only so long that dog story will work. Shut off the lights."

I held the chain while he checked for anything else that might give us away. I waited to pull it until he'd unlocked and opened the door. "You sure you can lock it again?" I walked past him and outside.

He followed and pulled the door shut. "I can't believe you asked me that."

Chapter 20

Tuesday morning, I was spared having to talk much about the Lindens 'cause everyone at Bell was buzzing with war news.

"Did ya hear?" Florence said as we were punching in. "We sank another Japanese ship. It was the *USS Washington* that did it for us this time, I think."

"Hey Betty." Helen punched her time card. "Isn't your brother on the *Washington*?"

Rose followed us to the locker room. "A boyfriend in North Africa and a brother at Guadalcanal. You've got the world covered, Betty."

"Yeah, lucky me." I stashed my lunch pail and purse. The Allies had won at Guadalcanal with heavy losses. But we'd won. That didn't mean Sean was safe, but since we hadn't gotten a telegram, the chances were pretty good he was at least okay. There'd been no news from Tom's family either. How many more lives did those two have?

Helen eyed Rose. "Don't you have family in Italy?"

Rose scowled. "Not the same."

Catherine came up beside me as we headed across the yard to the assembly building. "It's gotta be hard," she said. "Wish more of these planes were going to help our boys."

"They are," Helen said.

Catherine's expression turned bitter. "I've said this before. Most of 'em are going to the Soviets."

"But they're our allies," Rose said, as we entered the work area.

"It's only a matter of time before they switch," Catherine said, taking her place on the assembly line. "They can't help it. It's who they are."

"What's her issue?" Florence asked me, keeping her voice low so Catherine couldn't hear. With the racket that had started with the chains, it wasn't likely.

I glanced at Catherine. Dark, slightly exotic-looking, passionate. That was Catherine. Usually full of laughs, but sometimes she got funny, like now. "No clue. She doesn't like the Russians, that's for sure. But even my pop says he don't completely trust Stalin."

"Ike does. Don't your dad trust Ike?" Florence asked, lifting both eyebrows.

"He does." I focused on my job, very aware of Florence hanging at my elbow. But I couldn't look at her. Everybody trusted General Eisenhower. To say a word against him was like spitting on the flag. "You wanna know what's up with Catherine, maybe you should ask her. Otherwise, we gotta get to work."

Florence muttered something, but she stepped away.

The whistle blew for lunch. "I'm gonna go out and have a quick cigarette," I said to the others. "Save me a spot."

Outside, the sky was blue, the wind gentle, and the temperature was still warm. November seventeenth and I was out without a jacket. We were in for a heck of a winter storm for sure. Just as I was finishing my smoke, I saw a tussle at the front gate. I squinted. It was Anne, struggling with two of the Bell security guards. I thought I saw a box in her arms. It would cut into my lunch time, but I strolled over.

Anne was begging the men. "I just have to see her for five minutes. Please."

"I'm sorry, Miss Linden. We can't let you onto the site. Management orders."

She was shaking. Then she caught sight of me. "Betty, please. I need to talk to you. It's important."

"Guys." I looked at the guards. "Can't you bend the rules just a smidge?"

"No can do, Miss Ahern," the guard said. He did look like he regretted his words. "It's not worth my job for that."

Anne's eyes filled with tears and she clutched her box, silently begging me to do something.

"Tell you what." I pointed to a patch of withered grass just beyond the main road onto the Bell property. "I'll talk to her right there, where you can see. She's not inside, I won't let her in, you're not busting the rules, and she gets to talk to me. Is that good enough?"

The second guard seemed like he was gonna object, but the first one answered. "Good enough for me. We'll keep an eye out, though. One step inside and we call the cops."

I grabbed Anne's arm and hustled her to the designated spot. "Talk fast. What's so important you gotta bust in here to see me and interrupt my lunch?"

"I found this." She held out the box. "I was cleaning George's room, putting his things into piles to either throw or give away. This was way in the back of his closet, covered by old shoes." She bit her lip. "I don't know what to do with it."

"What's in the box?"

She wouldn't answer and shook her head.

"Can I look inside?" I didn't wait for an answer and peeked under the lid. Then I let loose. Words Mom didn't think I knew, but you didn't work in a factory and have a father at the Steel without picking up a few colorful phrases.

C-cards. The kind that you got when you were identified as being essential to the war effort, like doctors or the mail man. A C-card got you as much gas as you needed, no questions asked. The box contained dozens of them. If I took 'em out to look close, the guards would see for sure and that would probably get Anne arrested. In this quantity, though, I was sure they were fake. They had to be. A regular Joe like George Linden wouldn't have a box full of C-cards. "Who knows about these besides you?" I asked, voice low to avoid being overheard.

"No one, at least I don't think so."

"You don't think?"

"Well, Freddie asked me if I'd gone through George's things yet. Right after the police told us about George and again last night."

"You think he knows about these?"

126

"I'm not sure. He was awfully intense, kept asking me if I'd found anything unusual in George's possessions." Anne's eyes shone with terror. "What am I going to do?" she whispered.

Sounded to me like Freddie knew his cousin had something not quite legit, but either he didn't know exactly what or he didn't want to tip his hand. I re-covered the box and handed it to her. "You have to give these to the cops."

"I can't. What will they say about George? Or about the rest of us? This will kill my parents. Bad enough their son was supporting Hitler. To learn that he had contraband as well will crush them."

"You have to." I glanced over, but the guards were barely paying attention. "Ask for Detective Sam MacKinnon. He's homicide, but he's a straight shooter. Tell him what you found and where. He'll be fair with you."

"Why can't I simply throw them away?"

"First of all, you do that, and people will pick 'em out of the garbage and put 'em on their cars. Guaranteed. Second, it might relate to the murder."

"How?"

Could she really not see? Maybe she was too terrified. "Have you found any other black market items in George's things?"

She gave a slow shake of her head.

"Look, if these are fake, and I think they are, he was counterfeiting them. Or he had a supplier and was dealing them. Not only is that a crime, what if he sold one and it was discovered as a fake? The person who bought it would be madder than a wet cat."

"You think that person would be angry enough to kill him?"

"Maybe. Plus, these aren't amateur looking. A person would need the right printing equipment and knowledge of how to get all the right stamps and stuff. I think George was working with a supplier. That's why I asked about other things."

"Such as?"

"Ration books. Did he have a stash of nylons, access to rubber tires?"

She wiped her eyes. "Tires, I don't think so. Where would he put them? But there are still boxes of things to go through in his room and our garage."

She squeezed the box to her chest. "A couple months ago, George suddenly had all this money. I asked him and he told me it was none of my business and I shouldn't worry. You think it was related to these?"

"It's possible." Heck, it was almost certain. The production was slick, but George could easily have been the distributor. He could have been killed by a buyer who felt cheated or his supplier, 'specially if he was taking more dough than agreed. "Point is, there's a lot of cabbage wrapped up in counterfeiting. Where there's a lot of money, there's a good motive for murder."

"What makes you so sure Detective MacKinnon won't arrest Mama, Papa, and I because he thinks we were all in on it with George?"

"He's one of the good guys. If you weren't in cahoots with George, Detective MacKinnon won't try and make it look like you were." I patted her shoulder. "I bet he's gonna give you credit for turning this stuff in, too. You wouldn't do that if you were part of the racket."

She took a big, shaky breath. "Okay, I'll call him. Betty, do you think this had anything to do with the sabotage?"

I couldn't answer. Mostly 'cause I honestly didn't know. But it was one more fact to add to my investigation. "One more thing. Your car. Does it have a 'C' sticker on it?"

"I wouldn't know. George was the one who took care of the car."

"Try and find out, will ya?" It didn't make sense for George to have access to the C-cards and not use one himself. It would certainly explain where he got all his gas.

***

By the time I got back to the cafeteria I barely had time to bolt down my lunch, which spared me from having to talk about my meeting with Anne. The assembly line was no place for serious conversation. Dot tried to get me to talk on the bus, but there were too many people who might overhear us, so I put her off. It wasn't until we got off at the foot of Main Street that we were alone.

"All right, where were you during lunch and why did we have to wait?" Dot asked as we headed toward home.

I lit a cigarette and took a deep drag. "I was talking to Anne Linden." I blew out a stream of smoke into the cooling afternoon air. Cool, but more like early spring, not late fall. Like I said. Unnatural.

"What did she want?"

Should I tell Dot about this new development? After all, she prob'ly wouldn't run her mouth and she had gone with me to the garage. "She found a box of C-cards in her brother's stuff. I think they might be fake."

Dot halted and gasped. "Why would he have counterfeit gas ration cards?"

"Keep your voice down." I checked around, but the street was deserted 'cept for us. "Why else? To sell 'em." I resumed walking, puffing on my gasper as I thought.

Dot hastened to catch up. "But where would he get something like that?"

"I don't know. I don't think he made 'em." I quickened my step.

"Where are you going?" She sounded out of breath as she struggled to keep up, being so much shorter than me.

"I gotta talk to Lee."

"Because he knows where to get fake ration cards?"

"No, but he might have an idea how to find out."

We reached the Tillotson house on Mackinaw just as Lee was opening his door. He paused on the porch. "Detective Ahern. You look like you're in a hurry. Off to break into another Bund meeting house?"

"Ha ha. Look. If I wanted to buy a black market gas ration card, where would I go?"

He had been grinning, but it faded away as I spoke. "Why on earth would you wanna do that?"

I told him about the box of C-cards in George Linden's possession.

"Stay right here. Don't move." He went inside. A couple minutes later, he came back out, tugging on his cap. "Let's walk a bit. I don't think we need anyone overhearing this conversation."

We walked back down Mackinaw to Louisiana, where Lee hung a left. He didn't speak until we reached Conway Park, well away from anyplace we might be seen or heard. "What's this about C-cards?"

"George Linden had a whole box of 'em. Anne found it." I told Lee my idea about a possible tie between the cards and George's murder. "I don't think I'm nuts for considering it, am I?"

"No." He rubbed his bum leg. "She didn't find anything else?"

"She says not, but she's looking. I figure if I can find out where I could buy a card, I might find the killer."

Dot piped up. "I thought we were only looking for a saboteur."

"I think we've gotta look for both." I pulled out my deck of Luckys and offered one to Lee. He took it and I lit both of 'em. I didn't usually smoke this much, but my nerves were tighter than piano wire and the taste of the Lucky Strike soothed them. "I got a feeling the girls at Bell, and maybe even management and the cops, think George was killed because of the sabotage. If they're still fingering Anne for that, maybe they'd think she was involved in the murder, too. If I can show it was actually this black market stuff, not the sabotage, that'll most likely clear Anne of all of it."

"What if Anne was doing it all on her own?"

"I don't see it. She's been working at that factory for what, two months? Three? How come she didn't start causing problems sooner if she wanted to ruin things?"

"I don't know." Dot scuffed the ground. "She wanted to make sure people trusted her first."

"But they didn't trust her," Lee said. "At least not according to Betty."

Dot's glare cut through the falling light. "Whose side are you on anyway, huh? And you." She whirled to me. "You never liked her much. Now she's a dame in distress. Just 'cause she gave you money doesn't mean she's innocent. She coulda paid you just so you wouldn't believe she was involved."

Dot was right. I hadn't liked Anne much. So why had I agreed to help her in the first place? It was that look she'd had when they dragged her off the line and fired her. She'd been like a cornered rabbit, all wide-eyed and not understanding what was going on. It wasn't a look that could be faked, not like that. No one deserved to be framed and punished for something she didn't do. "It's not only the money, Dot." I said. "It's the difference between us and the Nazis. Everybody gets a fair shake. You know Sean and Tom. If they were here, what do you think they'd do?"

"Help her," Dot mumbled, scuffing the ground with the toe of her shoe.

"Darn right they would. Or at least they'd look for the guilty one. If that turned out to be Anne, well, then she has to take the punishment. But if it's not her, people need to know that. Tom and Sean aren't here. I am. They'd expect me to do the same thing they would."

Lee stared at me, expression unreadable. Then he turned to Dot. "They'd want us to help out. You know they would. Tom's one of my best friends. I don't think I could look him in the eye if I didn't."

There was silence cut only by whirring of night-time insects and the squawking of stray seagulls. Dot's gaze was fixed on the ground. Then she huffed and looked up. "Fine, I'll help. Not 'cause I like Anne Linden though. I wanna make that perfectly clear."

"Clear as my gramma's crystal goblets, the ones her mama brought from Ireland," Lee said without a trace of a grin.

Dot ignored him. "Could the guys in the Bund be the ones behind these fake ration cards?"

"What makes you think that?" Lee asked.

"George Linden was in the Bund and he had the cards. They need cash for their activities. Why not this way?"

I gazed at the empty park, hardly seeing what was in front of me. "It's possible I s'pose. 'Cept we didn't see nothing in their headquarters, or meeting room, or whatever the place was."

Lee leaned against a tree. "Could have been in the car bays. We didn't look there."

"We were too busy hiding." Scarface, Heavy, and Weasel didn't look like counterfeiters though. At least Scarface and Heavy didn't. They were muscle. I didn't know enough about Weasel to say what his role was.

Dot broke the silence. "What do we do next, Betty?"

"Simple." I dropped my cigarette, crushed it underfoot, and headed out of the park. "We need to find ourselves a black market ration card dealer."

Chapter 21

After dinner, while I cleaned up, Mom's sharp voice cut through the house. "Elizabeth Ann!"

Now what? Had Cat ripped up the garbage?

I tip-toed to the front door. Detective MacKinnon stood between Pop and Mom. He'd shown up at our home? That was worse than Mom finding a stray cat in the back yard. "Detective. Are you here to see me?"

"Who else would he be here to see?" Mom snapped. "Bad enough the entire neighborhood saw you dropped off by a police car, now a police detective is visiting the house. What are the neighbors going to think of us? You and I are going to have a talk about this later, young lady."

"That's enough, Mary," Pop said. "It's not the girl's fault the police want to talk to her." He ignored Mom's sniff of disagreement. "Betty, would you like me to sit with you while you talk to the detective?"

"No, Pop. It's okay. I met Detective MacKinnon last month when Mr. Lippincott...you know."

"Very well. Use the front room." Pop turned to the detective. "Can I get you a glass of water?"

"Thank you, but no, Mr. Ahern. Actually, would you mind if I spoke to Elizabeth outside? Not that I don't trust your family, but I'd prefer not to be overheard."

Mom sputtered. "Well, I never. We're law-abiding, God-fearing people in this house—"

"Of course, Detective." Pop opened the front door and gestured for me to follow Detective MacKinnon out.

The night air was cool, but dry. A few stars peeped through the clouds overhead. The nearest street light was a few houses away, giving enough light to see by, but not enough for me to make out the details of his puss. My breath steamed before me. "I'm sorry about my mom. Her world of 'what nice folk do' keeps getting smacked around."

"Perfectly understandable. Nice folk don't get visits from police detectives."

"Exactly. So, you have a question for me?"

"I'm sorry to bother you at home, Miss Ahern—"

"I told you last month, it's Betty."

"Betty." He flashed a grin. "Did you tell Miss Linden to bring me a box of C-cards?"

"I did." I told him about Anne coming to Bell. "I figured you were the best person to talk to, since they could be related to her brother's death."

"Did you see the cards?"

"I opened the box, but I didn't inspect them real close. Were they fake?"

"Yes." He pulled a pack of Camels out of his jacket pocket, tapped one out and patted his pockets, probably looking for a lighter.

I took out my Zippo and a cigarette, and lit my smoke. "Need a light?"

"Thank you." He leaned over to light his gasper then took a drag, blowing the smoke out of the corner of his mouth so it was carried behind him by the night breeze. "We searched the Lindens' property again. We found a box of contraband ration books in the basement, behind the furnace."

I let out a low whistle.

"Why do you say it's related to George Linden's murder?"

"I only said it could be. It's logical, isn't it? If he's selling counterfeit ration cards and other black market items, he'd have a lot of money on his hands. People who have a lot of money are often targets for theft and murder, leastways they are in the movies."

MacKinnon chuckled. "Still playing detective, are you?"

"No. Least I'm not playing." I flicked ash to the pavement. Should I tell him? It might make him take me seriously and slip me some news. "Anne Linden paid me fifty bucks to clear her over the sabotage going on at Bell."

"Not bad. But that doesn't make you a real detective."

"Why not? Not like women can't do it. Even Pinkerton hired a woman."

"I never said you couldn't do the job. Only that pay doesn't make you a professional. But that's not why I'm here." He pulled out a couple photographs. "You're right, of course. If George Linden was involved in black market deals, that could very well be a motive. Have you ever seen either of these men?"

I tilted the pictures so I could see them better. It was Scarface and Heavy. "Yeah. My friend Lee, he saw a guy who could be either of them with George." I gave a quick summary of the pamphlet campaign and how I'd followed them from Dingens Park to the garage. I left out how Lee and I had broken in. "They were with a third guy, real scrawny. I don't know his name yet."

"That was rather dangerous, you know." Detective MacKinnon slipped the pictures back in his pocket.

"They didn't see me. Who are they?"

"William Dunkel and Marcus Hoffman are known members of the German-American Bund. That itself is not illegal, but they both have records for petty theft, disturbing the peace, and, in Hoffman's case, assault. You say your friend saw them with Linden?"

"Yeah, but Lee doesn't know which one." Goosebumps broke out on my arms as the breeze picked up. Heavy—Hoffman—had a rap sheet? Considering I'd heard what I took as a threat against Anne, that wasn't good news. "Tell me. Was George using those C-cards for himself?"

"I think he was. We found a counterfeit C-card in a leather satchel under the front seat of his Ford. It had adhesive on the back. Somehow, he was placing it over the A-card in the windshield, most likely when he went to fill up. According to other papers in the satchel, he was passing himself off as carrying newsreel equipment."

At least George hadn't pretended to be a doctor or something.

"Anyway, did you ever see Miss Linden or her parents with an extra ration book? Or hear her talk about her brother's activities?"

"Never. Well, I didn't see 'em with any ration coupons at all. But Anne said something once about how her mother had been saving sugar coupons.

She wouldn't be doing that if she had all these books, would she?"

"Probably not. You said Anne hired you to look into this sabotage. Have there been any further incidents since she was fired?"

"No."

"Then maybe she was involved, either because of her brother or on her own initiative."

"I don't believe that." I tilted my head. "I also don't think Anne or her parents had any idea what was going on with the ration cards."

"Why not?"

"You'll laugh, but…it doesn't feel right to me."

"I won't laugh at all." His face was somber. "Instinct is a very powerful tool for an investigator."

I stuffed my hands in the front pockets of my pants, and rocked back and forth on my feet. I had to tell him about what I'd heard in the garage, but without admitting to breaking and entering, of course. "D'you think…is Anne in danger from these guys? In the Bund?"

MacKinnon's forehead wrinkled. "Why would you think that?"

"It's just, say the Bund is involved in something illegal. Something more than just passing out propaganda. If they think George blabbed to his sister, d'you think they might rough her up to find out?"

He narrowed his peepers. "Why do I get the feeling you're hiding something from me?"

I kept my mouth shut, but swallowed hard. If he asked straight out, I didn't think I could lie.

Fortunately, he didn't. "I suppose it's possible. I'll follow up with Miss Linden and tell her to call me if she sees anything suspicious."

Good enough. I relaxed a smidge. "Well, if that's all, I better get inside before Mom starts yelling. Don't think she won't light into you, too."

"I'm sorry if I got you into trouble."

"Don't worry about it." I headed for the house.

"Betty."

I stopped with my hand on the doorknob and turned back to look at him.

"If you find out anything else, I would appreciate you getting in touch

135

with me." He stepped over to hand me a card with the precinct address and phone number.

I took it. "Who said I was gonna keep looking? Didn't you just tell me I wasn't a real detective?"

"A First Ward girl like yourself giving up?" He took out some keys and opened the door to a black Ford. "Somehow I doubt that very much. Good night." He raised his fedora in a good-bye, got in his car, and drove off.

Chapter 22

I filled Dot in on Detective MacKinnon's visit the next morning on the way to Wheatfield.

"He came to your house? Bet your mom didn't like that."

"I couldn't tell what made her angrier. The police visiting or her finding Cat on the back step, meowing his fool head off."

"You never shoulda fed that cat. No way you'll get rid of it now."

I figured that, but I wasn't so sure I wanted to. I'd spent a bit of time sitting outside, scratching Cat's ears thinking about sabotage, George Linden, the Bund, counterfeit ration cards, murder, and if it was all related. Cat had filled out a bit since I'd started taking care of him. Rubbing the silky ears helped me think.

"I can't believe George was selling black market ration books, either," Dot said. She chewed her lip some. "I mean, he wasn't giving them to his family, was he?"

"I don't know. Least I don't think so. But maybe he was. MacKinnon said he found one of the C-cards in the Ford. I guess George fixed it in the windshield each time he went for a fill up." Must have been a good job if it fooled the station attendant. "Someone gave George the ration cards and coupon books to sell. But George stole a few for his own use."

"And got himself killed for it?"

"Could be. I mean, that's lost money, right? I hardly think he paid for those phonies fair and square." I arched my eyebrow. "Go on, chew that lip some more. It's gonna bleed you keep it up."

"It helps me think." But she stopped. "I'm having a hard time seeing where

137

the Bund and the sabotage come into it."

So was I. Even Sam Spade didn't deal with things this complicated, which made me think maybe it was a bunch of separate things that just happened to involve George.

"Detective MacKinnon has a point, though," Dot continued when I didn't answer. "Anne's fired, George is dead, and the sabotage has stopped. That can't be a coincidence."

"Assuming it's over and the culprit just isn't waiting and making us think we're safe."

Dot nibbled her lip again.

The morning passed in peace and quiet, as quiet as it got on the line, that is. I was working in a different building today, on the body assembly, riveting the exterior panels to the frame. It required some attention to detail, but was repetitive enough that I could let my mind wander a little bit. It had been more than a week since the last act of sabotage. Everybody seemed to think it was behind us. Everybody 'cept me.

After lunch, I returned to my place and took up my rivet gun. Then I smelled what I swore was smoke. Thick and sharp, like burning chemicals. Work had barely started again when a girl ran in, face streaked with black soot, hacking for all she was worth.

I dropped my rivet gun. "What's wrong?"

"Fire," she gasped. "Paint...fire...awful."

I sprinted out into the yard. Dot was working paint that afternoon. I skidded to a stop on the pavement. The paint operation was separate from where the fuselages were assembled and the big assembly lines were the final pieces were put on. It stood off in a corner of the Bell property, far enough away that the completed plane bodies had plenty of space to be put on their dollies and rolled onto the main floor. Red-orange flames leapt out of the building. Thick waves of dark gray smoke rose from the roof and the windows, covering the yard with its suffocating smell and robbing us of fresh air. This was serious. Without painted airplane parts, we couldn't do anything else.

More important, Dot might be in there.

Mr. Satterwaite stood beside me, peepers glazed, face slack. He was obviously in no mind to do anything useful.

Florence had followed us. "Holy moly." She froze and stared at the roaring scene.

I shook her. "Go call the fire department. Now. Go!" I gave her a little push and she staggered off. Then I faced the building. Where was Dot? Hopefully not inside. I couldn't help her if she was.

Girls streamed out of the building, clutching each other, doubled over with coughing. I grabbed one. "Dot Kilbride, where is she?"

The girl only shook her head, hacking too hard to answer.

"Helen!" I shouted over to her. "We gotta keep that fire from spreading 'til the firemen arrive. Grab some sand buckets and see if that hose on the side of the office stretches far enough. I gotta look for Dot."

Helen nodded and organized a few of the calmer girls into a bucket brigade. About twenty-five yards of asphalt separated paint from the final assembly lines. We couldn't save the paint building, but we needed to make sure the fire didn't spread. A few more girls had come out, all with scorched clothes and blackened faces. I stopped one. "Is anyone left inside?"

She shook her head. "I think we're all out," she said, voice creaky.

A quick visual search told me Dot wasn't in the group. "You seen Dot Kilbride?"

"No." She coughed. "Maybe she left by the back door." She staggered away.

I knew the door she was talkin' about. It led to the garbage bins. Dot wouldn't have gone that way, she'd have followed the rest of the girls. Wouldn't she? Or maybe that had been the nearest exit and she'd taken it. I raced to the back of the building. No Dot.

Damn. Where was she? I fought against the clenching of my heart. Some stupid saboteur was not gonna rob me of my best friend and future maid of honor. I ran around the building, squeezing between the wall and the fence. No girls. Flames and smoke poured out of the bottom floor windows, which had burst from the heat.

My vision was closing in. 'Cause of the smoke or the panic? I couldn't tell and I didn't want to spend time figuring it out. Just as I decided I was gonna have to fight through the flames and search the interior of the paint building, I spotted another knot of girls through the heavy smoke. They were stumbling, waving their hands feebly against the suffocating air. I sprinted over. "You seen Dot Kilbride?"

A girl pointed to a knot of bodies gathered well away from the inferno. "I think she's...over there."

I ran as though my life were riding on my speed. Sure enough, Dot was in the middle of the group, clutching her arm, tears on her face.

"Dot! Are you okay?" I pushed others aside in my haste to reach my friend.

Her sleeve was pushed back, the skin on her arm red and shiny. "I was tryin' to put out some of the fire and my arm got burnt. Not too bad, I think, but it hurts like the dickens."

I was no medic, but the skin was intact and not blackened. She needed some attention, but she'd prob'ly be okay. I turned to Catherine, who stood nearby, shirt filthy with soot, face sweaty and red. "Take her to the infirmary, will ya? I gotta help the bucket brigade until the firemen get here."

"Sure thing. C'mon, Dot." Catherine wrapped her arm around Dot's shoulders and led her away.

It seemed like forever that we carted buckets of sand and water. Helen and Rose manned the hose until the fire trucks turned up. Catherine returned from taking Dot to the nurse and joined the bucket line. Eventually, we couldn't see the flames any longer. The firemen came out of the building. One of 'em reported to the fire chief and they both went over to Mr. Satterwaite. I tagged along, staying far enough behind they wouldn't pay me any mind.

"The fire is out," the chief said.

"Is the building completely lost?" Mr. Satterwaite asked, mopping his shiny forehead. He was as out of breath as any of the bucket brigade girls, but he hadn't done much that I'd seen. I wanted to be generous and assume he'd been managing the response, but his breath smelled of whiskey and I had my doubts.

"The equipment is pretty much destroyed. It'll need to be repaired or, more likely, replaced. Of course any paint burnt up. The fire inspector will have more information once he concludes his investigation." The chief tilted back is helmet. "In the meantime, what can you tell me?"

Mr. Satterwaite's mouth opened, but nothing came out. Of course not.

I stepped forward. "I'm Betty Ahern, sir. I wasn't in the paint building, but I was working on fuselage assembly, over there, when we were told about the fire. " I spilled everything I knew and pointed him toward a couple girls who'd been working in the paint area who were able to share a little more. No one knew exactly when the fire had started. The first hint they had was the scent of burning paint. By the time they found the source, one whole corner of the area was ablaze and the smoke was thick enough to walk on. Most of 'em panicked and ran out. A few, including Dot, tried to beat back the flames. A couple more little fires popped up, joined together and before long the entire building was consumed.

No one knew how the fires had started. No one had been smoking, nothing hot or with a flame had been dropped on paint or thinner or nothing. It was like sprites had popped into existence and set the building to burning.

Which was completely and totally impossible.

The fire chief dismissed us and stepped away to talk to the inspector who had just arrived.

Mr. Satterwaite shook his head. "This is a disaster. Spread the word, Miss Ahern. You can all go home once the authorities are finished with you. Don't bother coming to work tomorrow. I'll have to call management and see how we proceed. We'll have to hire a temporary paint crew and I imagine nothing will get done until we get that up and running, and we replace any parts that were destroyed. We can't build if we can't paint." He shuffled to the main office, presumably to make his phone calls.

I stared at the ruins of the paint building. It was hard to believe someone hated little Bell Airplane so much, more than GM or the Steel, neither of which had faced this problem. But I couldn't ignore the blackened evidence before my eyes.

***

I passed on Mr. Satterwaite's news as we milled around, waiting to be interviewed. Dot hadn't returned from the infirmary. I sat on the floor in the hall outside the cafeteria, waiting for my turn while Florence, Helen, Rose, Alice, and Catherine jabbered around me. Whoever did this hurt Dot. Well, maybe didn't target her especially, but she was injured anyway. It had been bad enough when they'd fingered Anne as being responsible. Now whoever the real saboteur was had made it personal. I hadn't been this mad since...actually, I didn't think I'd ever been this angry, period.

"Anne must have snuck back on the grounds somehow," Catherine said.

"How?" Florence snapped. "Not like there are dozens of entryways to this joint. Every one of 'em has a gate and all the gates are guarded."

"I don't know how she did it," Catherine said, tossing her dark hair.

Alice drummed her fingers against the wall. "She coulda climbed the fence."

Florence's reply was sharp enough to cut metal. "Right, because the Anne we knew was the type to scale a fence." She eyed Rose. "You gonna tell 'em?"

"Tell us what?" Alice asked.

When Rose didn't speak, Florence did. "Rose's uncle. In Italy. He's a fascist. One of Mussolini's stooges."

The girls gasped and Rose shot to her feet. "So what? I told you, we ain't talked to him in years. And what about you?" She wheeled to Helen. "That cousin of yours in Berlin. You said you stopped being pen pals years ago, but what if you lied? How do we know you haven't been all cozy and he's not a Nazi, getting you to do his dirty work."

Helen's face reddened. "You shut your mouth."

They squawked at each other like Polish grandmas arguing at the Market, until Florence turned to me. "Betty, what about you? You must have some ideas."

"Yeah, I think you should all shut your traps because it's obvious none of us knows what's going on."

"Who died and made you queen?" Catherine asked.

I slammed my hand down on the floor and the slap echoed through the hall. Several other girls nearby turned to stare. "Least it wasn't the same person who made you stupid. It had to be someone who was working paint, or at least working here at Bell. That wasn't Anne Linden. And if all we're gonna do is hurl accusations at each other, we might as well walk off the line now for all the good it'll do."

Catherine balled her hands. "Are you calling me stupid?"

"Yeah, I am."

She glared. "You're just sore because precious little Dottie got herself hurt."

I jumped up and pulled back my fist.

The others came between us. Alice tugged Catherine away while Helen held me back and Florence grabbed my arm.

"I don't know what happened," I said. I relaxed and stepped away from the group. "I don't know who the hell is responsible for all this. But I do know one thing. I'm pretty damn sure it isn't Anne Linden."

Florence looked from the others to me. "As far as I'm concerned everybody who worked paint today is a suspect," she said. Then she faced me. "And just 'cause no one saw Anne doesn't mean she didn't sneak in."

Catherine's face was deep red. Mine probably was, too. Helen was pale as new milk and Rose's expression scornful. If it wasn't for the others, Catherine and I would certainly fight and I was pretty sure who'd come out on top of that. She might know how to scratch and slap, but Sean had taught me the value of a solid right hook.

"Elizabeth Ahern?" Suit One called from across the room.

I tugged my shirt and walked over to him. "That's me."

"This way." He led me to an office, the same muckety-muck's office where Detective MacKinnon had interviewed me last month.

"I understand you were the one who organized the bucket brigade until the fire department arrived. Thank you. It was very brave and took some fast thinking." He pointed at a chair.

I sat. "I had to do something."

"Of course." He took a seat behind the desk. "My name is Scott Devaney. I'm the senior vice president for safety here at Bell."

"Things haven't been too safe lately."

Mr. Devaney didn't look ruffled. "Your friend, Miss Kilbride, said you had a temper."

"You talked to Dot?"

"Yes, down in the infirmary. She's fine. The nurse said she could leave, but she refused to go until you'd been interviewed. I was going to talk to you last, but I think she should get home and rest."

He'd tried to be kind to Anne, too. I softened a bit.

"What was the argument about?"

"The others were talking about who mighta set fire to the paint building. Catherine, she's the dark-haired one, said it musta been Anne Linden. She said somehow Anne found a way to sneak back into the plant."

"You disagreed."

"Heck yeah." I stood my ground. "I wasn't all that sure Anne was guilty when you and the other guy took her outta here when she was fired. But I'm sure now. Then..." How much did I want to say? These were my friends. I didn't want them to be hung out to dry 'cause they might have family on the wrong side of the war. But I couldn't stay silent either. "The other girls' families got dragged into it. See, Rose has an uncle in Italy and Helen has a cousin in Berlin."

"Who might be working for the Axis and enlisted the aid of their relatives stateside."

"Exactly." I didn't want to believe it, but I'd be a fool if I didn't admit the possibility.

Mr. Devaney made some notes. "Tell me what happened."

There wasn't much to tell, honestly. But I recounted it all, from the first news to the last bucket of sand. "I didn't see Anne at all, not all morning. I go out for a smoke right after lunch. It's not real sunny, but it's bright enough that I'd see a girl crossing the field to climb a fence."

"What if she came over near the back of the plant?"

He was good. "I can see the paint area pretty clear from where I was smoking. There are only two doors in to that building and I could see both of 'em."

Mr. Devaney permitted himself a small smile. "If it wasn't Miss Linden, who do you think it was?"

I sat up straight. "I don't know, but my first suspicion would be anyone who worked paint. That stuff would go up fast. Had to be someone who was right there."

"Or someone who could slip in and out very quickly."

"I'd think it would be someone with a grudge against Bell, too."

"Or who wanted to harm the war effort."

"I can't think who fits that description. Not even the girls with foreign relatives. Most of us, we need these jobs and the money. Me, I got a brother overseas. My guy's over there, too."

"Except, as you so accurately pointed out, it had to be someone with access to the Bell facilities. That means one of these girls is guilty, despite what you think. Yes?"

Blast.

Mr. Devaney finished writing what had to be notes based on our conversation. "That's all, Miss Ahern. Thank you."

I stood. "How long are we gonna be down?"

"Hard to say. There's a lot of clean up to do. Then we have to get the paint operation running. After all—"

"Yeah, I know. We can't build planes if we don't have all the parts."

Chapter 23

While Dot and I waited outside the Bell gates for the bus to take us back to Buffalo, I stared down the road. What was I gonna tell my folks? The first two incidents had been minor. The fire was serious. They'd want me to quit work for sure. Well, Mom would, prob'ly. With the plant closed, even temporarily, what could I do?

Next to me, Dot cradled her arm. "Whatcha thinkin'? And don't tell me nothing 'cause I know that's not true."

"Tryin' to sort stuff out. How's the burn?"

"It's okay." She pushed up her sleeve to show the bandage. "They slopped some stuff on it. The nurse said it wasn't too bad all things considering."

"That's good."

"I heard you all argued pretty bad."

"It's nonsense. Stuff people say when they're scared and grasping at straws." Least that's what I hoped. I stuffed my hands deep into my pockets. It was downright warm outside in the sunshine. I didn't even need the coat and I'd considered going without it this morning. My fingers brushed the stiff edge of a crumpled wad of paper, too thick to be a receipt. I pulled it out and smoothed the wrinkles, expecting it to be a bit of trash.

It was the note I'd taken from the coat room a week or so back, the one with the funny script. The text stared at me, M, H, O, P, A, E and the number three. Something that looked like an O with a line through it and a backwards R. I'd seen the symbols before, but where?

Dot tugged her sleeve down. "What's that?"

"Something I found when I searched the lockers. Do these symbols look familiar to you?" I held out the sheet.

She bit her lip. "Yeah, I've seen script like that before." She paused then snapped her fingers. "The Broadway Market."

A light bulb might as well have appeared over our heads. "That Ukrainian vendor. He's got a sign, half this and half in English."

"Think he can tell us what it says?"

"One way to find out." The bus pulled up and we got on, paid our fare, and grabbed the first available seats.

Even on a Wednesday afternoon, the Market was busy. We threaded our way between grandmas in headscarves and moms with babies, a babble of accents all around us. The Ukrainian stall was on the far outside wall. The letters on the sign were a dead match for the paper in my pocket. I pulled it out and started to compare, trying to pair the strange letters to their English counterparts and work out the words.

The Ukrainian finished with his customer and came over to us. "Can I help you ladies?" His voice was thick with an accent I'd have associated with a Russian.

I suspected he'd have an issue with my lumping him in with the Russkies, though. "Yes, but not with your food."

"Speak for yourself," Dot said, her mouth practically watering at the selection of goodies. She pointed at a bun with sugar and nuts on it. "Can I get one of those?"

"Certainly." He grabbed a bag and a sheet of waxed paper. He grinned at me as he put the treat in the bag. "Are you sure I can't tempt you with something?"

"Can you tell me what this says?" I handed over the note. "It looks like the letters on your sign."

He wiped his hands on a towel at his waist, then took the paper. After a moment he said, "Yes. Is Cyrillic, the alphabet of my country."

"What about others, like the Russians?"

"*Da*, them too."

"If you translate it, I'll buy a bun."

He grinned. "Is a list of dates." He turned the sheet and pointed.

"November six and November seven. Here, list of mechanical parts. Chain, engine."

I nudged Dot, who was sniffing the contents of her bag, eyes closed. "The dates and places of the first two sabotage attempts." I looked at the vendor. "What else?"

"Down here, more parts maybe? Paint, riveting, electric, welding. At bottom, a sentence. Next shipment, mid-December. Find out number of finished planes." He handed back the note. "Is all there is. But this, this is serious, *da*? You work at this place? The writer, he not a very nice person I am thinking."

"Yeah, I do. No, he's not nice. But nothing you need to worry about, trust me." I wanted to jump up and down. The paper could only be the saboteur's. Her plans? Was that mid-December shipment the goal or a deadline? Possibly. I would even say prob'ly. "This is it, Dot. The Bell saboteur is definitely one of us."

Dot licked sugar from her fingers. "Do you know whose coat you took it from?"

I deflated a bit. "No."

"Why is it written in Russian? None of us are Russian, you know."

Deflation was replaced by a twinge of irritation. "What other languages use Cyrillic letters?"

The baker thought, tongue between his lips. "Russian, yes. Also many Slavic languages, like Bulgarian or Serbian."

Bulgaria or Serbia. How close were those countries to Italy or Germany? Why couldn't I remember a map? "Is it easy to learn Cyrillic?"

He spread his hands. "I would not know. I have never taught it."

Dot sighed and put the remaining half of her bun back in the bag. "It's a good way to hide a secret message. Write it in a lingo few people are likely to know. You'd only have to know the letters, not be from one of those places."

She had a point. The note-writer didn't have to be Russian or whatever. She, I was sure it was a she, only had to know Cyrillic. "Somehow we gotta figure out who at Bell knows this script. And we gotta figure out who killed

George Linden."

"Why? That wasn't part of your deal with Anne."

"Dot, I told you what I heard at the Bund headquarters. It sounded like they were threatening Anne. I can't let her get hurt. You don't have to come along." I turned to the vendor, who was hovering near us. "Can I borrow your pencil?" He handed it to me while keeping his attention on a new customer. I scribbled his translation on the back of the paper.

"Don't be silly. 'Course I'll help you." Dot stowed the bag with her remaining sweet in her pocket. "I just wanna make sure you know why you're doing all this."

"I know why." I handed the pencil back. "Thanks for the help."

He took it. "My pleasure. But aren't you forgetting something?"

I blinked.

He removed another sweet bun and put it in a bag, then handed it to me, his other hand outstretched. "Your roll. Five cents, please."

***

Dot continued to offer comments and questions clearly designed to bring me back to earth, but I remained optimistic all the way back to the First Ward. The note was the property of the Bell saboteur, at least to my mind. Now it was just a case of tricking someone into revealing her knowledge. Despite Dot's pessimism, I was confident I could figure out how to do that. Then I'd figure how the Bund fit into everything, assuming they fit at all. They were starting to feel like one of those red herrings from the pulps. Pesky enough to stick around, but not truly involved.

We got off the bus and started walking down Louisiana Street toward Mackinaw and home. Suddenly, Dot froze in place and stared open-mouthed down the street.

"What is it? You look like FDR just showed up in the First Ward."

She pointed at a male figure about half a block away. "Not FDR, but almost as surprising. Is that Freddie Linden?"

I looked in the direction of her finger. Sure enough, Freddie was meandering up the sidewalk, looking back and forth at the houses like he was following a tennis match or something. "Sure looks like him."

"What in the world is he doin' here?"

"We'd have to ask." I picked up my pace and called out. "Freddie, that you?"

He looked up and smiled, then hurried toward us. We met halfway between Miami Street and Mackinaw. "Thank heavens. I've been wandering around looking for you for almost an hour. I guess you're just getting home from work."

He'd come all the way from Kaisertown to find me? "Uh, yeah."

"Actually, we're coming from the Broadway Market," said Dot. "There was a fire—" She broke off as I stepped on her foot. "Ow, sorry."

"There was a fire? Where?" Freddie looked at her, then back to me.

"Nothing, it's not important." Freddie might not be involved with things at Bell, but that didn't mean we had to fill him in on the details. "Why're you looking for me?"

"It's rather embarrassing, actually." He tilted his face down, but looked up at me with what he must've thought was a boyish, whimsical glance. "I think Anne brought you a box of items from George's possessions, yes?"

Did he mean the box of phony C-cards? I didn't know what Freddie's angle was, but his whole look put me on edge. "What kind of items?"

He shot a furtive look over my shoulder, then another behind him like he wanted to make sure we were alone. Then he edged away from Dot and motioned me to follow. "It would have been, ah, some things that might appear to indicate George was up to something shady."

Definitely the fake cards. Instinct told me to play dumb. "I don't know what you mean."

He gave me a knowing look. "I see how it is. Well, if Anne *had* brought you something like that, what would you have done?"

"I'd have told her to turn them in to the police. Anything else would be criminal."

His expression was crestfallen. "Do you think Anne would bring you any other things she found? Not saying she has, but would she?"

This conversation was as irritating as the gnats that swarmed over the beach sand on a summer day. "Freddie, spit it out. What do you want?"

A flicker of annoyance crossed his features, lessening the similarity to Gary Cooper. "George had some goods in his possession before he died. He told me they were a business opportunity. I don't think he had time to take care of them, but they seem to have disappeared. Since Anne trusts you so much, I was hoping that if she found these things and brought them to you, you could give me information."

Did he really think I'd advise Anne to keep the loot? No way. But his words removed any doubts I had. George had been involved in a lot more than phony C-cards. I needed to talk to Anne. "Freddie, I don't quite follow. But I can tell you this. If Anne had brought me anything that looked like black market goods, I'd have told her to take it to the cops. Immediately. Do not pass Go. I'm sure you've noticed, but there's a war goin' on and fake ration coupons and the like are illegal."

His gave a dismissive snort, the know-it-all look definitely not like Gary Cooper. "Don't be silly. Counterfeit items, like ration books, only hurt the government."

"How do you figure?"

"Easy. Ordinary people need coffee, sugar, and all the other things. Fake coupons get them what they want, what they need. Sure the money doesn't go to the government, but who cares? The feds can get plenty of cash for the war. Nice people like Uncle Helmut and Aunt Louisa benefit, too."

"And the racketeers make a buck, right?"

"Of course. That's the way capitalism works." He glanced at Dot, who was standing a few paces away, just out of earshot, patiently waiting. "Then you can't help me?"

"Sorry, pal."

"Shame. Please give my best to your friend." He pushed past me and strode up Louisiana, headed for the bus stop.

Dot wandered over. "What's his deal?"

"I don't know." I watched Freddie's retreating figure. "But something tells me I oughta find out."

151

Chapter 24

The sweet roll made convincing Mary Kate to cover for me while I ran out after dinner pretty easy. After making sure I had enough for bus fare, I slipped out the back door. I thought briefly about negotiating with Jimmy for the use of his bike, the one he had for delivering papers. But although the evening weather was on the warm side, it could all go bad in an instant. I didn't relish the idea of riding, or worse, pushing, a bike through rain or wet snow. The bus it was. I decided to go alone. Arguing with Lee or Dot would delay me, and might cause me to miss the Bund.

Cat was sitting at the corner of the house, washing his paws. He stopped and fixed me with the kind of accusatory stare only a feline could.

"Yeah, I'm going out. And I'm going alone. What of it?"

Meow.

"I know I oughta take someone. But Dot and Lee will argue with me. They don't get it. If the Bund killed George and they think Anne knows something she shouldn't, she's in big trouble. I gotta find these guys and get to the bottom of it."

Meow.

I wrapped my scarf around my neck and threw the ends over my shoulders. "You're impossible." Here I was, talking to a cat. This job was driving me nuts. Cat watched me as I stepped around him. Then he disappeared behind the trash cans, flicking his tail as if to say, "Don't say I didn't warn you."

I caught the bus as it was about to pull away and worked out my plan while I rode to Kaisertown. I was playing a long shot and I knew it. But not only didn't I have another location for the Bund, it was the only place beside the park where I'd seen them. The sun was sinking over the lake, sky a rosy-purple streaked with clouds. No scent of snow. When it came, it was gonna clobber the city. Hopefully that old saying, "Red sky at night, sailor's delight" was true and I'd get home without a hitch.

When I got to South Ogden, the garage looked abandoned. While I loitered across the street, I looked for something I could slip in my pocket and use to defend myself, if it came to that. Not for the first time, I thought I'd made a mistake by not asking Lee to come with me. I needed to work on not being so impulsive. But he'd already almost been caught once. He wouldn't be keen on coming back. I had to know how deep George's involvement in the Bund was, and what their motive was for murder. If any.

I went inside a store on the way to the garage from the bus stop and bought a Coke. I tried to ask a few innocent questions about whether Weasel, Heavy, and Scarface had been around, but the counter clerk didn't know anything. I paid for my Coke and resigned myself to waiting.

The sun was almost completely down and my Coke bottle nearly empty when the trio appeared. I gripped the bottle by the neck. If things got rough, a hunk of broken glass in my hand was better than nothing. I double-timed it across the street. "Hey, you. Yeah, you three. I gotta talk to you."

The three of them stopped and turned. "Who the hell are you?" Scarface asked, voice kinda rough.

"You tell me your name and I'll tell you mine."

Scarface and Heavy glowered, but Weasel pushed forward. "Why should we?"

"I wanna talk to you about George Linden."

Weasel eyed me, and exchanged looks with the others. "C'mon in." He turned and opened the door.

I hesitated. "Why don't we talk right here, huh?" Being in the parking lot with the three of them wasn't perfect, but it was a heck of a lot better to be out in the open than shut in the garage. I clutched my empty bottle, feeling a little like I was Daniel in the lion's den. Hopefully God watched over fools, like they said.

Weasel shrugged and faced me. "That's Marcus Hoffman," he said, waving at the one I knew as Scarface. "And that's William Dunkel." He waved at Heavy. Detective MacKinnon had shown me pictures, but it was nice to get the names straight from the source. Marcus's beak-like nose had clearly been broken at least once and up close he was a little broader in the shoulder than William.

"Who're you, aside from being the one in charge?" I hoped the bravado in my voice distracted them from my knees, which wavered against my fight to keep them from knocking together.

"What makes you think I'm in charge?"

"You're the one yapping aren't ya?"

He chuckled, but it didn't sound like humor. "Patrick Flanagan. Friends call me Pat."

"An Irishman in the Bund?"

He spread his hands. "Anyone who's willing to take on the damned Brits is okay with me." A sly grin appeared on his face. "What can we do for you, sweetheart? With all the boys off to fight, are you looking for a friend?"

Marcus and William sniggered.

"Hardly." I tightened my grip on the neck of the bottle and took a step backward. Easier to break the glass and wield it as a weapon if they decided to rush me. "I told ya. I wanna talk about a guy named George Linden."

The sniggers faded, but Patrick kept his grin. "Sorry to say George is dead."

"Yeah, I'm aware. But you know him, or at least you did. He part of your little gang?"

Marcus cracked his knuckles.

Patrick waved him off. "Wouldn't you like to know?"

"I already do, to be honest."

"Then why're you asking?"

I shrugged. "I wanna hear it from you."

Patrick tilted his head, studying me. Not in a creepy way, more calculating. "He was, yeah. Linden had a good face. Clean, blond, pretty, the perfect poster boy for the Germans. Turns out, we was wrong about him."

154

"You know how he died, right?"

"Said in the paper he was stabbed."

"Way I figure it, he had to know his attacker. You gotta be close to a guy to stab him. He's gotta trust you. Did George Linden trust you?"

The three didn't move, but there was more knuckle-cracking, this time from both members of the goon squad.

"They found counterfeit ration cards and coupon books at his home. You know anything about that?"

Pat's stare was stone steady. "Why should we talk to you?"

"I happen to know the cops are interested in your little group. Talk to me now, and maybe I can convince them to look elsewhere."

He hesitated. "We don't get involved in stuff like that. Too much risk. We want to draw attention to the cause, but not that kind."

"What about sabotage? George's sister, Anne, used to work at Bell Aircraft. There's been a few incidents up there over the past weeks. Word is Anne got fired 'cause they thought her brother was pressuring her." I was hoping to provoke them into saying something incriminating. It didn't appear to be working. Maybe 'cause I was wrong and there was nothing to say? I edged back another step, ready to make my getaway. I was faster than Marcus and William. Prob'ly.

Patrick, however, didn't flinch. "If we ain't stupid enough to get into fake ration cards 'cause we want to stay outta the way of the law, we sure as hell ain't gonna piss off the army with sabotage." He took a step toward me. "It occurs to me that maybe you ain't so smart. You come down here all by your pretty little self?"

I held my ground, even though my nerves screamed at me to run away. "Hardly. I left a friend where you can't see him. I also told people where I was. I turn up missing and you meatheads are the first ones the cops'll come after."

Patrick stopped and licked his lips.

I had to admit his denials had the ring of truth. Both counterfeiting and sabotage were prob'ly too complicated for these fat-heads. "You said you were wrong about George. How so?"

Patrick spit. "He got himself some dirty friends. Friends that true Aryans don't need to have."

"What kind of friends?"

"Filthy little Jew boy." Patrick spit again. "We told George it was us or him. Linden chose the Jew. Something about a business opportunity that could set him up right."

George had a Jewish friend? That's right, Anne had mentioned it briefly when she hired me. "You get a name for this friend?"

"We don't talk to Jews," William said, voice surprisingly light for a guy his size.

"As you might expect, George and us parted company shortly after he made his decision." Pat's gaze was icy cold. "Now, we done you a favor by talking. I suggest you scram before we change our minds and decide to not be so friendly."

I almost said something, but for once in my life I thought twice about it. I looked between Marcus and William. I knew that look. Lee would definitely tell me to beat feet, and this time he'd be right.

***

The Linden house on Casimer was blocks away, but I hurried through the growing gloom, running over the bus schedule in my head. I had about thirty minutes before the next bus back home. I could make it, but barely.

Anne answered the door with her hair covered with a kerchief, wearing work pants and what was prob'ly one of her dad's old shirts. She had a smudge of dust on her nose. "Betty! I didn't expect to see you." She gripped the door. "Is something wrong?"

"I have a question. Can you talk?" I asked.

She paused, then came outside. "For a minute, yes. I'm trying to clean up after the latest police visit. They found—"

"I know. Detective MacKinnon came to see me."

"Why you?"

"I was the last person to see your brother and I found his body. He wanted to ask me about the C-cards since I was the one who told you to take them to him." Up close, I could see faint purple smudges under her eyes and tiny lines around her mouth that hadn't been there last time I saw her. "You okay?"

"I'm tired. Mama and Papa, well, they've been unable to function since George was killed, especially Mama. It might be a good thing I'm not working. It's up to me to do everything, including planning the funeral."

I tried to imagine planning Sean's funeral. I couldn't. My admiration for Anne and her personal strength went up a notch. "When's that gonna be?"

"The police released his body yesterday. We're skipping a viewing. The service will be Thursday, two o'clock at St. Casimir's. I would very much like you to be there. Dot, too."

Dot would prob'ly try and make an excuse, but I'd figure out how to convince her. "We'll be there. I heard the cops found more counterfeit ration books."

"Yes," Anne said, voice glum. Definitely flat and not like her usual. "You said you had a question."

"I just talked to a guy." Something told me Anne would be horrified if I said I'd been talking to members of the Bund, so I skipped that part. "You said George had a friend who was Jewish. Tell me about him."

Anne twisted a cloth in her hands. "There was a boy, maybe George's age or a little older. He came to the house one night."

"What did he look like?"

"As tall as George, but heavier. Not fat, just more muscular. He had dark hair and dark eyes. A very pleasant face. He had nice manners. His teeth were very white." The memory brought a smile to her face.

"Did you get his name?"

"No...wait. Yes. Joseph. But no last name."

"He go by Joe?"

"No, Joseph. That's how George introduced him to me. They were going out. We only said hello. And he mentioned how he'd always liked the name Anne." Her cheeks colored. "He said it was a pretty name, like me."

He'd flirted with her and by the look on her face, she hadn't minded. Joseph wasn't necessarily a Jewish name, but it was definitely possible. "He wasn't wearing a yarmulke or anything?"

"I only saw him for a minute." Anne had been looking off into the distance, remembering, but her focus came back to me. "They were in the hallway and I was going upstairs. His hair was dark and he was wearing a fedora. He could have been wearing one under his hat and I didn't notice."

Rats. "Okay, well, do me a favor. If this Joseph comes back, try and get a last name. If you do, come see me or call." I dug a piece of paper and a pencil stub out of my pocket, and wrote my address.

Anne took the paper. "Is it important?"

"I think so. I promise we'll be at the funeral. I might bring a friend of mine, too. You know, besides Dot. Tell your parents I said hello." I hustled down the walk and heard the door close behind me.

Anne might not know Joseph's last name and I might not be able to find him. But if he was friends with George, and maybe a business partner, if what Patrick told me was true, he'd be at George's funeral. Least that was the way it happened in the movies. I was gonna go. And I wouldn't even have to make up an excuse to talk to him.

***

My timing was perfect. Mom was out at the rectory when I got home, so I had time to feed Cat. I sat on the back step and lit a cigarette, thinking about what I'd learned that day. After he ate, he came over to rub against my legs. I scratched behind his velvety ears. "I dunno, Cat. This is getting complicated, you know?"

He meowed in agreement.

"Exactly. First it was just the sabotage. Now we also got murder, counterfeit ration cards, guys who'd like to bring a Nazi fan group back from near dead, and a German with a Jewish friend. It's too much."

He meowed again and butted his head against my hand, purring.

"What a first case."

Mom appeared from around the corner. "Who are you talking to?"

I looked, but Cat had already scampered out of sight. Smart animal. "Just myself. How'd it go at the church?" I crushed out my gasper and hoped Mom hadn't heard what I was talking about.

Either she hadn't or something else drove it out of her head, because she

158

didn't ask. "I saw Mrs. McClusky there. Did you know her son, Billy, has been discharged and sent home?"

"Why?"

"It turns out he was asthmatic. He couldn't keep up with the marching, poor boy. He's quite unhappy."

"I would imagine so."

"I thought maybe you'd go visit him."

I stared at her. "Why?"

"Well, I thought you might like a partner at all those dances you go to. I know you're friends with Liam Tillotson, but he probably doesn't dance much with his limp. Billy was always a good-looking young man." She went into the house.

I followed. "And a bully. Don't you remember the way he used to beat kids up if they didn't give him their lunch?"

Mom sniffed. "I think those stories were exaggerated, Betty."

"No, they weren't. I saw him. He might be a looker, but Billy McClusky is a horrible person. I wouldn't dance with him if he was the last boy in Buffalo. Besides, have you forgotten something?" I wiggled my left hand at her.

"Tom is an ocean away."

"So? You like him, don't you? What does distance got to do with it?"

"I do like Tom. And if he were here instead of in the army, it would be different. But..."

"But what?"

She stopped at the kitchen sink and faced me. "You have to admit it's a dangerous place for him. What if he doesn't come home?"

I opened my mouth to retort, but then saw the gleam in her eye. She was really concerned. "If Tom doesn't come home, then you can talk to me about other boys. But not Billy McClusky."

Mom huffed and her eyes filled with tears. "Elizabeth!" She stormed out of the kitchen.

I followed her to the front room, where she was attacking a hole in one of the boys' socks with pure vengeance. Tears glistened on her cheeks.

I knelt before her. "Mom, stop. Talk to me. I don't understand. I love Tom. I'm doin' my part for the war and helping the family. Why is that so hard for you to accept?"

She said nothing for a moment, but at least she put down her mending. Then she looked up. She was crying for real now. The sight took my breath away. "I'm worried about you, Betty," she said, wiping her cheeks.

"Worried about what?"

"I know you love Tom. I do, too. The war news…I worry every day about Sean, and Tom, and all those other young men."

I patted her knee. "I know. So do I."

"And then you go to work in a factory, like a man. The women at church, the older women, I see the way they look at you. I hear the whispering. Young ladies don't do that kind of thing. Then I saw the story about the fire and how it was set on purpose."

I hadn't seen that yet. Of course I hadn't been let into the paint building with the cops and the firemen around. I made a note to read the paper, but now I tried to focus on Mom. "Young ladies of their generation. It's all different now. Who else is gonna work the factories, make the things we need for this war? The young men are all over there. Pop and his friends can't do it all, you know that."

"What if you get hurt? What if Tom gets killed and you can't find another man? I want you to be a wife and a mother and be happy, Betty. It breaks my heart, thinking you could miss that."

My anger dribbled away. I brushed aside Mom's tears. For the first time ever, I thought she looked old and tired. I'd been focused on how I felt and completely ignored her. "Mom, listen, please. I'm sorry if I caused you any problems and I know you're doin' the best you can. But please understand. Tom's the guy. He's always been the one. I promise, if…if something happens to him, I'll let you play matchmaker. With anyone you like, but not Billy McClusky."

She laughed weakly.

"As for work, yeah, things are kinda grim at Bell right now. But they're gonna figure it out and it'll be swell. Promise. I'm not in any danger. Well, no more danger than anyone else who works in a factory. I can't sit at home and do mending. I'll go nuts. We all got our way of coping. This is yours." I patted the socks on her knee. "Working is mine. Sean and Tom are doin' their part. Let me do mine."

She reached out and cupped my cheek. "You're so strong, Betty. I envy you." She smiled, a bit watery, but the first real smile she'd given me in a while. "Any boy I want, huh?"

I hugged her. "Remember. 'Cept Billy McClusky."

Chapter 25

Thursday morning was weird, not having to report to work. I was determined to fill my day making progress on at least one, if not both, of my cases. Problem was, I didn't quite know what to do. Since the weather was still on the mild side, I sat on the front step, a scrap of paper and the stub of a pencil in my hands, an unlit cigarette in my mouth. I wrote out everything I knew plus all the things I needed to find out, a "to do" list of sorts. Cat must've known it was safe, 'cause he came out to helpfully rub against my legs.

Dot came by after breakfast. "Whatcha up to?"

I spoke around the cigarette. "Writing down everything I know so far and the things I need to do next, or at least figure out."

"Like what?"

I filled her in on everything I'd learned from visiting the Bund headquarters in Kaisertown, plus knowledge of the new man on the scene in George's murder, the mysterious Joseph.

"You went back to that garage on your own? You crazy?"

I waved off her concern. "It had to be done. I couldn't let them threaten Anne."

"Are they really doing that?"

"Dunno." I twirled the cigarette in my fingers, reviewing my list.

"Is that the kitty you've been taking care of?" Dot asked. She held out her fingers for Cat to sniff.

"Yep, this is Cat."

"Not a very good name." Dot wrinkled her nose. "What's on your list?"

I stuck the smoke behind my ear, since I couldn't hold pencil, paper, and gasper at the same time. "I have to figure out who's behind this sabotage. I wish I could get into the paint building and poke around."

"That's not gonna happen."

No, but Dot had worked there. "The fire started after lunch. You see anything suspicious?"

She bit her lip. "I don't think so. The morning was pretty standard. Catherine even commented that it was kinda boring. We broke for lunch at noon like always. We got back after lunch and had barely started up when someone smelled smoke, and all you-know-what broke loose."

It wasn't a lot of info. "Everyone came back at the same time?"

"Yeah. Least no one was so late that I noticed it."

Then not like the engine fire. But all that thinner and paint would go up like dry wood. The saboteur didn't need much time. "Who all was there?"

"Well, me and Catherine. I think Helen was there in the morning, maybe Rose, bunch of other girls. I could write down their names, I guess."

I handed her the pencil stub and paper. "I'd appreciate it."

She wrote, not looking at me. "I don't see how this is gonna help."

"If I can't get into the scene, I'm gonna have to talk to folks. 'Course I'll have to find 'em. That could be more complicated. If I can rule out Anne or the Bund, I can move on to other suspects for George's murder, as well as finish my job for Anne."

Lee came limping up the street, a lit cigarette trailing smoke behind him. "Now here's a pair of gloomy Guses. What's eating you two?"

I told him about the paint fire and the temporary closing.

To his credit, the horrified look on his face had only been matched by my brothers and sister. "Did they say how long?"

"No," I said, unable to keep the bitterness out of my voice. "They've gotta clean and get the paint back up so we can finish the orders."

Lee's response did not become a good Catholic boy. His vocabulary was more colorful than what I'd picked up from Pop and Sean. "What do we do now?"

"We?"

"Yeah. Dot and I are in this with you. Right, Dot?" He looked at her.

She tossed her head. "Of course I am."

"Okay." He rubbed his hands together. "Then all you gotta do is decide what problem you tackle first."

He was right. "The sabotage, I think. The way I see it, the threat to George coulda come from the Bund, maybe as a result of these problems, or those fake ration cards he had, or this mysterious Joseph. Seeing as the paid job is clearing Anne, let's put a name to the Bell saboteur. But to do that, I need to get back into the plant and that's impossible."

"Maybe you don't." He flicked away his cigarette. "You've been looking into this for a while, haven't you?"

I nodded, playing with Cat's tail.

"Okay, then you've already inspected the scene. They'd clean it up even if Bell was open and there'd be nothing more to see. You've asked questions of the others."

Dot was looking at him, her face creased with an odd expression. "What interests me is the rod in the assembly chain. We know someone coulda left the cigarette that caused the engine fire at almost any time. But the rod, that's trickier. It would take more time than dropping a lit smoke."

Lee tilted his head, face serious. Cat walked over and batted Lee's leg with a paw. He responded to the unspoken command by picking the animal up and rubbing its head. "It had to happen when no one was around. Lunch break. Would she need the whole hour?"

Funny how Cat always got what he wanted. "Dunno," I said. "If someone was missing for the whole hour it woulda been noticed, so I'd say no. When I inspected the area, there were scratches, like the chain had been pulled out and reset. But I don't know how long that would take."

He set Cat down. "I got an idea. Give me a few minutes and meet me at my house."

Dot glanced at me. "Don't you have to work today?" she asked Lee.

"Nah, day off."

"This what you want to be doing?"

He shot her a look I couldn't figure out. "Don't have nothing else to do."

He hurried off.

I turned to Dot and crossed my arms. "What was that about?"

"What?" She crouched down to tickle Cat under the chin.

"Questioning Lee. It's like you don't want him around."

"That's not it at all." She focused on Cat. "I just find it funny he'd give up his one day off to help you play detective."

"He's a friend." I took in her doubtful look. "He's trying to be helpful, is all. We should go."

We found Lee behind his house, an old bike propped in front of him as he fussed with the chain. Cat had followed us and went over to inspect Lee's activity.

"What's all this?" I asked.

"You said you thought the chain had been pulled out and reset. Well, I figured a bike chain is as close as we're gonna get to something similar." He obliged Cat with a scratch under his chin. "I figure we can run some tests. Each of us take a turn removing the chain, wait a minute, then put it back. We go as fast as we can. The time for the real saboteur is prob'ly some average of our three times. I'm making the assumption that maintenance keeps everything in pretty good shape, so I haven't figured on rust or nothing slowing things down."

"Makes sense to me." Good old Lee. I wouldn't have thought of his idea. "We're assuming the saboteur is a Bell employee. 'Cept we don't know why any of them would want to cause problems at Bell. I've never heard any of them criticize the war effort." Plus there was the note I'd found, written in Cyrillic. I still hadn't figured out if anyone at Bell knew that alphabet.

Lee stood. "You're assuming the war is the motive. What if it's something else? Maybe one of them has a grudge against the company."

I also straightened, as did Dot. "What kind of grudge?"

"That, Miss Detective, is what you have to find out." He dusted off his hands. "Dot, you go first. I'll time you." He looked at his watch. "Go."

Dot worked as fast as she could, pulling the bike chain off the big front gear. As soon as she did, she said, "How long do you want me to wait before putting it back on?"

165

I thought. "Thirty seconds."

She nodded and held off until Lee gave her the go-ahead. Dot finished and looked at Lee. "How'd I do?"

"Swell, Dot," I said. "How long, Lee?"

"Couple seconds over two minutes. We each should do this a few times, get a sense of slowest and fastest time."

We did it six times, each of us taking a turn. The slowest time was about three and a half minutes; the fastest was a couple seconds more than two. The sun rose in a cloudless sky while we worked and we shucked off our coats. Beads of sweat lined Dot's forehead. "This is great and all, but does it tell us anything?"

"Yes." I clambered to my feet. "We know that if it was one of the girls, she had to get it done in the time between when the lunch whistle blew and when everybody got to the cafeteria."

"What if it was someone from outside?" she asked.

"That person still wouldn't have a lot of time," I said. "He wouldn't be able to get into the assembly area until we were all gone and he'd have to be out well before we got back."

"Three minutes." Lee struggled to his feet. "I would think that's well within possibility for both types of candidate, an inside or an outside job." He brushed dirt from the knees of his trousers.

"Thanks for the help. Oh, are you doing anything this afternoon?"

A strange look crossed his face. "I told you I wasn't, why?"

"George Linden's funeral is today. Anne asked me to be there and it's possible this Joseph will be, too. I thought it would be good if all three of us went."

He glanced at Dot. "I s'pose I could. My suit's clean. No good movies playing."

"I thought you liked Bob Hope." Dot said. "His new one, Road to Morocco, is supposed to be funny."

"It's no fun to see a comedy alone."

Dot shot a look at me.

All this looking. What was up? "Swell. Then we'll meet you at the bus stop at noon?"

He nodded, wheeled the bike to the side of the house, then went inside.

Dot and I left, and walked down Mackinaw. "I guess I'd better find a nice dress," I said.

"Betty, do you think you're being fair to Lee?"

I pulled up. "What d'ya mean?"

She kept walking. "Isn't it obvious? He adores you. Didn't you catch that expression on his face?"

"He does not. He knows me and Tom are a done deal. You're imagining things."

She shrugged. "Didn't you hear him about the movie? How it's no good going alone? Right after I mentioned the Hope flick?"

She couldn't be serious. Lee?

"And you're taking him out."

"It's a funeral, Dot. Not a date."

"But it's somewhere with you. Look." She took my hands. "I'm only sayin' be careful, Betty. I know you wouldn't hurt him for the world, and I know you're devoted to Tom. I don't think I could bear it if the three of you wound up not talkin' to each other." She let go of me and walked off to her house.

Chapter 26

At home, I made a baloney sandwich for lunch, then I changed. Mom appeared in my doorway with a basket full of laundry. "Where do you think you're going?"

I buttoned up the only funeral-looking garment I had, a deep navy shirtwaist dress. I'd have to wear my stockings again. "I told you, I have a funeral to go to. For the brother of that girl at Bell, Anne Linden. Can I borrow your cameo?"

"Yes." Mom put the clean clothes on my bed. "What about dinner?"

"I might miss it." I brushed my hair and pinned it in place, then went to work on my makeup. I didn't have to look all dolled up, it was a funeral after all, but I ought to look presentable.

"Are you going to this thing by yourself?" The disapproving set of Mom's mouth told what she thought of that.

"No." I blotted my lipstick. "Dot is going and so is Lee. We won't be too late, either." I grabbed my purse and kissed her cheek. "See you later." I bolted for the door. After our talk last night, I understood her thinking. I also thought we'd come to an understanding. I wasn't going to a dance hall by myself. It was a funeral and I was gonna be with my two best friends. At a Catholic church. How much trouble could I get into at a Mass?

I met Lee and Dot at the corner of Louisiana and Miami Streets. Dot was dressed similar to me in a navy knee-length dress, but with a Peter Pan collar and a fuller skirt. Lee wore a black suit, white shirt and black tie, with a shiny black pair of wingtips. He offered each of us an elbow. "Ladies. I must say, I'm a lucky guy with the two of you on my arms."

"Flirt," I said. I caught Dot's eye and frowned. I was gonna have to have a talk with Lee. He was definitely sweet-talking us. But was it directed at me? A small, niggling idea took root in my mind.

We got to St. Casimir's well before the funeral started. I pushed my friends to take a seat in the back pew. I wanted to be able to see everyone and watch the whole Mass. Most of the crowd were strangers. I saw Helen with her parents and waved in greeting. She, Dot, and I were the only Bell employees there. Most of the guests were older, likely friends of Mr. and Mrs. Linden. I saw them up front with Anne. She and her mother were dressed in black with black veils. Mr. Linden wore a black suit and white shirt, like Lee's.

A couple of minutes before two, a young man walked in. He was also wearing a black suit, but he had something none of the other men did. A small, round black cap on the back of his head. If the overhead lights hadn't been on, I might not have noticed the cap against his dark brown hair. I nudged Dot, who sucked in her breath.

Anne came forward and embraced the young man, and led him up to the pew behind where the family was sitting. Yep, that had to be Joseph. There weren't any other guys around George's age present. He was prob'ly the one who caused George's split with the Bund. After all, how many Jewish friends could George have had?

The great thing about the Mass was that I didn't have to pay much attention. 'Cept for the homily and a few other things, it was exactly the same as Sunday, which meant my body knew precisely what to do. That freed me up to watch Joseph. He sat a in the pew behind the Lindens and took his cues from the people around him. As we sang the final hymn, the pall bearers, all of 'em older men, carried out the coffin and the Lindens followed. As soon as the singing was over, I shoved my hymnal in the holder.

"Where are you going?" Dot asked.

"To talk to Joseph." I hurried toward the young man, who was idly flipping pages in his hymnal. As I got close, I could see Anne had been right. He was good looking. I couldn't see the white teeth, but his dark eyes matched his hair and his skin was brown from working outdoors. Under the suit I could tell he was well-built, good shoulders. His hands were long-fingered and prob'ly strong. When he smiled, he'd be a looker. No wonder Anne had gotten all goofy when she talked about him.

I stood at the end of the pew, blocking one exit. A heavyset older woman sat at the other end, so he wasn't going nowhere. "'Scuse me. Joseph?"

He looked up. "Yes?" Before I could continue, he hefted the book. "An interesting selection of music. And your readings. I didn't know Catholics read from the Torah."

"We don't."

He smiled, showing a dimpled cheek. Definitely a cutie. "The first reading. Deuteronomy."

"Oh that. It's the Old Testament, that's all."

"To my people, it's part of the Torah." He replaced the books. "I suspect you didn't come over to talk theology."

"You were friends with George, weren't you? Anne mentioned."

"Joseph Weinstein." He held out a hand. "Yes. George and I were friends. Hopefully we were going to be more."

Dot and Lee had pushed their way through the crowd and entered the pew behind Joseph.

"I'm beginning to feel like you're ganging up on me. You know my name, but I don't know yours."

"Betty Ahern." I pointed. "This is Dot Kilbride and Lee Tillotson. Dot and I used to work with Anne, and Lee's a friend of ours." I noticed neither Dot nor Lee offered to shake hands.

"It's a pleasure meeting you." Joseph nodded at them. "I hope you're not intending to cause trouble. Surely you wouldn't do that in a place of worship. This isn't a synagogue, but I'd be most uncomfortable if a fight broke out."

"No, no fights." I glanced at my friends, who seemed perfectly happy to let me do the talking. "You know George's death wasn't natural and it wasn't an accident either, right?"

"I heard. The police came to speak to me this morning in fact." Joseph ran his fingers along the edge of the pew. "The detective said George's friendship with me might be why he was killed."

Around us, the church had emptied. Only a few people remained in quiet conversation. "We'd like to ask you a couple questions. Well, at least I would. Do you mind if we went somewhere more comfortable?"

He shrugged. "There's a diner down the street where we could get coffee. Is that acceptable?"

I agreed and we left, the three of us genuflecting and crossing ourselves before we walked out while Joseph looked on. He appeared intrigued by our actions, but not amused. Maybe he'd never seen Catholics at church before.

The coffee shop was on Clinton, less than a five-minute walk from St. Casimir's. The sun hung low in the sky and clouds had rolled in, and there was a definite chill to the air. I was glad I'd brought along a coat.

We ordered and crammed into a booth in the back. Joseph stirred sugar into his cup and set down his spoon. "What did you want to ask me?"

"Where'd you meet George Linden?" I blew on my coffee to cool it.

"He and some friends were passing out flyers on the street corner," Joseph said. "They gave me one before they noticed my yarmulke."

"Then you knew George was in the Bund," Dot said.

"I did. I tried to reason with them, explain why Hitler's Reich mustn't be allowed to succeed." Joseph sipped. "The others were not very open to hearing me. But George was different. We met again, just the two of us, a few days later."

"How'd you win him over?" Lee asked. "From what we heard, he was pretty committed to the Bund, at least at first."

"I told him stories," Joseph said, fixing Lee with a steady gaze. "Have you heard any stories from Germany, Mr. Tillotson? The ghettos?"

"A few," Lee said, returning the stare. "Some of the guys I work with, they got family over there who know Jews. Some have tried to help Jewish neighbors get out. A few succeeded. Others didn't."

"Then you know." Joseph paused, dropping his gaze to his cup. Then he looked up. "George didn't. It took a few meetings, but I gradually made him see that while keeping the German people downtrodden was not good, lifting them up at the expense of the Jews wasn't either. My people are not responsible for the problems of Germany. Yet we have been forced into ghettos, our possessions confiscated."

"That worked?" I asked.

"As I said, it took some time, but yes, eventually. George was not the most gracious of people." Joseph gave a faint smile. "He could be abrasive and rude. But that was, I think, mostly a defense against those who had picked on him as a child. Being different is hard when all you want to do is fit in. I understood."

I bet he did. "Did you know George was leaving the Bund? Was your friendship the reason?"

Dot spoke up. "And what did you mean you were going to be more than friends? You're not...you know."

Joseph laughed. "No, I'm not a homosexual. It's nothing like that. We were going to go into business. Through his father, George knew something of the butcher's trade. I knew about making food kosher and I have contacts who can help us with the koshering process. We were going to open a small grocery and delicatessen, catering to German Jews. You know, immigrants who had left Germany and missed the foods, but who needed kosher meats that are sometimes difficult to find in neighborhood markets." He looked at me. "The answer is yes, Miss Ahern. I knew he was leaving the Bund. I also knew it frightened him a little. His fellow members were not the most understanding people."

I'd met Patrick, Marcus, and William. They prob'ly weren't the only other members of the group, but if they were an example then I could well imagine the rest weren't too keen on George's leaving, either.

"What about profiteering?" Lee asked. He'd been quiet, taking it all in. "Did you know George was involved with that, too?"

Joseph frowned. "What do you mean?"

"Counterfeit C-cards and ration coupon books," Lee said. "That wasn't part of your business plan, was it?"

"No." Joseph drained his cup and set it down. "But now that you told me, something I didn't understand makes sense."

I glanced at Lee and Dot. "What?"

"One of my concerns about starting our business was money. You need capital to get started, to rent or buy a storefront, and buy goods. George assured me I didn't need to spend any time thinking of it. He had a plan and the money angle was covered."

"George was into the black market to earn the money you needed to start the business." I finished my drink and pushed the cup away. I hadn't seen all of the ration books, but I could easily believe George would make plenty of dough. More than enough to give him and Joseph a good start.

"You didn't know anything?" Dot asked, her tone betraying her lack of belief.

"I thought he was getting the money from his father or another relative. The Linden family isn't wealthy, but they aren't poor, either." Joseph spread his hands. "You don't know me and you have no reason to believe me. Had I known George was involved with the black market, I would have advised him to get out of that as well. I knew he wanted to make money, and we both were eager to start our business, but I wouldn't have approved of doing it that way."

"How bad did he want the cash?" I asked.

"Quite a bit. I gathered his father used to be moderately prosperous back in Germany. George had heard stories and, well, he wanted to help out his parents, I suppose. At least he always talked about how even simple things were so expensive and how his father used to be able to afford so much more. The prospect of owning a successful business was very appealing to him and he was impatient to get started. That's probably why he jumped at a quick way to get the money by dealing in black market goods."

From his expression, Lee had doubts. "Why're you telling us all this?"

"Because George was a friend. A flawed man, but a friend." Joseph laid some coins on the table, then checked his watch. "I must be going. It has been a true pleasure meeting all of you. I hope you are successful in your investigation, Miss Ahern." He slid out of the booth.

"What investigation would that be?" I asked, playing dumb.

Joseph was too smart to be fooled. "The investigation into George's murder. I'm not stupid. Why else would you be asking these questions?"

"Well, in that case, what if I have more questions? How can I find you?"

He took a pen from his pocket and wrote a phone number on a napkin.

"Call me if I can help. Have a good evening." He nodded in farewell and left the shop.

Lee waited until the bells over the door had stopped jingling. "Do you believe him?" He put some more money on the table, enough for all three of our coffees then stood.

"I want to. I think he's a nice guy." I stood back to let Dot out and followed my friends out into the evening.

"He is nice," Dot said. "I get the feeling you've got more to say, though."

"Sam Spade wouldn't believe a story just 'cause a guy in a nice suit told him one." I saw the bus pull up and I hurried to catch it.

I heard Dot puffing behind me. "Why didn't anyone tell me how much running was involved in this gig?"

***

Lee walked me to my door. I stood on the front step, watching as he escorted Dot to her house. He'd been in a funny mood since we left the diner where we'd talked to Joseph. Awkward, like he wanted to say something, but was afraid to. I tilted my head and peered through the falling light. He took off his cap, twisting it in his hands. Dot gave him a quick hug, then went inside. Lee hesitated a moment, took a couple steps backward, then jammed his cap on his head and shuffled off to his house.

That little niggling idea doubled in size.

I didn't need to check the clock to know I'd missed dinner. But someone, prob'ly Mary Kate, had put a plate in the oven to keep a portion warm for me. I heard the radio from the living room. Pop was listening to the news. Normally I'd've said hi, but I had other plans. I figured Mom had already left for her weekly Bible study group. I ate quick, scraped my plate clean, then snuck to my bedroom to change into work clothes. Then I grabbed my coat, tiptoed to the back door, and slipped outside. My thoughts ran left and right. Lee, Dot, the Bell sabotage, and George Linden's death. I needed fresh air.

I lit a cigarette. Why couldn't my first real case be uncomplicated? At least not all mixed up with life stuff. Something was up with Lee and Dot, and I was pretty sure I had nothing to do with it.

To take my mind off my friends, I forced myself to think about the case. Patrick Flanagan, the Irishman in the Bund. I knew the Irish in Europe were neutral 'cause they hated the Brits, but Patrick was an American. He'd acted like they'd thrown George out of the Bund because of Joseph, but what if that wasn't the case? What if George had wanted out and the rest weren't so keen to let him go?

I was willing to bet Patrick didn't live in Kaisertown. I wasn't sure he was a First Ward boy, but with the last name of Flanagan it wasn't a stretch. It was six o'clock. I was alone, but I'd confronted the Bund on their turf and nothing had happened. I knew enough folks in the neighborhood that I felt pretty safe walking around to see if Patrick was at any of the local hangouts.

After an hour, I'd visited four places, all of them nearly deserted, and my dogs were barking. If I stayed out much later, Mom would bust me for sure. But I couldn't quit yet. I stopped in a shop for a bag of chips and a Coke. "Say, maybe you can help me," I said to the soda jerk before he walked off. "I'm looking for a guy."

"You're gonna have to be more specific, sweetheart, even with so many boys off to war."

"His name is Patrick Flanagan. Weaselly looking guy. Dark hair, thin, sharp nose. Runs with some fat-heads from Kaisertown who're trying to bring back the Bund."

The soda jerk half-laughed. "Those idiots. I read about them. Any Irishman who thinks he's gonna get a better deal with the Jerries than the Brits will deserve it when old Adolf turns on him, too."

"Amen to that. Can you help me or not?"

He tapped his fingers on the counter. "I don't know his name, but I saw a guy matching that description down at O'Reilly's a few nights ago. Drank by himself. Got all snarly when we asked him to move down so's we could throw some darts."

I sipped at the Coke. "You think he's there now?"

"Might be. You aren't thinkin' of going over there, are ya?"

I shrugged. "Is it dangerous?"

"It ain't dangerous so much as it's not a place for nice single girls, if you catch my drift."

"Who says I'm a nice single girl?"

He shook his head. "If you're set on this, I'd go now. It's kinda early, so you'll prob'ly be okay. After nine o'clock it'd be a diff'rent story."

I thanked him and flipped him a coin. Then I grabbed my Coke and headed out. I'd been visiting bars for the last hour and nothing had happened. How bad could O'Reilly's be?

Pretty bad. O'Reilly's was a dirty hole in the wall place on Louisiana Street. The windows hadn't seen a cleaning in months. When I went inside, I was sure the floor hadn't either. The weak lights left deep shadows along the wall, and I hesitated inside the door. Maybe this wasn't such a good idea. I could still hightail it out, no one had seen me. But then I might miss the chance to find Patrick. I swallowed and pushed aside my second thoughts. *Buck up, Betty.* This wouldn't take long and surely some of the fellas in here would stick up for a girl on her own, wouldn't they?

A few old geezers sat eating off greasy paper at the tables. A bartender chatted with a customer at the bar, too heavyset to be Patrick, but maybe they knew him. "'Scuse me," I said.

"Hey there doll," the man said. He smelled like beer and stale sweat, and his face was pockmarked. He grinned at me with a mouth full of yellow, crooked teeth.

"I'm looking for someone," I said.

"Yeah? Well, you mighta found him."

I stepped away, ready to bolt for the door. "Thin guy, name of Patrick Flanagan."

The bartender eyed his customer, who was not Patrick. He better not try and tell me it was.

Fatty leered at me. "Any guy who'd leave a pretty thing like you ain't worth looking for." He gripped my wrist.

Fortunately, Sean had taught me a few tricks. I lashed out with a foot, catching him right above the ankle. While he howled, I smashed his arm against the edge of the bar, right where my brother had taught me. As I expected, his numb fingers let go of me and I pushed him away. "I'm not the girl for you, pal." I turned to the bartender. "Do you know Patrick Flanagan? Or should I move on?"

He stared at me, then jerked his head toward a solitary figure in a booth near the back of the bar.

"Thank you." I walked over and knocked on the frame of the booth. "Fancy meeting you here."

Patrick looked up from his beer. "I could say the same. You didn't strike me as the kind of dame who hung out in a place like this. Then again, I saw you just now. You handle yourself pretty well."

I slid into the booth, hoping my face didn't give away the butterflies in my stomach. "Thanks, but you're right on the first try. I was looking for you so I had to lower my standards."

He gave a mirthless chuckle and took a gulp from his drink. "Why do you need to see me?"

"George Linden."

"What about him?"

"Last time we talked, you made it sound like it was no big deal, him walking away from the Bund."

Patrick's shoulders twitched. "More where he came from."

"'Cept he's dead. He walked away from you, and next thing you know he's lying like a gutted fish in a Kaisertown alley."

Patrick didn't answer.

"Know what I think? You had big dreams for this little club of yours. Then your perfect Aryan, George, turns up with a Jewish friend. Next thing you know, he's leaving you in the dust. Made you mad, didn't it?"

Patrick growled.

"You said you weren't in on the counterfeiting or the sabotage."

"Yeah."

"That doesn't mean you weren't angry. Maybe you tried to convince George to stay. You got together, you had words, next thing you know you're sticking a switchblade in him."

Patrick was breathing hard through his nose. It made a wheezing sound.

I knew I was pushing my luck, but I channeled Philip Marlowe. "How did it feel, getting thrown over for a new friend? I didn't think Irish boys hated Jews as much as the Nazis do, but I bet it couldn't have felt good. You had this whole plan for glory and George Linden left you high and dry. Am I right?"

He slammed his hand down. "Shut your filthy mouth."

"Not so casual now, are you?"

"You bitch." His breath was really wheezing now. His one hand gripped the heavy glass, the other clenched in a tight fist. "Linden was an idiot. I tried to make him see. He started saying how maybe we were wrong, maybe the Nazis were wrong, the Bund was misguided. It might not be a bad thing for the Allies to run all over Germany like the Germans had done to those pigs in France."

I stood and took a step back. Sean had taught me that space was your friend if you thought you were gonna get in a fight. "You tried to convince him to stay?"

Patrick took a couple deep breaths to calm himself down. "Even threatening him with Marcus and William didn't make a difference. He walked."

"When was this?"

"Last Friday. He came to the garage, said he was done. I told him he was making the mistake of his life. He didn't listen." Patrick took a drink and wiped his mouth with his hand. "Guess I was right."

"What makes you say that?"

"Not four hours later he turned up in that alley. I say the traitorous little bastard got exactly what he deserved."

I studied him. He was awful satisfied with himself. Because George was dead or because he ordered the hit? I wasn't sure. "What do you want with Anne Linden?"

He smirked. "Who said I wanted anything with her?"

"Little birdie told me you were gonna pay her a visit. See if she knew anything from her brother that could get you in trouble." Like information that could get Patrick and his goons sent down for murder?

He played with his glass. "I haven't made up my mind. Why? You got a problem with me talkin' to her?"

"Anne doesn't know anything. You stay away from her."

"Or what?" He challenged me with his stare.

"You'll deal with me." Not a great response, but all I had. I turned away and exited O'Reilly's with as much dignity and swagger as I could.

Chapter 27

Friday morning and nowhere to go. They were prob'ly still cleaning up at Bell. The day dawned brisk, but with a clear blue sky and soft lake breeze that promised another mild day.

Absolutely unnatural.

With the younger kids in school, Mom spending her morning with the Ladies of Charity at church, and Pop at work, I had the house to myself. I made my bed, had breakfast, and washed the dishes. Then I went outside to sit on the back step. Cat came to greet me and I rubbed his ears. My mind was a fog and I wasn't sure what to do. Not for the first time, it struck me that since the cops hadn't arrested Anne, the job I'd been hired to do was over. Then again, she'd asked me to find who was responsible and I hadn't done that. I also needed Bell Aircraft back in business, as did most of the other girls. In addition to the cops, Bell must have hired investigators. They'd be slow, though. They needed stuff like warrants and had to follow rules. I didn't.

George's death, that wasn't my thing. Lee and Dot would be horrified that I'd walked into a place like O'Reilly's on my own. Anne had told me to lay off. I'd talked big last night to Patrick Flanagan as a bluff, but that was all it was. If he decided to hunt down Anne, there was nothing I could do about it.

Cat meowed and nuzzled my fingers. There was nothing more to be done about the sabotage. As far as I was concerned, it was an inside job, but I was at a dead end until I could get back to Bell. I was convinced, based on little more than my own gut instinct, that George Linden's murder was a separate incident and I had two real options: the Bund or the black market. I decided to focus on the ration cards.

Risky, using profiteering to fund his business idea. 'Specially since he had to have worked for or with someone. A press, the ink, and paper would've been hard for a guy like George to come by. He'd gotten the goods from somewhere, prob'ly to sell and return the cash to his supplier in exchange for a part of the profit. That person coulda demanded to be cut in on the butcher shop, maybe threatening to expose George's cash source if he was left out. 'Course he would've had to do it in a way to keep his own nose clean so he could keep running his illegal business. Who would that be and where would I find him? If he did demand to be dealt in, and George had refused, was that motive enough for murder?

I stood and Cat meowed in protest. "Sorry." I went inside to fetch a coat. I'd visit the cops. Detective MacKinnon worked out of a building on Main Street. He would be able to give me information on potential black market sites. I'd given him the scoop the night of the murder. It was time for me to see if MacKinnon was willing to share some info in return.

At the precinct, I gave my name to the sergeant at the front desk and told him I needed to speak to the detective. He picked up a telephone receiver and spoke. Less than five minutes later, MacKinnon came out. "Miss Ahern," he said. "Is there something wrong? Or do you want to add something to your statement?"

"Neither." I looked around. "You got a good place we can talk for a minute?"

"We can go upstairs to my office."

"I'd rather not. I'm not sure anybody here knows my folks, but last thing I need right now is my mom finding out I was here."

He didn't say anything, but led me outside and around the corner into a small alley next to the building. It had warmed up and the corner was out of the wind. "This more what you had in mind?"

Over the lake, gulls cawed, a lonely sound. "Yeah, thanks." To cover my shaking hands, I dug my deck of Lucky Strikes out of my pocket and tapped one out. MacKinnon took out his lighter and his own cigarettes. He lit mine first. "Thanks," I said. "I got a question for you. All that fake ration stuff you took from the Linden house. You find out where it came from?" I asked.

"No." He blew out some smoke. "It's not my department, but since I can't rule out a connection with the murder, I've been working through our known black market contacts trying to trace it. So far, nothing. Why, do you have information for me?"

"I dunno. You said George was using one of the C-cards for himself."

"Correct."

"How likely is it that was part of his pay? For selling the rest."

MacKinnon thought. "I wouldn't think it likely at all. If George had been caught with a fake gas ration card, it would draw attention to the operation and perhaps expose the rest of the counterfeiting."

What had Anne told me about her family's baking? Her mother must have been saving her sugar ration coupons. "What about the ration books? Could he have been paid with those?"

"Possibly, but still unlikely. It would be easier to claim you'd traded or saved coupons for food items. But still a risk if someone noticed the coupons were fake." His eyes narrowed. "Why do you ask?"

"I think I told you Anne said they saved their sugar coupons. What if George gave his mother a black market coupons without her knowing it? She thought she was saving them 'cause she'd have a few extra, but really he was slipping them into the family supply."

"Would he do that?"

"I didn't know him well, but if he didn't think he was getting paid enough for his work, maybe. Or he coulda been trying to give his family a little extra. Maybe his mom said something about how she missed not being able to bake a favorite dessert or he was tryin' to make family life more comfortable."

MacKinnon ashed his gasper. "It's a possibility. If he stole the ration books, that would cut into the profit for the person he was selling them for. War profiteers would view that as theft."

"Would they kill him for it?"

"They might issue a warning first, and I'm not talking about the kind of warning a beat cop gives out. The warning from a profiteer leaves more bruises and broken bones. But if they'd already done that and he continued to steal, or if the theft was serious enough, they might."

I took a last draw from my smoke. "Or they intended to warn George and things got outta hand."

"Also possible." He dropped his and ground it out with his foot. "Why are you asking me?"

I rubbed out mine on the side of the building. "I'm thinking is all. Where does the most black market activity happen?"

"The profiteers move around. We've made several arrests down on the Buffalo River near South Michigan Avenue. That's one of the more popular places because—" His peepers widened a bit, then narrowed again. "You're not thinking of going down there, are you?"

"Me? Detective, what an idea." My innocent tone rarely worked with Pop, but Detective MacKinnon didn't know me as well. Maybe he'd buy it.

"Miss Ahern." He stepped closer, not threatening exactly, but definitely making a point. "I know you fancy yourself a private eye and that's fine as far as it goes. But a young woman has no business going into an area where there is known profiteering activity. Especially by herself."

"Don't you worry, Detective. I wouldn't dream of it." Going by myself, that is.

***

I left the police precinct and strolled down Main Street. I stopped here and there to look into the department store windows, but my brain didn't register what I was looking at. I was too busy thinking.

Investigating any black market activity down by the river would have to done in the dark. In fact, I might have to wait on that for a different night. Lee was at work and I had to convince him to go with me. He wasn't likely to be excited about the idea, so it could take a while to swing him to my side. Dot was outta the question. Not only would she flat out refuse, she wouldn't be very helpful if things got out of hand. I'd have to have a good story to tell Mom and Pop for that one, since I was sure to be out late. No, this excursion would take some planning.

A girl across the street waved at me. "Betty, over here." It was Alice.

I checked for traffic, then jogged across to meet her. "You killing time downtown too, huh?"

She gave a rueful grin. "Well, I gotta do something with my free time. It's a little depressing, though. Even with me working I can't afford half this stuff and God only knows when the next paycheck's gonna come. If it ever does."

"It'll come. They'll get things back up and running."

"Do you know something or are you just being confident?"

"It's mostly confidence. But look." I slung my arm around her shoulder. "The army wants those P-39s. So do our allies. They'll get things cleaned up, get the paint shop back working, and we'll be on the line in no time."

"I hope so." She hitched up her purse. "Say, there's an ice cream place up there. You got time to have a milkshake?"

I checked my watch. It was eleven o'clock. "Are you buying?"

"I got enough cabbage for that."

"Then I got time."

Ten minutes later, we were sitting in a corner booth, milkshakes in front of us. Hers chocolate, mine strawberry. "Thanks," I said. "You didn't go to George Linden's funeral."

"Helen saw the announcement at St. Casimir's. We talked about going, but in the end it felt weird. Not like we were good friends."

"Dot and I went, and we weren't close to her."

Alice sucked on her straw. "I know he was her only brother and we felt bad that Anne got the hook, especially now that it's likely it wasn't her after all. We didn't think she'd be happy to see us. Then again, if she'd bothered to get to know us, maybe we would have stuck up for her and she wouldn't have gotten fired in the first place."

"She was shy."

Alice was silent. I could tell she was working up to ask me something, and I had a pretty good guess what, but I wasn't gonna offer information. Eventually, she spoke. "Helen told me Anne hired you to find the person behind the sabotage. That true?"

"Yep."

"Have you learned anything?"

I hesitated. Technically, Alice was in my pool of suspects. But she was the least sneaky person I knew. Even less than Dot. If I zipped my lip to everyone, I might cut myself off from some useful dirt. "Sort of. Logically, the person would have had to be working those areas, or at least working at Bell, all three days. On the same shift as the incidents."

"Makes sense. Could she have let the person in?"

"She'd still be involved. We're a pretty tight-knit group. Don't you think someone would've noticed a stranger? I think it was an inside job."

Alice made a "hmm" sound, which I took for agreement.

Lee's words, that maybe it wasn't about the war, came back to me. "Tell me, have you ever heard anyone complain about Bell? I mean something so bad they'd try and take the company down?"

"Nope. I mean, girls gripe about Mr. Satterwaite all the time, of course. But the whole company? Sometimes someone'll say how she wishes we didn't have to work all the time, but that's just being tired."

To my mind, Mr. Satterwaite deserved all the complaints. If the problems had centered around him, like wrecking his office or something, I'd have dozens of suspects. "What about anyone talking down about the American war effort?"

Her forehead creased. "What do you mean?"

"I dunno." I cast about for an example. "Maybe someone who lost a relative in the war and she's bitter. Or someone who doesn't think the U.S. should even be at war in the first place. Stuff like that."

She swirled her straw in the melted remains of the ice cream. "Most of us are happy to be doing our part. I mean, we don't all have brothers or boyfriends overseas like you do, but even if we don't we want to help our boys."

I stabbed what was left of my milkshake with my straw.

"The only person I ever hear crabbing is Catherine. That isn't about the U.S. though. She don't like that the Soviets buy P-39s, and the Americans don't seem to have any problem selling 'em to the Red Army."

I'd heard a few of Catherine's rants, so I knew exactly what Alice was talking about. "She sure does get worked up. I don't know why. She isn't even Russian."

Alice blinked. "Didn't you know?"

"Know what?"

"Her grandmother came over just before the Bolsheviks overthrew their old czar. I think they called themselves White Russians, the folks who supported the czar against the Reds."

"But Ramsey isn't a Russian name."

"You know how lots of immigrants changed their names before they got to Ellis Island? I guess they did it so they didn't stick out so much and they've gone with Anglicized versions of Russian names ever since. That's why she's Catherine to us, but that's not what's on her birth certificate or what she's called at home."

It hadn't happened with a lot of Irish immigrants, but Pop talked about a few Polish guys at Bethlehem whose grandfathers had changed their names to better fit in the new country. "What's her name?"

"Kateryna. Kateryna Ivanova Razumovsky." Alice finished her shake and checked the wall clock. "I'd better go. Thanks for spending time with me, Betty. I'll keep hoping you're right and the next time we see each other it'll be at work." She gathered her coat and purse, and left.

I sat in the booth, poking the melted ice cream with my straw. Catherine was Russian. Heaven knew she made a lot of anti-Soviet comments. Was that the same as being anti-Russian? I suspected not. I hadn't paid enough attention in history class to remember much about the Russian revolution. The czar had been killed, along with his whole family. The nobility didn't come out too good, but then they rarely did. Was Alice telling me Catherine's family was Russian nobility?

I laughed. Catherine was the type of person where if that was the case, she'd have made sure we all knew it. Not that it would have changed her social standing. She was still a working-class girl, same as the rest of us. But she'd have wanted us to know her family had money, or at least it used to.

The note I'd found, the one in Cyrillic. Had that been Catherine's coat? I didn't remember if I'd ever seen her wearing it. Did her grandma teach her Cyrillic?

Noon. I'd go down to the river and check out the scene. Then I would go see Dot and find out if she knew anything about Catherine's Russian family. Catherine. Bright, bubbly, fun-loving, slightly sarcastic, and a bit temperamental. Could she be a saboteur? On the surface, I wouldn't say she had the personality. Still, the Russian angle was interesting.

Chapter 28

The Buffalo River wasn't big as far as rivers went. Deep enough for barge traffic to the mills, but not very long or wide. It started up near Buffalo Creek on the other side of the city, then meandered it's way south of Kaisertown, through the First Ward, and eventually linked up with Lake Erie, wrapping around a little spit of land that was home to the grain elevators and other industrial buildings. The river was spanned by two bridges in the First Ward, one at Ohio Street, not too far from my house, and the other at South Michigan.

I traced the route of the river in my mind. If I wanted to conduct some shady business, like black market ration cards, where would I go? Not to the bridge area at Ohio. Too much traffic, too many buildings. I might be spotted. There were businesses and a park along the water. In the dead of night would it be deserted enough? There were bus stops. People working the night shift at the grain elevators or other businesses would be taking Ohio. Not enough in the way of privacy.

Detective MacKinnon had mentioned the area near South Michigan. On the far side of the bridge was the General Mills plant, which filled the air with the scent of Cheerioats, the cereal they'd started making last year. There would be people around. But what about the other side, 'specially underneath the bridge piling?

I hopped on the bus and rode it to the stop on South Park closest to South Michigan. I was lucky that the temperature had stayed mild. Walking down by the water with a brisk wind in the wintertime would freeze your nose off in a New York minute. In the middle of the day, there were a fair amount of people and trucks, including half a dozen or so in the parking lot at the cereal plant. On either side of the bridge, there were parking lots littered with dry leaves, cigarette butts, and other trash. I poked around, but didn't see anything out of place.

I crept down the bank toward the water, eyes peeled. There, near the bridge pilings. Tire tracks, heavy by the impression depth. A scrape of black paint on the concrete. The ground had thawed and I could see boot treads in the mud, a heavy sole like a workman's shoe and several different patterns. Men, by the size of them. A truck, at least one, and more than two people. What had they been doing hanging out down here? I looked around, the breeze blowing my hair across my face. I held it aside. At night it'd be dark. Some light from over at General Mills and the streetlights, but not a bad location if you wanted to engage in some funny business.

A man dressed in coveralls and wearing a wool hat leaned over the concrete railing separating the street from the adjacent lots. "Hey, what are you doin' down there?"

I squinted and looked up. The guy was Pop's age, the clothes worn and stained. He wore a tattered blue coat and held a dented lunch pail in his hand. "I'm just lookin' around."

"Well, get up here 'fore you fall in the river. It's November, missy. That water ain't warm and I don't fancy taking a swim to save you."

I clambered back up the embankment and over the railing. "Thanks, but I know how to swim. You work around here?"

He had a plug of tobacco in his mouth and he spat to the side. "Over at General Mills for the last ten years. Long enough to know you don't go climbin' down near the water."

"Always in the day?"

"I alternate between days and overnights." He spat again and glanced down to where I'd been. "Look at it down there. All wet and boggy. 'Course you ain't the first person I seen down where she oughtn't be. Would you believe there was a truck in that very spot the other night as I was coming to work? A truck, I tell you. And two grown men who oughta know better. I paused and hollered that the shore patrol wouldn't like them mucking

189

around underneath the bridge like that, but they didn't pay me no mind. Idiots. One of these days I'm gonna come to work and they'll have found a dead body. It'll serve 'em right."

A truck and two men? Jackpot. "You see any of 'em clearly?"

"Nah." The man rubbed his chin. "The guy who seemed to be in charge, he was older, but I couldn't see much in the dark. He told me to scram if I knew what was good for me. I walked off. They wanna get busted by the cops, or fall in the water and get themselves killed, that ain't my problem." A whistle sounded over at General Mills. "I gotta go. You stay away from that water, missy. You hear me?"

I smothered a smile. He coulda been my pop. "I hear you. Thanks for the tip."

The man headed off to work and I studied the spot by the bridge. Between what I'd seen and what the man told me, I needed to pay a nighttime visit. Sooner rather than later.

***

I decided to hoof it back to the First Ward. I had some heavy thinking to do and that was best done alone, not on a bus. Plus, it gave me the opportunity to bask in the sun and walk down Ohio Street in view of the lake. Lake Erie could be fierce in the winter, but mild days like today there was nothing better than watching gulls swoop over the sparkling water to help me sort my thoughts.

It was time to divide my forces. Assuming the forces would agree to being divided.

I reached Louisiana Street and walked past Conway Park. Ahead, near the corner of Mackinaw and Louisiana, I spied the very people I needed. Dot and Lee. From what I could see, they were engaged in a heated conversation. Uh oh.

I flicked away my cigarette as I approached. "Okay you two, knock it off. What's goin' on?"

Dot's face was red, a sure sign she was steamed about something. "Nothing important."

Lee, on the other hand, had the same look Jimmy and Michael got after a good scolding. Mulish and sullen.

"C'mon, don't be coy," I said.

He shot a look at Dot. "It's nothing. Whatcha been up to?"

I was pretty sure I knew the score. Dot had delivered a lecture and Lee hadn't liked it one bit. "Checking out the bridge at South Michigan." I told them about my newfound friend at General Mills and his tip about the men and trucks.

Dot worried her lip as I spoke. "Maybe I'm dim, but I'm confused. What do phony ration cards have to do with the sabotage at Bell?"

"Nothing. Least I don't think so. It's two different incidents, which means you're not gonna like what I have to say next," I said.

"Oh?"

"Dot, I need you to do two things. First, find out where Catherine lives and spend some time tailing her."

"Catherine Ramsey?"

"That's her."

Dot's forehead creased. "I don't understand. Why?"

"Did you know she was Russian?" I asked.

"Nope. The way she talks about the Reds, I wouldn't have thought it. She hates 'em."

"They're not the same," Lee said, breaking into our conversation. "Reds and Russians. I mean, all Soviets are Russian, but the reverse isn't true."

"I don't get it," Dot said. "Soviets, Russians, they're all fighting Hitler so what's the difference?"

Lee leaned against a street light post. "Prob'ly depends on why her family left Russia." He was such a history nut. "If her family supported the Czar and the nobility, they might be White Russians. It could be possible she'd hate the Soviets. What does she say about Stalin?"

I exchanged a glance with Dot. "I've never heard her talk about Stalin in particular, but she's always sayin' how it's a shame Bell supplies P-39s to the Reds."

Dot clearly wasn't buying it. "I still don't understand. What does this have to do with George Linden?"

"I don't think it has anything to do with him and that's my point," I said. "We're chasing our tails trying to connect the Bund, the sabotage, the black market, and George's murder."

"It's not?"

"No. That's why I need you to find Catherine and follow her. What she's doin', who she's talkin' to, stuff like that. Frankly, I can't believe she's smart enough to do all this on her own."

Dot shrugged. "What if she sees me?"

"Talk to her. See if you can get her to say anything that'll connect her to the damage. Oh, and show her this." I pulled out the Cyrillic note from my purse.

"See if she reacts. Got it." Dot pocketed the note. "Anything else?"

"Yeah." I glanced at Lee. He prob'ly wouldn't like this next bit, 'specially if I was right about his feelings, but it was necessary. "After that, I want you to go over to Kaisertown and follow Freddie Linden." I gave her the address of the shop where he worked. "He came around askin' about those ration books that George had. Either he's tryin' to cover for George or take his place. I wanna know if he meets with anyone or does anything that'll point us in the right direction."

Lee pushed off the post. "I'll go with her."

"No, I need you for something else."

"Like hell," he growled. "I'm not gonna stand by while Dot goes and follows a maybe-saboteur and a maybe-black marketeer. It's too dangerous."

"She'll be fine. It'll be daylight and there will be plenty of folks out and about. I need you for something else." I faced Dot. "You'll be okay, won't you?"

She tilted her head, peepers flicking between Lee and me. "Yeah, no problem. You don't want me to talk to either of 'em?"

"Not unless you have to," I said. "I rely on you to make up a good story if you're seen."

"I still think I should go with her," Lee said, crossing his arms.

I shook my head. "A girl on her own won't draw as much attention."

He glowered at me. "What d'you need me for?"

I took a deep breath. "I'm gonna go down to South Michigan by the river tonight after dark and I need you to come with me."

Lee gaped. "Why on earth would you be goin' down there?"

I talked fast. "I spoke to Detective MacKinnon earlier. He said they'd made a lot of arrests down there for black market activity."

"So?"

"Remember those ration cards and coupon books? George had to get 'em from somewhere. I figured someplace where the cops had already busted people would be a good place to start. A guy at General Mills told me he'd seen men down there, so I figured I'd take a look for myself."

"Are you off the rails? You're gonna go down to the Buffalo River, at night, alone, to a place where there are known criminals?"

"Not alone. I'm askin' you to come with me." I could almost see steam coming out of Lee's ears. "Look, Dot is going to be in public places during the daylight. She doesn't need backup. I do. Be grateful I'm askin' you in the first place."

He didn't blink. "If Sean were here, he'd paddle your backside for even thinking of it."

Sean wasn't much better, but at least Lee hadn't mentioned my fiancé. 'Course Lee was dead right. Sean would not be happy with me if he knew what I was up to. He'd taught me to rabbit punch and protect myself from guys I didn't care for. He'd always said he couldn't see me as a happy housewife. But this was different. This was going down to a place that would have been dodgy under any circumstances, never mind deliberately looking for trouble.

Dot was watching both of us, but Lee only had eyes for me. His jaw was set and he looked much older than his nineteen years.

"George got those ration cards and books from somewhere. Detective MacKinnon told me he'd stolen at least one C-card. What if he'd filched coupon books, too? Those things are worth serious dough. Don't you think if the supplier found out he'd be more than a little angry? Maybe enough to kill?"

For a moment I thought he was gonna lay into me and drag me home.

"Fine," he said. "I'll go. I'll meet you right here after dark. You leave without me and I'll paddle you myself."

Chapter 29

After leaving Dot and Lee, I puttered around the house for a bit. Mom found lots for me to do. Cleaning, mending, getting stuff ready for dinner. I did it all with only half a mind on my chores. The other half wondered what Dot had found out and worked on how I was gonna sneak out for the trip to the river later with Lee.

The phone rang about two o'clock. "I'll get it." I dove for the receiver. "Hello?"

"Betty, it's Dot. Meet me at Taylor's Drug Store. Corner of Louisiana and Seneca."

"When?"

"Now."

I glanced around. "Dot, that's blocks from here. I can't—"

"Look, I'm here with Catherine. You either get here or not." She hung up.

It'd take me a good twenty minutes to walk to where Dot was. I peeked in the front room. Mom dozed by the radio. Maybe if I borrowed a bike I could get there and back before dinner. I went looking for Jimmy.

He was in the back, playing with Cat. "Hey Betty. Watch this." He tossed a ball of wadded up newspaper toward Cat, who jumped and batted it away.

"Swell. Can I borrow your bike?"

He picked up the ball of paper, while Cat watched him, tail swishing in anticipation of the next throw. "Why?"

"I gotta go somewhere and I gotta get there fast. I'll be back in time for your evening paper route."

"Sure. It'll cost you a dime."

"What? That's not borrowing." The little thief.

He shrugged. "If you took the bus it'd be a nickel each way. Seein' as it'd cost you no matter what, I might as well get your dime."

I dug the coin out of my pocket and flipped it to him. "Crook."

He caught it and grinned. "Don't be late or I'll charge you another nickel."

I grabbed the bike from where it rested against the house and pedaled off. My brother the business man.

I arrived at Taylor's ten minutes later, puffing a bit. I saw Dot as soon as I walked in. She was sitting in a booth with Catherine and Florence. She waved at me. "Betty! Fancy seeing you here. Come and join us."

She wanted to play it as a chance meeting. I could do that. I calmed my breathing. It wouldn't do to be gasping for air if I was supposed to have chanced upon them. "Sure. Whatcha all up to?" I slid into the booth.

"Gabbing," Dot said. "About work, of course. Wondering when we're gonna go back."

Catherine arched an eyebrow. "I don't usually see you in this neighborhood."

"I was bored, same as you I expect. Borrowed my brother's bicycle to get some exercise. If I have to mend one more pair of trousers I'll go mad." I leaned back.

Florence sniggered. "You got any new ideas 'bout who's responsible?"

I shook my head. "You?"

"Nope. I hope this doesn't shut us down for good."

"It won't. I'm sure Mr. Satterwaite is working just as fast as he can to get us back." I eyed Catherine. "Is this what you do every day?"

She sipped from her green Coke glass, half filled with fizzy black liquid. "Sort of. That and think that maybe we're on the wrong track."

"Oh?"

"Yeah. We've all been focused on Anne, but as you pointed out, she wasn't around for the fire. I'm thinking there's a suspect everyone is overlooking."

Dot squinted at her. "Who?"

Catherine's answering smile was sly. "Betty."

I froze. Was she serious?

"Don't be stupid, Catherine," Florence said. "Betty wasn't near the paint building that day. No way she'd risk Dot getting hurt."

"Just 'cause you didn't see her doesn't mean she wasn't there. After all, those first two incidents happened where she was working. I know for a fact that she has a tube of South American Red lipstick and we all know she smokes." Catherine sat back, arms crossed. "As for Dot, maybe Betty didn't know her friend would be in the paint building. Or maybe she forgot. Gotta be hard to remember all that stuff when you're trying to wreck things."

Dot piped up in a harsh voice I'd never heard before. "Why on earth would Betty want to ruin things at Bell? Her brother is in the Navy. Her fiancé is in the Army. I can't think of a person with less of a motive."

Catherine's shoulders twitched. "Aren't the Irish neutral in this war? Isn't she Irish and proud of sayin' so? Some folks say being neutral is as good as fighting for the Nazis."

That did it. My voice came back. "My pop works for the Steel," I said, tone harsh.

"Just 'cause your father works for Bethlehem Steel doesn't mean you aren't a disloyal bitch." Catherine's grin was malicious. She was enjoying skewering me. She didn't even need to believe it. She just liked throwing out the words and seeing what happened.

Dot shot to her feet, no easy task considering the closeness of the booth. "You take that back. Right. Now."

"Cool it, Dot." I laid a hand on her arm and tugged her back down. "Tell me, Catherine. Why haven't you told everybody your family is Russian? I thought the Russkies were on the side of the Allies. If we're talking about things you've hidden, let's talk about that, huh?"

The grin slid away, replaced by a vicious snarl. "You don't know what you're talking about. Only a fool thinks all Russians are the same. You might be a traitor, Betty Ahern, but I never thought you were a fool. I'd watch out if I were you." She tossed a couple coins on the table and stalked to the door, shoving two little kids out of her way in the process.

"You made her mad, Betty," Dot said. "I don't know if she's your saboteur, but I do know she's got an awful temper. I'd be careful if I were you."

Florence tilted her head and shot me a look. "I didn't know her family was Russian."

"Yep," Dot said. "Her name's Kateryna Ivanova Razumovsky."

"Is that important?" Florence asked.

"I dunno," I said, gazing at the door. "I honestly do not know."

***

I got Jimmy's bike back in plenty of time, even though I rode Dot double on the way home. He was waiting in the back yard, Cat swatting at the crumpled ball of newspaper. "Thanks for the rental."

He took the bike back. "Sure thing, sis. Any time."

"You gonna charge me a dime every trip?"

He slung his pack of newspapers over his shoulder. "'Course I am. You have a job, you can afford it. Consider it an expense." He took off before I could answer.

The little brat.

On the way home, Dot had confided she hadn't had much success with Freddie. He hadn't been working when she stopped and the owner hadn't known where he was. "I'll try again later," she said. "You be careful tonight."

"I will. Lee'll be with me."

"I'm not only talking about watching out for black marketeers. You be careful of Lee's feelings. Remember what we talked about." She walked off home before I could answer. I remembered. As if I didn't have enough to do. Find a saboteur, a murderer, and sort out relationships. 'Cause I was pretty sure I wasn't the one who had to be careful of Lee's feelings.

The first part of the evening was uneventful. We had dinner, I washed the dishes, and I sat quietly reading my Bible while Pop read the paper and Mom sewed. Around nine I yawned. "I'm pretty sleepy. Think I'm gonna hit the sack early. 'Night."

Pop shot me a quizzical look, but Mom didn't react at all. "Pleasant dreams. Lots more to do tomorrow since you're still off work."

I went to my room, where Mary Kate was already asleep. I changed into work clothes as quietly as I could. I waited five minutes, then climbed out the window and crept around the corner of the house. I wasn't watching my

198

feet, which is how I stepped right on Cat's tail. He yowled and fled, setting the metal garbage cans knocking in his path. I ducked around the side of the house and heard the back door creak. "What is it, Adam?" Mom asked, her voice a little faint. She hadn't left the living room.

"Nothing," Pop's voice was louder.

Please don't come around the house, I prayed.

"Stray cats, I'd expect." The door creaked and shut.

Thank you Mother Mary. I tip-toed away from the house and down the street.

Lee was waiting for me, exactly where he said he would. He'd put on a dark gray shirt and the trousers he prob'ly wore to work at GM. He was smoking while he waited. "You're late." He stamped out the gasper.

"Nearly blew it stepping on the cat's tail. Let's go."

We double-timed it down to the corner of Conway Park, then over to Ohio and up to South Michigan. "Is your leg okay?" I asked. He hadn't complained, but I knew he didn't usually walk this fast. It was quite a bit warmer than it should be, even at night and close to the water. I heard it lapping at the shore, but the absence of gulls crying put me on edge.

"I'm fine. Keep your voice down."

We reached the bridge. The area was deserted, the glossy black water of the river like a mirror in the night. Occasionally, I heard a splash from something jumping into or out of it. We found a pile of junk covered with overgrown grass and tucked ourselves behind it to watch. "Lee, before anyone gets here, thanks for coming with me," I said. "You didn't have to."

"Yes, I did." He eased himself to the ground. "I can't let you roam around on your own."

I glanced around and the moonlight sparkled off the end of a broken bottle. I picked it up. Not the best weapon, but better than nothing. "You want me to look for another one?"

"I got my knife, I'm good." He lifted an eyebrow. "You thought I was gonna come down here with nothing?"

That was Lee, Boy Scout prepared. "Since it's just us for a minute, I gotta talk to you about something."

He studied the water. "What?"

Here goes nothing. "I wanna make sure you know I'm gonna marry Tom. You know, soon as he comes home. I love him. You know that, right?"

That got his attention. "Of course I do. Don't be stupid. Why else do you think I made that promise?"

I took a breath. "Dot thinks you're sweet on me. That's why you're doin' all this."

"Oh she does, does she?" His voice was flat and emotionless.

"Yeah, 'cept I think she's got it wrong." He didn't say anything, so I plowed on. "I think the one you're sweet on is her."

He averted his gaze.

"Am I right? C'mon, you can tell me." I paused. "I saw you when you walked her home the other night. The look on your puss. It reminded me of Tom."

When Lee spoke, his voice was tight. "We gotta talk about this now?"

"I think we do." I shifted a bit. "Have you said anything to her?"

The darkness hid his expression. "There's no point."

"Don't say that. I'm sure if she knew, she'd feel the same way."

"Dot loves to dance, to go out and do things. She needs a guy who can keep up with her." His bad leg twitched. "I'm not going to be cutting a rug any time soon."

"Lemme talk to her. I'm sure—"

He whipped around to face me. "Don't you dare. I'll get over it. Nothing I'm not used to by now." The silence was strained, awkward. Neither of us said anything, letting the sound of water and nighttime traffic wash away the tension. When Lee spoke again, his voice was neutral. "You see anyone?"

I didn't know exactly what he was thinking, but I could tell he definitely wanted to get off the subject of Dot. "Nothing."

"I don't mind saying I'd love to know whose brainchild this was. Black market ration cards."

"How long you think we should wait here?" I asked.

"At least an hour, maybe 'til midnight."

* * *

We waited, but no one showed. Eventually, we gave up and headed back home. "Well, that was a waste of time," I said. "Should we go again tomorrow?"

He twisted his neck, maybe trying to work out stiffness from watching. "Might as well. It's a good place. Right by the river, not a lot of activity at night. It'd be real easy to slip in on a small boat, unload, and have a truck waiting."

"Then I'll see you tomorrow?"

"I'm working daylight shift, but I'll come by after supper. Don't step on the cat sneaking back into your place." He gave me a quick hug and walked off to his house.

I kept a sharp eye out for Cat when I got home. He was nowhere to be found, prob'ly still mad 'cause of his tail. I eased myself through the window. Mary Kate was tucked in, dead asleep. I peeled off my clothes, got into my nightie, said a quick prayer, and climbed into bed.

Chapter 30

I woke up Saturday not sure of what day it was. This not-working thing was messing up everything, including my ability to track time. Mom loved it. I had plenty of time to help with breakfast, do laundry, clean the house, make lunches for the younger kids and, most of all, listen to her litany of complaints: everything from the prices of stuff at the market to the conduct of the war to the fact I didn't have a boyfriend. She musta gotten up on the wrong side of the bed. I tried to point out that I had a fiancé.

She waved her hand, dismissing my protest. "He's not here. Now Billy McClusky—"

"Mom. We agreed. I'm not gonna go out with Billy."

"Fine, what about the Tillotson boy? I know, the issue with his leg, but he has a good job. And he's a handsome young man."

"I will admit that Lee is a better choice. But I'm pretty sure his heart is elsewhere." I heaved a basket of wet laundry out of the back door. After I pinned it on the line, I snuck out front for a smoke. Cat followed me. "I don't know what I'm gonna do with her, Cat." I scratched behind his ears and he nuzzled my hand. "Any chance we can convince the Axis to call off this whole war thing so Tom can come home and I can get on with my life?"

A shadow fell across me. "Are you talking to a cat?" Anne asked.

"He's a better listener than people some days." I shaded my eyes as I looked up. "What are you doin' here?"

"I had to see you. This was with our milk bottles when I got them this morning." She held out a plain white envelope.

Inside, was a typed sheet of paper. "We know your son was stealing from us and we know the police took the merchandise he had. You owe us one thousand dollars. You have until the end of the week to pay up or return the merchandise. We'll be in touch." No signature. I turned over the sheet. No marks. No writing on the envelope. "That's a lot of dough to come up with."

"I know."

"You or the cops find any money stashed in George's stuff?"

She crossed her arms tight across her chest. "There were a few dollars in his wallet and twenty dollars in fives in his dresser drawer. That was it."

No money. Lots of ration books and C-cards, not including the one Detective MacKinnon said they found in George's car. "Anne? How many ration books does your family have?"

"Four, one for each of us. Same as with anyone else."

"Who does the shopping?"

Little lines creased her forehead as she thought. "It depends. Mama does odd errands. You know, if we need something on the spot. But George did the regular shopping. He said since he had the car, it would be easier for him to get the stuff home. Plus Mama doesn't like grocery shopping. The prices of everything are so distressing. She would make the list, hand it to George, and he went."

"You never went with him?"

"I was often working. That was another reason he did the shopping." She paled. "Oh my gosh. You're thinking he used some of those phony ration books for himself, aren't you?"

"It never seemed like you had more than the normal amount of rationed items?" Mom would have noticed right off the bat, but maybe Mrs. Linden, not being used to scrimping and saving, wouldn't.

"No. Well, Mama did say once or twice how nice it was he was able to bring home extra coffee or sugar, especially since Papa likes his morning cup and his desserts. She assumed he'd saved up the coupons or traded for them. So did I." Her eyes shone and her lip trembled. "All the while, it was because he was stealing, wasn't it? Whoever gave him the books to sell found out and demanded money, but George couldn't pay it back. That's why he was killed."

"Slow down. It's a possibility, nothing more." I examined the paper again. It was pretty unremarkable. Plain paper without a letterhead or watermark and typed on the same kind of machine that was prob'ly used in dozens of offices. "I talked to Joseph after the funeral."

"What did he say?"

"Did you know George was going into business with him? Kosher meats?"

"No, but that would explain why George often asked Papa about the logistics of butchering. Papa isn't a butcher himself, but he was an accountant at a big meat-packing company when he was in Germany. He knew some about the business." Anne wiped her eyes. "Is that why he was killed?"

"It's another possibility. His friends in the Bund. They wouldn't be too happy if George was leaving, which he was. I can't imagine it'd be better if they found out he was flying the coop 'cause he was going into business with a Jew." I threw my cigarette butt into the gutter and handed back the letter. "Have you talked to any of the gals from Bell?"

"I saw Rose one day. She was mailing a letter, she said. What if…"

I waited. "What if what?"

"Well, I was thinking. Mussolini is a fascist and a Hitler ally. What if Rose is connected to the sabotage that way? A friend or a relative who convinced her to help her native country?"

I eyed her. "I thought of that. She says she hasn't written any of her family."

"She would say that, wouldn't she?"

Anne was right. Unless I could catch Rose in the act of mailing a letter, though, I'd have a hard time proving she was lying.

Anne took a deep, shuddery breath. "What should I do with the note? I don't have that kind of money. Neither do my parents. It's true we're a little better off than some, but not like this."

I stood and brushed dirt off my pants. Cat wound around my ankles, but when I ignored him, he stalked off, tail swishing back and forth. "You need to get in touch with Detective MacKinnon and tell him." I pointed at the paper. "Meanwhile, I've got some things to check out." I hoped Lee would be up to another trip to the river. This time, I planned to have more than a broken bottle for protection.

***

Lee wouldn't be home from work until almost four. Meanwhile, Mom continued to find stuff for me to do. So much that when she mentioned going to the market for some shopping, I jumped at the opportunity. Anything to get outta the house. I stopped by Dot's to see if she wanted to come with me. On the way, I told her about the results of the previous night and Anne's visit earlier.

"A thousand bucks?" Dot froze picking over some sad-looking vegetables. "Holy mackerel."

"Yup." I reviewed Mom's list. I'd already picked up everything on it. Now I was poking along so as not to make it home too fast.

"I didn't know those coupon books were worth so much."

"Coupon books and the gas ration stickers. I guess it depends on how much George was selling 'em for and how many his supplier gave him to get rid of. Pop told me once that profiteering is a big deal."

She followed me to the cash register. "This whole thing is crazy, you know that, right? The sabotage, the Bund, black-market goods, murder. It sure would make a good spy picture. Anne thinks Rose could be involved?"

"Because Italy and Germany are allies, yeah. I can't believe it's all connected. Not every last bit of it anyway. It's too much." I handed over my coupons and money, took my bags, and headed out. Hollywood might make a movie with all these elements, but it was too complicated for real life. Least I hoped so. Otherwise, I was gonna call Warner Brothers and see if they wanted the rights to the story.

"You can't?" Dot asked, when we were back on the street.

"George being killed. I think that could be the black market stuff or the Bund. I don't see him as Bell's saboteur."

"Hmm. You might be right about that."

Dot might have preferred to take the bus. I wanted to delay my arrival home as much as possible, so we hoofed it. The weather was okay, a bit overcast. My view of the lake was blocked, but a few gulls foraged for scraps along the streets. "You have any luck with Freddie Linden?"

"Oh, I forgot. I went back to the deli in Kaisertown, and he was there. I didn't know if he'd recognize me, so I kept outta sight."

Smart move. "He go anywhere?"

"I'm not sure." She turned from Broadway to Jefferson. Some kids pulling a wagon loaded with cans rattled past us. "He was at the deli for a couple hours. Then around dinner, he ducked out. Thought I heard him say something about getting food."

"Wouldn't he be able to eat at work?"

"That's what I thought. When he left, he was walkin' pretty fast, not payin' attention to anything so it was easy to follow him. He went to a locksmith's shop on Dingens. He went inside, stayed maybe fifteen minutes, then left, and headed back to work. I followed almost to the deli, but when I was certain that's where he was goin' I turned around and went home. If I didn't make it back for supper, Ma would skin me alive."

"You weren't able to see him later?"

"No, I'm sorry, Betty. I couldn't come up with a good reason to leave again. You know how my folks are."

"'S okay, Dot. You did great." I squeezed her arm. She did look a bit disappointed. Freddie had left work under false pretenses, gone to some locksmith, then gone back to work. Huh. What had he been doin' and what did he do later? Based on his actions and his questions, he'd known a lot more about his cousin's black-market activities than he let on.

"You gonna answer me?" Dot asked, clearly a bit put out.

"Huh? Sorry, I was thinking. What did you say?"

"You struck out last night at the river. What're you gonna do now?"

"I wanna go back tonight. I'm hoping Lee will help me out again." If he didn't strangle me. "As for the saboteur, unless something happens to prove me wrong, I think that's gonna have to wait until we're back to work. I can't shake the feeling one of us is behind that."

Dot paused at South Park, looking for traffic. "I hope it's Catherine."

"Why?"

We hurried across the street. "She put my back up. Accusing you? That was way outta line."

It was easy to underestimate Dot, with her pinup girl looks and cheerful nature. I was lucky to have her on my side.

***

I was sitting on Lee's doorstep when he got home that afternoon. Cat followed me over. I'd considered shooing him away, but changed my mind. Not that I thought Lee would ever lay a hand on me, but maybe he'd be less likely to argue if faced with a furry opponent.

He pulled up short when he saw me. "This can't be good."

"Why can't I have come over to see a friend?"

"Oh, I dunno. You've had a lot of hidden motives lately." He narrowed his peepers. "Or are you gonna tell me this really is a friendly visit?"

"Not exactly." I took Cat off my lap and put him beside me, where he issued a meow of complaint and stalked off, tail held high.

"Now what?"

"Don't flip your lid, but I wanna go back to that spot on South Michigan tonight."

"We were just there. It was a bust."

"You said we could go back. And there's been some new developments." I told him about the note Anne's parents had received.

He scrubbed a hand through his hair. "Come on in. Don't worry. My dad's not home and Mom's at the church rolling bandages or something." He led me into a kitchen that didn't look all that different from mine. White appliances, black and white squares on the floor, scrubbed wooden table, and a crucifix over the doorway. He dropped his lunch pail on the counter. "How much did they ask for?"

"One thousand dollars or the stuff back."

"Because everybody's got that lying around. No chance of returning the goods?"

"Not now the cops have it."

He sat and stretched out his legs. "By going back, what are you trying to do?"

"Put a name to a face or at least get a name." I sat across from him. "I give that to the cops, then they can make the bust, and the Lindens are in the clear. At least on that front."

"You don't wanna get involved?"

"I'm not crazy, Lee."

His raised eyebrows and half-smile told me he didn't quite buy it.

"Okay, I might be a little crazy. But I'm not stupid. If these guys killed George, the last thing I want to do is let them see me." I paused. "You'll do it, then? Go back with me?"

"You'll go anyway, so yeah, I'll go. You wanna get down there early again, make sure we get a good hiding spot?"

I nodded.

"Okay. I'll come over to get you, tell your folks we're going to a movie or something."

It was a good ruse, but… "Don't make it sound like a date."

"Why not?"

"I don't want my mom to get her hopes up."

Chapter 31

After dinner, I mentioned that Lee and I were going to the pictures. "*Road to Morocco* is still at the theater downtown."

Mom put down her knitting. "You're going out with Lee Tillotson?"

"Just as friends." Inspiration struck. "He's asked me for advice and we're gonna talk about that, too."

"What kind of advice?"

"Turns out Lee is sweet on Dot." It was almost comical how Mom's expression soured. "He wants to know the best way of asking her out. We're going to screen the flick and see if it's a good date movie."

Mom resumed her knitting without another word. Okay, so maybe Lee hadn't specifically asked me for advice, but he was interested in Dot and maybe we would chat about that on our way to the river.

Lee showed up in plenty of time to maintain the fiction of the movie. Mom didn't look up from her knitting, but he talked shop with Pop while I finished getting ready. It wasn't a date, but no sense in looking like a slob. There was a definite bite to the air, so I wore one of Sean's old jackets.

"Good night, Mr. and Mrs. Ahern." He led me out of the house. He was also in a heavy jacket, the collar turned up to keep his neck covered. "Are you sure you want to do this? We really could go to the pictures."

"You're not getting off that easy, bub. Let's go." On the way, I told him about the results of Dot following Freddie Linden.

"I hope Dot was careful," he said. It was too dark to see his face real clear, but I had no trouble picturing his expression of concern based on his voice.

"I'm sure she was. Why, you worried?"

"Aren't you?" He didn't look at me. "Freddie knew about his cousin's shenanigans. No doubt in my mind. My question is did he want George to stop or did he want a cut?"

I halted. "Huh?"

Lee faced me, breath steaming. "Think about it. Freddie came to see you and asked about the ration cards. He knew George had 'em. Only two possibilities. Freddie wanted to turn everything in and spare his relatives embarrassment, or he wanted the action for himself. Either way, I think we need to consider him a suspect."

It was exactly the idea I'd been tryin' to avoid, but Lee's logic was spot on. "Freddie killed George to make him stop, or he killed George because George wouldn't give him a piece of the pie."

"Or because Freddie wanted to take over."

The thought made me ill. "That's sickening."

"It's only a possibility. I'm not sayin' that's definitely what happened. But you already suspected Freddie was up to no good or else you wouldn't have asked Dot to tail him." He came closer, his face shadowed, but his expression softened with sympathy. "Cheer up. I might be wrong. I prob'ly am. On another note, tell me more about Catherine. What's she like?" He resumed walking.

I stayed beside him. What I didn't say is that he'd vocalized a thought I'd had and pushed aside. Not 'cause I liked Freddie, but 'cause it was terrible, thinking such a thing could happen between cousins close enough to be brothers. "She's a funny one. One minute she'll be ready to fight, the next she acts like nothing happened."

"But she's definitely Russian? I wonder what kind. Being White Russian—that is, folks who supported the nobility—wasn't real popular. Still isn't."

"You think Catherine's family was nobility? No way. She'd lord it over us if that were the case. It's how she is."

"No, not that. But maybe her family had ties to the White Russian faction somehow."

"Be serious."

"It would definitely explain why she hates the Soviets so much."

It would. I didn't know enough about the Ramseys, or Razumovskys, to say one way or the other. But anybody who met Catherine knew within five minutes that she despised the alliance with the Reds. It was something she and Winston Churchill had in common, a distrust of the Soviets.

"Did she work the areas in question on the days of the sabotage?"

I tried to remember. "She was at Bell. I know that much. And if she's right, that it coulda all been done by someone who was at the plant anywhere, I guess she's as much a suspect as anyone."

He thought a second. "Rose. You're sure her family back in Italy is fascist?"

"No. Helen has family in Berlin, too."

"One suspect who might want Bell to stop supplying one of our allies. Two more who might be Nazi or fascist supporters 'cause of family in Europe."

"How'm I supposed to find out if that's true?"

He didn't have an answer to that. We were almost at the end of Miami Street by now. "Worth creating a map of everyone's movements," he said.

"Sounds like you believe the sabotage and the murder are separate. That's not what I thought at first, but it's what I've come to believe."

"Yeah. We should prob'ly stop talking now."

We walked the last block in silence. I hoped anyone who saw us would assume we were a couple out for a stroll. It wasn't the prettiest place, and it was well after dark, but I could hope.

We found ourselves a pile of wood pallets to hide behind underneath the bridge. Between that and the shadows, we would be almost invisible. "Did you bring your pocket knife?" I whispered.

"Yep. I don't see any bottles for you to use this time, though."

"I'm all set." I pulled out Sean's switchblade. I'd pinched it from his dresser drawer. I didn't intend to show up this time without some sort of means of defense.

Lee wisely kept his yap shut.

Time slid by, as did the moon overhead. There wasn't a lot of cloud cover and the silvery light glimmered on the water, making the whole scene a set of sharp shadows and hard edges. The scent of cereal was thick. Like Bell and Bethlehem, General Mills worked all hours. Just as I thought tonight would be a bust same as last night, an old Ford truck pulled up. The headlights were off, but the moon was plenty bright enough for the driver to see where he was going. A couple minutes after the truck arrived, another car parked on the little strip of grass. Two men got out of the truck, both heavyset. I couldn't see their pusses, but each wore a squashy cap, the same kind as Lee's and what I'd seen newsboys downtown wear when they hawked their papers.

A third man got out of the driver's seat of the second car. An orange-red dot betrayed the presence of a cigarette before he crushed it underfoot in the withered grass. He opened the back door and another guy appeared, maybe the head honcho. He was taller than the others and much thinner. He wore a long overcoat with the collar turned up. He approached the two men from the truck. The driver disappeared around the corner of a building.

"Good evening, gentlemen," the tall man said. In the crisp night air, he sounded like he was only feet away, not yards.

"Let's get this over with," one of the truck men said in a gravelly voice. "I don't like being in the open. You got the goods?"

"As long as you have the money."

The truck man handed something over and Tall Man looked at it.

"Can you see what they're doing?" I asked Lee.

He shook his head and laid a finger against his lips.

Tall Man put whatever it was, most likely a pouch or an envelope of some kind, in his coat. "New product is in the trunk. Same price, same cut as the last time."

I wiggled a bit, trying to see. They'd gone around the car and lifted the trunk lid. It completely blocked my view.

"Betty, stop making so much noise," Lee hissed.

"I need to see what they're doing. If I just—" I didn't get the chance to finish my sentence. A dark shape appeared behind Lee, something in his right hand.

"It's rude to skulk in the shadows," he said. "Why don't you come out and say hello?"

I looked at Lee, who was as still as a statue. I clasped my hand around the knife in my pocket.

"Please don't," the man said, voice a touch weary. "You pull whatever's in your pocket and I'll have to shoot your friend. That will cause a mess for everyone. My boss won't like that." He nudged Lee with a booted foot. "Get up and move."

If Lee was afraid, I couldn't tell. His face was marble as he reached down and gave me a hand up. The three of us marched over to the group by the vehicles, who'd fallen silent at the sound of voices.

We stopped maybe ten feet away from them. The man from the bridge came around front. In the moonlight, I could see his right hand clasped a little snub-nosed revolver. Good thing I hadn't gone for the knife.

"What do we have here, Lloyd?" Tall Man asked. He sounded like someone who had unexpected visitors for tea, not a man who'd been interrupted in a clandestine exchange by the Buffalo River.

The men from the truck growled.

"Snoopers," Lloyd said. "We haven't gotten any further than that."

"We're not snooping," I said. "We were walking by the river. We saw your cars, got scared, and—"

"Young lady." Tall Man's voice was amused. "No one takes a stroll under the South Michigan Street Bridge at night. Lloyd, search them."

Lloyd patted me down, checking all my pockets. He was a pro, that was for sure. The search was brisk. He didn't leer and he didn't try to get frisky. 'Course he didn't find much on me as I'd left my purse at home. But he did take Sean's knife.

He fared better with Lee. He had his wallet on him, including all his ID. Lloyd pulled out the card and read it. "Liam Patrick Tillotson. Nice Irish name. I see you're a First Ward local. Address over on Mackinaw." He replaced the card and handed the wallet back, smirking while he did.

"Mr. Tillotson." Tall Man exhaled a cloud of smoke. "Why don't you tell me the real story?"

I exchanged a look with Lee. He shrugged, a gesture that said, "Might as

213

well, all they can do is shoot us." I cleared my throat. "We were looking for you."

Tall Man focused on me. "Is that so?" The men from the truck grumbled louder. Tall Man held up his hand to silence them.

"Okay, we didn't know you were, well, *you*. We heard this was a spot where a person might be able to get some goods."

Tall Man pulled a silver cigarette case and matching lighter from his coat. "What kind of goods?"

"Ration cards," Lee said. "Black market ones."

"Are you in the market?"

I glanced at Lee. "We're in the market for information."

Tall Man lit his gasper, puffed, and blew out a thin stream of smoke. "Whatever made you think you could find it here?"

Time for a gamble. "We, or at least I, knew George Linden," I said.

Tall Man *tsked*.

"More specifically, I know his sister. He worked for you, didn't he?"

Tall Man blew another thin stream of smoke. "For a while. Our relationship came to an unfortunate end."

"You know anything about that end?"

Lloyd's hand, the one that held the revolver, twitched.

Tall Man, however, didn't move. "I might."

"Wanna tell me?"

"What's in it for me? For me to give you information without getting something in return hardly seems fair."

I glanced at Lee again. This time, he shut his eyes. He knew me too well not to suspect what I was gonna say. "Well, I hear George had some of your merchandise when he died. You'd like it back."

"Go on."

"A trade. I get your stuff back, you tell me what you know about George's death. Sounds pretty fair to me."

A muscle in Lee's jaw twitched. Someone who didn't know him would think it was stress. I knew better. He was wondering how I was gonna return something I didn't have.

Tall Man studied me, the moonlight reflected in his eyes, which were dark as wells. Maybe not the eyes of a killer, he had Lloyd for that, but ones that belonged to a man who'd order my death with as much remorse as he'd feel stepping on a cockroach.

"We got a deal?" I asked.

He ashed his smoke. "Fair enough. You return what belongs to me, all forty-eight books, I'll give you whatever information I have."

"How do I find you?"

"There's a bar at the corner of Clinton and Fillmore Streets. Leave a note with the bartender and I'll contact you." He nodded at Lloyd. "You can give the young lady her knife back."

Lloyd tossed the knife at my feet, where it clattered against the gravel.

Tall Man took a step closer. "Under normal circumstances, I'd invite one of you to keep me company while I wait. However, thanks to Lloyd, I know exactly where to find Mr. Tillotson. Try and double-cross me and you'll regret it to the day you die. I won't have Lloyd kill you. I'll send him after your friends, starting with young Liam here. I assume you're friends since you're together. Understand?"

I bent down to retrieve the knife. Then I straightened, swallowed hard, and locked my knees to keep them from knocking together. "Yeah. I understand."

***

We didn't walk back to Mackinaw. We bolted. I didn't think Lee could move that fast. I was wrong. I kept checking over my shoulder, expecting to see Lloyd and his revolver behind us, but there was no one. Not even a seagull.

As soon as we reached the safety of our street, Lee whirled around and grabbed my wrist. "What the hell are you thinking?"

I yanked myself free. "I was thinking about not getting shot. You're welcome."

"What would I be thanking you for?" It was impressive how he sounded as angry as Pop when he laid down the law for the younger boys, but Lee never raised his voice. "How the hell are you gonna return something you ain't even got?"

At that point I knew how mad Lee was. The worse his grammar got, the more excited, or the angrier, he was. "Calm down."

"Don't you tell me to calm down. Elizabeth Ann Ahern, I oughta—"

"You oughta what?" I stood toe-to-toe with him. No one trotted out my full name except my folks. "Sean taught me to fight dirty, remember? You might be bigger than me, but if you think I won't take every advantage, and that includes your bum leg, think again."

We stared at each other for at least a minute, him breathing heavy trying to calm down, me determined not to give in. I knew it was a low blow and I'd never do that to him, but I damn sure wasn't gonna let him bully me, either. I thought maybe underneath the anger, I could see a little glimmer of fear in his eyes. He and Tom had gotten into a lot of serious scrapes, but he'd prob'ly never had a gun pointed at him before.

He closed his peepers and leaned against a light post. "Fine." He opened them. "But I sure do wanna know how you're gonna pull this one off, Betty. Have you considered that the information he's gonna give you is that he killed George? Or more likely, he sent that Lloyd to do it?"

"I have. Two things. First, Lloyd had a gun tonight. Not a knife."

"Doesn't mean he didn't have a knife the night George died. It was a neighborhood, not a deserted bridge. Maybe he took a knife because a gun was too noisy."

It was a fair point. "Do you think George trusted this guy, Tall Man, whatever his name is? Better yet, do you think he trusted Lloyd?"

"Only if he was an idiot," Lee said. "What does that have to do with anything?"

"If George had been shot, yeah, I'd have no problem believing Lloyd coulda done it. And you're right, I bet Lloyd knows how to handle a knife, too."

Lee's eyes narrowed.

"It doesn't make sense," I continued. "If I don't trust you, why in the world would I let you get close enough to stab me?"

"You wouldn't. But maybe Lloyd and George were standing far apart, Lloyd pulled a switchblade, and lunged."

Something to ask Detective MacKinnon. In that situation, George woulda had time to defend himself and surely there were ways the cops could tell. "I s'pose it's possible. But you gotta admit, it's just as possible that George trusted who killed him and that's not Lloyd."

Lee's blood pressure seemed to have come down. At least he wasn't steaming at the ears any more. "Maybe Lloyd, or Tall Man as you call him, wasn't involved. Betty, that still doesn't explain how you're gonna give back something that the cops have. Don't tell me you think you're gonna steal those ration books out of police headquarters. Or are you gonna get your cop buddy to help you?"

"Don't be silly." No way I'd do that. And I had no intention of just turning this whole thing over to the police. This was my job. I started toward my house. "I'm gonna counterfeit 'em."

Chapter 32

Pop worked second shift on Sunday. We went to early Mass so we could do the big family dinner before he went to work. Mom noted I was unusually quiet and Mary Kate had to pinch me to keep me from falling asleep during the sermon. In my defense, I was bone tired. I'd gotten home late the previous night and after I'd climbed in my window, it had taken a long time to fall asleep. Not so much because of visions of Lloyd and his snub-nose revolver, although that didn't help. More because of Lee's reaction to my proposed "solution" to providing the store of black market ration cards. The only thing that prevented him from yelling was the time. I could still see the look in his eyes as he'd stalked off, and it cut me as deep as a knife blade. He was one of my best friends and I mighta pushed him over the edge with the idea of forgery.

Between trying to figure out how to pull that off, the late-night trip down to the South Michigan Street Bridge, and guilt over Lee, I hadn't gotten much sleep. I peeled potatoes for Sunday dinner with my eyes half shut, while Mary Kate set the table.

Mom came into the kitchen to check the meat. When she walked away from the stove, she stopped and gave me a beady-eyed stare across the sink and pot of potatoes. "You're half asleep standing there, child. What's the matter? Are you sick or something?"

I was saved from answering by the ring of the telephone. "I'll get it."

It was Mr. Satterwaite. "Paint operations have been restored. We're reopening the plant on Tuesday."

"Then they caught the saboteur?" There'd been nothing in the morning

218

Courier-Express.

"No."

"Then why're we opening? Do they think they'll have a better chance if Bell is open as usual?"

"I'm not at liberty to say, Miss Ahern. There will be parts for assembly on Tuesday morning. If you still want a job, be there. If not, I'm sure we won't have any problems replacing you." He hung up.

I laid the receiver in the cradle. I was going back to work. Heaven knew I was happy, but I hadn't positively identified the saboteur yet. Had the higher-ups? If not, did they think they could solve the mystery any easier with us around? Were they hoping for another incident? What if one of us got hurt? I was still on the hook for finding an answer for Anne. Being back on the assembly line and around all my suspects would make that easier. I'd talk to Dot later, work up a plan for smoking out the person responsible.

We ate dinner at noon, then Mary Kate and I took care of the washing up. Afterward, I grabbed my coat from the closet. "I'm going out," I called. I didn't wait for an answer. The sun was shining. It wasn't ridiculously warm, but it wasn't cold, either. I could see the birds in the distance as they swirled and glided over Lake Erie. Normally by now, no gull was daring enough to tempt the winter winds on the lake, but the warmth had everything wrong side up. I'd gotten too old for snowball fights and sledding, but I missed the snow. With luck, it'd get back to a normal temperature, I could wrap up my sleuthing, and return to life as it should be. As close as it could get with a war going on, anyway.

I hadn't heard from Tom or Sean lately, but I wasn't particularly worried. According to the news, the Allies continued to push Hitler's Afrika Korps west. The US was shoving the Japanese off Guadalcanal. A lot of the action of the past few days centered around the Soviets and Stalingrad. I was interested of course, but nobody I knew was fighting there.

I needed the time to think, so I skipped the bus and walked to police headquarters downtown. Did detectives work on Sunday? They had to. Crime didn't stop 'cause it was the Lord's day. "I need to see Detective Sam MacKinnon, please," I said to the sergeant at the entrance. He told me to wait and phoned someone. A few minutes later, MacKinnon appeared. "I gotta speak to you. It's about George Linden."

MacKinnon took me by the elbow and led me outside. "Miss Ahern, you are an intelligent young woman. But you're going to get both of us in trouble."

"Even if I can help you out?"

"Somehow I get the feeling you aren't here to give me what I need to close this case."

"Well, I might. If you can help me first, that is."

He crossed his arms. "Help you how?"

I hesitated. "Are you handling all the black-market stuff you found at the Lindens' house?"

"Sort of. We seized it as part of the homicide investigation, but war profiteering is outside our jurisdiction. We'll assist the feds if they need it, of course. Why?" His eyes narrowed.

"Well, I kinda met the guy in charge of the operation last night. You know, down by the Buffalo River, the place you told me about."

"Do I want to know how you did that?"

I told him the story. Well, most of it. I left out Lloyd and the threats, and made it sound like I'd only observed, not talked to them directly. I also left Lee out of things. He was already mad at me. No need to make it worse by giving his name to the cops.

"Miss Ahern, what am I going to do with you? I don't think you need me to tell you that was incredibly dangerous."

"I know, I know. It seemed like a good idea at the time. But I have a question."

MacKinnon shook his head and sighed. "Yes?"

"Stabbing. You gotta get right up close to the person you're killing. It's not like with a gun."

"Right." He relaxed a bit, but still looked more than a little put-out. "A good shot can hit his victim from feet or yards away. It depends on the accuracy of the weapon. Even a long blade requires the killer to be a lot closer. As you so aptly put it, the killing is more personal."

"Can you tell if George tried to protect himself?"

"We can. They're called defensive wounds. Let me show you." He took a pen out of his jacket pocket. "If I stab you, what's your first instinct?" He jabbed the pen at me.

I put out my hands to block him.

"Exactly, you try to protect yourself. Look at your skin."

I did. A line of blue ink ran across my palm. "You drew on me."

"If it had been a knife, it would be a cut. That's a defensive wound."

"Did George have any? Defensive wounds?"

Detective MacKinnon replaced his pen and hesitated, like he was tryin' to decide whether or not to tell me. Finally, he spoke. "No."

I thought over what he'd said. "Then it's not crazy to think George knew his killer and trusted that person enough not to try and protect himself. Least he wasn't expecting trouble and the killer might have been too quick."

Detective MacKinnon's lips twitched like he was fighting a smile. "If I didn't know better, Miss Ahern, I'd say you were after my job."

***

I left Detective MacKinnon and headed home. First, I stopped at the five-and-dime and bought some paper that would look like the covers of ration books, at least if you didn't look too close, and a bunch of newspapers. Back on Mackinaw, I stopped by Dot's.

She came outside as soon as she saw me at the door. "Did you get the call from Bell?"

"Yup. Tuesday morning we go back."

"It's good, right? That must mean they found the saboteur and it's safe now."

"They didn't. I asked Mr. Satterwaite. He was his usual prickly self, but he told me they didn't."

She gaped. "Then why're we going back?"

"He didn't say, but my guess is that someone in charge thinks they'll have better luck figuring it all out once we're all back to work. Try and draw the saboteur into the open, that kind of thing. How's your arm?"

She rolled up her sleeve so I could see the half-healed burn marks. "How're they gonna make sure none of us gets hurt?"

"Relax. We'll figure it out."

"We?"

"Yes, we. In the meantime, I need to ask a favor. I need you to go to Kaisertown and tail Freddie Linden again."

"Whatever for?"

I told her about my talk with MacKinnon and my deduction. "We know George was selling black-market ration stuff. I don't think he would have let those guys get close enough to him for stabbing. That leaves his friends in the Bund and his cousin."

"Why would Freddie do such a thing?"

"Money." I tapped out a cigarette and lit it. "I think the argument Anne overheard was George and Freddie fighting about the ration cards. Freddie wanted in and George wouldn't share."

"You think Freddie killed his own cousin over money?"

"Oh, Dot." I reached up and patted her cheek. "I know you've seen *The Maltese Falcon* and other detective pictures with me. When it comes to money, some people will kill their own mother."

She gasped.

"Remember, George was killed in Kaisertown, and both George and Freddie live there." I paused, but she said nothing so I continued. "Anyway, I'm not positive. But I need to know where Freddie goes, who he talks to. Specifically, I need to know if he goes to this address and leaves any messages." I handed her a slip of paper with the address of the bar Tall Man had told me about the previous night. "Don't talk to him, you understand? Just follow. If he sees you, pretend like you're shopping, or something."

She took the address. "What about the Bund guys? You want I should go by the garage?"

"No. Stay away from there. I'll handle them. Can you go take care of following Freddie this afternoon?"

"Mom don't need me for nothing, so I can go now." She glanced at the shopping bag full of paper. "What are you planning to do?"

"Me? I've got to find a way to dummy up a box of ration cards."

Chapter 33

I sent Dot off, providing her with some bus fare. I needed to start keeping count of my expenses if I wanted to treat this detective thing as a job. Then I went home. I remembered what the box Anne had found looked like: plain, brown cardboard. "I need a box, Cat," I said, as I rifled through my neighbors' trash piles. "A regular box, that's all." Cat merely watched me, a complete lack of interest on his face as he started to wash his whiskers.

Lee appeared. He was holding a box. "You're talking to the cat again."

I straightened and took a drag from my gasper to buy time to come up with a response. I blew out the smoke and said, "I thought you weren't gonna speak to me again after last night."

"I thought about it, but I changed my mind." He brushed the hair from his forehead. "You know I think this is pretty reckless and I'm not keen for you to keep at it. But I know better than to try and change your mind. If I can't get you to quit, I might as well help you out, maybe prevent you from getting hurt."

I grinned at him. "And it's a reason to hang out with Dot. The two of you being sidekicks."

His cheeks reddened and I didn't think it was from the breeze. "Anyway. I figured you were gonna need a box for those fake books."

"Don't you have to get to work?"

"I'm off." He held out the box. "You want this or not?"

I searched his face, trying to see if he was messing with me. But he seemed sincere. I took it. "You have time to help me with these?"

"What should I do?"

It was exactly the kind of apology I would have expected from him. Nothing sappy, just back to work. "We need to fill this so it looks like it's got ration books in it. At least, on the surface. I don't think Tall Man will go through every last book to be sure."

"What about the C-cards?"

"I'll have to stall on those. I don't have what it takes to fake 'em. Hopefully I'll be able to pass these off, get the information I need, and get outta Dodge before he notices they aren't real fakes."

"Real fakes. You know how funny that sounds, don't you?"

"Shut it, wise guy." I flicked away my cigarette butt. "When Anne showed me the box, it was full to the top, everything stacked real neat."

He took the box from me, set it on the ground, then took out his own ration book. He held it out at different angles, like he was trying to picture how it would fit. "You've got a problem."

"What's that?"

"The paper you bought isn't gonna work. You need to fake the printing on the covers. You don't have the right tools for that."

"Damn it." I sat next to Cat, who immediately stopped his washing and butted his head against my hand. I rubbed his ears. "Mom's got old books of ours. What if I take off the covers?"

"That won't work either. Your names are on 'em. These gotta look like fresh books, never touched." He sat on the ground. "You need at least eight covers. You can fake what's underneath. Stack up blank paper or something. The top needs to look like the stuff they took from the Lindens. And those are with the cops."

"Yeah." I scratched Cat under the chin. "But I know a guy who might lend us a hand with that."

***

I took Lee with me when I went back to police headquarters.

"What is it this time?" Detective MacKinnon asked when he came down to meet us. "Who's this?"

"Detective Sam MacKinnon, this is a friend of mine. Lee Tillotson. Lee and me have known each other for ages."

"Does he make the third musketeer with you and Miss Kilbride?"

"You mean like in the Don Ameche movie?"

MacKinnon closed his eyes and his lips moved in silent words. Then he sighed. "Something like that. What do you want?"

I glanced at Lee, but his expression clearly said this was my show. "Remember those ration books you took? The ones I asked about when I was here earlier? Do you still have them?"

"We do. Why?" MacKinnon asked.

"Well, see we, I mean I, was hoping to borrow them."

"No way. Even if I wanted to, they're in the evidence locker. I can't get them out."

"Not even just a few?" I checked with Lee, who held up eight fingers. "Say about eight."

The detective narrowed his eyes. "What for?"

I hesitated, then told him about our scheme.

"Absolutely not." MacKinnon glared at me, then Lee, who shrugged and said nothing. "Here I was thinking you were doing pretty well for yourself. I can't believe you'd put yourself in danger like this. And you." He stabbed his finger at Lee. "Letting her do it. That doesn't make you a very responsible friend."

Lee grimaced. "Detective, you've met Betty. I understand you worked with her last month on something up at Bell. Do you honestly think I had a say? Best I could do was tag along in case it all went off the rails."

Detective MacKinnon grumbled in response.

"Be reasonable, Detective." I had to get those ration books or I was sunk. "You've got the books. I know where the guys who gave 'em to George Linden are."

"You said. At the South Michigan bridge. We'll have to stake out that location, that's all."

"Well, you could. 'Cept I already know how to get in touch with 'em."

MacKinnon's eyebrows bunched together. "You told me you only saw the men. How does that give you information on how to contact them?"

Lee broke in again. "We talked to 'em. Did she leave that part out?"

MacKinnon's language woulda made Pop flinch.

I wasn't gonna be turned away. "Okay, so I didn't tell you everything. Point is, I told Tall Man—"

"Who is that?" MacKinnon's face had turned an interesting shade of purple.

"He's the guy who looks like he's in charge. Anyway, I told him I could get the books, all forty-eight, and he said I should leave a message at this bar to contact him."

"Forty-eight? We seized forty-five books."

Well, damn. I'd thought it was a whole new delivery, but George must've had enough time to sell a few of them. No matter. Not like Tall Man was going to get the chance to count 'em anyway. In my head, I brushed aside the numbers. "Never mind. Here's the plan. You give me eight books. I need 'em for the top layer in the box 'cause I can't fake the cover printing. I'll dummy up the bottom layers so it feels like the box is full of books. I'll send the message and when he tells me to come, you follow along. I'll give Tall Man the goods and get his information. You get to make a bust for war profiteering and you get the same information about George for your investigation. We both win." I shot a sideways look at Lee. "Sounds like a deal, if you ask me."

"It's not the best plan I've ever heard," MacKinnon said. "What if he goes through the box?"

"You'll be there. Hey, you got a better idea?"

MacKinnon closed his eyes and his lips moved again. Maybe he was saying a silent prayer for patience. Mom did that when the boys were being particularly difficult. Then he looked at me and shook his finger in my face. "All right. I'll loan you the books. But if you try and make this exchange without me, so help me I'll arrest you for interfering with a police investigation. Understand?"

"Yes, sir." I didn't doubt he'd do it, too.

***

Like I asked, Detective MacKinnon fetched eight of the books and handed them over. They were wrapped in brown paper. I guessed so his boss didn't know what he was doing. "Remember," he said, holding tight to the books when I tried to take them. "I'm sticking my neck out for you. Don't let me down. This all goes right, it'll be fine. Something goes wrong and I lose these, my captain will have my badge. And your hide."

"I'll leave the message at the bar later today, but I don't know that Tall Man will get in touch with me right away. 'Course it's Sunday and the place might be closed, but I'll do what I can."

"You call me the minute he does." He wrote down a number on a little card. "Your family has a telephone, don't you? I expect a call. No striking out on your own with this."

"Yes, sir. I will." I took the books and the card, and left.

Lee and I went back behind my house. Cat watched us from his perch on the back step. We cut stacks of newspaper so they fit in the box real tight, then we laid the books from Detective MacKinnon on top. As a last check, Lee closed the box, picked it up, and shook it. "Sounds good and I think it's about the right weight. If Tall Man, as you call him, shakes this box, it had better be what he expects."

"You think he'll check that close?"

"I dunno." Lee set down the box. "He doesn't expect any trickery from you. He'll definitely open the box to see what's in it, but he might not do anything beyond that."

"Let's hope not." I looked up as Dot came into the backyard. "You're back. What did you find?"

"I'm not sure I found anything."

"Did he see you?"

"Maybe, but I did like you said. I looked in the windows of a store like I was checking things out. For all Freddie Linden knew, I was just another shopper out for the afternoon." She sat next to Cat and tickled his chin. Then she pointed at the box. "What's that?"

"We'll tell you in a minute. What about Freddie Linden?"

"He's weird." She went back to tickling Cat, who purred and stretched his neck so Dot could get at more of it.

Lee lit a cigarette. "How so?"

"He's got a job, don't he? I know it's Sunday, but he didn't go nowhere near anyplace that looked like he worked there. He stopped at a butcher's, got some sausages, then walked in circles. Down Clinton, all the way to Fillmore, up Fillmore to Oneida. Around the block back to Clinton, and back over to Fillmore. Then home. Like he didn't have a care in the world. It was crazy."

Clinton and Fillmore, that's where the bar was. "Did he go into a bar?"

"Not for long, but yeah. It's more like a tavern, I think they serve food. I didn't want to follow him in case he saw me. He hadn't reacted at all when I was trailing him, so I don't think he recognized me, but what business do I have in a tavern?" She patted Cat on his head and dusted off her hands. Cat meowed in protest.

"Did you go into the tavern after Freddie left?" Lee asked. He had tensed during her recitation. "You're sure he didn't see you?"

"No. I didn't want to lose him. But he wasn't in there very long, a minute maybe even less." She chewed her lip a bit. "He sure didn't act like he saw me. Like I told you. Not a care in the world. He wouldn't be that way if he thought he was being followed, would he?"

Lee relaxed a smidge. The boy could say whatever he liked, but I knew he was smitten and not with me. He and Dot were perfect for each other. But playing matchmaker would have to wait until I'd cleared my plate.

A minute was plenty of time to drop off a note if he'd written it ahead of time. It wasn't illegal to go into a bar. If Freddie had left a message for Tall Man, the bartender wasn't likely to tell me. He was prob'ly on Tall Man's payroll. "You did good, Dot," I said.

She pointed. "Your turn. What's in the box?"

Lee and I told her about our plan to meet Tall Man. "I guess that means I gotta run over to Clinton and Fillmore. If I leave now, I'll be back by dinner."

"I woulda left the note for you if you'd said something."

"I wasn't sure I could get Detective MacKinnon to play ball." I looked for a place to hide the box. I didn't need Mom or Mary Kate finding it before I was ready for my meeting. I shoved it behind the garbage, which wouldn't get picked up until next Thursday. I was sure Tall Man would contact me before then. "If Tall Man asks who left the note, I want him to recognize my description. Plus, you've done enough with tailing Freddie."

Lee leaned on the house. "You think it's possible Freddie killed his cousin over these ration books?"

"Yeah, what about the Bund?" Dot asked.

"I've met the guys in the Bund and I think they've got as much in the way of smarts as a box of rocks. Sabotage and murder are way beyond them."

Dot and Lee glanced at each other, then back to me.

"I think it's very likely Freddie wanted in on the whole black market scheme. He wants the money. Anne told us he's got expensive tastes and he as much as said he'd do it in a heartbeat if he could get away with it." I scooped up Cat and nuzzled him, then let him leap down to the ground. "I go back to the fact you gotta get close to someone to stab. That and Detective MacKinnon told me George apparently didn't try to defend himself."

"He trusted his killer," Lee said.

"Either a close friend or a relative," Dot added.

"Exactly." I fished coins from my pocket and checked for bus fare. "Hopefully I'll find out which tonight."

Chapter 34

Lee insisted on going with me. "Twice you've gone out on your own and you're lucky nothing happened. I'm going."

We didn't talk. I stared out the window as we rode the bus to our destination. The weather might be warm, but the sun was going down early, same as it always did this time of year. It'd be close to dark by the time I got home. I'd spent a lot of time on the bus lately. I wondered if I could make the walk faster. Prob'ly not.

We got off at East Eagle and Fillmore, and chose to walk to the rest of the way. It would give me a chance to check the place out as well as collect my thoughts. I needed to be at the top of my game. The note I'd written to Tall Man before I left home was in my pocket. "Your package is ready" is all I'd said. I hadn't given him my name so signing it was pointless. How many deliveries from a girl could he be expecting anyway?

Dot's description of the place as a tavern was accurate. What Pop would call a "working man's establishment." Reasonably well lit, there were a couple of tables in the middle of the room. Booths lined the back wall. It was a place I coulda gone on my own, no sweat. The wood was darkened with smoke and being rubbed by countless hands. Tarnished brass rails were on the walls. The seat cushions in the booths were worn thin at the edges, so they showed white against the maroon. There were taps at the bar for beer, Budweiser, Labatt's, Molson, all staples of the Buffalo bar scene, what with us being so close to Canada and all. An older guy with a bushy beard was at the bar talking to the lone bartender, a guy who looked old enough to be in the service during the Great War, slick black hair going gray at the sides and a heavy, grizzled five o'clock shadow. One of those guys who needed to shave twice a day just to come close to "clean shaven."

He curled his lip when we entered. "We don't serve dames and this ain't a place for romance. Now scram."

"I have a message," I said.

"Yeah, for who?"

I didn't have a name. "The tall man." Lee waited by the door, hand in his pocket, as I walked up to the bar. I made sure to leave a lot of space between me and the old guy, in case he wasn't just a drunk who started throwing them back before dinner.

The bartender scowled and moved toward me. His limp was worse than Lee's. "Give it to me."

I handed over the paper with my note.

"Wait here." He gimped off through a door behind the bar.

I didn't say anything while I waited. The old guy studied me with a watery-eyed stare and sipped his beer. I had expected to be told someone would be in touch, not to wait. Did that mean Tall Man was on the property? Would he demand delivery on the spot? That would be uncomfortable.

The bartender came back, the heavy step of his right foot making him sound like a peg-leg pirate. "Tonight, midnight. Same place."

"Wait, did you say tonight?" If that was the case, I'd need to stop at police headquarters before I went home and hope Detective MacKinnon was still in. I wasn't gonna to use the pay phone here and risk being overheard talking to the cops. Boy, would MacKinnon be sore if I wound up having to make this meeting without him.

"Tonight. You got the goods, don't ya? Isn't that why you came here?" The look on the bartender's face said in no uncertain terms that it better be the case.

"Yeah, I just didn't expect a meeting so soon."

"He don't like to wait."

"Right. Well, I'll see you tonight."

He chuckled. "You ain't gonna see me, girlie. But I'm sure you've met Lloyd before and he'll make sure the boss is happy. Least you'd better hope he's happy."

The two men set to laughing. It was all I could do not to run out.

***

We weren't that far from Kaisertown, so I talked Lee into moseying by the garage. The last time I'd talked to Patrick, he'd been up front about how he'd been mad at George and not all that sorry he was dead. But that was a far cry from doing the killing.

"Good thing I came with you," Lee said.

"I've done this before on my own. I can't always have a buddy."

"Yeah, yeah. I told you. You were lucky. Third time's the charm and all that, and I'm not talkin' about good things."

Maybe I was wrong, but Patrick didn't feel like a killer. Not that I'd put it past an Irishman to get violent, but there was too much of the weasel in Patrick's face. He'd talk. He might even throw a few haymakers. More like he'd set his bully boys, Marcus and William, to the task of roughing someone up. But killing, in particular stabbing? That required a level of cold-bloodedness I didn't think Patrick had in him.

Marcus was locking the door when we got there. He looked smaller without his buddy. He wouldn't give me the time of day if the others were around, but maybe I'd have better luck if he was on his own. "Marcus. Fancy seeing you here."

He stared at me, not a flicker of recognition in his eyes.

"Betty. You know, the friend of George's sister? I talked to you the other day when you were with William and Patrick."

That must have sparked something for him. "Yeah, I remember now." His voice was soft for such a big guy. "You worked with Georgie's sister."

"Right."

"Bell Aircraft." He sounded ridiculously proud he'd remembered. Then he frowned. "You accused us of faking stuff and, and..." He fumbled for the word.

"Sabotage. It means breaking stuff on purpose."

"But we didn't do nothing like that." His heavy black eyebrows beetled.

"I believe you. I have another question. This one's about George."

232

"What about him?"

"Between you and me, how mad was Patrick? Really, really mad or just a little bit?"

"He wasn't happy." Marcus's expression had gone from anger to puzzlement, as though I was moving too fast for him. "See, Patrick is the guy with all the ideas, but he said no one was gonna listen to an Irishman about how they should support the Germans."

"He didn't ask you or William to be the front man?" Lee asked.

"Nah, he said we was too stupid looking." It was a matter-of-fact statement. Maybe Marcus was too used to being called stupid for it to hurt. "Patrick said we needed a good-looker, a German one, and someone who could sound good when he talked. That was why we picked George."

"What about George's cousin?" I asked.

"His cousin?"

"Freddie Linden. Looked a lot like George, 'cept his hair is a bit darker and he's a little shorter."

"Oh him. Nah. He didn't like the Bund 'cause of the leader who went to jail. He said we was a bunch of losers."

Marcus fell silent. After a moment, I prompted him. "Eventually George lost interest."

"Yeah." Marcus scuffed his feet.

"He wanted to go into business with a Jew."

"Yeah. Joseph sounded kinda nice, but he's a Jew. How nice could he be?"

Very nice, as a matter of fact, but I didn't press the point. "Patrick hunted him down and they had a fight, didn't they? He didn't mean to kill George, things just got outta hand." I was spinning the story for him, but I hoped that with his guard down, Marcus would either confirm or deny things without asking questions.

He cocked his head, a puzzled glint in his eyes. "Naw, it couldn't have been Patrick. I mean, yeah. He was real mad, but he couldn't have been the one who killed George."

Lee frowned. "Why not?"

Marcus hung his head. "Patrick and I, we got ourselves arrested for

233

trespassing. We were in jail that night."

I shot Lee a look. "Where did this happen?"

"Bethlehem Steel." Marcus continued to stare at his gigantic feet. "We went back to pass out more flyers. Someone called the police and they got us all. I had to call my ma to come to Lackawanna to post bail. She didn't like that."

"I'm sure she didn't." Lackawanna had its own police, but it couldn't be that hard for Detective MacKinnon to confirm Marcus's story. "What about William? Was he with you?"

"Nah, his ma made him stay home. William ain't afraid of most people, but his ma is real scary when she's mad. I'd be scared of her if I was William."

"Thanks, Marcus." I turned to walk away and Lee followed me.

"I'm real sorry about George," he said. He sniffled and I turned at the sound. Was the big lug crying? He was. "He was kind to me once. It's too bad he got himself killed."

I stood stock-still as the lumbering Marcus wiped his nose. Tears made it all shiny. Well, I'll be darned. The only thing that could have surprised me more was learning Hitler had sent Winston Churchill a birthday present.

Chapter 35

L ee and I managed to finish everything I wanted to do, including talk to MacKinnon, and got home in time for dinner. Afterwards, I met up with Dot and Lee outside Lee's place. Dot wanted to go with us to the river that night, but Lee and I talked her out of it. "This guy's never seen you. I don't want to spook him with a new face. And I don't want you getting in trouble with your folks if it don't go as planned." The last argument proved to be the winner, but I had to agree to fill her in on all the details on Monday. Given Lee's expression when she proposed going, I would have tied her up if I had to. "There is one thing you can do for me, though."

"Name it."

"You were at all three accidents. I want you to go back and think real hard about who was around. See if you can remember anything now that some time has passed and things are calmer. You know, jog a memory or two."

"Sure thing, Betty." She was such a doll.

I gave the box of fake books to Lee for safekeeping. Then I went home and did all my regular things. Once Mary Kate was sound asleep, I pulled on the same clothes I'd worn last time and snuck out.

Cat met me at the corner of the house. "*Meow?*"

"Go back to doing whatever it is you do at night. I don't need you waking up the neighborhood. Go on, shoo."

He stalked off, tail in the air like I'd insulted him or something. In cat speak, I prob'ly had.

Lee was waiting for me at the corner, box in his arms. "You all set?"

"Yep."

"You bring that switchblade again?"

"'Course I did. I'm not dumb, you know."

He raised his eyebrows, but wisely kept his mouth shut.

We didn't talk and maintained a brisk pace down to the bridge. I considered asking Lee if he wanted me to carry the box, but decided against it. He wouldn't appreciate me talking like I didn't think he was up to the task.

When we got to the bridge, things were quiet as a graveyard. The moon slid behind a bank of clouds, only to come out a few minutes later and spill silvery light over the scene. The only sound was the lap of water against the shore, the ever-present smell of Cheerioats in the air. No sign of the cops or Tall Man and his gang.

Lee put the box on the ground and stood over it. "Where are they?" His fingers tapped against his leg.

"Who?"

"The cops, that's who. You think they'd be early."

"Shh." I craned my neck, looking. Not a soul could be seen. They were either not here or hiding real good. "We won't see 'em until they're ready."

"What if they're not here?"

"MacKinnon said they'd come. We gotta believe they will. I'm not keen to hand over a box full of newspaper. Tall Man gets this back, he's sure to discover the contents. Thanks to your wallet, he knows where to find us. Or where to send Lloyd."

"'Cause that's so much better."

I don't know how long we stood there. Long enough that I saw a bad guy every time a shadow moved. My nerves were like piano wire. Didn't any of these guys know how to be on time? What a time for the temperature to go back to something like normal. My hands were frozen and my toes felt like tiny ice cubes inside my shoes. Good thing I'd worn my winter coat and a wool muffler. If Tall Man or Lloyd didn't show up soon, Lee and I were gonna freeze into a couple of statues

The rattle of an engine cut the night air. I elbowed Lee. A car pulled up, and I recognized the Chevy emblem in the moonlight. The headlights were off. Lloyd got out of the back seat, looked around, then said "Coast's clear" to someone inside. A moment later, Tall Man emerged from the other side of the car. "Good evening. I see you didn't have much difficulty contacting me."

"Not especially." I glanced around. "Don't you guys own a watch? The guy at the bar said midnight."

"I wanted to make sure we were alone." Tall Man tipped his head toward Lloyd, who melted away into the night. Looking for people who shouldn't be there. Those cops better be good at hiding 'cause I didn't want to be in the middle of the gun fight that was sure to happen if they were found.

Tall Man pointed at the box "Is that the merchandise?"

"Yeah," I said. Like last night, Lee looked like he had lockjaw.

"Bring it here."

Lee started to pick up the box, but I stopped him and took it myself. If our friend found out the box was full of fakes, I didn't want him striking Lee.

"Put it down and back up."

I placed the box at Tall Man's feet and returned to Lee's side. I held my breath while Tall Man opened the box. Please don't look at everything, I thought. Then I said a quick prayer. I needed all the help I could get.

But Tall Man only glanced at the top layer. Seeing the ration books, he grunted and refolded the flaps. "Where are the C-cards?"

"I couldn't get those," I said. "The cops had already handed them over to the feds."

"Pity. Oh well, there's more where they came from."

"You said you had information about George Linden."

"I did." A grin played around Tall Man's thin lips.

Lee spoke up, voice harsh. "You gonna tell us, or do you plan to welch and have Lloyd shoot us?"

"Tut, tut. How very rude of you."

"I don't trust what I can't see."

"Very well." Tall Man beckoned with a gloved hand. Lloyd came out of the shadows near one of the bridge pilings. "George Linden. What a shame.

He was my best distributor."

"A little bird told me he was stealing from you," I said.

"Unfortunately, yes. A C-card for his personal use, a couple of ration books. We had a very stern talk about that."

I wondered if "stern talk" was code for Lloyd had roughed George up. Prob'ly not, though. Tall Man wouldn't want too many questions asked if George suddenly had broken fingers or a black eye. But I was sure it had included threats against Mr. and Mrs. Linden, and Anne, too.

"Anyway, water under the bridge as you might say."

"That doesn't tell me who killed him," I said. My voice sounded a bit on the sharp side.

Lee coughed into his hand to cover up the word. "Cops?"

It was a good question. Where the heck were they and what were they waiting for?

"I'm afraid I don't know the answer to that."

"You lied to me," I said. "You said you had information."

"I said I didn't know who killed him." Tall Man tugged on his gloves and nodded toward Lloyd, who picked up the box and headed for the car. "My information is more along the lines of possibility. Before George was killed, his cousin came to me."

"Freddie?"

"He wanted in on the operation, to be a distributor like George. I said I didn't have any current openings, but I'd keep him in mind if one came up."

"He prob'ly wasn't real happy with that answer."

"No." Tall Man smoothed his overcoat. "I suggested he talk to George, see if a partnership could be arranged."

"Did he?"

"My dear, I have no idea. Of course George was killed only a few days later, which means I do indeed have an opening. Now that the product has been returned, I'll be able to send Lloyd around and see if the young man is still interested. His cousin's death may have put him off the job. The danger, you understand."

Unless the danger to George had come from Freddie in the first place.

Lloyd closed the trunk. Tall Man moved to the car and motioned to the driver. "It's been a pleasure dealing with you. I'm always happy to make room in my operation for smart people such as yourself. If you fancy making some money, leave a message, same way as you did today." He opened the car door.

If Detective MacKinnon didn't hurry, he was gonna miss his chance.

Spotlights lit up the area and uniformed cops materialized out of nowhere, guns drawn. "Stop where you are. Put your hands against the car." MacKinnon's voice was deafening. He must have been using a megaphone. The driver bolted, but ran right into a couple of officers. Lloyd spun in place and took a couple steps backward, but another cop grabbed him and wrestled him to the ground. Tall Man merely grimaced and held up his hands, as two more cops covered him with their guns.

While the uniforms cuffed Tall Man, Lloyd, and the driver, MacKinnon strolled out from behind a warehouse.

"Nice of you to show up," I said. My heart was going like gangbusters, something I hadn't noticed until that moment.

"I've been here the whole time. I saw you and Mr. Tillotson arrive as a matter of fact."

Lee's face turned red. "Yeah? How long were you gonna let that go on? What if he'd had his goon shoot us?"

"No need to shout." MacKinnon grinned. "If there had been any hint of a threat to you or Miss Ahern, my officers had instructions to intervene. As that didn't happen, I wanted to get as much information out of the suspect as possible. You two did an excellent job."

Lee sputtered, but I laid a hand on his arm. "We did an excellent job of doing your dirty work, you mean." Lee muttered an oath and stomped off. His leg must've been hurting, because his limp was more noticeable.

MacKinnon gazed after him. "Is he okay?"

"Yeah, he's prob'ly just a little stiff from all the walking and standing, never mind carrying that box." I poked the detective in the arm. "It was mean, you know. Not telling us you were here."

"Had you known, you would have given us away by looking around or through your body language. This way, you didn't have to act."

It made sense, I s'pose, but it was still unfair. "By the way, did you get a chance to check those names I gave you?"

"The arrests in Lackawanna? Yes. Marcus Hoffman and Patrick Flanagan were arrested for criminal trespass on the day George Linden was murdered. They spent the night as guests of the Lackawanna police."

"So it wasn't Marcus, it wasn't Patrick, and it wasn't that guy or his goon." I nodded to where Tall Man, Lloyd, and the driver were standing while cops searched the car.

"No. But thanks to you and Mr. Tillotson, I'll be paying another visit to Freddie Linden tomorrow."

"I really am mad at you, you know. I oughta bill the city for services."

MacKinnon chuckled. "Good luck with that."

Chapter 36

Monday morning, I rushed through my chores, then I trotted over to Dot's house. Even if Lee hadn't been working, I'd have left him alone. I suspected he was still sore at me after last night.

Dot, however, made a perfect audience for the story. "I can't believe the cops didn't tip you off. I bet Lee wasn't very happy."

"You got that right." We were sitting on the front step. Cat appeared and pawed at my leg until I reached down and scratched behind his ears.

"For someone who said she doesn't like cats very much, you sure spend a lot of time fussing over that one." Dot held out her hand and Cat obliged with a head bump.

"He's grown on me." If I ever opened a real office, having a cat around might help clients feel more comfortable. Unless cats made 'em sneeze or something. "Did you think about those accidents like I asked?"

"Yep. Just a sec." Dot got up, went in the house, and returned with a pad. "I wrote some notes, tried to put together a timeline."

"That's swell." I took the pad. She'd gone above and beyond. For each day, she'd listed out times of when stuff had happened and who she remembered seeing.

"Okay, here's the first thing. The engine fire." She resumed her seat. "Nothing much happened in the morning. Florence was one of the first to leave for lunch. She didn't dawdle once the whistle blew, and she was in the cafeteria when I got there. Afterward, we left together, so I don't see how she had much time."

"What about the others?"

"Alice and Helen are kinda the same. They were behind me, but they were together the whole lunch hour. But here's where it's interesting." She tapped the page. "As we were walking out, Rose said she'd forgotten something and went back. Then I had to go to the ladies' before I could get my lunch. When I came back from the lockers, I saw Catherine. She looked like she was coming from the assembly building, but she left with the rest of us, so she musta gone back, too."

"What about Rose?"

Dot wrapped her arms around her legs and drew her knees up to her chin. "She didn't come into the cafeteria until after I got there. She said it was 'cause she couldn't find what she was looking for."

"Which was?"

"She didn't say, just that it wasn't important. But she was gone plenty long enough to light a cigarette and set up the fire. Plus she smokes Camels and wears red lipstick. If you're right about her having relatives back in Italy who might support Mussolini, there's your motive."

That was two good suspects for that day: Rose and Catherine. "What about the dolly chain accident?"

"I think that one was set up. That rod didn't come from the main assembly area. We all left for lunch around the same time. Catherine was the slowpoke that day. I don't know where she fell behind, but she didn't get to lunch for a good five minutes after the rest of us."

Dot was right about the rod. Where would it have come from? I tried to remember. "There was a whole pallet of struts in the yard that morning." There'd been discussion on how best to move them and when. "I think Rose said the bundles were heavy, so they were gonna have to get a forklift to carry them. Which means she must have gone over to inspect them." She could have filched one. I hadn't seen her, but that only meant she could have taken it unseen.

"And she left lunch early, said she had to use the ladies'. Plus, remember? A couple of the girls said they saw someone with dark hair, or wearing a dark bandanna, skulking around the assembly line."

"Both Rose and Catherine have dark hair. Doesn't Rose wear a dark blue bandanna?"

Dot nodded, face solemn.

"What about the others?"

Dot stretched out and Cat climbed into her lap. "I don't remember anybody being missing. Not that they weren't, but I didn't notice them."

"But that means a lot because if someone who was supposed to be there wasn't, you'd have noticed that." I thought a moment. "As long as the saboteur stole the rod from that pile early and hid it, anyone might have jammed it in. Except it wasn't until we fired things back up after lunch that there was a problem."

"I can't work out how any of the others had the time."

Rose and Catherine were still looking good. I was honest enough to admit that I didn't want it to be Rose. She was a hard worker and smart. Sure, she had a temper, but only when people made dumb mistakes or were lazy. "Rose and Catherine are friends. Do you think Rose knows Cyrillic?"

"I dunno. Why?"

"That note. I'm betting not many of us know Russian, so writing it in Cyrillic is a good choice. Maybe they're in it together and that's their code."

Dot cocked her head. "Perhaps. Could also be Catherine who wrote the note or someone used Cyrillic to try and frame her."

"Hmm. But if Rose is the culprit, would she frame a friend?"

"Are they really friends?" Dot shrugged. "Lots of options."

So many possibilities. "Is this all?"

"No, the last incident, the paint fire." Dot played with Cat's tail, but she must've pulled a little too hard because he hissed and jumped away. "Sorry, kitty. Anyway, here's where it gets tricky. I worked paint that day. I'll swear on a stack of Bibles none of the others did."

"Not Rose or Catherine?"

"Nope. I don't know where they were, but it wasn't the paint building."

"Don't tell me we've got another saboteur."

"I don't think so." She flipped the pad to another sheet. "This is a sketch of the building. The fire started here." She pointed to a corner. "At first, you'd think someone would have to be inside the building, but there's a window. Underneath is where they store thinners and things that need ventilation. I'm thinking someone could light up say a rag or bit of rope, or even a cigarette, toss it in the window, and you've got a fire."

I studied the drawing. "All they'd need to know is the thinners are there."

"Exactly. Anybody who's ever worked paint knows that. I'm sure both Rose and Catherine fall into that category."

"And even if they didn't, not like it's a big secret." I leaned over to give her a hug. "Dot, did I ever tell you you're amazing? Rose and Catherine. Those are the names that keep coming up."

"Aww, don't mention it." She scuffed her feet, but the gleam in her eye was pleased. "I can't believe it of Rose. She's always works so hard. Why would she do this?"

"I dunno. All I can think of is the family she has back in Italy, that they're fighting for the Axis. Or she's a secret Mussolini fan." I'd never had a political conversation with Rose. Unlike Catherine, she didn't talk about the war much. I'd always thought this was nothing more than a good job for her. Then again, I could be wrong.

We sat in silence for a few minutes. Cat had clearly forgiven us, because he had come back and was pestering us equally for attention. Thinking of the word "cat" made me focus on Catherine. She was pretty clear that she didn't like the Nazis, but she disliked the Soviets with equal, if not greater, feeling. Why was that? I couldn't just bust out and ask her "Is your family White Russian?" but there had to be a way of getting to the bottom of her dislike.

Dot broke the silence. "What are we gonna do?"

I turned to a fresh piece of paper. "Now? We're gonna set a trap."

Chapter 37

From Dot's, I went to Lee's house and left a note for him to meet me at the drugstore near the corner of Clinton and South Ogden as soon as he got home. Then I hopped a bus to Kaisertown. I knew Freddie worked at the deli between Clinton and Weimar. I had to hope he was there today.

The Linden family had money in Germany. Enough that they'd skedaddled to keep what they had when it became clear the Nazis were on their way to taking over. Anne and George remembered that life. Did Freddie? If his family had been in the same situation it would definitely be a step down being a counter boy in a neighborhood deli. It was easy to see where he'd get jealous if he saw his cousin with dough. Jealous enough to kill? Freddie played the role of the almost-brother real well. Somehow I had to pierce that shell and pull it back to see what was underneath.

I got to the deli and peered in the window. Freddie was behind the counter wrapping something in paper for a fat, old, gray-haired woman. I watched him hand it over, all smiles. Then he set about wiping down the top of the case.

I entered the store and set the bells over the door to jangling. I went straight to the counter. "Do I need to take a number or something?"

Freddie looked up. "Betty. I'm surprised to see you here. I thought you lived over in the First Ward."

"I do."

"Don't they have delis over there?"

"I wanted to try something different." I made a show of studying all the

245

different meats and sausages. "To be honest, I wanted to talk to you, too."

He paused, rag in hand. "What about?"

"Kinda public here. Can you take a break?"

He studied me a second, then tossed the cloth aside. "I'm going outside for a couple minutes Mr. Mueller." He didn't wait for an answer, but came around the case and disappeared through a side door.

I followed him. "Must be nice working for a boss who doesn't mind you walking out."

"I'll be back." He leaned against the building. "What's this all about?"

"Your cousin, George. He was into black market goods. But you knew that."

Freddie stiffened. "I don't know what you're talking about." His voice was icy.

In my previous dealings with Freddie, I'd pegged him as arrogant. A bit snobby. He wouldn't give information to just anyone, 'specially not a working-class Irish girl. But he'd want to *appear* important, maybe more important than he was. Maybe if I goaded him a bit, he'd spill just to make himself feel better. "Oh, come off it. You said the two of you were like brothers. Why wouldn't he have shared that information? I mean I could see him not wanting his folks or his sister to know, but you?"

He licked his lips. "George was getting ready to set up a business with his friend, Joseph Weinstein. One day he mentioned he needed money and it seemed like he had it only a couple weeks later. I wondered."

"Plus he drove everywhere. Didn't you ever think about where the gasoline came from?"

"Sometimes." He narrowed his eyes. He wasn't at the breaking point.

"Your family and George's came to the States together. They had money. Maybe you didn't? Maybe you had to work and you saw George with all this stuff. Pretty natural to think why not me?"

Freddie pressed his lips together and I could almost see the steam coming from his ears, like in the cartoons they showed before the pictures.

"You never asked him about it? There's a war going on. He doesn't even have a job." *C'mon, say something.*

"I asked once. He said he had sources he couldn't talk about."

"Illegal sources, you mean."

Freddie'd gone real still, barely moving. "What's your point with all this?"

"I'm curious. Like a cat, you might say." I took a step back and leaned against the opposite wall, arms folded hoping I looked easy and relaxed.

"You know what they say about curiosity and the cat."

I chuckled. "Yeah, I do. But cats have nine lives, too. Anyway, I find it nuts you didn't feel a tiny bit jealous, if you know what I mean. There's your cousin, practically your brother after your folks died, and he's got all this dough. He's not sharing, and you're busting your hump down here wrapping sausages. I'd get tired of it after a while." I paused. "You ever ask him to give you some? To let you in on the action"

Freddie didn't answer.

"Go fifty-fifty? Even sixty-forty? I mean, you had to know there was enough for both of you. You must have the patience of a saint if you never asked. Saint Frederick. Is there a Saint Frederick? I'd have to look that up—"

"Shut up!" Freddie's face was flushed and his breath whistled in his nose. "Yes, all right? I asked. He had money for movies and girls, nice clothes. He drove that damn car all over Kaisertown, showing off. I knew he wasn't getting it from a job, so I asked. He told me he could get me a deal, but no can do when I asked for a piece of the action. It wasn't his call. He wouldn't even introduce me to his supplier." He took a step toward me.

I took in the fire in his eyes, his heavy breathing. Suddenly goading Freddie didn't seem like a smart play. Crap. If I was right, I was standing in an alley with a killer. Had anybody seen us go out? Could anyone hear us? It was too risky to stick around and find out. "You know what? Never mind. I gotta run." I hurried back through the deli and out the front door, leaving him in my dust. Time to try something else.

***

I headed down to a pharmacy on South Ogden across the street from the garage. I checked their clock. It was not quite one. I had hours to wait for Lee, assuming he decided to join me. He prob'ly would. I bought myself a

Coke and a box of Cracker Jacks and settled in to wait. If the clerk threw me out, I'd have to find another place.

Lee walked in shortly before one-thirty. "Just a sec." He went and got his own snacks, then sat down next to me at the counter.

"Didn't expect you for hours yet. You leave work early? Don't tell me you got yourself fired."

"Nah." He took a swig of his Coke, then belched. "I figured you might be up to something, so I said I wasn't feeling too good and left."

"I can give you some cash to make up for the lost wages."

He shook his head as he took another gulp, then opened his bag of potato chips. "What's the plan?"

I brought him up to speed on my talk with Freddie. "He didn't come out and admit anything, but I gotta believe he's involved in this somehow. He was definitely jealous enough, especially after George told him to take a hike."

"Then what are we doing here?"

I pointed at the garage. "Marcus and Patrick have solid alibis, but William is still a suspect. I don't really think he's our guy, but we need to cross him off the list."

"How do you plan on doing that?"

"Trickery of course." I finished off my Coke and Cracker Jacks. The prize turned out to be a plastic soldier. One of my brothers would like that, so I slipped it in my pocket. Lee followed me out the door and across the street.

I'd seen William and Marcus go into the garage while I waited, so I knew they were inside. I planned to play it by ear. I knew Marcus had been in jail the night George was killed. William didn't seem all that bright, so tripping him up oughta be easy.

I opened the door without knocking. "Hey guys, I...what's going on?"

They were piling stuff into boxes. All the flyers, stacks of plain paper, and whatever other junk was lying around. A stack of boxes was by the desk, prob'ly already filled. Marcus paused in his task. "What does it look like? We're clearing out."

"Why's that?" Lee asked, peeking into the top box in the stack.

248

Marcus shrugged. "Bund's finished. The cops busted Patrick last night for sticking up a liquor store. He was tryin' to get cash for us to keep printing the flyers. 'Cept the owner of the store had a shotgun under the counter. Held him there 'til the cops showed. We figure there ain't no point in continuing without him."

William grunted and hefted another box onto the stack, which swayed.

Lee took a step aside. "You might wanna start another pile, pal. So someone doesn't get hurt when that one falls over."

William grunted again, took the top box, and started another tower.

"What do you two want anyway?" Marcus asked. He'd gone back to emptying the drawers of the battered wooden desk. A few chewed pencils and some rubber erasers were scattered on the top, along with a ball of rubber bands.

Marcus wasn't even tryin' to play the tough guy. Without Patrick, he seemed to be sort of deflated. Lost. Both of 'em. Part of me wondered why they'd bother with all the junk, but I focused on my task. "Same thing I did last time. I've a few questions about George Linden."

Marcus frowned. "I told you, me and Patrick were in jail that night."

"Yeah, but what about him?" I pointed at William. "What were you doing?"

William blinked, eyes a bit dull. Clearly not a lot of thought going on in that noggin. "What d'ya mean?"

"George Linden." Lee rapped on the box for emphasis. "We already know he was part of your group, then he had a change of heart. We know that didn't sit well with Patrick. Your buddy there has an alibi. So does Patrick. What about you?"

William's mouth hung open a bit. "What about me?"

Oh brother. I was surprised this guy managed to get his shoes on the right feet in the morning. How could he have killed George? But I plowed on. "Here's what I'm thinking. You knew George had scrammed. Patrick was mad. He sent you to talk George into coming back, the two of you argued, and bam! you shot him. How close am I?"

"I didn't shoot nobody." William's bass voice was pouty, like Jimmy when Mom told him no at the store. "I don't even got a gun, for pete's sake."

Lee and I exchanged a look. Either he didn't know George had been stabbed, although I couldn't think why he wouldn't, or he was playing dumb. I took one look in the big oaf's face. He wasn't playing. He was dumb.

"My mistake," I said. "Guess we gotta keep looking. Let's go." Lee and I headed for the door.

"Is that all?" William asked, clearly puzzled. It was prob'ly a common thing for him.

Lee opened the door. "Yep, that's all we needed. Thanks, fellas." He held the door for me, and we walked out to the parking lot. The sun was out, but the temperature was dropping. A few seagulls that were pushing their luck with the good weather poked around for scraps. Lee turned up the collar of his coat. "Well, that was a waste of time."

"Not really." I stared at the gull. "It isn't William. That leaves one suspect standing."

"Freddie."

"Uh-huh." We needed to get him to confess. To do that, I was gonna need Anne's help.

Chapter 38

Lee and I talked strategy on our way to Anne's house. "One thing's for sure," he said. "Freddie Linden is a hell of a lot smarter than William Dunkel. We're gonna need a real trap for him."

"I know. And don't ask. I'm not sure what that looks like yet. We gotta talk to Anne."

Iron gray clouds had come in while we walked. I took a deep breath. The air lacked that dry, yet damp, quality that meant snow. The longer the snow took to show up, the more likely it would be a doozy of a storm. I made a mental note to find our shovel and make a warm hole for Cat to hide in when it did.

The windows at the Linden house were covered by curtains, the grass of the tiny front yard still sorta green because of the mild weather, although it was dying at the edges. Mr. Linden answered the door. "*Ja?* Oh, Miss Ahern. You are looking for Anne, yes?"

"If she's here. This is a friend of mine, Lee Tillotson."

Mr. Linden held the door open. "Anne!" he called. "Visitors." He turned to us. "A cup of tea, maybe? We have a little coffee, if you'd rather have that. It is not even mostly chicory."

I glanced at Lee, who shook his head. "No thanks, Mr. Linden. We're okay."

He sighed. "Why do you want to speak to Anne?"

"I'm hoping she can help us. You heard from the cops?"

"Nothing. Anne, she works all day, trying not to dwell on things. I would have hoped we would know who did this to our son by now, but maybe we'll never know, *ja*?" He turned as Anne entered the hallway.

"Betty." She wore an apron and wiped her hands on a towel. "Who's this?"

"A friend. Lee, this is Anne Linden." I glanced at him. "Uh, your pop said you've been working hard. Maybe we can give you a hand."

She tilted her head. "That's all right. It's not difficult work. I know you didn't come all the way over to see me only to help me pack up my dead brother's belongings. You wouldn't have brought a friend for that, either."

Drat, why couldn't she get the hint. "Oh, we didn't come over special." I fumbled around for an excuse. "See, Lee's mom has a weakness for those strudels and, uh, we came to get some. Then I realized you lived nearby, so I figured I'd introduce you to Lee. I've told him all about you and the, uh, things we've talked about. He wanted to meet you."

"I did?" Lee asked.

I stepped back, right onto his foot.

He sucked in his breath. "Yeah, I did."

I prayed that Mr. Linden was too good-natured to notice the awkward tone of the conversation. "Why don't you let us come help you? That way we can catch up and you'll have the chore done in no time. Many hands make light work, my mom says."

Her expression was puzzled, but cleared as she worked through my words. She beckoned us toward the stairs. "Thank you. Freddie finally had some time to sort through George's clothes for what he wanted to keep. I'm boxing up the rest for the St. Vincent de Paul Society."

The room she led us to was small, with one window that looked out the side. A twin bed was in one corner, an open wardrobe half full of shirts and trousers was in the other. Clothes were neatly folded and piled on the bed and a small wooden table that must have served as a desk. A ladder-back wooden chair was pushed under it and a banker's lamp with a green-glass shade was in one corner. She waved at it. "Do either of you need a lamp?"

"Don't you think your father will want that?" I asked.

"No, he has one." Anne's face was pinched and gray, fine lines had settled in around her mouth.

"No one's helping you?"

"Every time Mama looks at anything that used to belong to George, she cries." She went back to folding shirts. "What do you want?"

I brought her up to date on everything I'd learned, including the arrest of George's black-market supplier and Tall Man's info that Freddie had been interested in getting involved.

Anne frowned, but continued to fold. "No, I can't believe it. Freddie? He's always been a stickler for following the rules."

"He as much as admitted it to me," I said.

She dropped the shirt. She recovered quick though. "Okay, so he wanted to make money. What does that have to do with George's death?"

Lee eased down on the bed. "We're wondering if he wanted in the black-market organization bad enough he created an opening."

"You think he killed George?" Anne clutched the shirt, folding forgotten. "No. I don't believe it. I won't believe it. Those two were like brothers. More than brothers."

"Money has a way of coming between a lot of brothers," I said.

The quiet surrounded us, the faint clink of dishes the only noise. Finally, Anne said, "Even if I believed you, what do you want of me? You must want something or you wouldn't be here."

Her reluctance to play along was strange. Sure, she'd only hired me to clear her name, but wouldn't she like to see her brother's killer brought to justice? "We need to put Freddie in a position where he spills his guts. Either he confesses or we learn he didn't do anything." And if he hadn't killed George, we were back to square one, but I didn't tell her that.

"You know him as well as George did," Lee said. "You know the right pressure points, what we can do to make him confess."

She glared at him. "If he has a confession to make. I won't help you beat a lie out of him."

"We're not asking you to," I said. "Anne, I know this has gotta be hard to hear. But Freddie's our best suspect right now."

"I didn't hire you to put my cousin in jail." She threw aside the shirt. "I hired you to help with the situation at Bell."

"Yes, but I told you that might mean finding George's killer."

"Who is not my cousin. Have you made any progress on the job I paid you for, or are you too focused on sending Freddie to prison?"

The words stung. "I have, as a matter of fact. Dot and I have a plan for Tuesday when we go back to work." I didn't bother pointing out that she had been cleared already since she hadn't been a Bell employee when the paint fire happened. I needed her help and that meant not getting her angrier than she already was.

She went back to folding, her face a mask that hid her thoughts. Was she gonna tell us to scram, that we were plain crazy? Or was she gonna help us? It felt like forever, but she finally spoke up. "Fine. I'll help, but I'm not so sure you're going to get what you expect. I simply don't believe Freddie is a killer."

I exchanged a look with Lee. She might not, but we sure did. "Swell. Lee and I were putting the finishing touches on a plan." Slight exaggeration. I chewed my fingernail. "You think you can get Freddie to come over later?"

"Maybe."

"Here's what I'm thinking. We know he's interested in the whole black-market deal. You give him a call and tell him you found another box of ration books the cops missed."

"How will that help?"

Lee nodded. He knew where I was going with this idea. "Tell him you don't know what to do. Should you call the cops or not?"

"Then tell him you can't deal with it anymore," I added. "See what he says. I bet he jumps to help."

"He won't if he sees you two, especially you, Betty," Anne said. "Not after what you told me."

"We'll be hiding," I said. "When he asks you for the box—"

"If he asks for it."

"When. He'll do it. Anyway, then you say something like you can't believe George would do that. Ask if Freddie knew, what he woulda done if someone approached him."

"Basically, you need to get him to say not only would he sell, but he'd do anything for the opportunity," Lee said. "Including bumping off his own cousin."

"I don't know. I hired you to clear me, Betty," Anne said. "Not only do you have nothing to show me on that, but my brother is dead, and now you're trying to convict my cousin. Maybe you just need to give me my money back and we'll call the whole thing off."

What? No. She had to want her good name back, not to mention her job. And what right-thinking sister wouldn't want to know who bumped off her brother? Not being happy to think her cousin was guilty I could understand, but hadn't she said she wanted her name clean even if George had been involved? "Anne, think about it. We almost have an answer. Don't you want to see all of this to the end?"

She frowned.

"I have an older brother. If someone killed him, I'd want that person behind bars. Even if the killer was another relative." I watched her face, still as stone. What was going through her head?

Lee watched the two of us. "Anne, I understand this is a lot to take in. But Betty is right. You need to let it play out. Could be we're wrong and Freddie is innocent. Wouldn't you want to find out?"

At last, Anne nodded. "Very well. What are you going to do?"

Thank goodness. Her lack of excitement about the prospect bothered me a little, but I brushed the feeling aside. "Lee and I will hide. If Freddie says anything that makes him look guilty, we'll jump out and grab him. Then we'll call the cops."

"And if he doesn't?" she asked.

"Then we'll leave and not say another word. I'll give you back your fifty bucks and we're square. Deal?"

"Okay." Anne looked at Lee, doubt all over her face. She'd seen him limp into the room. "You think you can do that? Jump out and hold him?"

Lee grinned. "Oh, yeah. Trust me. I only look gimpy. I can handle anything Freddie decides to throw at me."

Chapter 39

Lee and I killed time helping Anne pack up George's clothes. When she left with a full box, Lee pulled me aside. "This harebrained plan has more holes in it than Swiss cheese. It could put you and Anne in danger if Freddie's really a murderer."

I noticed he left himself out, but didn't say anything. Men. "I know, but it's the best I can come up with on short notice."

He shook his head. "Betty, I love you like a sister, but the next time you get the bright idea to play dime-store detective, you need to read some Raymond Chandler or Dashiell Hammet before you go off all cockeyed. Not just watch movies."

Despite Lee's concern, the plan started off perfect. Anne was a little worried Freddie would want to see the nonexistent box, but I was pretty sure he'd agree to take it sight unseen. Anne called the deli and told Freddie to come over before dinner. "He said he'd be here in about half an hour."

I checked the grandfather clock in the Lindens' living room. It was five o'clock. Should I call Detective MacKinnon now or wait until Freddie had confessed? I'd wait. If I was wrong, or we couldn't get him to 'fess up, MacKinnon wouldn't be all that happy I'd wasted his time.

A thought occurred to me. "We prob'ly should get your folks out of the house," I said. "We don't want them around while we're getting their nephew to admit to killing their son."

"Mama and Papa go over to a friend's house for dinner, cards, and drinks every Monday night." Anne straightened a lace doily on the chair back. "They'll be gone before Freddie gets here."

256

Sure enough, Mr. and Mrs. Linden headed out well before five-thirty, leaving us to wait.

"Here he comes," Anne said from where she'd been looking out the window.

"He's right on time," Lee said. "Must be real excited." He nudged me and we went to hide around the corner in the dining room. Out of sight, but not out of hearing.

The front door opened. "Freddie, thank goodness you're here," Anne said. The door closed.

"Anne? You look funny. Is something wrong?" Freddie asked.

"I found a box in the basement, tucked way behind the boiler. More ration books. I'm sure they're fake. The police must have missed it in their first search."

"Well, what do you want me to do? Can't you—"

"You have to take it, Freddie. I can't handle any more."

Anne's voice was perfect. Tight and edgy, like she was about to fall apart. I couldn't see her face, but I could imagine that porcelain complexion white with fear.

Footsteps. It sounded like Freddie was circling the room. Then he said, "Where is the box?"

"In the basement. I can't lift it."

"I don't understand. You said before—"

"Freddie! I know what I said before. This is something I need you to do. Please."

"Anne, you already know I'd do anything for you. But given everything—"

"I need to get it out of the house before Mama finds it. If she does, she'll call the police and..." Anne paused, her intake of breath clear as day. "Please. I'm begging you. You have to help me."

"What's gotten into you? You weren't this nervous when—"

"It's nothing." Anne took another deep breath. "Betty came to see me and I'm a bit unsettled, that's all."

"Speaking of her, she's trying to get to the bottom of what happened to George."

"Yes." Her voice dripped scorn. "Don't worry about it. I told her I didn't want to see her again."

"What if she goes to the cops? Sounds like she's got it all figured out. It could mean real trouble for—"

Anne interrupted yet again. "She knows nothing. Yes, she believes you wanted a part of the black market money from George. When he wouldn't share, you killed him so you could take his place. But she doesn't have proof. It's nothing to be worried about."

"If you say so." His voice sounded a more relaxed than it had. "Are your parents at home?"

"They went out."

"Good." His volume returned to normal. "Maybe I need to take care of Betty Ahern. She came to see me at the deli, you know."

"No, I...I didn't." A different note came into Anne's voice. Was it worry? Maybe she was worried I'd put myself in danger and she'd feel guilty if something happened to me. "What did she say?"

"Nothing you haven't told me. I think she was digging. I almost let her get to me, but I stopped myself in time."

Anne's exhale was heavy with relief. "Good. Now about these ration books."

"I'll take them. After all, we can't risk the police getting in the way. The government has plenty of money." He chuckled, a dry, mirthless sound. "Who does it really hurt, forged ration books? Everybody wins. People get to buy the things they need, we make some money, and it's not like the government is losing. They're still getting their share. All this rationing is just a way for them to inflate prices and exert control. If you think of it, they're no better than the Nazis."

Oh, I so wanted to see Anne's expression, but Freddie hadn't confessed yet. Lee and I had to stay hidden. And why did he keep saying we? He must have a partner, a friend of his maybe.

"George didn't understand," Freddie continued. His bitterness was unmistakable. "He was like a brother, but he never took me seriously. You were right about that. I only wish...well, never mind. Are you sure you don't want me to take care of the Ahern girl?" There was a snap, then the sound of something slapping against flesh, as though Freddie was hitting something against his open palm.

"Freddie, put that away," Anne hissed.

"I could do it quick, just like George. I'd go to the First Ward and wait for her to get off the bus. She's not as smart as she thinks, putting herself in danger all the time. She didn't even bring a friend when she cornered me at work. I could pull her into an alley. One little jab, like with George, and..."

That was our cue. Lee and I came out. I expected to see Freddie, maybe red-faced, facing down his cousin. Despite Anne telling him to put it away and the knowledge he'd stabbed George, it was a bit of a jolt to see him with a switchblade in his hand.

Lee pushed me back. "Betty, see if there's a phone in the kitchen and call the cops."

Freddie snarled and lunged.

Anne shrieked. Lee whipped out his own knife. I shoulda known he wouldn't have come to a meeting like this without it. Lee was good and he'd been a Boy Scout. He'd brought it to the meeting with Tall Man and he'd be prepared for a possible killer like Freddie.

Lee and I were no strangers to street fights. Looking at the way Freddie held his knife, like he was gonna slice off a hunk of meat at the deli, I knew he didn't know anything. Freddie might have taken his cousin by surprise, but he wasn't gonna beat a good First Ward boy.

Well, not under normal circumstances. In the street, Lee could move freely. But here, in the Lindens' cluttered living room, it was different. Lee would have to dodge furniture and stuff. With his bad leg, he wasn't the most nimble guy. Plus, as an amateur, Freddie could do more damage accidentally than Lee could do on purpose. One wild swing was all it would take, and boy, was Freddie swinging.

Lee circled, sleek as a cat, looking for an opening. Freddie's wild cuts kept him at bay. Then Freddie darted in and just as I feared, Lee's leg caught on a chair and he stumbled. Freddie slashed through the air and a thin line of red appeared on Lee's left shirt sleeve. But he caught his balance quick and didn't flinch.

They grappled and crashed into a table. A vase hit the floor and shattered. Anne cried out again and looked like she was gonna get in the way, but I grabbed her arm and hauled her over to me. "You stay outta it. Lee knows what he's doing."

"He'll hurt Freddie!"

"No, he won't." I looked around. There was a broom standing against the wall near the kitchen. I grabbed it. I couldn't use it, though. In all the hoopla, I might hit Lee. But I'd be ready if Freddie somehow got the upper hand.

They had broken apart, an overturned ornamental table between them. Freddie went back to waving his knife wildly. Lee circled, occasionally darting in, but Freddie's unskilled technique kept Lee out of reach. Blood dripped from the cut on his arm, but it wasn't his knife hand and it wasn't slowing him down any that I could tell. If something didn't happen, this could go on all night. Why didn't Anne call the cops?

I shifted my grip on the broom handle. I could take down Freddie without a hitch. Problem was, the men were darting around so much I had just as much chance of blasting Lee as Freddie.

A growing panic in Freddie's eyes told me he knew he was outta his league and looking for an escape. He suddenly threw his knife at Lee blade first, a half-hearted attempt at best. He whirled and took a step toward the front door. Blocked by jumbled furniture, he changed direction and headed toward the kitchen, maybe figuring on making his escape through the back.

This was my chance. I hefted the broom as though it was a Louisville Slugger, and swung like I was batting clean-up down at Civic Stadium. The broom handle connected with Freddie's midsection and he went down like a sack of flour.

Lee came over to sit on Freddie's back and pinned his arms. "Thanks for the assist." He looked at Anne and winked. "Told ya I only looked gimpy."

Freddie threw a frantic look at Anne and started babbling in German. As he spoke, her expression turned stony. "*Sei ruhig!*" she snapped.

I looked at her. "What did he say?"

"He…he was trying to explain, begging me to forgive him," she replied. Freddie's eyes widened. "Anne! What—"

"I told you to be quiet," she said, tone scathing. "I have to think, I have to—"

The front door crashed open. "Police! Hands in the…Miss Ahern, what the hell are you doing here?" Detective MacKinnon entered, gun drawn, but stopped when he saw the boys on the floor and me holding a trembling Anne and the broom.

"Hiya, Detective. What're *you* doin' here?" I asked. After all, it wasn't like anybody'd had the chance to call 'em yet.

"My job," he grumped, but he didn't holster his gun. "If you remember, it's my responsibility to catch criminals."

"You mentioned it before." The presence of half a dozen armed police officers calmed me right down. It was all gonna be okay. I slumped against the wall. "Why didn't you tell me you were coming? I would've waited for you."

"We've been building our case for days. I told you last month, the police aren't in the habit of sharing every bit of information we have with the public." He lifted an eyebrow. "Not even a member of the public who fancies herself a private dick."

I shrugged and spread my hands. "I'm not gonna apologize for busting in on your collar. But if you're looking for George Linden's killer, Lee's got him pinned right there. You can cuff him if you want. I won't mind."

MacKinnon holstered his gun and pulled out his cuffs. "Miss Ahern, you and I are going to have words about this." Lee got to his feet and MacKinnon cuffed Freddie, then pulled him up.

"Sure thing, Detective." I patted Anne's back. She was stiff as a board, face drawn, paler than new milk. Shock, I s'pose. Not every day you found out your practically-a-brother cousin was a killer. "I still think I oughta bill the city for services, though."

Chapter 40

O
f course I told Dot all about it on the bus to work on Tuesday. As usual, she made a great audience, gasping in all the right places. "Lee didn't get hurt, did he?" she asked at the end.

"A cut that looked worse than it turned out to be. It was pretty clear Freddie didn't know how to handle that knife. He could jam it into someone, but not actually fight."

She sat back. "How did Anne take it?"

"Pretty bad." Anne had been a wreck. After the cops left, she'd collapsed in a shaking, gasping heap. Lee raided the liquor cabinet for "a little bit of something" to put in the tea I fixed her.

"Betty? What is it?"

"Nothing, just…" I nibbled my thumb nail. "I can't shake the feeling I missed something."

"You're crazy." Dot's expression was tinged with exasperation. "What about Detective MacKinnon?"

His reaction had been harder to judge. On the one hand, we made his job a whole lot easier by sitting on his suspect. On the other, he was pretty steamed I'd beaten him to the punch again. "This is twice, Miss Ahern," he'd said. "You aren't going to give up this line of work, are you?"

"Not as long as I'm good at it, Sam."

"Excuse me?"

"I figure as long as you and me are gonna be working side by side, I might as well call you by your first name. Don't ya think? Feel free to call me Betty."

He didn't have an answer to that.

Dot leaned back in her seat. "All we gotta do now is catch the Bell saboteur. How're you gonna do it?"

Good question. I'd racked my brains all Monday night trying to think of an idea, but nothing that came to mind seemed like it would work. "I don't know. We gotta make it look like it's a good opportunity, but not too good."

"Why not?"

"We make it look too good and whoever it is will get suspicious." I watched the rippling brown grass whip by. There'd been a frost over night and the wilting leaves glittered in the morning sun. My money was on the idea that if presented with an opportunity, the saboteur would jump, no matter what the actual impact to production. Because of that, I had to push her toward a possibility of my making.

We arrived at Bell and got our assignments. "Riveting," Dot said in disgust. "I hate riveting."

I understood. You had to sink the rivets in the metal just right then it had to be sanded to make sure the plane body was smooth and aerodynamic. It was tiresome and repetitive. Me, I was back on engine installation. Unless I could swap. "Hey Helen," I called. "Where are you today?"

"Riveting."

"Wanna switch?"

She stowed her lunch and closed her locker. "Why would I wanna do that? Where are you?"

"Engine installation."

"I hate engines. So messy and I can't get the oil outta my cuticles for nothing."

Why couldn't anything be easy? "I know, what you mean." How could I get her to swap places with me? "I gotta say, it'll have one benefit today."

She tilted her head. "Yeah? What's that?"

"Our saboteur has already struck there. She's prob'ly moving to another area."

She thought. "You got a point. I'm tired of having my work interrupted."

"Then switch assignments with me. If I'm right, and the saboteur is moving through different parts of the factory, you'll be in the clear and have a nice, peaceful shift."

"And you won't? Never mind." She grinned and waved me off. "Yeah, okay, fine. I'll switch."

Now Dot and I would be in the same area. Step two, make body assembly look like a good place for sabotage. If I was right that the previous attempts were acts of opportunity, I had to make it look like a prime option. Mentally, I cursed myself for not spending more time planning my next move, but hey, the best Hollywood detectives sometimes had to improvise.

Rose and Catherine, my prime suspects, stood nearby. Perfectly positioned to overhear me. I nudged Dot and we slowed. "You think there's gonna be any more trouble?" I asked her, making sure I'd be heard over the noise of girls filing in.

Thankfully, Dot was quick on the uptake. "I sure hope not. They must've checked all the machinery and tools last week. You know, made sure everything was working."

"Well, I hope they looked over the air hoses on the rivet guns. You know, over in the fuselage assembly building. Some of 'em were looking pretty worn before we left. One of those blows, and it'll be a humdinger of a mess. Just our luck if they can finally get the parts painted and we can't get the planes put together."

Rose and Catherine remained deep in conversation, but Dot and I had walked right by 'em. They couldn't have missed it. But both headed in a different direction.

Dot chewed her lip. "They aren't following us."

"It doesn't matter." Well, hopefully it didn't. Maybe I was barking up the wrong tree. But I had to try something. "Every other time it was the afternoon when we had problems. I bet nothing happens until after lunch."

"Then what are we gonna do?" Dot took her place and picked up a gun.

I did the same. "We just gotta wait, hope one of 'em is the saboteur, and she took the bait."

***

The whistle blew exactly at noon. Dot and I hung up our guns, but we walked real slow to the door, making sure everyone filed ahead of us. I had no intention of going to the cafeteria. It didn't look like Dot did either.

Finally, the building was empty 'cept for us. "Where should we hide?" she asked.

I checked around. Wherever we chose had to cover us almost entirely. It wouldn't do for the saboteur to show up and find us standing around.

She tugged my sleeve. "Over there?" She pointed to the line of half-assembled fuselages.

"They might see our feet. But it'll work." I dragged her over behind where a part of a plane stood, at the far side of the assembly area near the doors where they'd be put on the dollies and shipped across the yard to the main assembly lines. There were stacks of struts and metal on the ground nearby. Our upper bodies would be behind the plane, our feet hidden by everything else. I crouched down and peered around the cover. A long line of rivet guns hung in front of me. Perfect.

Dot took a spot beside me. "How long you think we gotta wait?"

"Whoever it is has to eat, come up with a reason to leave the cafeteria early, make it down here and tamper with those guns in time to vamoose before she's seen. I don't expect anything to happen until maybe fifteen minutes left in the hour."

That didn't mean we could yammer and fill up the time. Our culprit might show up early. Fortunately, the creak of the door and footsteps in the nearly silent building would be heard long before the person got close. I hoped we'd made it sound like a good enough opportunity. If the saboteur was trying to make things look like accidents, wouldn't fraying lines be a good bet?

We waited. My stomach grumbled and my legs cramped. Fifteen minutes down, then thirty, then only fifteen minutes to go. If nothing happened soon, we'd have to try again tomorrow.

The door opened, then shut and footsteps echoed across the floor. Dot nearly jumped up, but I put a hand on her shoulder and laid a finger over my lips. Not yet.

I didn't recognize the feet and legs that walked up to the line of rivet guns.

So many girls wore the same dark blue pants and heavy black shoes. A hand picked up one of the guns and a bit of gold glittered in the light. I recognized that ring. Catherine had one exactly like it. Her grandma's, she said. I heard a faint hiss that sounded like air escaping a balloon. A hole in one of the air lines? Sounded like it. Bingo.

I stood and moved around the pile, motioning Dot to come around from the other side. "Hey, Catherine. What are you doing here?"

She started, the rivet gun falling from her hands. "Oh, nothing. Just checking things out. I heard you this morning talking to Dot about the maintenance and thought I'd take a look to be sure."

"You aren't working over here today."

"I had some time to kill. Finished eating early. Everything looks good, so I guess I'll get back to it."

I glanced at the clock. Ten minutes until the whistle blew again. "That's it? You came by to check?"

"Yeah. I'm as concerned as everyone else, you know. I don't want the place shutting down again." She took a step away, her left hand behind her back.

Dot came up behind Catherine and grabbed her wrist. "Then why are you holding an awl?"

Catherine must've used the sharp tip of the tool to puncture one of the hoses. As soon as the gun had been fired up, doubtless the air pressure would have caused a bigger rupture, maybe leading to further damage. Catherine pushed Dot to the ground. She shoved the line of rivet guns at me so I had to duck, then darted for the main doors and outside.

Girls were starting to filter out of the cafeteria. "Stop her!" I waved at the fleeing Catherine. "She's the saboteur!"

Everybody froze, although gasps cut the frigid air. *C'mon girls, don't just stand there*. I stopped and looked for something to throw. A box of wooden chocks, used to wedge under the landing gear during final inspection, was at my feet. I picked up a set and threw them at Catherine's legs. They whirled like a set of bolos from a jungle movie, collided with her back and sent her to the pavement. I sprinted over to grab her before she caught her breath and got up.

Mr. Satterwaite trotted up, breath puffing like a steam engine. "What's all the racket? Miss Ahern, explain yourself."

I grabbed Catherine's arm. She was sputtering in Russian, almost certainly words that were not appropriate for nice young ladies. "Here's your saboteur, Mr. Satterwaite."

"Catherine Ramsey? Why on earth would she do this? You must be mistaken."

Dot jogged up, her face a little pink from running. "No, she isn't, Mr. Satterwaite. We saw it, Betty and me. We saw Catherine over in the fuselage assembly building, near the rivet guns. She had an awl in her hand. After she ran off, I checked the air hose. It has a hole in it, new. If we hadn't been there, she might have done even more damage."

Mr. Satterwaite looked from Dot, to me, to Catherine, who I'd hauled to her feet, hissing and spitting like a wet cat. The rest of the workers gathered in the yard. "I still don't understand," he said.

"Her name isn't Catherine," I said. "It's Kateryna Ivanova Razumovsky. She's Russian."

Rose pushed her way to the front of the crowd. "That doesn't make any sense. So she's Russian. Big deal. Why would she want to hurt the war effort? The Russians are our allies."

"They're Soviets, not Russians," Catherine said, still fighting to free herself from my grasp.

Helen, Florence, and Alice had joined Rose. "Soviets, Russians, aren't they the same?" Helen said. "They're still allies."

Catherine stopped twisting and shot her a look of pure loathing. "They aren't the same. You don't understand. The Soviets are animals. They'll betray you the minute you turn your back on them. They don't deserve our help."

Dot's forehead puckered. "What does she mean by 'help'?"

I looked at her. "The Soviets buy a lot of P-39s." I turned to Catherine. "You didn't want the planes to get to the Russians, did you? You thought if you shut down things here at Bell, they'd stop selling the P-39 and the Russians would be outta luck."

"Yes, damn it." Her breath came hot and heavy, crystallizing into clouds in the air. There was a red mark on her cheek from when she'd hit the ground.

Florence had the same expression on her face as Dot. "But why? What've you got against the Soviets?" she asked Catherine.

"They killed my grandfather," she spat. "He was an officer in the Czar's army. He tried to protect the imperial family during the 1917 revolution. My grandmother had already fled the country with my father, but *Ded* stayed behind. Lenin's goons shot him like a dog in the street. *Babushka* got to America eventually, but she had almost nothing. Her heart broke when she found out *Ded* had been killed. My father, he dropped out of school to go to work. Had my grandfather lived…let's just say everything for my family would have been different."

Alice wiped her eyes. "Catherine one of us could've gotten hurt bad. Dot got burned. Don't you care about that? Don't your friends mean anything?"

"I didn't mean for anyone to get hurt," Catherine said, still defiant. "That's why I always did stuff when no one was around. Once the machinery was back in action, it would break pretty fast before anyone got injured. The paint fire, that got out of hand." She glanced at Dot. "I'm sorry you got burned, but I'm not gonna apologize for what I did. Besides—" She clamped her lips shut.

I studied her. "Besides what?"

Catherine mashed her lips together and refused to speak. But the fire in her eyes was intense. I knew that look. Catherine was mad and not just 'cause she was caught.

Mr. Satterwaite looked like he'd been smacked in the face with a wing strut. "I guess…I guess I should call the police." He hurried back to his office.

Catherine tugged in my grasp. "You gonna let go of me?"

She was twisting like an angry chicken, trying to break my hold. "Not until the cops come," I said. There'd been a rush of triumph when I'd taken her down, but her story drained it all away. I thought of my grandfather, how I would feel if I found he'd been shot just for doing his job. Horrible, that's how. "I'm sorry about your grandpa. I understand now, why you hate the Soviets so much. But Catherine, do you think he'd have approved of what you did?"

"The Molly Maguires were pretty violent, weren't they, Betty?" she asked. "Tell me, if one of them had killed a relative of yours, how would you feel? Wouldn't you be mad?"

Mad, sure. Bitter enough to wreck an entire factory, put people out of work, and cause innocent people like Dot harm? No. Least I hoped I wouldn't be.

Chapter 41

M r. Satterwaite let us celebrate Catherine's capture by getting back to work. Dot grumbled as she picked up her rivet gun. "Doesn't he believe in fun?"

It was okay by me. I didn't feel much like celebrating. I thought the finale to my first big break as a private dick would make me giddy, not grumpy. I couldn't shake the feeling I'd missed the boat somewhere.

When the shriek of metal on metal announced my third botched rivet, Dot stopped to look at me. "What's eating you? I'll bet you haven't messed up three times this year. Now it's three in one day?"

I paused. "Something's not square."

"Yeah. Your work. Mr. Satterwaite's gonna have kittens." She hefted her rivet gun. "Get your head outta the clouds. You did a good job. Now you better get back to puttin' these planes together. Unless you've got another detective job."

When I got home after work and walked in, I heard voices from the front room. "Hey, I'm home." I stopped in the archway.

Detective MacKinnon sat on the couch next to Mom, holding a cup of had-to-be-weak coffee on his knee. He and Mom were chatting, but the thin line of Mom's mouth told me she was only being polite. "You have a visitor. Again," she said, voice sharp. She took the half-empty cup from him and headed for the kitchen. She paused as she passed me. "We'll talk about this later, Elizabeth. What are the neighbors going to think with the police dropping by every few days?"

Oh boy. Like it was my fault MacKinnon had come to visit. "Detective, what a surprise," I said. "Is there something you need?"

He motioned to the couch. "Please, Miss Ahern. Sit, would you?"

I thought a moment, then went to the couch, sitting and crossing my legs at the ankles like a lady, despite the fact I wore my work pants. "Yes?"

"I'm sorry to cause a problem for you by dropping by," he said, shooting a look toward the kitchen. "But I have a few issues I'd like to chat about related to our arrest of Frederick Linden. On second thought, let's go outside."

Once we were on the sidewalk, I faced him. "You think I can help with Freddie?"

"I do." He crossed his arms. "We've been talking to Mr. Linden and he's been saying some interesting things."

"Such as?"

"He wasn't acting alone. Problem is, he sounds so desperate to pin the blame on this other person, his statement isn't very credible. At least not to my captain. My colleagues think I'm making mountains out of molehills and Linden is doing what every criminal does. Try to shift the blame."

I studied him. "And you think I can help you?"

"Well, yes. You're a smart girl. I think maybe you have some of the same thoughts as I do."

I knew it! It had been too easy. "Funny you should say that. The Bell saboteur was caught today. I was talkin' to my friend Dot and I said I felt something was off."

MacKinnon lifted his eyebrows. "That we've missed something? Or rather, somebody?"

"Yeah." I wasn't loony. MacKinnon, the experienced pro, had the exact feelings I did. This wasn't over by a long shot.

"I have an idea," he continued. "I think you can help me out. But it may be a tad dangerous. I understand if you'd rather cut your losses and walk."

I thought. I had fifty bucks. I had solutions for both crimes and I believed I was mostly right. But not completely. I took a deep breath. "What's the plan?"

***

An hour later, MacKinnon dropped me off at the corner of Casimer and

Barnard, a few blocks from the Linden house. "You're clear on what you have to do?" he asked.

I smoothed my skirt, having changed into nicer visiting clothes for the evening's task. The envelope in my pocket was a lead weight. I didn't want to give up the cabbage, but I had to sell my story. "Yeah. Just don't wait too long before you interrupt."

He gave me a tight grin and waited for me to exit the car before driving off.

I walked to the Linden house practicing my script in my head. Bottom of the ninth, bases loaded. I didn't need a home run, but a bases-clearing stand-up double would be good.

I knocked on the Lindens' front door surprised my hand wasn't trembling. After a minute, Anne answered. "Betty. I didn't expect to see you tonight."

"Spur of the moment decision. May I come in?"

"Sure." She held the door open, then led me to the front sitting room. "What's this about?" She sat on one of the chairs, where a piece of embroidery was draped on the arm.

I swallowed around what felt like a golf-ball sized lump in my throat. "I, uh, I thought I should return this." I held out the envelope. "It's the fifty bucks you paid me." I'd scraped together some cash to replace what I'd spent in expenses.

She didn't take the envelope, face a mask of puzzlement. "I don't understand."

"You hired me to clear your name. I didn't."

She laughed, a brittle sound or was that my imagination? "I saw a story in the paper this afternoon. They caught the saboteur at Bell. That wasn't you?"

"Well, it was, but I botched the job."

"Catherine Ramsey's Russian, it said. Who knew?"

"I think you did."

Silence. Anne was good. She didn't bat an eyelash at my accusation. "I'm not sure I understand what you're saying."

"I don't know why you egged her on. But I'm pretty sure you not only knew she was Russian, but you got her to do the dirty work. She wouldn't even give you up when we pinched her."

More silence, but Anne's face smoothed and grew cold.

"Was that first incident your idea, the fire at the engine installation? Was the sabotage for the Bund or someone else? 'Cept you got fired. You needed a stooge. Catherine fit the bill."

"You're insane," Anne said, tossing her head back.

"I mean, with her family background it's pretty natural for her to hate the Soviets. I'm sure it wasn't hard to get her to play along. What'd you give her to keep quiet?" A flare of anger at the memory of Dot's injury calmed my nerves. I clasped my hands in my lap.

"You need to leave." Anne's tone of voice was cold and flat.

"Do you hate America that much?" I looked around the room. "Do you like causing trouble? Or did someone offer to pay you and you're greedy, like Freddie?"

"This conversation is over," Anne said. "On second thought, I will take my money back. You are clearly delusional." She stood and snatched the envelope from my hand.

This wasn't working. I needed to get her to say the word, any word, that would help MacKinnon make his case. It was clear to me now that Anne was a very practiced liar. She'd conned her family, Freddie, Catherine, me, the cops. I'd never out-lie her. She was too good to be manipulated. Heck, if MacKinnon and I were right, and I was increasingly sure we were, she'd been doing the manipulation all along. I needed to rattle her. A full broadside might do it. An accusation she couldn't talk her way around. "You killed your brother."

"Freddie already admitted to that," she said. "You were here."

"Yeah, I heard. 'Cept you kept cutting him off before what, before he fingered you? Oh, you prob'ly didn't stick the knife in George. I think Freddie did the deed. But you led him down that path, didn't you?" My brain was working overtime. "The black market. George wanted dough to set up the business with Joseph. After that, he was gonna quit. But you liked the extra goodies, the money. You wanted him to keep it up. Maybe you tried to convince him and he turned you down?

Anne walked to a dark wood table by the wall. She ran her fingers over the wood. She didn't say anything, but I didn't need her to. Instinct told me I was right.

"You stole ration books. I know there were some missing 'cause what Tall Man asked for and what I got from MacKinnon didn't match. When George said he was out of the business, you appealed to Freddie. To his sense of outrage. To the brother-sister bond you two had. You got him to stab George down that alley. You'd take over the black market affairs, Freddie was your leg-man, and you'd split the profits. How close am I?"

"You think you're smart, don't you?"

My breath came fast, heart pounding. MacKinnon told me he'd be outside the front window where he could see me. I brushed hair behind my ear, our prearranged come in signal. As far as I was concerned, Anne had confessed.

MacKinnon didn't appear. He ought to be in place by now, so what gave? I plowed on, hoping he was biding his time, not out of position. I couldn't string her along forever. "I'm not as clear on the sabotage, though. Unless…was that for the Bund? Did they pay you?" Her silence was grating my nerves. Nick Charles would've known just what to say to crack her. Damn.

"You know," she said, voice as light as if she were commenting on the weather, "you talk too much." She turned. There was a small, pearl-handled revolver in her right hand. Not big, but prob'ly enough to do the job.

I sprung up and brushed hair from my forehead again. "Calm down, Anne. Let's talk about this." Where the hell was MacKinnon?

"I'm done talking. And so are you." She jerked the gun in the direction of the chair I'd vacated. "Here's what's going to happen. We're going to take a little walk together, you and I. But it's getting late. The streets aren't safe."

"Then what?"

Her answering smile was cold as ice and sent a chill down my spine like when I walked the lake shore before the water warmed up. How had I ever thought she was pretty and innocent? "I'm afraid you'll be found tomorrow morning, the victim of some dirty cutpurse. I was right. You're good, Betty.

You're right about the black market. As for the sabotage, Catherine was never shy about her views. One day, I told her to do something about it and made a few suggestions. I planted the idea, even suggested I'd help with the cover up, but the actions were all hers. As for the Bund," she spat. "They're too moronic to do anything, but they are a useful distraction."

Lee wouldn't believe it, but I was speechless. I believed her every word, but at the same time I was stunned. She'd been such a good actress. I'd always thought she looked like Marlene Dietrich, but Dietrich was nothing compared to Anne Linden.

"Overconfidence is going to be your downfall," Anne continued. "If you believed me to be the person you just described, why did you come alone?"

I wasn't alone. I'd brought backup. Where was MacKinnon? Not here, that's for sure. I'd be damned if Tom was gonna get a letter saying I'd been taken down by a street thief, or worse yet, a slip of a girl like Anne. "What I don't understand is, why hire me?" I needed to keep her talking while my mind raced and prayed MacKinnon would bust in.

Her shoulders twitched in the tiniest of shrugs, but the gun didn't move. "What better way to clear my name? I thought you were smart enough to uncover Catherine, but not enough to figure out I was behind it all. Plus, if you liked me that would be a stamp of approval in the eyes of the others. I'd be above suspicion. A person like you wouldn't be friends with a traitor."

"You weren't nervous Catherine would talk? Freddie's family, but Catherine's not loyal to you."

"She'd be a convicted criminal. Who would believe her?"

I'd been used. That made me angrier than being held at gunpoint. To hell with MacKinnon. I'd handle this on my own. I waited as Anne reached for the doorknob.

I pounced and slammed her into the wall. But the weak, dainty physical image was as false as the sweet, innocent look. She was tough. I latched on to her gun hand, pushing it away from my face and toward the ceiling. With a "pop" it went off. I felt the air ripple past my cheek and smelled the acrid tang of gunpowder. *You can make your entrance any time now, Detective.*

Anne and I fell to the floor. Did she have more shots? I didn't want to find out. I'd worked long enough at Bell that I knew I could overwhelm her eventually. But she had the gun. I watched as the barrel slowly, but surely turned toward my face. Anne's finger tightened on the trigger.

Tom, I'm so sorry. I squeezed my eyes shut.

The door burst open and slammed into Anne as the gun went off again. Bits of plaster fell as the ceiling cracked. A shadow fell over us.

"Police, drop it." MacKinnon loomed overhead, his own revolver drawn. "Are you okay Miss Ahern?"

I scrambled to my feet as MacKinnon kicked the gun from Anne's hand, then hoisted her up and cuffed her. "What happened to brush-back-your-hair-and-I'll-come-in?" My heart hammered and the blood pounded through my body. I knew I was being rude, but I was so jumpy I didn't care.

"Sorry." MacKinnon had the grace to flush with embarrassment. "The forsythia in the front made it impossible to hide where I intended. I had to find another spot, one where I could keep an eye on you."

I gulped air and collapsed onto the couch. Anne, now cuffed and stiff as a board, glared at me, not saying a word, but I was too overwhelmed to pay her any mind. "Now I'm definitely gonna bill the city for services."

MacKinnon dragged Anne toward the door. "You'll be okay. Good job. What's the line? Here's looking at you, kid?"

I sighed. "Wrong movie, dummy."

Chapter 42

MacKinnon dropped me off at the corner of Louisiana and South Park. I wouldn't let him come any closer to the house. "My mom is already sore at me, which means she's prob'ly sore at you. I'm doin' you a favor."

"I truly am sorry I left you out to dry like that." He had apologized all the way home. Frankly, I'd gotten over it before we'd even left Kaisertown, but I wasn't gonna tell him that. I'd caught a murderer, a saboteur, and a criminal mastermind. I was too jubilant to be mad. I wasn't exactly sure what would happen to them, but sure as anything it'd involve jail.

"Remember, you owe me." Once I got out of his car, I hustled over to Dot's house. She and Lee were on her front step. I brought them up to speed on what had happened with Anne. I fixed Dot with a stare. "I told you something was wrong."

She looked properly ashamed.

I didn't tell Mom or Pop what had happened. They would read about Anne's crimes in the paper, along with the news about Freddie and Catherine. They didn't need to know I was involved and I didn't put it past Mom to storm police headquarters to give MacKinnon a piece of her mind.

That evening, after supper was over and the dishes washed, I retired to my room. I took out pen and paper, and wrote a letter to Tom.

Dear Tommy,

I got your last letter. I'm so glad to hear you are okay, especially with everything I see on the newsreels. I hope you got all the sand taken care of.

Things have been pretty interesting here. We had a bit of a dustup at Bell this month. Turns out one of the girls was sabotaging the works because she doesn't like the Soviets, and they buy the most P-39s. It took a while, but they caught her. I don't know if it'll go as far as treason, but Catherine is going to jail.

This German girl, Anne, was originally accused of the sabotage and was fired. Then her brother was murdered. They thought maybe Anne's brother was forcing her to commit the sabotage because he was part of the German American Bund. You know, those crazies who support the Nazis. Anyway, turns out that wasn't the case at all. George, the brother, was into black market ration books and gas cards. He was going into business with a Jewish friend and leaving the Bund, and he needed the money to get started. But then he got a crisis of conscience, or maybe he made enough money, and he was getting out.

Anne wasn't so keen on that idea. She liked the extra cash and the goods from the ration cards. She manipulated their cousin, Freddie, into killing George. She was gonna take over the black-market operation and she promised to split the dough with Freddie. When he got caught, he sang like a canary because Anne was all set to let him take the fall on his own. Madness, isn't it? I can't believe what people will do for a little cash, some sugar, and a bag of real coffee.

It was Anne who gave Catherine the sabotage idea, too.

Oh, it looks like I've adopted a stray cat. Or been adopted by one. You know how cats are.

Anyway, I wanted to let you know that the excitement isn't all in your part of the world or in the Pacific. Before you get worried, I'm okay. I think Mom wanted me to start dating Billy McClusky since he was discharged from the Army, but I had a talk with her and I'm pretty sure she's given up that idea.

I love you. Stay safe and write when you can.

Always your girl,

Betty

I folded the letter and slipped it into an envelope, dotting it with a little of my favorite perfume before I did. I hadn't lied. Everything I'd written was a true account. I'd merely left out my involvement. There was no use telling Tom about my new career as a private dick. He'd only worry and he had other things to think about. There was plenty of time to tell him the score.

You know, after I got a little better at this detective thing.

Acknowledgements

Thank you to the wonderful team at Level Best Books—Harriette Sackler, Verena Rose, and Shawn Reilly Simmons. You're all so wonderful to work with. I'm glad you invited Betty to join the LBB family.

Many thanks to the Niagara Aerospace Museum and David Ebersole for providing a glimpse into how the P39 Airacobra was made and the layout of the facility, as well as tidbits of trivia that will surely make it into stories to come. I've taken some creative liberties for the sake of the tale. I hope I am forgiven.

Much gratitude to my critique group—Annette Dashofy, Jeff Boarts, Tamara Girardi, and Peter WJ Hayes for your encouragement and support. I'm often asked what advice I'd give to new writers and I always say, "Find people you trust to give you honest feedback." My stories would not be the same without these talented writers.

Thanks to Sisters in Crime and Pennwriters. Another piece of advice I give is for new writers to join professional organizations, especially in their genre. Both these groups have given me knowledge and support. I could not do what I do without my tribe.

A special shout out to SinC sibs Martha Reed and Susan Thibadeau, and fellow Mysterista blogmate Keenan Powell. Without Martha and Susan's "Short Story Challenge" in 2016, Betty would never have come to the page. Keenan and I traded stories before submitting to *Mystery Most Historical*, which we both appeared in. She was the first person to urge me to put Betty in a novel.

Post-humous thanks and love to my grandmother, Betty Lederman. She was a real-life Rosie the Riveter who really did work at Bell Aircraft and provided my inspiration. I wish I had taken the time to learn more of her story when she was alive.

Last, but certainly not least, thanks to my family, especially my husband Paul, for enabling me to go on this mystery-writing odyssey. You've put up with my quirks and let me go on adventures. Much love to all of you.

About the Author

Liz Milliron is the author of **The Laurel Highlands Mysteries** series, set in the scenic Laurel Highlands, and **The Homefront Mysteries**, set in Buffalo, NY during the early years of World War II. *Heaven Has No Rage*, the second in the Laurel Highlands Mysteries, was released in August 2019. The first book of the Homefront Mysteries, *The Enemy We Don't Know*, was released in February 2020. Soon to be an empty-nester, Liz lives outside Pittsburgh with her husband, two children, and a retired-racer greyhound.

You can connect with me on:
◯ http://lizmilliron.com

CPSIA information can be obtained
at www.ICGtesting.com
Printed in the USA
FSHW010727020420
68727FS